It was just a bit of
Now sl

When the Mask Falls

Caroline O'Breackin

When the Mask Falls

Copyright © 2018 by Caroline O'Breackin

Cover design by Chris Mitchell Photography
Edited by Paul Feldstein

ISBN: 978-1-9996445-0-5

A catalogue record of this book is available from the British Library

All rights reserved. No part of this publication may be reproduced, distributed, or transmitted in any form or by any means, including photocopying, recording, or other electronic or mechanical methods, without the prior written permission of the publisher.

Caroline O'Breackin Publishing
Holywood, County Down

Printed in the United Kingdom

First Edition

First published in 2018

FASTPRINT PUBLISHING
Peterborough
England

Printed on FSC approved paper by
www.printondemand-worldwide.com

www.carolineobreackin.co.uk

Dedication

It seems to me; that dedicating a novel, is a not actually a delightful way to show gratitude to a person who has been instrumental to the process of producing a book, as it should be. But rather, an elegant way of alienating all those who thought they should have been mentioned, but weren't.

So, I will simply write this, if you helped, in any way at all, then I thank you; this book is for you and I will forever be in your gratitude. However, if your contribution amounted to a big fat nothing, if you couldn't even muster a simple word of encouragement or follow me on social media, then I bring shame on you!

Kickstarter

There is a group of wonderful individuals that must get a mention, and that is everyone that supported and funded me through my Kickstarter campaign. However much you pledged, your donation is very gratefully received and it is thanks to you that I was able to launch my book so successfully. I can't mention everyone, there were so many of you, but here is a personal thank you to some of my top supporters:

Mum and Dad
Joy and Edwin Mitchell
Elaine Lynn
Ken Titmuss
Jennifer and Matthew Grumball
Lara Curry
Emer
Mandy
Karen Smiley
Owen McMahon
Wilma
Robert Titmuss

Thank You

Acknowledgements

There are a few people that should be acknowledged as without them this book would not be in your hands today:

Firstly; Chris Mitchell Photography, for not only producing the amazing photography and cover design for this book, but mostly for putting up with me as I changed my mind and fussed over the design so incessantly. His hourly rate was seriously compromised by the time I was finally satisfied. My only hope is that I haven't put him off doing it all again for the next novel.

I also have to thank Susan Feldstein for evaluating my novel and giving me the encouragement I needed to actually finish it.

Thank you to Paul Feldstein for editing my manuscript so brilliantly, and for squeezing it in over Christmas too.

My beta readers are due a thank you too, as without them I would have never finished the book, and the story wouldn't be half as good as it is today.

Also, thanks to all that encouraged me in whatever way they could, whether it be a Facebook follow, a word of encouragement or feedback along the way. However you supported me, I thank you wholeheartedly.

chapter one

He watched her tremble as he pressed the gun firmly against her temple. She was still holding his unlocked phone in her hands, her eyes wide with fear. He snatched the phone from her shaking hand and tossed it noisily onto the walnut dresser.

'I wasn't…'

'Save it.'

He was past *I wasn't* and *I didn't.*

He sighed wearily, took a final glance into her tearful eyes, and pulled the trigger.

The Boss, as he demanded he be called, threw his hand towel over his shoulder and stepped in front of the full-length mirror in his bedroom. He was naked except for his open white shirt, boxer shorts and now empty shoulder holster. He was uncomfortably close to fifty, although he worked hard on his appearance. *Not bad,* he thought, as he smacked his tight gut with his hand. He pulled back the end of his nose and peered inside, a little more hair in some places than he would've liked, but overall, *not bad at all.*

His vanity was distracting, and he knew it, but he had a much bigger problem, bigger than unwanted nose hair anyway. She called herself Pixie and she was fast bleeding out on the floor in front of him.

Of course, in a perfect world she'd have been lying under him right about now, telling him he was the best she ever had, instead of ruining his recently waxed, solid wood floor. A pity really as she had been, by far, his favourite.

There was a lot to like about Pixie. Apart from her stunning beauty, and the fact that she was as horny as a dog with two dicks, she was smart, and he could rely on her. Unlike some of the others, who could be a little lackadaisical with their ETA, she was always bang on time, and today was no exception. Twenty-eight minutes after he hung up the phone, his doorbell rang and there she was. Ironically, if she had been running late, they might not have been in this unfortunate mess, but in a rare instance of disorganisation, he was delayed, so he'd had Eddie escort her to his room.

He'd been in the ensuite, freshening up, when Eddie dropped her off, and less than a minute later he had joined her in his bedroom, only to catch her with her hands on his phone. She was a very beautiful young girl, probably only just legal. Her smooth milk chocolate skin and long black hair added an air of class, more lawyer than hooker. Her face had been a picture of confusion as she attempted to protest her innocence. He wasn't interested, he might once have been, years ago, showed a little compassion maybe. This wasn't the first time he had caught a call girl snooping, or stealing, and he did what he always did when someone disrespected him, and slid his .22 Springfield from his holster and pulled the trigger.

He tutted as the limp hooker slumped to the floor, revealing an ugly pattern of blood and brain splatter on his bedroom door and wall.

'Such a shame,' he said, sliding his antique Sarouk rug with his bare foot, across the polished wood floor and away from the expanding pool of blood. He mopped his brow with the towel on his shoulder then tossed it over her face.

He shook his head as he replaced the gun in his holster and sat back on his queen size, hand carved mahogany sleigh bed, his back propped comfortably against the plump collection of red silk scatter cushions.

Her face may have been spoiled but the rest of her was still very nice to look at, he thought, and he gazed over her still corpse, the chocolate colour of her skin beautifully complimented by the dark wooden floor and the oozing red blood pool that was growing around her. He tilted his head and took hold of himself in his right hand.

I pay a hundred quid a night for a hooker and I end up taking care of business myself, where's the justice in that? he thought to himself as he gritted his teeth for the grand finale. *At least one of them would get a happy ending tonight,* he thought. Well, sort of.

Feeling slightly more satisfied, he stepped over Pixie's lifeless body and hit the call button on the intercom by the door,

'Boys, I've some trash that needs taking out.' He paused for a second. 'And bring a mop.'

He shook his head and stepped back over her before heading to the bathroom for a shower.

'Such a shame.'

He could have removed the girl's dead body himself, and he might well have done twenty years ago, but he had three boys on the payroll, no use having them sitting idle.

When he got out the shower, Pixie and all traces of her had gone and they had been replaced by a lovely lemony, bleachy scent. He took a deep breath and pulled on a white robe and his leather slippers before walking over to the window.

His number one, Eddie, was outside, leaning into the back of his Sky Engineers' van. Apart from his trademark jeans and Superdry biker jacket, he was also wearing a pair of blood stained latex surgical gloves. He watched him slam closed the back doors of the van and wipe his brow with the sleeve of his jacket.

He had found Eddie, twelve years ago, beaten half to death and begging for spare change under a railway bridge in Newport. He had pulled the twenty-two-year-old out of the gutter, and he was so far gone he was probably only a couple of needles away from a lethal overdose, but The Boss had got him clean, sorted his and his mother's dealer's debts and since then, Eddie had been working that debt off. Eddie was a smart kid, in another life he could have really made something of himself, but when you choose meth over books, you've only got one future ahead of you.

He turned away from the window and headed out of the bedroom and down the red carpeted hall to his quaint kitchen. Antique oak cabinets joined in the middle by a large range cooker lined the walls, and an oak centre island stood on terracotta tile. It was traditional, just how he liked things, not that he used the kitchen much.

Standing over the Belfast sink was Danny, who was peeling a pair of blood stained latex gloves off his giant black hands. Danny came along not long after Eddie, and he did a great job of helping keep Eddie clean in the early days. He had found Danny starting a fight in the street with a gang over the result of a pool game, one man versus five. He was brave, but not the sharpest tool in the box, and what he lacked in intelligence he more than made up for in his three-hundred-pound body of muscle. So he put him on staff too.

He had always intended to stop at two, and for years things worked well, easy, slick, but last year Danny spent some time at her majesties pleasure for aggravated burglary and he had found himself temporarily relying on Eddie alone.

Waiting in the airport car park one drizzly afternoon, he couldn't help be seduced as he watched a young, long-haired, skinny kid work his way along a line of parked cars, methodically manipulating the lock, relieving the car owners of their most poorly hidden possessions, one after another, as bold as brass. In minutes he had lightened the load of more than ten cars. He liked him instantly and made his mind up there and then to give the twenty---year-old, white South African, a job. He chuckled to himself as he recalled TJ immediately fleeing the scene in a spunky little Mercedes that he had just robbed.

And then there was the Barrister – an old school friend called Ash. Judge Henderson and four bent cops were also on the payroll. The Boss had a tidy little team working for him at his house in Redmarsh Road. So tidy in fact that he hardly felt like he needed to be at work there some days, and on those days, just as he had intended today, he liked to indulge himself in some of life's little pleasures. He would have to settle for a brandy and a cigar in front of the fire instead. *Not quite the same,* he thought.

'Make sure you get rid of her properly this time, Danny,' he said to the giant man in his kitchen.

'Eddie wants to take her for a swim in the canal.'

The Boss nodded and relaxed. Eddie was the smartest of all of them, and he knew he could rely on him whatever the situation. He had become very fond of him over the years and thought of him almost like family. Now, more than ever, he needed things done right and he was glad Eddie was running things for him.

'Danny, where's TJ?'

'Wiv some cops, they called 'im saying they had some information or somefing.'

'Thanks Danny, I'll be in the other room.'

'Aight.'

He shook his head and wondered if elocution lessons would be a waste of money for Danny. He walked out of the cosy little kitchen and through to the living room, a perfectly gentlemanly room, his sanctuary.

The fire was already crackling in the stone hearth, filling the room with an oaky smell and a comforting, billowing heat, just what he needed on this cold Devonshire evening.

He took a seat in his favourite of the two leather chairs that faced the fire, and placed his glass down on the walnut inlayed side table, before sliding out the drawer and helping himself to his preferred winter cigar, a Monte Two. He ran the unlit cigar though his fingers and under his nose as he listened to Eddie's new car wheel spin on the drive.

With the cigar in one hand, he struck his Zippo lighter and gently rolled the tip in the top of the flame to warm it before taking his first heavenly puff. Odours of leather and spice filled the room and he couldn't help but inhale deeply and enjoy as much of the warming scent as he could before it escaped.

'Heaven,' he said, as he closed his eyes and let the smoke escape from his mouth.

chapter two

'Tea's ready!'

I don't know why I bothered shouting, even in my most booming voice I had no hope of competing with Sara's and Ben's stereos, both barking hostile 'melodies' through the walls and ceiling in a bitter struggle for musical supremacy.

'Tea!'

Once upon a time, my two little cherubs, the apples of my proud eye, would sit at the kitchen island begging to help while I cooked. Stirring, mashing and mixing or, when there was nothing left to do, drawing cute pictures of houses and trees and ponies, eagerly anticipating the results of mummy's efforts. Then, one dark day, my little angels turned into Satan's pawns, minions of the devil. They became teenagers and I became their housekeeper, taxi, cook, social secretary; their slave. Life would never be the same again in the Walker household.

Still no sign and tea getting, if not already, cold. *Time for plan B,* I thought, and dropped to my knees. The fuse box was under the stairs and I had become quite accustomed to squeezing myself into the cupboard with my torch, reaching past the hoover and the filter coffee maker that, apart from the day it was unpacked, had never been used, and pulling the cover off the electric box. Third switch from the right disabled the electrics upstairs and moments later a heavenly silence filled the house.

Silence never lasted long in my house, and minutes later a stampeding army thundered down the stairs, voices shouting incoherently at each other and at me. I reversed out of the cupboard, dusted my jeans and readjusted my pony tail.

'Tea's ready.'

They both grunted, and I followed them into the kitchen. They slumped in their chairs and I sat opposite.

'Where's Dad?' Ben poked at his lamb chop with his fork.

'He's working late.'

'He said he would drop me at Steve's.'

'I can take you.'

'Humph.'

'Well, if you are dropping Ben, you can drop me at Stacie's, it's on the way,' said Sara.

'What's wrong with your car?' I said.

'Nothing, just thought I might have a few drinks.'

'Ok, that sounds nice.'

And that pretty much summed up our evening's polite dinner conversation. We continued our meal in silence, well except from the constant bleeping from mobile phones that had become a recent, but uninvited, guest at the dinner table.

'This is shit,' Ben announced, in his least grateful tone as he got up and banged his, mostly uneaten, plate of food down by the sink and marched out of the kitchen.

He got no argument from me. I hadn't eaten meat since a farm trip with my parents when I was eight, so it probably was shit, but I wouldn't know. My vegetable grill was very nice, but somehow, I couldn't see the little carnivore trying one.

There was still no sign of Michael when I started to clear the plates, no surprise really, he was rarely ever home these days, so I wrapped his plate with cling wrap and placed it in the microwave for later. I cleared the rest of the dishes, stacked the dishwasher and washed up the last few items that wouldn't fit.

I had been looking forward to a quiet evening in with the iron, but Ben and Sara were both eager to get out and driving them around for twenty minutes or so seemed a small price to pay for an empty and peaceful house, so we all piled out into the cold winter night and into my new Audi TT, a guilty offering for poor neglected Alice, compensation from an absent husband. What would I get next time I complained about the state of our boring marriage, I wondered? Maybe a Florida beach house or a private jet, but how about a loving and attentive husband? Not unless Harrods have started stocking them, I suspect.

As per my explicit instructions, I obediently dropped Sara off first at the pre-arranged spot just out of sight of her friend's house; my delightful eighteen-year-old, who once wore pig tails and pretty pink dresses, now strode down the street with more piercings than I could count, wearing a pair of knee high leather, stiletto heeled boots, with more buckles than were strictly required, and were probably too high to walk in anyway, a skirt that was arguably too short and a thin jacket that was definitely too light for this November evening. My sweet angel.

My sixteen-year-old son was slightly easier to please and I dropped him only two doors away from his friend's house wearing a pair of dirty Doc Marten boots; laces trailing behind him, filthy jeans that I had offered to wash, only to be told that's how you're supposed to wear them, a hoody that, on the back, instructed the reader to do something that I am convinced is physically impossible and no jacket. Apparently, it is cool to be cold these days.

Having completed my taxi duties, I turned the car around in the road and started in the direction of home. That ironing wasn't going to get done without at least some input from me; well sometimes it did, but only when I was day dreaming, in which case it was a beautiful Brazilian man, six-foot-tall, shoulder length black hair and a body as hard as granite. Now I think about it, the ironing didn't get done then either.

The car drove itself while I day dreamed of Andre standing by the ironing board, all tanned, in his tiny y-fronts, and before I realised it I had missed my turn off, well, three turns actually, and I was heading into town. I cursed and searched for a suitable place to turn. My headlights found a car park to my left which offered a perfect turning spot, so I flicked the indicator on and pulled in.

The car park belonged to a pub, it was quite full, which seemed odd to me as drinking and driving were certainly not a recommended combination. In any case, I found a bit of space at the back which I turned into, manoeuvred the gear stick into reverse position, and just sat there, the car eagerly awaiting my instruction.

Watching in the rear-view mirror, I saw a young couple, maybe in their early twenties, exit the pub. They were holding hands and laughing together, and looked very much in love. We used to be like that, me and Michael that is, but that was more than eighteen years ago. These days we were lucky to get out at all, even if it was my fortieth birthday. I wracked my brain trying to remember the last time we went anywhere at all together. My memory failed me, but it was a long time ago, I can be sure of that.

The pub looked friendly enough and I imagined what it might be like on the inside; people drinking, laughing. Sod it, the ironing could wait another day, not that anyone would notice the difference, most of the clothes looked the same when I had finished assaulting them with the iron anyway. So I turned the engine off, picked up my handbag from the passenger foot well and stepped out into the car park. A little flutter rippled through me; I hadn't been to a pub on my own since before I had met Michael and here I was heading straight for the door. I dropped the car keys into my handbag and ignored all the safety warnings my brain was currently issuing as I pushed through the heavy door.

Oh Alice, what are you doing?

The pub was disproportionally quiet considering the volume of cars in the car park, but I walked over to the bar and sat myself on a bar stool. A very young and handsome bartender quickly appeared, smiled inanely, and asked 'What would you like?'

Hmm, what would I like? So many possible answers, but I suspect he was only offering me a drink, so I ordered a white rum and diet coke.

If I'm honest, I was feeling more than a little self-conscious. This was not how I remembered going to pubs when I was younger, and that flutter of excitement had turned into a nervous stutter.

I fixed a stare on the beer mat that eloquently reminded me, as if could forget, that I was sitting in the Fox and Cub Pub; I wonder how many units of alcohol it would take to make someone forget the name of the pub they were in, that they would need a beer mat to remind them. Too many, probably.

I'm not usually a drinker and the rum and diet coke had an instant effect on me and I dared myself to look away from the mat. Maybe it was a symptom of my age, but when I was a kid I would have happily walked into some of the roughest dives. Now I just feared the worst wherever I was. The pub seemed nice enough though.

The music in the bar was soft and melodic, not gratingly insistent as I had grudgingly become accustomed at home. There was no TV, and as such no battle over the remote control, no pile of dishes taunting me in the sink, no hunting for dirty socks in the devil's lair that I used to refer to as *Ben's room*.

However, despite the good indicators of a decent environment, and the accumulative effect of my beverage, I still wasn't fully at ease and my fingers were tapping, independently of me, against the wooden bar. I just wasn't used to doing nothing and I made a deal with myself to leave as soon as I had finished my heavily priced drink, and go home to my comfort zone, the ironing board and the movie, just as originally planned.

I needed something to do in the meantime, and reading the labels on the bottles of spirits that hung upside down along the full length of the bar was not going to adequately fill the time it would take me to finish this drink, so I settled for the staff notice board that was only just in view. Learning about the dramas that currently affected the Fox and Cub was hardly stimulating reading, although I secretly wondered why Gary needed to change his shift at such short notice, I guess I might never know the answer to that, and my eyes started wandering again. They found a man who was also sitting alone. He had harsh, staring eyes and tight, frowning skin and I found myself wondering what might have made him so tense – money, or girls maybe?

Just like me, he was sitting at the bar, exactly six stools away actually. His left leg was twitching up and down and his finger was tracing the rim of his pint glass. For a moment I found him quite intriguing, but only for a moment, because the man suddenly looked up. My gaze urgently diverted back to the beer mat.

I could feel heat radiating from my cheeks, and my normally lethargic heart had started pounding like a drummer. God, I hope he hadn't seen me looking at him.

I picked up the glass and gripped it between my sweaty hands as I fixed a stare on the beer mat; my eyes couldn't get me into trouble there. Besides, my drink was nearly finished, and the beer mat would do to keep me entertained until I took my last mouthful and trudged back to boring, but familiar-ville. Drinking alone in a bar was definitely not for me, so next time I'll just stick with the housework.

With a huge sense of relief, I finished the drink, put the empty glass down on the beermat and leant down to retrieve my handbag from the floor; a Harrods sale would have been less traumatic than this spontaneous evening out, but as I sat back up the barman had rematerialized and was waiting for me wearing his ridiculous grin.

'Can I get you another?'

I opened my mouth to say no thanks, but a deep, male voice answered for me,

'Yes, and a pint of Stella.'

I glanced round in the direction of the unsolicited voice; it belonged to the stranger who *had* been sitting six stools away, but who was now perching on the stool right next to mine.

chapter three

TJ pulled up on the drive and parked between his boss's imperial blue BMW M6 and the Sky engineer van at just after eight. He was burning with excitement following his meeting with Pull and Whiteman, two local detectives that TJ had made 'friends' with. Well, friends as long as there was enough cash on the table, and tonight there had been, and then some. His pockets felt light, but he knew it would be worth it; the boss would be very happy when he heard his news.

It was a last minute meeting at their choice of location; a nice secluded spot along the River Exe, free of CCTV, and busy bodies. By day, a cute little place to walk the dog, but by night, a popular location for dealers and addicts. Tonight, the spot had belonged to TJ, Pull and Whiteman.

Sucking the last bit of life out of his cigarette, he flicked it onto the ground behind him as he climbed out of his blacked-out VW Golf. He glanced down the line of parked cars searching for one in particular, but Eddie's was missing. *Ah shame*, the South African thought to himself, he would have to rub his nose in his success later.

He could never understand what the boss liked so much about Eddie; he was so cocky, so arrogant, lording it about the place in his fancy car, and getting all the best girls. He rarely even got his hands dirty these days, that was TJ's job, and Danny's, while Eddie stayed back at the house smoking expensive cigars and drinking and laughing with the boss, laughing at *him*, probably.

It made his stomach turn while he thought about it, then he remembered his news and that perked him up. It was TJ's turn to be the star now. That made him smile and he pulled up his shoulders and strutted down the drive, past the bubbling water fountain, to the solid oak front door.

Danny was waiting for him in the kitchen, a beer already out of the fridge. Danny was a good guy, he liked him, maybe not the sharpest tool, but if you needed someone to watch your back, Danny was your man. He tapped the top of the tin with his fingertips before snapping back the ring pull and taking a long mouthful of the cold, fizzing beer.

'Howsit? Where's Eddie?'

'Working.'

'And the boss?'

'Front room,' Danny answered.

'Good mood?'

'Ish.'

'He will be just now, come on, you don't want to miss this.'

Danny necked the last of his beer and hauled his giant body out of his chair to follow TJ out of the kitchen. The door to the front room was closed, as it often was. TJ knocked and waited impatiently for his boss's deep voice to invite him in.

'Hey Boss.'

He was sitting in his usual leather chair, his fat cigar poised on the edge of a heavy glass ashtray that was balanced on the arm of his chair. His head turned to TJ, his tired looking face flickering in the light of the fire.

'TJ, make this quick, I was about to head home.'

'Ja sure.'

He shifted nervously, this was not quite the reception he was expecting, but he persevered, the boss was surely going to change his attitude when he heard what he was about to tell him.

'I just came from meeting Pull and Whiteman, the cops I told you about before.'

'I know who they are TJ, get to the point?'

He started to feel even more nervous now; how did he always do that, make him feel this way?

'They said they have a witness that has come forward, said she saw you with Molly McGiven the night she was shot. They say the witness has photos on her phone to prove it.'

That got his attention; he sat forward in the chair and his baggy eyes widened as he stared straight at TJ.

'A witness. Who?'

'I don't know yet, the boys say they can find out her name and get the photo for me,' he paused. 'If the price is right.'

He stood up out of his chair and faced up to TJ,

'What price, what do they want?'

'They want two thousand.'

Now he was in uncomfortable territory and he felt a bead of sweat form and roll down the back of his neck. He had already paid the cops fifteen hundred out of his own pocket. He knew the boss would never agree to the first offer and he added a bit for barter room, but this was a big gamble. He should never have done the deal without running it past The Boss first, he knew that, but he had got over excited and let himself get carried away. He had been caught out this way before, but there was no way the Boss wouldn't want her name and address, or the evidence, surely.

'Fine,' he said. 'Two thousand, but I want it yesterday, understand.'

TJ smirked, sighing on the inside, as The Boss strode across the room to a safe built into the wall. He watched eagerly, breath baited, as The Boss punched in the code, opened the heavy steel door and lightened the safe by two thousand pounds in used notes. Even better than he imagined, a done deal and five hundred in his own pocket for his trouble, easy.

'Yes sir.' He said impatiently, as the boss riffled the cash with his fingers. 'It'll be done.'

'Now, I've got to go. Run the whole thing past Eddie when he gets back and see how he wants to handle things.'

Eish, why did he have to be brought in?

'This is shite, I can do it on my own, I don't need Eddie to babysit.'

'I'm sure.' The Boss raised his left eyebrow and grimaced. 'Or, I could just hand it *all* over to him and Danny, I need these things handled right TJ. Eddie knows how I like things done.'

'Fine, I'll talk to him tonight when he gets back.'

'Good,' he said dropping the pile of notes into his hand. 'Good.'

Without so much as a smile, The Boss turned his attention to his pilot jacket draped over the back of the other chair, pulled it over his arm as he passed TJ, and squeezed past Danny, who was almost filling the doorway behind him, and just marched out the front door, straightening his coat as he walked, not even a *good job*, no *attaboy*, not even a *see you later*. And now Eddie would take half, no, more likely all the credit for his work, once a-fucking-gain.

Turning on his heels, he growled as he punched Danny square on the arm before storming back into the kitchen and throwing his sulky self deep into a chair.

He grabbed at his Glock 41; the same one Eddie had, dumped it on the table with a thud, necked his beer and sparked up a fag. He took two deep drags on his cigarette before Danny appeared in the doorway.

'Sorry bro,' the South African said, flicking ash on the tiled floor.

'Eddie's ok, you know.'

Not for long, he thought, staring at the gun on the table, not for fucking long.

'Ja, I'm sure.'

'You just got to get to know 'im.'

'What are you still doing here anyway?'

'I'm waiting on Eddie, there's a hooker in the van, needs got rid of.'

'Another one? Well, I'm here, come on, let's go now.'

'He wanted to wait till after eleven.'

'Bollocks to that, come on, sooner done, sooner we can all get the fok out of here. Where's the keys?'

Danny eased the van keys out of his straining back pocket and tossed them over to TJ. He grinned as he tossed them playfully in his hands.

'Come on, what you waiting for?'

He noticed Danny sigh, but with Eddie gone, he could take charge again, and strode out the door heading straight for the van, buzzing once again.

chapter four

The barman delivered our drinks and scarpered quickly, leaving me alone, in silence, with the stranger. My freeze or flight instincts argued amongst themselves as I flailed pathetically in this unfamiliar territory.

'I should probably, have to, maybe, get home, maybe?'

'I saw you looking at me.'

My hand started shaking in my handbag as I felt around for my keys; they were there a minute ago, shit, where were they.

'I'm sorry, I wasn't, I mean, I didn't…'

Where were those damned keys?

'I'm Jonny.'

Oh no, he wants to know my name, just go, forget the keys, it's only a couple of hours walk home from here.

The silence was painful.

Do something, Alice, he's looking right at you, he'll think you are crazy.

'I'm Susanna.' My hand stilled in the bottom of my handbag for an awkward moment, mid-search.

What happened, who said that, who the hell is Susanna? Jesus Alice. That drink must have really gone to my head, what the hell was I thinking?

'Nice to meet you, Susanna.'

'Er, oh.'

The stranger, Jonny, was an unremarkable man to look at. He was tall, maybe six foot, or thereabouts, and had a stocky build. His narrow blue eyes told a story of their own and they made him look weary and jaded. He had just the right amount of stubble though, and light brown, not too short hair.

'Stood up, were you?' he quizzed.

'Oh, no, I'm not meeting anyone, actually I have to....'

'Not married?'

Why would he think that? I ran my fingers over the hand that had now long abandoned its mission of finding my keys, no wedding ring, oh, and then I remembered leaving it by the sink when I washed the dishes.

'No,' mouth said. Yes, actually you're married, brain interjected, for twenty-one hap - well twenty-one years. 'You?'

'No.'

'Girlfriend?'

What are you asking him that for?

'Nope, just me, all alone.'

'Aw.'

No, no, no not *aw*, my mouth suddenly had its own agenda, I took a gulp from my second rum and diet coke.

'So, what are you doing here?' he said.

'I don't know, actually.' At least that was true.

He sniggered, 'Fair enough, what about your job, what do you do?' he said.

I swallowed hard, what the hell was I doing? This was crazy.

'Not much, just a boring shoe shop assistant, but actually....'

'I thought that would be a girl's idea of heaven, working in a shoe shop.'

He smiled warmly, and boy what a smile it was, the harsh look he had started with simply melted away as his smile stretched from ear to ear, forcing every other muscle in his face to look just as happy as his mouth did, including the cute dimple that just appeared in his right cheek. Its persuasive powers were not limited to his own face and I found myself relaxing and smiling right back at him.

'What about you?'

'I work in security.'

'Oh.'

'Oh, is right,' he laughed.

'Sorry, I didn't mean…'

'Security. The one job guaranteed to bring an end to a perfectly fine work conversation, trumped only by insurance or accountancy.'

My hand briefly touched my lips as I giggled. That's it, no more alcohol for me, the last time I had giggled like that I think I was in high school and was being chatted up by Darren Ringwood.

'Burglar alarms and stuff?' I asked.

'Something like that.'

'Well, I suppose someone has to do it.'

'That's true.'

He smiled again, oh that dimple, I wish he would stop doing that.

'You have a nice smile,' I said.

That's it mouth, you are properly fired.

'So do you. I could look at it all night. Another drink?'

'No, I've still got this one.' I said looking down at my empty glass, Jesus where did that go? 'Oh well, I'm getting a taxi home now anyway, why not.'

Brain, you're fired too; accessory by lack of intervention.

He beckoned the barman with two fingers who swiftly obliged us with another round of drinks; my third. This was an unprecedented amount of alcohol for me in one night, but I was starting to enjoy my illicit and spontaneous meeting with Jonny and contrary to my initial assessment, he was coming off more and more sweet and lovable as the evening went on, and less and less predatory. Maybe it was that slight hint of a Welsh accent that he had or maybe it was just the rum.

He gazed intently, his infectious smile never once faltering, while I told him all about shoes and the occasional insane customers that thought they could squeeze their giant feet into a delicate size five shoe. Not sure how much he was *really* listening, but he gave a good impression and laughed in all the right places, so that was pretty encouraging.

'So where are you from, you didn't grow up round here?' I said.

'Oh, no. I grew up in Newport, but my mum is from London, guess I just kept her accent.'

'So what kinds of things does a guy in security actually do?'

'Oh, I hate to talk about it, it's so boring and I wouldn't want to risk having you slip into a coma, but I can show you how to defend yourself using only your thumbs.'

I held my hands out and looked puzzled at my innocent, but apparently, deadly thumbs. They certainly didn't look like they should be tucked in an assassin's tool box and I'm pretty sure Bruce Willis would have much rather used a gun in *Die Hard*, but still, handy to know, I guess.

'These thumbs?'

'Yes, here.'

He leant forward and took my hands in his. His gentle but strong hands. Pulses of electricity sparked and rippled down my arms and through my melting body.

Oh my.

He was looking straight at me and like a stunned rabbit, I was caught in the headlights, lost in those dreamy blue eyes.

The phone in my handbag snapped me sharply out of my delightful trance and back to reality when it started playing the crazy frog song at full volume. My cheeks burned as I snatched it out of my bag, urgently hitting answer to bring a welcome end to the embarrassment. Crazy frog was a dare from Sara that I had never got around to deleting. I made a mental note to do it straight after this.

The caller ID informed me that Sara was calling.

'Hello?'

'Mum, you need to come and get me now, Stacie is such a bitch, I'm never talking to her again…'

'Ok, ok, no problem, I'll be there in a bit.' I reluctantly dropped the phone back into my bag and my heart sank. That was the end of my night of fun. Familiar-ville called and reality was missing its slave.

'I'm sorry, I have to go.'

'Everything ok?'

'Undoubtedly, but duty calls, and when duty calls…'

'I come running?' he finished.

'Sorry.' I said trying not to look too drunk as I slithered off the bar stool, my hand firmly gripping the edge of the bar. 'Thanks for the drinks. It was really nice meeting you.'

'You too.' He smiled again, that bastard.

I couldn't help but smile back as I carefully headed for the door. Just one foot at a tipsy time, any slip up now could bring about the end of what little dignity that damned frog had left me with.

Relieved to have made it to the door, I rested my hand on the handle for a second. The handle brought a certain sense of security and I enjoyed it briefly before I reluctantly yanked the door open.

'Wait!'

I spun round to see Jonny bouncing straight for me. He placed the cardboard coaster my drink had rested on in my free hand and smiled, his wonderful smile, before blushing and turning back to his stool. Which offered my first opportunity to check out the rear view. Not bad.

Eyes, you belong to a married woman.

The fresh, oh who am I kidding, the bloody freezing November air hit me like a slap to the face as I stepped outside, bringing with it a slight sense of sobriety and a huge sense of guilt. Thankfully though, not enough sobriety to convince me to drive my own car, and I made my way over to a taxi rank at the end of the road, hopped straight into a waiting cab and gave the driver Stacie's address.

The cab was warm, thank God and I cozied up in the back as the driver pulled into the late evening traffic.

I was still clutching the illicit beer mat when I pulled on my seat belt. There was just enough light in the back of the car to take a proper look at it. Jonny had written a mobile phone number on it and the words;

Call me, if you like, Jonny.

Argh! I do like, but Jonny, even though I may or may not have accidentally led you on a bit tonight, you will not be seeing this married woman again, sorry, and I tucked the coaster into the very bottom of my handbag just in time for Sara to bounce into the back of the cab.

Tears flowed as she fired incomprehensible teenage babble at me. Not being proficient in this new language of the damned, I missed almost every word, but still, a mother has a job to do and I put my arm round her shoulders and listened to her drivel all the way home.

Thankfully, once on our drive her phone found our Wi-Fi and she continued her ranting on Facebook.

Shutting the door behind me, I slipped out of my heavy winter coat and dropped my handbag by the front door.

'Where have you been?' The voice was coming from the front room and belonged to my husband.

Michael, aka Mr Mundane, had made it home, and was sitting in his chair in front of the telly, with his dull charcoal grey tailored trousers, lacklustre white shirt and safe grey silk tie, loosened and hanging across his chest like a saggy noose.

'I was at Jackie's.' I lied.

'Oh right. I was worried.'

'Sorry, it was last minute.' Change the subject; lying definitely not your strongest talent. 'Did you find your tea ok?'

'Yes, I did, but I got something at work. Where's Ben?'

'At Steve's.'

Mr Mundane nodded and turned back to the telly, I took my leave and went upstairs. It was getting late, so I filled the bath and lay back in the foamy, lavender scented water and dreamt of Jonny aka Mr Dimple.

chapter five

TJ reversed the van as close to the edge of the river as he dared and pulled on the handbrake. It was dark, and the place was deserted, except for one late night dog walker who had braved the cold evening with his very large Brindle Boxer.

They waited patiently in the van, Pitbull rapping lyrically from the van's speakers, while the dog finished up his business and they disappeared out of sight.

'When are you going to learn to drive anyway?' TJ said over the bass.

'Tried three times didn't I, not my thing.'

TJ nodded knowingly to himself – definitely not the smartest tool in the box. Danny was sitting in the passenger seat staring blankly through the windscreen. His leg was twitching, and not even in time with the riotous beat, making TJ more than a little uncomfortable.

He took a good look out the window; the picnic area in front of the van was empty, aside from the obligatory pile of dog poo bags beside an overflowing bin. The well-trod path along the river was clear to the left and a glance to right confirmed it was the same.

To hell with this, he thought, *the coast was clear, why was Danny still sitting there.*

'What you waiting for?' TJ said.

'Eddie usually dumps 'em in the canal, says they never get found there.'

'You know something, I'm getting tired of hearing that loser's name, just get the bitch out the van and into the shitting river, would ya?'

Danny mumbled noisily under his breath as he pushed open the passenger door and hopped down into the sharp night. TJ didn't ask him to repeat himself; he knew exactly what he had said and chose to ignore it, this time.

He sparked another cigarette and dangled it out of his open window, watching via the rear-view mirror as Danny opened the back doors. A few minutes later a gentle thud confirmed the body was out of the van and he turned and leant out the window to get a better look, but he could only see the end of the black body bag peeking out from under the door.

Laughing to himself, he watched the floor show unfold. Even considering the size of him, Danny was struggling to get the body off the ground and eventually, after dropping it twice and a lot of cursing, he gave up trying. *This was better than TV*, TJ thought as he took a long drag on his fag.

'Eddie usually helps me.' Danny called, his head peering round the side of the rear door. 'It's not that easy once they go stiff, ya know.'

'It's a hooker, bro, maybe ninety pounds at best, I think you can handle it.'

In between glancing up and down the street for possible witnesses, he watched Danny drag the body awkwardly across the grassy bank until he got close enough to the edge to kick roll it in. A gentle splash followed, then the rear doors slammed shut and Danny walked back along the side of the van dusting his hands against his thick thighs.

'Excellent,' TJ said, as he flicked his spent fag butt.

Danny hauled himself back into the passenger seat. *Another job well done*, he thought, *and without the help of Eddie, imagine that.* He felt most satisfied, lit another fag and smugly drove the van back in the direction of the house.

He eyed Eddie's car as he pulled into the drive and he couldn't help but feel a deep sense of satisfaction. The look on his face would be priceless when he told him his news.

This should be good fun, he thought.

He didn't have to wait long either, the handbrake was barely on when Eddie appeared at the front door, a beer in one hand and a giant grin all over his face, *smug bastard.* Eddie was already sauntering over to the van as he flung open the door and hopped onto the tarmac.

'Hey TJ, Danny, where've ya bin?'

'Just got rid of that hooker for ya.'

Eddie slapped him on the shoulder, 'Great, thanks.'

So fake, he thought.

'Laters ya'll.' Danny said, waving as he walked across to his own car, a beaten-up Ford Focus. Eddie waved back with one finger.

'Ja, also the boss says I need to speak to you, I did a deal with two cops for some evidence and the name of a witness, said I should run it by you, he wants it done yesterday.'

'Good job, man. No problem.' He said beaming. 'Seems you don't need me here then, talk about it tomorra?'

'You going now then?'

'Looks like I got some free time, gonna head over to The Green Room for a drink, you wanna come?'

'Nah.'

'Tomorrow then,' Eddie said as he headed to his car.

TJ leant up against the van, nodded and waved. Smug bastard.

chapter six

It took me less than half an hour to dry off after my shower, scrunch some moose into my unruly hair and pull on my favourite old jeans, top and vans. I bounced down the stairs, fully aware that the clock was ticking. I darted into the kitchen; stew bubbling nicely on the range, check. Spuds in the oven, check. Plates with knives and forks set out on the table, check. I opened the fridge and pulled a Boddingtons from the plastic ring that bonded it to its five friends, snapped back the ring pull and poured it into a tall glass for Mr Mundane, who was currently sitting in front of the telly watching the news.

A loud blast from a car horn outside demanded my attention and I dashed the beer through to Michael.

'Right, I'm off. Dinner will be about twenty minutes'

He barely looked away from the telly as I passed him his drink,

'Ok, see you later, where are you going again?'

I leant forward to give him a quick kiss on the cheek.

'Jackie's, for book club, see you later.'

He nodded and took a mouthful of beer as I sighed and left him in his comfortable chair.

I picked out my warmest coat, the white one with the fake fur lining, and pulled it on, grabbed my bag, my keys and a chilled bottle of white I had retrieved from the cellar earlier and looked back at Michael, his eyes still fixed to the giant TV screen, I sighed again, was this really my life?

The cab hooted again, he was clearly more impatient than me, but only just, and I dashed out the front door and across the lawn. I gave the cabbie Jackie's address and slumped into the back seat.

Jackie was my absolute best friend, had been since school; she owned the shoe shop I worked part time at for the past twelve years. I was heading over to her house for book club; our regular Friday night date where we drank wine, moaned about our husbands and, very occasionally, we talked about books.

If I recall correctly, we only really discussed a book once and that was only because it was *Fifty Shades of Grey*! The book was *all* we could talk about that week, it was the closest I would ever get to having a Mr Grey of my own and that's for sure, and right on cue, my mind flashed up an imagine of Jonny's smiling face, which of course I dismissed immediately, with a disapproving frown.

While the taxi turned out of the street, I popped open my hand bag to drop my keys and phone inside, the beer mat Jonny had given me was still there, sitting proudly at the top.

Call me, if you like.

I pushed it to the bottom of my bag and closed it quickly.

Call me, if you like.

Still on my first glass of wine, I nursed the rim as my eyes wandered absently around Jackie's smartly decorated front room. Her husband, Alistair, was noticeably missing, probably upstairs watching TV in the bedroom, as he was usually instructed to do on a book club night. Jackie and Lara sat at right angles to me on the overstuffed, cream sofa, and Gilly sat opposite me on a matching chair.

I put the nearly full glass down on the floor by my feet and pulled a purple cuddle cushion into my arms as my eyes continued to drift round the room, only barely taking notice of the photos of Jackie and her family that stood proudly on the mantel piece, and the fire that crackled comfortingly below it.

My preoccupied brain was, of course, thinking about Jonny, again, and no matter how hard I tried, my mind's eye was not going to let me shift the image of his cute dimpled face, and the beer mat that was skulking guiltily in the bottom of my bag.

I listened absently to the girls' drunken giggles. I am not even sure what they were laughing about, but one of their husbands, Jackie's, I think, had committed a terrible crime by the sounds of it, probably forgot to put the bins out or forgot to compliment her on her hair, or some other random and inconsequential act. I let my mind mosey back to Jonny, beautiful Jonny and his beautiful smile. I'll bet he didn't forget to put the bins out or complain about lumpy mash.

'Alice?' Jackie's voice echoed in my head. 'Al!'

I was back in the room and Jackie was kneeling in front of me, staring straight at me, where was everyone else?

'You alright?' she said.

I sat up in the chair, 'What happened to Lara and Gilly?'

'It's half eleven, they went home,' Jackie said frowning. 'What's up, you've been quiet all night?'

'Nothing.'

'Nothing, my arse, spill.'

She stood up and perched opposite me on the edge of the chair, her wide, staring eyes boring holes into my brain. Maybe that was her plan, if I didn't give up the information willingly, she would just steal it straight from my mind.

'Come on.'

My fingers tangled involuntarily. I wanted to tell her, what harm could it do, she was my best friend and maybe if I talked about it, I would be able to get him out of my head and get back to normal. Whatever that was.

'I met this guy,' I said.

'What? Where?' Her eyes widened further, if that was possible, and her jaw near hit the floor, clearly not what she was expecting me to say.

'In a bar.'

'You, in a bar?' she said. 'What's he like?'

'His name is Jonny, he's nice, and has an amazing smile.'

'Alice Walker? I am shocked at you.'

I reached into my handbag and pulled out the beer mat, 'He gave me this.'

Jackie took the beer mat, her eyebrows looked like they were about to spring off the top of her head, it would be ok if they did, her enormous gaping mouth would have caught them easily enough.

'Are you going to call him?'

'What? No, of course not.'

'Why not?'

'Now I am surprised at you,' I said.

'So what if you are married, why shouldn't you have a bit of fun.'

'I told him my name was Susanna. It *was* kinda fun. But at Michael's expense, no, it's so wrong.'

'That's true,' she paused, 'but only if he found out.'

'You are terrible, I should just burn this, I don't know why I haven't already, to be honest.'

'Alice.' Jackie looked deadly serious. 'You are married to the most boring man on the planet, call him, have a bit of fun, no one would blame you, you deserve it. Believe me.'

I sat back in the chair and thought about it for a second. Then in a flash Jackie had grabbed my handbag off the floor beside me.

'Hey, what are you doing?'

I jumped out of the chair and grabbed for the bag, but I was too late, she had what she wanted and dropped the bag to the floor dashing out of the room, my phone in one hand, the beer mat in the other.

I gave chase, shouting and grabbing at her as I ran after her, but she was quicker than me and seconds later she had locked herself in the downstairs' toilet. I banged frantically on the door,

'Jackie, don't you dare!'

She didn't reply. I thundered on the door again.

'Jackie, I swear, get out here now.'

I could hear her giggling, but she didn't reply, then I heard a noise that made my stomach turn over – the message alert on my phone.

'Please, promise me you didn't,' I shouted, my head leaning against the door.

I could hardly contain my relief when the lock finally clicked and the door opened, revealing my soon-to-be ex-best friend smirking in the doorway with my phone in her left hand.

'Here.' Her cheeky smile grew, and she nodded as she handed back my phone. 'You'll thank me one day.'

I looked down at the screen, the messenger app was still open, and I scrolled, with horror.

11.34 Hi Jonny, it's Susanna from the bar. I would really like to see you again.

11.35 Hi Susanna. I didn't think I was going to hear from you again. When are you free? Jonny

11.37 Monday afternoon – for coffee?

What had she done? Now I had a date, sort of, my heart cartwheeled with the excitement, but my head was screaming at me, cheater, cheater, filthy cheater.

'I can't go Monday, I have to work.'

'Well, as your boss *and* your best friend, I am officially giving you the day off, and any other day you want to go see the lovely Jonny.'

The phone beeped again,

11.39 Sounds perfect, come to mine for 2? Flat 36 Winchester Appts, Winchester Street, can't wait. J

chapter seven

The trade had taken a little over twenty seconds, not what TJ had imagined at all, he wasn't expecting a grand reunion, but he thought twenty seconds was a bit disappointing, considering it had taken him and Eddie, who had insisted on coming with, more than half an hour to drive there This was *supposed* to be his moment of glory, what an anti-climax.

Still, they were true to their word and he had what he came for; a piece of paper with the name and address of the witness written on it and a photo, which clearly was The Boss walking with Molly McGiven. The time stamp placed him with her 31 minutes before she was found dead, damning indeed.

He had made sure to keep his back to Eddie during the exchange, since he had already paid the guys in their meeting before, but Eddie was smart, he would think there was something wrong if he didn't hand over the money and he would start asking questions, prying. Today TJ was smarter.

They all nodded to each other and he turned and jogged the fifty yards or so back towards the car. The route he had chosen was really overgrown and he quickly became aware of how dumb he must look as he struggled to run through the long grass and thick shrubs, so he settled down to a fast walk.

His brand-new Nike trainers and the bottom of his Levi's were wet from the damp grass by the time he climbed into the passenger seat beside Eddie, but he didn't care about that. He had his prize.

'Sorted?' Eddie said.

'Sorted,' he replied.

'Where to?'

TJ looked at the piece of paper he had been given, '28 Church Street.'

Church Street was on the other side of town; he would have to sit in the car for at least another half an hour with Eddie while he made small talk, so he leant forward and pointed to the car's radio.

'Can I?'

'Sure, whatever.' Eddie smiled.

He half smiled, turned the stereo on, found a station he liked and ramped up the volume as far as he dared without making it look too obvious that he was being antisocial; he hated the radio, but it was sure better than the alternative. He had to admit though, Eddie really knew how to shift his car and they sailed across town in no time. His radio idea worked well too, and they had hardly spoken a word to each other for the entire journey; that was until now.

'Do you know what this girl looks like?' Eddie said, turning the volume down on Ed Sheeran's latest track.

'Nope, just that she is in her early twenties and blonde.'

'Well, that sure narrows it down round here,' Eddie said laughing.

He had a point. No denying that. Smug Bastard.

'So, what then?' TJ said.

He hated asking, but he had been so wrapped up in his deal that he hadn't thought about the rest of it.

'That's easy.' Eddie said pulling over into a side street. 'What's her name?'

'Nancy Reed.'

'Ok. Wait here a sec.'

He sighed, here comes Eddie to save the day again. He glared out the window, watching as he disappeared down an alley.

They were in the middle of town and people were milling about as you would expect on a Saturday afternoon, teenagers on in-line skates weaving in and out of the crowd, tired looking mothers pushing buggies and dragging their toddlers around, couples just out for the afternoon. An old lady cursed and threw out her stick at the teenager on skates as he cut her off, he just laughed. Then his eyes caught a young girl, maybe late teens/early-twenties who was walking down the road in the direction of the car.

She looked comfortable in sexy red heels tucked under her tight jeans; *she must wear heels a lot,* he thought. Her shoes matched the close-fitting top she had on, partially concealed under her heavy winter coat. He liked her shoulder length, perfectly straight red hair; it matched her perfectly made-up eyes. He imagined looking closer into those eyes, his hand running through that hair, down her back. He bit his lip as he imagined what else he might like to do to her.

He waited patiently for just the right moment before he threw the car door open, nearly, but not quite, knocking her off her feet. A moment later he was out of the car, apologising profusely and introducing himself to her in his thick South African accent, the girls always lapped it up. He was still laughing about the close call with the girl, called Katy, when Eddie arrived back at the car with a bunch of flowers.

'Hey,' he said. 'I'm Eddie.'

'Who's the lucky girl?' she said, checking him out.

'Oh, these...' Eddie said.

'They're for his wife,' TJ told Katy, before shooting Eddie a scornful look. 'You can wait in the car; I'll be there in a minute.'

'Nice to meet you,' Eddie said to Katy before he disappeared behind the wheel.

'Shame, I've gotta go,' TJ said. 'I'd really like to buy you a drink though, you know, say sorry for nearly knocking you down.'

She paused for a second. Her dark eyes rolled into the back of her head, then she smiled, and dug into her handbag for a piece of paper and a pen.

'Give me a call.' She said, scribbling her number down and handing it to him.

TJ smiled, 'I definitely will.'

She waved the tips of her fingers and continued along the street the same way she had been heading. TJ turned and watched her go.

'Eish, rear view, just as good as the front,' he said quietly to himself before snapping out of his lustful gaze and hopping back into the car.

'Nice girl,' Eddie commented.

'My girl.'

'Easy,' Eddie said as he threw his hands up. 'Just saying.'

That put him in his place, TJ thought.

The large bunch of flowers had found their way onto the back seat.

'What's with the flowers?'

'They, are for Nancy.'

Brilliant, TJ thought as they pulled back into traffic. Why didn't he think of that?

The flowers worked a treat too; Eddie just pulled his scarf over his face, hopped straight up to the door, rang the bell and asked for Nancy.

Moments later she was gushing at the front door and TJ had surreptitiously taken a bunch of photos of her, just in case they needed them later.

Stage one done, stage two – stalk the do-gooding bitch, wait till she's alone and snatch her clean off the streets, easy peasy.

chapter eight

Disappointingly, there was not much stalking to be done, and the prize went to, guess who, that's right, good ol' Eddie, for another moment of genius.

The card with the flowers had invited Nancy to meet her *secret admirer* behind a pub that had burned down about a year ago. A nice secluded spot, no cameras and no witnesses. Eddie scored again. But he wasn't getting the home run; this was still going to be TJ's victory.

'What time did you say?' TJ said.

Eddie was calmly reading the newspaper.

'Half eight,' he said, looking up. 'What time is it now?'

'Twenty past.'

Eddie nodded and went back to his paper.

They had come in TJ's Golf GTI – **G**ood **T**imes **I**mplied! and he *was* going to have a good time tonight.

He peered through the windscreen, staring at a cat attacking a paper bag about fifteen feet in front of them. The cat was having the time of its life, drawing back, waiting, pondering, then when the moment came it wiggled its bum and pounced, gathering up the bag between its paws and rolling around on its back. So elegant, he liked cats, liked their graceful arrogance; the ultimate sociopath.

It was getting cold in the car, so TJ turned up the heat before blowing into his gloves. He hated the cold and, at this time of year, he hated this country. Drizzly, damp and cold. Every winter he longed to go back to Cape Town. He had gone a few years ago, but realised he hated it there too, despite the excellent weather he hated the place, and he came straight back to England; the land he now officially called home, despite the bitter cold.

The heater fired a continuous and welcome stream of warmth into the car and TJ pulled off his gloves and held his hands across two of the vents to absorb as much heat as possible. He swapped his hands for his gloves and after holding the open end of his gloves over the vents for a few minutes, he slipped his cold hands back into the warmed gloves.

It was eight thirty-two. He searched the car park from his seat, no sign of anyone, *she wasn't coming* he thought, Eddie fucked up. The thought made him smile. TJ was right; they should've just grabbed her at the house when they had the chance. He hated all this messing about, *just get the job done and get out, that was the way to do things*, he thought.

Five more minutes, he thought, *five minutes and I'm leaving, then we do it my way.*

He didn't get his five more minutes and seconds later a short but perfectly formed blonde appeared at the entrance to the car park.

He nudged Eddie, 'Yo, that her?'

Eddie peered over the top of his paper, 'Looks like it.' He folded the paper and dropped it onto the floor of the car. 'Ready?'

TJ nodded and watched Eddie spring out of the car and across the crumbling tarmac, heading straight for her.

They were talking, and he wondered what Eddie might have said to her, she didn't run away like you would expect, in fact she continued towards him. Stupid girl didn't have a fucking clue. He pressed the button and the passenger window slid down so he could better hear what was being said. Nothing much at first, just some mumbling. Then Eddie had his arm behind her and was guiding her towards the car, she seemed to be quite happy to walk with him. How did he do that? Then he must have said or done something she didn't like as she turned and started to walk quickly back towards the car park entrance, and to safety.

'Speak up, damn it!' TJ said.

Eddie followed her, she sped up, but it was too late, Eddie quickly had his hand over her mouth and after a bit of a tussle, he had the girl under his arm and was carrying her back to the car.

'We just want to talk,' TJ could hear him say to the wriggling girl, who was shouting obscenity into his gloved hand.

TJ hopped out of the car and rushed round the passenger side to open the back door for Eddie. She was going nuts by the time he arrived, but Eddie still had a firm grip of her. She wasn't getting away, no matter how hard she fought or screamed. He dashed back round to the other side of the car and climbed into the back seat, handcuffs ready, he met Nancy in the middle and snapped the cuffs round her wrists securely while Eddie held her mouth shut and her body still.

She was quite the fighter and Eddie practically had to sit on her to stop her kicking and punching him. He just let her wear herself out.

TJ was quickly back in the driver's seat, 'Ready to go?' he said.

'Yep, somewhere nice and quiet I think.' Eddie said, still managing to firmly hold the crazed girl in the backseat.

By the time they arrived at the riverside, she had finally tired and stopped fighting. As Eddie held his gun against her head for insurance, he climbed off her and slowly removed his hand from her now quiet mouth.

TJ leant into the back to watch; he was struck by how pretty she looked, even though she was panting heavily, and her wet face was puffy and red.

As she found her breath, Eddie leant forward and whispered into her ear, and she nodded manically with wide eyes, allowing them to check her bag.

TJ searched the bag for her phone, and pulled out an iPhone; he removed the battery and sim and smashed the rest of her phone against the dash board before tossing it out the window. It made a satisfying splashing sound as it hit the water, which reminded TJ of the hooker and made him smirk.

Turning back, he looked her up and down, thought for a second and decided he had plans for Nancy, plans that didn't require Eddie.

'I can handle it from here,' he said.

'You sure?'

'We're done, I'm just taking her home, right?'

'Yeah,'

'Well, even I can't screw that up surely.' Eddie looked straight at him and cocked his head, looking unconvinced. 'You're not going to give me any trouble, are you sweetie?'

She shook her head and tentatively whispered 'No.'

'There, see.'

'Well, ok.'

TJ dropped Eddie back at his place before heading back into the night with the lovely Nancy handcuffed in the back of his car, young, pretty, restrained, just how he liked 'em.

chapter nine

Jonny's flat was on the top floor of what appeared to be a fairly new apartment block, and was positioned about half way along a long hall, which had a strong new carpet aroma. No letter box in his door, or in any of the others for that matter, they must get their mail delivered elsewhere. There was a door knocker right above the flat number; 36, and a bell.

I had been standing on the wrong side of Jonny's door, procrastinating, for far longer than I should, examining it intricately, trying to decide which would be the best way to alert him to the fact that I had arrived, door knocker or bell?

Of course, the real reason I hadn't knocked or rung the bell was that I was seriously considering a different action altogether; the option of utilising neither, turning on my heels and getting the hell out of there. Back to my not-so-little-anymore hellions and my safe, dependable and void of love or excitement marriage.

My heart was begging me to ring, knock or just break the flipping door down, but my brain was busy reminding me of the wedding ring I had hidden in the bottom of my handbag. A small band of gold, more than twenty years old, holding me to a sacred contract I had once made, a contract which my flaky heart was currently dead set on me betraying.

The heart won, and before my head had a chance to formerly protest, my trembling right index finger was firmly pressed against the doorbell.

Oh my god, I'm really doing this.

My stomach faltered. I was so nervous, it was like I had never been on a date before. I had, of course, but that was over twenty years ago. My stomach turned again and for an awful moment I was convinced I might deposit the roasted vegetable quiche I'd had for lunch on his doorstep, not a good start to a date.

I held my lunch down and about a minute later my heart stopped as the door opened. Jonny stood in the doorway with wet hair, wearing a black pair of combat style trousers, a slouchy grey hooded top, and a green towel wrapped round his shoulders. My heart sighed; he wasn't even half as good looking as my overactive imagination had made him out to be over the past couple of days.

'Hey,' he said.

Then there was that smile, and, oh my, that dimple, and I was now standing in front of the most beautiful man alive. My imagination took a bow and my heart enthusiastically gave it a high five.

'Hi.'

I melted.

'Wow, you look nice. Come in.'

I should hope so, I thought. I'd been working on this just rolled out of bed looking gorgeous look for hours; plucking, shaving, curling, moisturising, painting and struggling to decide between two almost identical pairs of jeans, it had been a mammoth undertaking.

'Oh, thank you.'

Cautiously I stepped in; cautiously, mostly because of the heels that were far too high for me, but that I was assured by Jackie made my bum look great in these jeans, but also because stepping across that threshold meant I was seriously contemplating committing a cardinal sin.

'I couldn't believe it when you texted, I haven't been able to get you out of my head since last week.'

That's interesting I thought, *neither had I.* I grinned at the thought.

His flat was nice-ish, I guess. The new carpet smell was still there but was now mixed with a vanilla scent. Cream carpet and magnolia walls, no pictures or anything decorative, bland, functional, but nice, but then I am not entirely sure what to expect from a single man's flat, maybe he had just moved in.

I took my coat off and Jonny offered his hand to take it from me. His warm hand touched mine and I caught his gaze for a split second. I smiled, pure magic.

'I'm sorry, I'm running a bit late,' he said, breaking the tension and waving at a black leather sofa with red and black striped scatter cushions. The sofa was placed directly in front of a wooden coffee table which was in front of large screen TV. 'Grab a seat. I'll be back in a sec.'

'No problem.'

I exhaled heavily as he disappeared through one of only two other doors, one, I assumed one was for the bedroom and the other a bathroom, while an arch opened into the kitchen.

It felt good to let go of all that built up anxiety, although my nerves were still in tatters and I started to wonder what on earth I was doing here. Mr Mundane crept into my thoughts, but he was no threat to my dishonesty, as in my head he was sitting in his chair complaining about lumpy mash.

I perched myself on the edge of the sofa and had a nosey at what he kept on the magazine shelf of his coffee table, nothing too interesting, a couple of newspapers, a chess set and a monopoly game, a couple of DVD's and a collection of remote controls. The coffee table had two little drawers in it and I wondered what he kept in there as I waited for him to come back, which he did, only seconds later, wearing a smarter t-shirt and no towel.

'Can I get you a drink?'

Hell yes, I need a drink.

'Yes, thank you.'

'Red or white?'

What happened to the coffee?

'Oh, red, please.'

I watched, head tilted slightly to the side, as his rear view disappeared through the arch into the kitchen.

'I haven't had lunch yet, are you hungry?' His voice echoed from the kitchen.

'I'm fine, but you go ahead.'

He returned with an open bottle of red and two glasses. Expertly, he half-filled each glass and handed one to me, sipping from his own.

'Chorey-Les-Beaune, someone gave it to me, it's quite nice,' he said. 'What do you think?'

I gave it a good sniff, that's what you're supposed to do isn't it, and took a sip.

'Um, that's nice.'

There was that smile again, inciting all those primal instincts that we married ladies are supposed to suppress.

He disappeared back into the kitchen and after a couple of moments he returned with a single slice of toast.

The mother in me suddenly stood to attention.

'That's your lunch?' I said.

'Yeah?'

'One slice of toast?'

'I didn't have a chance to get anything?'

'Don't you have anything in there you could make a sandwich with?'

'I usually just buy one.'

'Oh,' I said, taking a long mouthful of wine.

He sat beside me on the sofa and we started talking and laughing, turns out putting a slice of bread in a toaster is the closest he had come to actual cooking. It was quite a shocking revelation, and not one I think I believed, but hey, it got the conversation started and the more we talked, the more I relaxed. I was starting to really enjoy myself and him, it shocked me how much actually.

'...and then, he stuck his finger out the window and swore at me? Can you believe it?'

I couldn't answer; I was laughing so hard, and trying to keep from spitting out a poorly timed mouthful of wine. I kept hold of my wine and as the giggles subsided I found my hand on Jonny's knee, I looked up and we locked eyes for a second.

Suddenly, my mouth was very dry. I licked my lips and searched urgently for something to say that would break the unexpected, heart shuddering tension.

'So, you play chess?' I asked, pulling my hand away.

Jonny's eyes glanced at the chess set under the coffee table. 'Er, sometimes, used to.'

'Any good?'

'I do alright,' he said coyly. 'Why, you wanna play?'

'If you like, I don't know if I'm any good though.'

'All right,' he said, pulling the coffee table closer. He opened the box and pulled out the chequered board.

I picked up the bishop and the rook, 'So where do these two go?'

He chuckled and placed them on the board with the other pieces.

'How about a wager?' he said, oozing in confidence. 'I win, I get to see you again.'

'And what if I don't want to see you again?' I smirked.

'Then you better hope you're better at this than me.' He winked playfully.

'All righty, you're on,' I said, moving the king's pawn forward two squares.

He did the same. 'So, when you're not picking up strange men in bars or working in a shoe shop, what do you do with yourself?'

'I'm pretty boring really, I go to book club at my friend Jackie's house, usually on a Friday, and I like movies.'

'Book club?' he laughed affectionately. 'I'm gonna have my hands full with you.'

I hit him with a pillow, 'Don't be mean.'

'Sorry, sorry,' he was still chuckling. 'What books do you read?'

I moved my king's knight. 'Well, I like any crime thriller, but apart from when we read *Fifty Shades*, we girls normally just drink wine and bitch about men.'

'Oh really, well, I'd better behave myself then.'

'Yes, you'd better.'

'Or maybe not Mrs Grey.' he said, with more than a twinkle in his eye, while moving his king's bishop.

God, I hope so, I thought as the game progressed.

I looked on in disbelief as he moved his queen's bishop diagonally across the board.

'Check.' I grinned as I took his bishop with my knight.

'Hey!'

We spent the next few moves laughing and talking; it was really nice, and I felt connected to him somehow. Jonny was only thirty-five years old; it seems I found myself a toy boy. I figured I might be pushing my luck by trying to pull off younger than that, so I deducted four of my actual years and settled for thirty-six. Seemed plausible enough.

The board was looking decidedly empty as we moved into the end game, more white than black though, I am proud to say. There was only one way he could win, as far as I could see, and I wondered if he had seen it. I considered my next move carefully.

Maybe I shouldn't have hustled him at the start, maybe I should have told him I was chess champion for Devon and runner up in the nationals when I was sixteen, but then why not, he didn't even know my real name, what was one more lie?

I picked up my rook and rolled it in my fingers; glancing up, I looked into his eyes, and his not-so poker face. I put the rook down next to his only knight and sat back.

'You sure?' he said.

'Yep,' I said, my head bobbing.

They would be desperate to hear all about my coffee date on Friday, no doubt Jackie would have ratted me out to the others at some point during the last few days. They probably held a weekend summit to discuss my unexpected and improper behaviour. Forget about the unrest in the Middle East, the bankrupt world or starving children in Africa, my love life would be all they cared about.

I watched with intrigue as he studied the board, he shot me a wry smile, rubbed his hands together and picked up his king's bishop and slid it across the board.

'Checkmate!'

'Argh,' I said. 'I was hoping you hadn't seen that.' I lied.

'You owe me a second date.'

He grinned as he topped up my wine glass; thank God they were only small glasses.

'Do you still want to know how to defend yourself with only your thumbs?' His eyes widened.

'Oh yes, you didn't get the chance to show me before.'

He shuffled along the sofa and I held out my hands just like I had in the Fox and Cub.

'Well, there are a couple of things you can do actually,' he said, leaning forward.

He took my hands in his and that surge of electricity was back, powering through my body, and like a defibrillator restarts a heart, the sudden pulse of electricity had awakened the woman within, who immediately assumed jurisdiction over every part of me.

My eyes locked onto his. The intoxicating scent of his spicy aftershave seduced the last of my senses and I was powerless as he leant forward and unexpectedly pressed his mouth gently against mine.

chapter ten

It took me by surprise, but I didn't stop him kissing me; my body, especially my mouth, was now solely under the authority of Susanna, and she was ecstatic. Then he stopped and jumped off the sofa, his eyes pointing at his feet.

'I'm sorry,' he said. 'I don't know what came over me.'

'That's ok.'

But it wasn't, I didn't want it to stop, his kiss was heavenly, so soft and gentle. I couldn't remember ever being kissed like that, and it wasn't the sort of kiss you would ever forget. I never wanted it to end.

'I can't believe I just threw myself at you like that.' He stood up, his eyes darting all over the place, as I sat floundering in the awkward silence.

'I'm sorry, I should go,' he said, walking to the door.

A little confused, 'Wait, it's your flat, you can't leave. It's my fault, really, I'll go.'

Damn it, so close.

I found my bag on the floor and headed quickly to the door. At the last minute I glanced over at his sad crumpled face as I put my hand on the door handle and secretly hoped that I had done a better job of concealing my sad face than he had. At least I could honestly say I didn't cheat though, right? I slowly pushed down on the silver handle and pulled open the door. I paused for a second, but he didn't stop me. Damn it.

As the door closed quietly behind me I sighed and walked slowly along the hallway to the stairs, plodded down all three flights and out to the car park.

I sat still in my chilly car for a few quiet moments while I cursed myself.

It's for the best I thought, as I started the engine. Me, having an affair, how ridiculous. But I did like him, no, that's a lie, I really liked him, ah well, it just wasn't meant to be.

Then a knock on the window scared the proverbial crap out of me. I clutched my pounding heart as I dared to look round.

Jonny was staring in at me and my heart skipped, he had come after me, but then he held up my coat and it sank again as I wound the window down, just be cool.

'I'm really sorry,' he said.

'Honestly, its fine, is that mine?' He still hadn't given me back my coat.

'Will you come back up,' he said. 'Please?'

I relaxed into a smile, but on the inside, I was cheering, and I turned the engine off, stepped out of the car and followed him back upstairs.

'I guess I do owe you a second date.'

Take two.

We stood just inside the door and things suddenly felt awkward between us, like they had when we first met.

'It's just…' he said, knocking back the last of his red wine and placing his glass on the coffee table.

'What?' I said.

'It's just,' he said, swaying nervously on his feet. 'I just don't want to ruin everything on our first date. I was hoping I might at least get to a third or fourth before I screwed it all up.'

He laughed nervously.

'Well, if it makes you feel better, technically, we're on our second date already.'

'That's true.'

'So, what do you want to do? On our second date?'

He didn't answer, but I suspected we both knew the answer to that, at least I hoped I did. But was I bold enough to go for it, that was the real question? I was already well out of my normal pattern of behaviour just by being here, I hardly even recognised myself.

Do it, do it, do it, Susanna cheered me on.

I took a deep breath.

I stepped forward and held his hands in each of mine, the electricity was back, and I looked up into his eyes. 'You know. I think, if you want something, you should just go for it. Life's too sh…'

I never finished that sentence, I am glad to say, because his lips were pressing against mine again, his hands round my waist. We were kissing again, slow and gentle at first, the raspberry undertones of the wine still lingering on his soft lips. I wrapped my arms round his neck, closed my eyes and enjoyed his tender lips as they explored mine.

His hands slid onto my back and I melted deeper into a more intense, passionate kiss. He walked me backwards towards the sofa, his hands getting more urgent. He easily freed my top that had been neatly tucked into the top of my jeans, and I felt myself tremble slightly as his warm hands slid under my clothes, brushing against my tingling skin. He lowered me backwards onto the sofa, then he was on me, his heavy body pressing against mine, I was willingly pinned to the sofa as his lips searched urgently, working over my neck, my face and my mouth, as my inner woman trembled. I yanked his top over his head and explored his hot, sweaty back with my fingers as I kissed his salty chest. Eyes closed, he arched and groaned as I dragged my fingernails slowly down his back. His strong hands found my thighs, teasing all the way to the top. The button on my jeans eagerly popped open, followed by the zip and I purred as he ran his hands all over me, pushing away my panties and jeans.

My head tipped back, and I bit my lip as I felt every inch of him fill me up. I held on tightly round his shoulders, my fingernails digging into his hot skin as he brought me panting and growling, higher than I had ever been before. He called out with his final powerful thrust, sending Susanna cartwheeling in a euphoric, dizzy frenzy.

Still tingling and a little breathless, he kissed me firmly on the mouth and wrapping his strong arms around me he nestled his head against my shoulder and gently slumped on top of me as I moaned softly. I held him tightly and kissed him on his head before dropping my own head backwards onto the arm of the chair. My eyes closed, and I waited, still giddy, as the blood supply gradually returned to the rest of my body.

Several minutes passed and I had finally regained enough energy to speak, but what do you say to the first man to show you how good sex could be?

'Oh God.'

'Jonny will do.'

I laughed and slapped him on the arm, so predictable, but God was right, no man had ever made me feel like that before, especially not Michael.

Shit, Michael. The man I devoted myself to, promised to love, honour and obey, more than twenty years ago. The father of my kids, the man who thought I was currently at work. Poor Michael. I looked down at Jonny and then at the crime scene; clothes and cushions scattered across the floor, and my stomach turned, this was a terrible thing I had done, my inner woman now nowhere to be seen, just the guilt fairy pointing her righteous little finger at me.

What had I done?

Jonny knelt back, holding my hands, his soft blue eyes staring straight at me, that irresistible smile beaming with desire. I couldn't help it and smiled right back, but the guilt was still eating me up.

'You ok?' he said.

No actually, I'm not ok, I have just done the most terrible thing, but he wasn't asking Alice, forty-year-old mother of two, he was asking thirty-six-year-old, free and single Susanna, and she was most fine indeed.

Susanna smiled, 'Oh Yes.'

His face relaxed and his mesmeric smile returned, 'Good.'

Then his hands were on my face, he was kissing me again, but more softly this time. Susanna grabbed his arms and pushed him off the sofa and onto the floor. Towering over him, her hungry eyes fixed on his. With eyes still locked, she kissed his mouth, then his neck and worked her way all the way down as he massaged my breasts, and before I knew it we were doing it all again.

I like being Susanna.

chapter eleven

'Well?'

The Boss held out his hand to his guest by way of offering him a seat. It was a rare occasion that he invited anyone into his den, but he had known Ash for over thirty years and he was one of the few people in the world that he genuinely called a friend, and right now he knew he could do with at least one.

The just-lit fire crackled and spat, filling the room with a wonderful pine scent and a welcome warmth. Ash took his time and dropped his expensive leather case beside the spare leather chair and stepped closer to the fire.

Ash stood an inch or so taller than him, and was much more athletically built, and had a head full of jet black hair that any fifty-year-old would be jealous of, including The Boss, if he was honest. That's what living the bachelor life did for you he guessed.

Ash kept his poker face as he warmed his cold hands in front of the fire, while The Boss poured two glasses of scotch, his hand steady as a rock, while on the inside he was trembling like a leaf.

Through necessity, he had trained himself long ago to maintain a cool exterior and today he was doing well, especially as Ash was always the one person he had struggled to fool, so he made a point to straighten up and sit confidently forward in his lazy chair.

He had been friends with Ash, or Ashley Banks, since secondary school. There was nothing he didn't know about the guy and vice versa, and he loved him like a brother. But today he wasn't visiting as a friend, today was a business meeting. Today he was going to find out if an arrest warrant had been issued with his name on it. Today he would find out if he was to face a murder charge.

'Ash?'

They had lost touch when they went to different universities as kids, but ten years later, he had found himself in a little bother, and just by chance stumbled across his old pal, Ash, who as it turned out had very conveniently become an excellent defence barrister.

His old friend remained deadpan as he took his glass of scotch and sank deeper into the cherry brown leather chair beside him.

'How's the missus, and the kids?' Ash said.

'You know how the boy is, you probably see him more than me.' He laughed heartily. 'But, you didn't come here to ask me about the wife and kids.'

Ash laughed. He was right about that. Ash had never got married or had kids, that he knew about anyway, and he liked it like that. His bulging wallet proved aphrodisiac enough to a lot of woman and what showing off didn't get him, the cash itself usually did. No hassle, just good times. The Boss was right about his son too. Ash was good at his job, but the boy was starting to really push his luck. It was only a matter of time before the kid either got much, much better at nicking cars, or he ended up doing a stretch in jail.

The Boss shot Ash his most intimidating, cut the bullshit stare.

'Fine, fine. Straight down to business then.' Ash lifted his glass and swirled the dark liquid playfully around the edge; he took a long nose full of the wonderful rich aroma before sipping the aged scotch.

'Ash!'

'All right, all right, spoil my fun why don't you. You're fine, you're off the hook, they dropped the case.'

He tried to never show emotion, but he was finding it increasingly challenging to contain the grin that was emerging on his face, and decided, given the circumstances, that he would let it slide on this happy occasion and give grinning a go, after all, it's not every day you get away with murder, is it?

'Seems the witness that placed you on North Street at the time Molly McGiven went missing, has, in fact, now gone missing herself, so now they have no case against you.' He raised one eyebrow as he spoke. 'You wouldn't happen to know anything about that, would you?'

'No!' he protested. Ash's remaining eyebrow joined the first. 'Actually, I really don't, when did she disappear?'

'You really don't know?'

'No.'

'Well, I hope not, because that would make things seriously troublesome for you, if they were to find out, that is.'

The rare smile had vanished, and he was starting to feel a little uncomfortable; he sure hoped Eddie had done his usual good work, but he made sure he didn't show his uncertainty to his barrister.

'Apparently, the girl was last seen on Saturday night. She caught a cab to meet with a guy she knew, and the cabbie said he dropped her off at the side of the road and left her there. Then no more sightings.'

'What about the guy she met? Anything about him?'

'Nobody knows who he is, so they haven't spoken to him yet.'

'Excuse me for just a moment.'

He stood up from his chair and left Ash in front of the fire. He had a really bad feeling in his gut and needed to make a phone call.

In the kitchen he pulled out his iPhone and searched for Eddie's number. The phone only rang twice.

'Yup?'

'Eddie, listen, I know you went out with TJ on Saturday to talk to that witness, I need to know exactly what happened?'

'You talking 'bout Nancy Reed?'

'Yes, what happened?' He was pacing across the kitchen, this was going to be bad, he just knew it.

'Nothing much, we got her to meet us behind that pub I burned down a couple of years ago, the Dog and Duck they called it. She arrived, I threw her in the back of the car, we drove to the canal, trashed her phone. I had a friendly word like and then TJ took her home.'

'You didn't go with him?'

'No, why, what's happened?'

'She's gone missing, that's what's happened.'

'Oh fuck.'

'Yes. Fuck. Sort it!'

He hung up. Fuck was right; he started to feel sick and stomped out of the kitchen. He took a deep breath before walking down the hallway to the front room where Ash was just finishing his scotch.

'Everything all right?'

'Yeah, peachy. Listen, I am heading home, been a long day, you know.'

'You sure you don't want to blow off some steam at The Club?'

'Strippers and scotch?'

Normally he would have jumped at the chance, but not tonight, not after that news.

'Not really in the mood.'

'You sure?'

'Another time. I'm just going to head home.'

'Suit yourself.'

Ash picked up his case and affectionately tapped his friend on the shoulder, 'Smile, you're off the hook, again.'

He faked a smile, 'Thanks Ash.'

'No need to thank me, bill's in the post.' He laughed heartily as he left.

The Boss waited for him to leave, then got his coat, gloves and keys and walked out to his car. He sat in the driver's seat, the conversation with Eddie still working on him. He started the engine, but he had too much running through his mind to drive.

If that witness had gone missing, it would only be a matter of time before the police came knocking on his door again, and then he would be in the frame for two murders.

He dropped his head back against the headrest and exhaled. Maybe it was just a coincidence and she would turn up with just a little amnesia, as was the original plan. He wasn't convinced though, TJ was a bit too spontaneous, a bit too impulsive for his liking. He had hoped he could control the crazy side of TJ, take advantage of it even, but right now he was starting to regret keeping him on staff.

Eddie would sort it, he had to.

chapter twelve

'Hello?' I called as I walked through the front door. 'Anyone home?'

The usual stereo battle was in full swing, so I assumed that Ben and Sara were home from school and college already. I wondered if they even noticed when I wasn't here. Michael's car was absent from the drive, so I rushed up the stairs to jump in the shower.

As the warm water washed away any physical evidence of my betrayal, I considered the full implications of what I had just done. Jonny was a nice guy; he was funny, interesting to talk to, easy on the eye and very good at the other stuff. A satisfied grin broke on my face. That was an understatement; he was VERY good at the other stuff.

Michael was, well Michael; he was safe, he was secure, he was well off, but that was it. He was certainly not exciting, and I wondered if he ever had been. He barely seemed to notice me these days and I couldn't remember the last time we had had sex, or even went to bed at the same time for that matter.

I was eighteen when we met, he was twenty-seven. He was fairly rich even then and I enjoyed being spoiled with expensive gifts, fancy hotels and nights out. I think that's what attracted me to him, and if I'm being honest, it was probably what's kept me interested for so long.

Six months later he asked me to marry him and I said yes without a second thought and dropped straight out of university, abandoning my dream of being a vet and starting a new life as a kept woman.

I remember the look on my parents faces when I told them. I will never forget it. Mum almost choked, and Dad just went pale and quiet. I think he thought it was just one of those things I needed to *get out of my system*. I never did, I loved Michael then. I don't know if I still do.

Twenty years later, and now I have an eighteen-year-old daughter of my own and I wonder how I would react if she told me she was going to drop out of college to get married. Probably not much differently to my mum, to be perfectly honest.

I towelled myself off and climbed into my comfortable, makes my bum look big jeans, an oversized Bon Jovi t-shirt, baggy fleece and my slipper boots and plodded down the stairs to start dinner.

My phone buzzed in my back pocket as I opened the fridge to see what we had. I was not optimistic; it had been quite a few days since I had been shopping. I left the door gaping and pulled my phone out and looked at the screen; it was a text message from Jonny and my heart started tap dancing with joy.

I miss you already, Jonny.

Wow, my whole body clenched with excitement as I remembered the afternoon we had just spent together. I'd only been gone an hour and he was already missing me.

The fridge offered a chicken, that would do nicely, and I pulled it out and plonked it on the kitchen island, leaving my hands free to return Jonny's text.

Me too.

I put the phone down, put on some sterile plastic gloves from a box I always kept handy and unwrapped the chicken. I hated the slimy wet feel of the chicken on my hands. I hated the feel of any meat to be honest, but chicken always felt worse to me, not much I can do about that though when I live in a house of carnivores.

I found a roasting tray in the cupboard under the island and unceremoniously dumped the poor dead bird into it before shoving it into the roasting oven.

From the kitchen I could hear a key rattle in the front door; must be Michael coming home and I tugged the gloves off as I walked out to find him pulling his coat off and hanging it on the coat stand.

'You're back early, nice day at work?' I said, my wife 101 course had taught me the script well.

'Yes fine, yourself?'

He had clearly lied. He looked awful, like he had the world resting on his shoulders. Over the past few months he had aged disproportionately fast, and now he was looking closer to sixty than forty-nine. I longed to ask, but I had learnt long ago that he had a bit of a temper; the hard way I might add, so I learned to keep my mouth shut these days, life was simpler that way. I also learned long ago that eventually he will work out whatever it is that's bothering him, and then we all just get back to normal, so I just stick to my supportive wife script.

'It was ok.' I lied too, walking back into the kitchen. Actually, it was flipping amazing. My stomach clenched as I thought about it again.

'Were you working again today?' he said.

'Yes, I'm not long back.'

I guess neither of us were on first name terms with the truth today.

My phone vibrated loudly against the counter top and both our eyes shot straight to it, I chose to play it cool and ignore it and he looked back up at me with that disapproving look he reserved especially for occasions such as this.

'I don't know why you insist on working; don't I provide well enough for you and the kids?'

And there it was, again. I have got used to spotting that look. He hated me working, but what was I supposed to do all day. I hate all that mumsy, house-wifey stuff, and I was no good at it anyway. I don't do *ladies that lunch* either, I tried it but all they ever seemed to talk about was hair appointments, nail appointments and where they were heading for their weekend – they were just a bunch of money obsessed bitches.

'Of course you do, and I am always very grateful for everything you do for us,' I said – this script had been well rehearsed. 'I like working though, that's all.'

'You're impossible sometimes.' He shook his head. 'What time should I expect dinner?'

'I've only just put the chicken in, maybe an hour and a half.'

'Fine, call me when it's ready. I'll be upstairs, in my loft.'

'No problem.'

I watched him turn and head for the stairs. His loft was his office in the roof space, which he had renovated not long after we bought the house. He kept it locked; no one was allowed in there, not even me. I dread to think what he kept up there and I never looked. There could be dead bodies for all I knew. I giggled to myself at the thought, more likely, knowing Michael, it was just a dart board and a load of invoices and VAT returns that hadn't been filed yet. I never thought accountancy needed to be so private, maybe he had the Prime Minister's receipts up there, or some movie star, you would never know with Michael.

His footsteps disappeared up the steps and I waited for the lock to click on the loft door. Then, only once I was sure he was safely ensconced in the roof, I lifted the phone and checked my message. As I suspected, and had hoped, it was Jonny.

When can I see you again?

Yippee, he wanted to see me again, and I him, desperately. It made me feel a little giddy. I indulged the thought as I yanked a bag of potatoes out of the pantry. I wanted to run round there right now, but that would look desperate, and be impossible, given I had just started dinner for my family – I must keep reminding myself about them. I couldn't go tomorrow either, it was the anniversary of Dad's death and I had promised to meet Mum. Even if I wanted to, there was no way I would cancel that.

How about Wednesday?

For dinner? I'll order in, no toast, promise. J

For dinner? What would I tell Michael? I would think of something.

I could bring some stuff with me and cook if you like.

I thought he might appreciate a home cooked meal for a change, he didn't even eat a sandwich unless someone had prepared it for him and tucked it into a little cardboard box beforehand.

Hope you're a better cook than me, 7 ok? J

I'm terrible, but I think I can do better than toast, see you at 7.

Suddenly it was Christmas eve, and I was a five-year-old all over again, waiting for Santa to come down the chimney, only I wasn't a child waiting for Santa, I was forty and counting the days to when I could see Jonny again. All I needed was a good enough excuse to be out for the night mid-week. I lifted my phone and started texting.

Hi Jackie, any chance you might want to do a stock take on Wednesday night, say around 7? □

I figured the cheeky face at the end might mean I wouldn't have to spell it out, I was right.

Stocktake, eh? Is that what they are calling it now? Take it you had a nice coffee date; I noticed you didn't come back to work!

Sorry about that, but yes, it was most satisfactory!

You dirty bitch xox

Dirty bitch maybe, but Susanna had needs, and I figure it would be inhumane to deny her. That's my line anyway and I'm sticking to it, besides I was having fun, a not too common event for me these days. I was owed.

While the chicken rested, I laid the table in the kitchen; we rarely used the dining room, only for very special occasions like Christmas, Easter or the Queen visiting – she might one day, you never know.

I buzzed the intercom on the phone to let Michael know dinner was ready; thankfully he rounded up the kids on his way down from his loft, so I didn't have to shout up the stairs this time.

I carved the chicken and piled all the butchered bits of meat into a bowl, which I handed to Ben as he entered the kitchen. He looked at it like it was toxic waste, but walked it over to the table anyway. Sara took the bowl of peas; Michael the gravy and I quickly mashed the potatoes and joined them all at the table with my mushroom pastry.

Sara and Ben were both wired up to their mp3 players so the chances of getting any meaningful dinner conversation out of either of them was completely out of the question.

Michael sat quietly, wolfing down his food, his eyes fixed to the plate until he finished. His head lifted, and he looked at me with strange eyes, a look I hadn't seen before.

'Is everything ok with you?' he asked.

'Yes fine.' I said. 'Why do you ask?'

'You just look different somehow; I thought you might be coming down with something.'

'I feel fine.'

'Probably best to make an appointment with Dr Bentley, just to make sure. I'll set one up for you tomorrow.'

'No honestly, I feel fine, no need to bother him. Maybe because of dad, or just that time of the month.'

'Hmm. I had forgotten about your dad.'

Dad or woman's problems, both were effective conversation stoppers with Michael, and today I got a double whammy. He had no idea when my time of the month was or that the medication I was on meant I hadn't had one for going on four years. He and Dad had always had a passionate dislike for each other, but since he died twelve years ago, it was a no-go topic of discussion for him. Never nice to speak ill of the dead. Feeling conversationally castrated, he got up quietly from the table and hurried out of the kitchen.

'It's because you're smiling.' Sara said, without looking up from her plate.

'I thought you were listening to your music?'

'I was, then I stopped,' she said. 'Thanks for dinner.'

Surprised by her interest, I stood back and watched her strut out of the kitchen, followed immediately by Ben, who had said not a word, as usual.

I sat by myself at the table forking over my mash potatoes, thinking to myself.

I was smiling?

That's what Sara said. Didn't I usually smile? Was I that miserable normally? Was this the effect Jonny was having on me already?

I made a note to be less happy at home in future and cleared the abandoned dishes.

chapter thirteen

Not one surface in the decadently adorned room was devoid of at least one tee light, most had three or four and TJ was busy flittering from one collection to next, lighting their tiny wicks, one by one, until every inch of the room was touched by their flickering orange glow.

The window was open a crack and the voiles shimmied in the light breeze. He stood back, one hand on his hip, and admired his work.

'Very nice. Very, very nice, don't you think?'

He didn't wait for an answer, he didn't expect one, and strode out across the room to flick off the dimmed electric light. The room fell into complete darkness, except for the tiny flickers of light coming from the candles; it looked like a scene from a movie he had once seen.

'Even better.'

TJ had brought his CD player into the room and lifted the collection of CDs he had fetched with it and started shuffling through them in his hands.

'What do you think? I've got Franz von Suppe, Mozart, Edvard Grieg or maybe Saint-Saëns?'

He paused and considered it for a second.

'No, you're right; Saint-Saëns it is. My favourite. Just the thing,' he said, sliding the CD in.

His favourite track, *Danse Macabre*, began moments later. It was ominous yet beautiful. He pocketed the tiny remote control and swayed along with the foreboding tones of the violins.

He glanced across at Nancy for the first time since he had unlocked his parents' bedroom door. He had been looking forward to this visit all afternoon.

'Dinner shouldn't be long now, Chinese ok? Course it is, everyone likes Chinese food. Or maybe you want to eat after?'

Nancy was wearing his mum's beautiful red silk robe and was lying on her side in a foetal position on the black bedspread. His eyes explored her trembling body; her beautiful eyes, her neck, her shoulders and down to her hands and feet. taped together behind her with parcel tape. Her wide, reddened eyes followed him as he swayed towards the bed and sat down beside her.

She flinched as he ran his cold hand over her hair and across her swollen and bloody face.

'Still sore?' he said. 'Shame, I did tell you to be quiet, you didn't leave me any choice really, did you?'

She closed her eyes and nodded slowly.

'Maybe you will behave better this time.' He said nodding, 'I think you will.'

He brushed her face again as he found the end of the tape that covered her mouth and put a finger to his lips to remind her to keep quiet. She gasped for air as he pulled it slowly away from her lips, but she didn't speak, she knew that was not allowed.

'Thirsty?' he asked. as he lifted a glass of water from the bedside table. She nodded, and he lifted her head from the bed with his free hand and held the glass to her lips, tilting it just enough that she could take a couple of sips of water.

'That's better,' he said. 'See, I want to take care of you, just as long as you do what you are told, so I won't have to discipline you.

'Now, what did we decide – food first or after?'

His phone vibrated in his pocket, interrupting his train of thought. He yanked it out and looked at the screen before tossing it onto a chair by the door. He wasn't interested in talking to anyone tonight, tonight was just for him and Nancy.

'I think after, don't you? Yes, definitely after. Now then, let's get you ready.'

He opened his mum's dresser drawer and pulled out a lipstick. Winding it up carefully, he gazed intently at the colour, a dusty pink, then over at Nancy who was sobbing silently. He shook his head.

'Definitely not.' His phone vibrated again, but he didn't take notice as he rummaged for a better choice, *something a little redder*, he thought. He found another and wound it up to check the colour, 'too purple.' He kept rummaging and found what he was looking for, a brilliant dark red.

'Much more you, I think, don't you?' he said.

He smiled and sat next to the girl, holding her head firmly with one hand as he gently painted her dry, shivering lips with his mum's red lipstick.

Finished, he sat back to admire his work.

'Beautiful. Just beautiful. You should always wear this colour. It matches the robe too.'

He stroked her greasy hair and wiped a solitary tear from her puffy face with his thumb. She kept her eyes closed, but he could feel her skin tremble when he touched her.

'You're frightened. Don't be. I want to take care of you, please don't be afraid of me, I will look after you, you're very special to me,' he said, cupping her face with his hands. 'Smile for me, your face is so pretty when you smile.'

She forced a half smile as another tear fell from her eye and followed the line of the cut on her cheek. TJ kissed away the tear.

'Nearly ready,' he said, rolling her gently onto her back.

She stopped breathing as he trailed his hands softly across her body; along her neck, following the rise and fall of her breasts and down her waist to the belt that held the robe closed. She bit her lip when his fingers found the knot and deftly untied the belt, brushed away the silk to reveal her bruised and naked body.

'Just beautiful,' he said, sitting back approvingly.

The CD player had moved onto the next track and TJ used the remote control to re-start track two and the thumping beat started up again.

She turned her head away and her muscles tensed as his hands starting to explore her quivering body.

'Do try to enjoy yourself this time.'

The doorbell rang out and he leapt up from the bed, allowing her a moment to relax a little and curl up on her side.

'Dinner time,' he sang. 'Now, promise me you won't scream or shout, we don't want a repeat of last night, or do I have to put the tape back over your mouth? You may speak now.'

'I. I. Promise,' she stammered.

'Good girl,' he said as he leant forward and kissed her lightly on the cheek. 'Wait here, I'll be back, and then we can start having some fun.'

chapter fourteen

The music paused, TJ locked the bedroom door and bounced down the stairs, skipping over the bottom two steps as he hummed the tune of his favourite song. Heading merrily for the front door he couldn't stop a giant grin from stretching across his face. He wriggled his fat wallet free of his back pocket in anticipation of his food delivery. He liked Chinese food and he liked Nancy, so he was a happy boy tonight.

Absently, he yanked open the door but as soon as he saw who had rung the doorbell he quickly tried to force it closed again. He was too slow and not strong enough to hold Eddie back, as he easily forced his way past him and into the house.

'Where is she?'

'Yoh, get the fok out of my house.'

Eddie pushed him out the way and hastily headed down the hall, TJ in pursuit. Eddie led him into the kitchen, repeatedly calling out for Nancy.

'Where is she, you sick bastard?'

'Fok jou.'

'Cut the African crap TJ,' he said. 'Nancy?'

'She's not here, now get the fuck out.'

TJ could feel his blood surging as he followed Eddie out of the kitchen and back down the hall towards the front room.

'Nancy?'

'I don't know who you think you are coming in here,' TJ said, trying desperately to keep his cool. 'The doors there, now get out before I do something you regret.'

'Don't you dare threaten me,' Eddie said. 'Nancy!'

Eddie paused for a brief second before charging up the stairs, going from one room to the next, he flung the doors open, searching like a man possessed, until finally he came to the last door. It was locked.

'That's my mum's room; she keeps it locked when she's away.'

'Nancy!'

Eddie paused, his head slightly cocked, listening, but there was just silence.

'Satisfied?' Silence. 'Now go.'

Eddie stabbed TJ's shoulder with his finger. 'You are a sick, fucking freak, and when I find out where she is and what you did to her, I'm gonna kill you myself, that's if The Boss doesn't get to you first, you got that?'

'Yeah, whatever.' TJ forced a playful smile. 'Don't trip on your way downstairs.'

Eddie turned to the stairs and TJ shook his head as he watched him stomp one step after the next. Eddie was nearly half way down when TJ heard a muffled sound coming from the bedroom, and he held his breath while he watched to see if Eddie had heard it too. He had.

'What was that?'

'Now you're hearing things, old man.'

TJ felt panic set in as he heard a loud thud come from the bedroom.

'Fok,' he muttered under his breath. 'Ontwil, ek gaan sny wat hoere fuckig keel.'

Ignoring his Afrikaans rant, Eddie turned on his heels. He didn't need a translation as the tone said it all, and he charged straight up the stairs, two by two. TJ tried to block him, but he was like a bulldozer as he powered straight through him, knocking him clean off his feet.

TJ jumped straight up again and grabbed Eddie just before he pounded against the locked door, but Eddie was ready for him and TJ took a sharp blow on the side of his face which sent him reeling backwards against the stair bannisters.

'Fok!'

His face felt like it was on fire, but he clambered back to his feet as Eddie hit the door with his shoulder. The door cracked under the force, but it didn't open.

'Nancy, you in there?' He shouted again.

TJ threw his arms round Eddie and dragged him away from the door, spun him round and threw his best punch, straight into Eddies stomach, forcing him to double over. He took a chance and got a swift knee into his chest throwing him backwards towards the top of the stairs. Lunging after him, he saw an opportunity to push him backwards down the stairs, but Eddie grabbed him as he charged and managed to swing him down first.

Grappling for the banister, TJ stumbled over a couple of steps and just managed to stop himself from tumbling all the way down. He could hear Eddie pounding the bedroom door as he hastily pulled himself onto his feet. One more punch and Eddie was through the door.

'Fok sake,' he cursed, as he charged after him.

In the few seconds it had taken him to get through the bedroom door, Eddie had already un-taped Nancy's hands and was frantically working on the tape round her feet.

'No!' he shouted as he lunged for Nancy's feet, but Eddie grabbed him and swung him back out of the room. 'She's mine.'

'You're a sick bastard,' Eddie said, pushing him with both hands back down the corridor. 'Just shut her up, that's all you had to fucking do. Just shut her up and take her the fuck home.'

'You're calling me sick?' TJ panted while he caught a breath. 'Golden boy has a conscience, well halle-fuckinglujah. The gospel according to Eddie; thou shalt kill but not enjoy. You're the fucking freak.'

He saw Eddie coming for him and quickly jumped out the way before he got a hand on him.

Nancy was free and the frail looking girl had appeared behind Eddie. Wrapped tightly in the robe, she was hugging herself and crying –was she was expecting Eddie to protect her?

'Delivery!'

Downstairs, an older delivery man had appeared inside the front door. He looked just like Mr Miyagi from the *Karate Kid*. TJ sighed loudly.

'Fok. Go away.' TJ shouted returning his stare to Nancy and Eddie.

'Twenty-two fifty.'

'I said go away,' TJ said again, keeping his eye firmly on Eddie and Nancy

'Twenty-two fifty,' he repeated.

'Jesus Christ.' TJ physically guarded the top of the stairs as he found his wallet and tossed it down the stairs.

'Keep the change, now piss off.'

'Very good.'

The Chinese man left the white plastic bag on the floor inside the door, quickly extracted three notes, dropped the wallet by the bag and scurried away.

Eddie had moved in front of Nancy and they were both starring straight back at him.

Two against one, he thought, *not good odds, but worth a shot given the circumstances.*

Eddie broke the standoff first and lunged straight for TJ, who hopped sideways, leaving the stairs open for Nancy to take a dash for freedom. TJ grabbed at her arm and swung her round, but she lost her footing and fell awkwardly against the top banister, yelping as her body cracked against the wood. She looked TJ square in the eye, a cold desperate stare as her body flipped clumsily over the banister and she dropped over the edge. Eddie turned his head and winced as her body thumped onto the ground, forcing out a blood curdling scream with her final breath.

When he looked over she was lying perfectly still, with one leg folded under her. Her eyes were open, still staring. He quickly hopped down the stairs, followed by Eddie, and dropped beside her. His hand found her neck. There was no pulse. He looked back at Eddie, his hands tensing into fists.

'See what you did?'

'What *I* did. You are crazy. Anyway, probably did her a favour, better than being fucked by a sick pervert on his mum's bloody bed.' Eddie turned his back and marched out towards the door. 'I can't wait to tell the boss, he's just gonna love this, you dumb fuck. You better make sure you watch your back from now on, that's my advice. He will not be happy to hear about this.'

'Me? Maybe you should watch yours. You're not smarter than me Eddie, you think you are, but I know stuff about you, guy.'

'Whatever man.'

Eddie slammed the door behind him leaving TJ alone with his Chinese takeaway and Nancy's dead body.

TJ retrieved a single container and the free chop sticks from the plastic bag and sat on the bottom stair, right next to Nancy, picking heartily at the chicken chow mein for two.

'You just watch out Eddie,' he said under his breath. 'You are gonna pay for this, you can be damn sure of that, first chance I get, I'm watching, and you won't even see it coming.

'Smug bastard.'

chapter fifteen

I was running late, as usual. My hair was still folded up in a scrunchie waiting for a brush to bring some order to it, and I still had on my purple spotted fleece pyjamas, matching robe and slippers, when I trotted downstairs to make a very quick cuppa. If it was very quick, I might even have time for a shower before I left.

Michael had already left for work by the time I made it downstairs, as was usual these days, but instead of coming down to a completely empty kitchen, I was met by a steaming mug of tea and an enormous bunch of all my favourite flowers, filling the kitchen with an incredibly comforting aroma of roses and Yorkshire's finest brew.

I picked up the little card that leant up against the flowers and sat down on the swivel stool, cup of tea in hand and read:

Thinking of you today

A lump formed in my throat as I read the words. Whilst Michael had never exchanged a civil word with my dad, he knew how upset I had been when Dad died and had always been really supportive of me and the kids, and even now, after all this time, he remembered how hard this anniversary was for me. Perhaps I didn't give him enough credit sometimes

Dad's death had hit the family like a wrecking ball. To say it devastated everyone would be a huge understatement.

It's funny, because in many ways, we had all prepared ourselves for Dad to one day just not come home. We had all talked about it when we thought Dad wasn't listening, and we had all tried to talk him into getting a different job. Mum especially had always dreaded the day she got that knock on the door; everyone married to someone on *the job* was the same.

But Dad didn't die in the line of duty like we had once feared he would. He didn't die slowly of a horrific disease either, or have a sudden heart attack or stroke. He committed suicide; he took his own life, aged just fifty-eight and only two years away from proudly retiring from the force as Detective Chief Inspector.

News of his sudden death wasn't gently brought to Mum either, not by a grieving colleague in the comfort of her living room as Mum had once dreaded. It came in the form of a gut-wrenching screech from my sister, Gayle, who was unfortunate enough to find his lifeless body in the basement, dangling from the roof by electrical cable.

No note was left, no obvious signs of unhappiness, no depression, no warning, no nothing, just the painful fact that he had gone, and for no fathomable reason.

Gayle especially had never fully recovered from the trauma and had eventually moved to Jersey with her husband and two kids to escape from it. It hadn't worked for her and to this day she still couldn't talk about Dad without breaking down.

I had made some degree of peace with it, and Mum had too, but even after all this time I just wish I had known what was so awful in his life that he had felt he couldn't ask for help, couldn't even tell anyone and felt compelled to take such drastic action. It just wasn't like him; I didn't think so anyway, but then, I guess, that's what everyone says.

I smiled at the flowers, thanked my absent and uncharacteristically thoughtful husband, grabbed the mug of tea and hurried back upstairs to get dressed. Time was ticking.

Mum was dressed and ready in a pretty white dress with red flowers and matching red shoes. She had even had her silvery hair professionally done when I arrived to pick her up from her sheltered flat, half an hour away, in Honiton. She always made an effort for Dad and today was clearly no exception.

Dad's grave was in Taunton, near the home Gayle and I had grown up in, and once I had collected her and her large bucket of gardening tools, we headed off.

Mum was quiet on the journey; she always was until after we had visited Dad, then she would suddenly find her voice and talk your ass clean off. I enjoyed the temporary, but reverential silence.

Mine was the only car in the small car park at the gates of the cemetery, and apart from an elderly man and his little scruffy dog, we were the only ones visiting any of the more than one hundred graves in the cemetery. In fact, the whole place looked like it had been almost entirely abandoned, as many of the sites had become overgrown and the paths had certainly not been mown for a while. Even the metal gates had started to decay and rust. It was a depressing sight, and I made a mental note to find out who maintained the land and stick a flea in their arse about caring for it.

Given the crumbling state of the place, I felt compelled to clear a few of the other graves as well as Dad's. Some didn't look like they had been visited or cared for in a great many years and I wondered what had happened to the people who once looked after them, perhaps they were dead too by now, so sad. Quietly, together we weeded, tidied, cleaned and de-cluttered around Dad's grave and memorial stone.

The scruffy dog was called Sherlock, a very friendly little fella. He was named after the elderly mans deceased wife's favourite detective, so he told me. I scratched Sherlock's little tummy while I watched my mum finish up. She was an old lady herself now and I wondered how much longer it would be before she was there beside him. I stifled a tear. I would miss the judgemental hypochondriac, but hopefully not too soon.

Dad hated flowers, but he had always loved his herb garden, so Mum had decided to grow one for him right there where he lay. It always looked a terrible mess at this time of year and we usually ended up pulling most of it up, ready to re-plant next spring on his birthday. This year was no exception, and after saying a few words, we headed quietly back to the car with two bags of rubbish and our large collection of tools.

'So, what's suddenly made you so happy, my girl? You're not pregnant again, are you?' she said, as I helped her into the passenger seat of my car.

'Mum!'

'Well, the last time you had a glow like this, you told me a week later you were expecting Ben.'

'I'm not pregnant, mum.'

I closed the door and walked round to the driver's seat shaking my head. Heaven forbid, pregnant was the last thing I wanted to be, or could be for that matter, not according to the nice doctor who inserted my contraceptive implant anyway.

Should I tell her where my glow had come from? I wondered. My Mum was not usually the most discrete person in the world, but she disliked Michael almost as much as Dad had, so I was pretty confident she wouldn't be the one to let it slip, but then again, after a few sherries at Christmas she could say anything. No, better to keep it to myself. I would have to think of something else to keep her imagination satisfied for now, and I sighed as I opened the car door; this was going to be a long day.

chapter sixteen

Wednesday was delivery day at the shop and Jackie and I had just spent the last two hours stacking box after box of shoes, in between serving the occasional customer that had come in.

Michael hated that I worked in a shoe shop, said it embarrassed him, especially as the shoes Jackie sold were high end and I would often see some of his associate's wives when they came in. I didn't care; in fact, I think his attitude just made me more determined. Maybe there was a rebel in me somewhere.

Jackie had added a few new lines in the run up to Christmas and we sat and admired them over lunch. I loved looking at shoes, no doubt about that, and I liked the idea of fancy high heels, but if they had a heel over an inch I was in big trouble. Still, that didn't stop me giving it a go and I regularly like to hobble about the house in the latest pair of Manolo's or Alexander McQueen's. Jackie was different, very elegant and had truly mastered the four-inch heel totter. She needed to though, as without the heels she was only a tiny five-foot-two.

'So, Alice Walker,' oh no, she whole-named me, I was in trouble. 'Are you going to tell me what happened on Monday at Jonny's, or do I have to beat it out of you with the pointy end of a Valentino?' she said, strutting across the shop in a pair of Sophia Webster's latest insane creations.

I sat watching from behind the counter, tugging the foil lid off a Dairylea Dunker I had brought for lunch.

When the Mask Falls

'You'll have to beat it out of me, all I'm saying is that we had a good time and I'm seeing him again tonight. As you already know.'

'Yes, but I want details, did you sleep with him?'

'Jackie!' I exclaimed, scooping a pile of cream cheese out of the pot with a tiny cracker.

'Means yes. Was he any good?'

'I hardly even know him.' My cheeks were on fire, change the subject, stat. 'My mum was a pain in the arse yesterday, but thanks for the day off.'

'She always is, but was it good, I mean was it like *really* good?'

'I think I will call the council and see if I can get someone to look after the cemetery, it didn't look like anyone had given it a second look for months.'

'Better than Michael?'

Oh yeah, but still not telling, and still holding the same flipping cracker.

'So sad, all those graves just covered in rubbish and overgrown with grass and weeds.'

'Fine, don't tell me.'

'I won't.' I said, finally popping the cracker in my mouth.

'So you did then?'

'Yes, detective Jackie, I did have sex with my new lover, are you satisfied now?'

'I am, but my question was, were you?'

Her right eyebrow rose unnaturally high on her head; I worried it might fall off and I changed the subject again.

'How's Alistair these days?'

'He's fine, thanks; he's in court all this week, so I've hardly seen him these past few days.'

Jackie slipped the new shoes off and placed them back in the shop window display.

'I hate my old shoes now,' she said, pulling a sad face.

I laughed and dipped another cracker as my phone vibrated in my pocket.

'Is that him?' Jackie seemed more excited than I was.

I checked my phone, but it was just a text from Sara.

'No, it's just Sara saying she's got a date tonight and she's not coming home till late.'

Jackie sat down beside me, found a squished cheese roll in her handbag and peeled it out of its cling film covering.

'Has she told you she's gay yet?'

'No, the other day I thought she was going to, but then she clammed up and disappeared up the stairs.'

'Do you think you should just tell her you already know, make it easier for her.'

'Yeah, but what if I'm wrong?'

'You are not wrong, I promise you.'

'Hmm, maybe,' I said, gazing across the shop.

Jackie re-wrapped her half-eaten cheese roll and tossed it dramatically into her bag.

'I'm not eating this crap; I'm going next door, want anything?'

I shook my head, my Dairylea Dunkers were all I had allowed myself today for lunch, just enough to keep me going and hopefully, I would look as slim as possible for my date tonight. It was not to be though as five minutes later Jackie returned from the shop next door with a tuna baguette for herself, two cups of dishwater infused tea and a box of custard filled donuts.

'Damn you woman, I wanted to look good for tonight,' I said, picking out the fattest looking donut and shoving it in my mouth. No one can resist a custard filled donut, well I can't anyway.

chapter seventeen

I flew up the three flights of stairs, desperately trying to stay upright in my ridiculous new heels as I made my way up to the third floor, flat 36, a carrier bag packed with goodies in each hand.

The queue in Marksies had been ridiculous, far longer than I had left time for, and I was now running late, as usual, fifteen minutes of Jonny time already wasted, damn it.

Michael was expecting me back late from my *stock take*, but he was expecting me back and that meant I had to keep an eye on the clock; no getting carried away like last time and definitely no getting drunk.

With both hands unavailable, I pressed the bell with my nose and stood back, tingling from head to foot like an expectant five-year-old waiting for the gates of Disneyland to open.

The door swung open and Jonny stood in the entranceway, grinning from ear to ear,

'I thought for a minute I'd been stood up.'

'Sorry, there was a queue.'

'God, I've missed you.'

The bags hit the floor as I was swept up into Jonny's arms, moaning with pleasure, our lips glued together like a pair of horny teenagers, as our kiss lingered far longer than a *nice to see you again kiss* should.

'Hmm, I've missed you too.'

I closed the door behind me before I dropped down onto my knees to gather up the bags and the grocery items that had spilled out.

'Ooh, I like where this is going.' Jonny said, that dimple deeper than ever.

I hit him on the leg with a garlic baguette,

'You're terrible.'

'What? So, what's for tea?'

'Tagliatelle Carbonara.'

'Ooh, yummy, what's that?' He said taking the bags from my hands. 'Kitchen's through here.'

I rolled my eyes. 'It's pasta in a creamy sauce.'

The kitchen was quite small, but functional and stylish with its high gloss white cabinets and black countertops. Just how I imagined his kitchen would look. The most startling thing about his stylish kitchen was that it looked like it was brand new; either he was an obsessive cleaner, or a bachelor who genuinely never cooked.

'I thought you were kidding when you said you didn't cook?' I said, unpacking the bags.

'Wouldn't even know where to start.'

'What, really?'

'Yep.'

'So, what do you eat?'

'Take out.'

'Oh my god. Then I am long overdue here. Pass me a saucepan.'

'Which one's that?'

'Now you must be kidding.'

'Of course, I am.'

But he wasn't, and he just knelt down, staring blankly into the cupboard with all the pots and pans.

'At least you picked the right cupboard.' I smiled, nudging him out the way and pulled out a medium and a large sauce pan. 'Didn't you ever cook with your mum?'

'Er no.'

'Well look, I don't know how much use you will be in here, so why don't you just grab a beer or something and go and sit down and I'll shout when it's done.'

'You sure?'

'Yes, go.'

He smiled and so did I as I watched him leave, that tight butt just seemed to get better and better each time I see it. I dragged my eyes away and returned to the job of cooking tea.

I started with the sauce and once that was simmering, the broken garlic baguette found its way into the oven and I started boiling a pan of water before giving the sauce a stir. Everything looked good, so I found a spoon and scooped a small amount of sauce out of the pot for tasting. Delicious, just a touch of salt and pepper and nearly done.

'Five minutes,' I shouted out, and seconds later Jonny was standing in the kitchen door. I could get used to this.

'Smells great,' he said, sliding his arms around my waist and kissing my neck.

'Are we still talking about the food?'

He laughed, 'What can I do?'

'Bowls?'

'On it, I know what they are.' He winked. I can't believe he didn't even know what a saucepan was, but it didn't matter, it was cute.

I threw the fresh tagliatelle in the boiling water and just a few short minutes later it was ready to drain. Jonny had found some bowls and forks and was standing in the kitchen door clutching a handful of DVDs.

'Didn't know what you would like, so I got a selection.'

Hmm, I looked at the choices; *Noah*, *Captain Philips* and *The Lone Survivor*, how does one choose between three such great looking movies. Easy, Tom Hanks wins every time, in my DVD player anyway. Can't beat him.

'Gotta be *Captain Philips*,' I said.

'Good choice, I'll set it up.'

The pasta was done and in the absence of a colander I made do and used the pans lid to drain the water. Miraculously, only a few strands managed to snake out through the tiny gap and into the sink, then I dumped the pasta straight on top of the sauce and gave it a quick stir before rescuing the garlic bread and serving the lot.

I grabbed both bowls and headed through to the living room to deliver dinner.

I was speechless. Jonny had been a busy boy while I cooked, the main light had been replaced by a few candles, their pretty flames quietly flickering, some light jazz simmering in the background, Tom Hanks was paused and ready on the TV and two glasses of white wine stood elegantly on the coffee table just begging to be drunk.

'Wow, I'm impressed.'

Jonny smiled and fetched the garlic bread and we unpaused the movie and snuggled into the sofa with our bowls of pasta.

'Oh my God!' Jonny said.

'What, what happened?' I said turning around to see Jonny shovelling the pasta, quick as you like, into his mouth.

He paused for a second, 'This is so good,' he said. 'Marry me, seriously, right now.'

I grinned; it was quite satisfying to get such good feedback, addictive actually.

I turned back to the telly to find Captain Philips boarding his ship and about to start a horrific journey and I just about managed to stop myself shouting at the TV, *don't do it*, but of course, if he had just turned around and gone home to his wife, that wouldn't have made for such a good movie.

It was so nice to just snuggle in front of the telly, a rare treat for me.

As the wine ran out, the movie was drawing to a sensational conclusion and me being typically me, the tears started flowing for poor Captain Philips and his terrible dilemma. Poor Jonny immediately assumed he had somehow done something awful and rallied to make it all better, but no hugs or tissues were going to stop these tears, only the credits had the power to do that, but I appreciated the extra tight hug.

Credits rolling plus a handful of tissues and the drama was over. I glanced at my watch, it was nearly ten already, Michael would be wondering what was taking so long at the *stock take*; I checked my phone, which had accidentally been left on silent, and my heart sank. Two missed calls from Michael and a text from Jackie, holy crap.

Call me, right now

Shit, what had happened? I excused myself to the hall and quickly hit the call button.

'Jackie? It's Alice.'

'Oh, thank god. Michael called me, he said he had been trying to get hold of you and was worried because you hadn't come home yet. Are you still with Jonny?'

'Yes, what did you tell him?'

'I told him you had too much to drink and I had brought you home to mine to sleep it off.'

'What, why did you tell him that?'

'It just came to me, enjoy your sleep over with Jonny, and don't forget to fake a hangover in the morning.'

'Not funny Jackie...' but the phone had already gone dead and I was left standing in the hallway outside Jonny's flat, apparently with nowhere to go tonight, and my stomach sank. What was I getting into, all this lying, it just wasn't for me, it was too stressful.

I walked back through Jonny's door and there he was, with that smile stretched addictively across his gorgeous face, a fresh bottle of wine in his hand and all my anxieties just seemed to dissolve.

'Everything ok?'

'Yes, fine,' I lied. I was effectively homeless and definitely a lying bitch.

'Shall I open another bottle?'

I considered the question for less than a tenth of a second,

'Yeah, why not.'

At least I wouldn't have to lie about the hangover.

A couple of glasses later and most of the candles had gone out, my shoes had been kicked off and I was having the time of my life being swung around on the carpet, giggling like a teenager, almost in time to the jazz music that purred from Jonny's CD player. And better still, I had forgotten about my ever-growing pit of lies and the fact that I was homeless for the night.

Turns out, that wasn't going to be as much of a problem as I might have imagined. Exhausted from busting my very inadequate moves, I called a time out and slumped on the sofa. Jonny slumped next to me and I snuggled into his arms while I caught my breath.

'Thank you for a really fun night,' I said.

An awkward silence engulfed the room and I looked up at Jonny.

He licked his lips and looked intently at me, 'Stay Susanna,' he said tentatively. 'For the night.'

Asking a homeless woman to stay the night is like asking Donald Trump if he wants to earn himself a few million quid. I looked back into his eyes, that cheeky minx that ruled my womanly ways woke up and starting chanting loudly in my head. I couldn't deny her and reached up with my hand and gently pulled his head towards mine until our lips were touching.

He had my answer, spoken in the only true universal language, and he took my hand and led me quietly away from the sofa and into his bedroom. I closed my eyes and took a sharp breath as I was laid down gently down on his bed. Don't ask me what the rest of his room was like, I only noticed the feel of the silky sheets beneath me and his bright blue eyes. He climbed on top of me and we were kissing again, not the animal, haven't had sex for months kind of kiss that we shared on Monday, this was a slow and tender, we've got all night kind of kiss.

That night we didn't have sex, we made love, a wonderful, not going to stop smiling for a month, kind of love. The rest of the night I lay back in his arms and we talked and laughed until I fell asleep.

I woke up the following morning, exhausted from only a few hours' sleep, dehydrated for lots of reasons and alone.

Where was Jonny?

I pulled back the duvet and found my jeans and the top I had been wearing the night before and pulled them on before opening the bedroom door. Light flooded in, half blinding me and almost beating me back into the bedroom. I squinted my eyes and pushed forward while they adjusted to the dazzling morning light.

I found Jonny standing at the toaster in the kitchen wearing the same jeans he had been wearing last night too. He must have heard me come in because he looked over sharply and caught me standing in the doorway, admiring the view.

'Oh no, you're up already. I was going to surprise you with breakfast in bed.'

'I can go back there, if you like.'

He grinned, 'ooh yes please.'

'Down boy.' I grinned as I turned and headed back to bed.

Breakfast in bed was a rare treat, another one, but life went on whether I wanted it to or not and I had to get to work so I dragged my hung-over self out of bed and reluctantly collected up my things.

'I had a really good time.' I said, swinging both of Jonny's hands in the door way.

'Don't go.'

'I have to go to work, and so do you.'

'Then I'll quit.'

I frowned and leant forward to kiss Jonny goodbye. As soon as our lips touched his hands were on my back and I was being wrapped up tightly in his arms, I was starting to melt, but I had to stay strong, I had to get to work.

I found his hands and unwrapped myself from his arms.

'Miss you already,' he said.

I grinned as I pulled the door closed behind me. Every muscle in my body begged me to go back in, but I dug deep and summoned the strength I needed to pull away from the door and skipped merrily down the stairs and out into the cold to my frozen car.

chapter eighteen

Eddie reached inside his leather jacket, his narrowing eyes fixed firmly on the trembling club owner as he withdrew his Glock 41 from his belt holster. He tapped the muzzle of the gun impatiently against the desk in time with the thumping beat that was being pumped in via speakers in the ceiling, and repeated his question.

'Where. Is. My. Fucking. Money?'

'I told you, I'll get it. I promise. Just one more day, please, I beg you.'

'Robson, I hope you're not trying to take advantage of my good nature?'

'I promise. Tomorrow, I'll have it tomorrow.'

He sauntered across the office, his eyes glued to the man in the swivel chair, watching for any sign of movement, any sign he had a weapon tucked into one of those desk drawers, or in his coat, any sign he might make a grab for it. He didn't flinch.

'I might be able to help you.'

He turned and walked back across the office and stopped in front of the two-way mirror in the wall. He cocked his gun as a convincing reminder for him to play nice and with one eye trained on Robson, he watched the floorshow through the two-way mirror.

He smirked as a very attractive, scantily dressed girl served a drink to a suited, slightly balding man, probably in his late fifties. Eddie recognised her straight away, her name was Brandi (with an i), or at least that's what she had told him.

She teased the man as she stretched over his shoulder with his drink, lightly brushing herself against him and offered him her trademark, pants-tightening smile. It worked like a charm and after some notes changed hands, she climbed onto his lap and gave him the treat he had paid for.

He ended his gaze with a blink and took in the rest of the buzzing room.

'Looks like a busy night for you?'

Robson lowered his head.

'I'll bet I could find a couple grand in your tills, easy.'

'I need to pay the staff, please, tomorrow; I will have it, all of it.'

Robson had started sweating profusely and he wiped his face on his sleeve.

A knock at the door only added to the tension in the room and Robson shot a frantic look at Eddie.

Eddie holstered his gun and beckoned the unexpected caller inside.

The volume of the music had shot up as the door was opened, revealing a stunning and very tall black woman. The music muted again as the door closed behind her.

He let his eyes wander for a moment; her red streaked black hair tumbled over her shoulder, leading his eye past her bright red lips down to her barely contained breasts, where his eyes paused for a further second.

'I just wondered if your guest would like a drink.'

'No. He's just…'

'Actually, that sounds very nice, what's your name?' Eddie interrupted, reassigning his eyes to her face.

'Chelsea.'

'Well thank you Chelsea, that's very hospitable, a shot of your finest Irish Whiskey, neat.'

'It would be my pleasure.' She purred, winking deliberately over her shoulder as she left.

Eddie felt something stir and shifted his stance and the conversation back to business.

Robson jumped as Eddie slammed both his hands firmly onto his desk and leant forward.

'I *could* come back tomorrow, but my time is not free, and neither is my boss's compassion, if you understand what I'm saying.'

Robson sat back in his chair and attempted a smile as he licked his lips, thinking quickly.

Chelsea interrupted them again when she re-entered the room, balancing Eddie's drink on a silver tray. She placed the glass slowly on the desk, her soft skin brushing his as her hand withdrew. She paused deliberately, allowing him a moment to take in her beautiful scent and a close-up view.

'Anything else I can do for you?' she said, raising an eyebrow.

Jesus, he was tempted, she was beautiful, and he was only human, but he was on a schedule.

'Maybe next time.' He forced himself to say.

'Can't wait.' She said, swishing her hair over her other shoulder as she left again.

'Jesus Robson, how do you get anything done working in here?'

He shrugged.

Eddie leaned further across the desk, forcing Robson to shrink deeper into his chair, and directed a piercing stare straight into his eyes.

'I'll be back tomorrow, for what I'm owed and an extra quarter for my trouble and good will,' Eddie said. 'I'm sure I don't need to remind you what happened the last time someone fucked me around. You've got a good deal here, be a shame for it all to go up in smoke.'

Eddie stood up and necked the whiskey before turning on his heels and marching out, slamming the door loudly behind him.

As he snaked through the crowd towards the exit, he spotted Chelsea teasing a group of very drunk lads. One was wearing an 'L' plate on his head, an instant giveaway that they were on a stag do. She spotted him and blew him a kiss as he pushed past, he smiled back and picked up the pace. Outside he took a good lungful of the crisp air and half jogged up the steps onto the street, past the huge but oblivious bouncer.

The brisk November air had hit him in the face; it really dampened his mood. His car was parked across the street and he hopped through the evening traffic towards it, yanking at his car keys as he moved. His phone was vibrating insistently in his pocket and as quickly as he closed the car door he had pulled out the phone and cursed at the caller ID.

'Yes?' he answered.

'Eddie, you have my money?'

Eddie sat back in the seat, unclipped his holster and gun and tucked them securely under the passenger seat.

Staring absently into the rear-view mirror he answered the question, 'Tomorrow.'

'Listen Eddie, we go back, you're like a son to me, but I am starting to wonder, you're not getting soft on me, are you?'

'I'll have it tomorrow.'

'You used to be my go-to guy, don't start letting me down now.'

'I said, I'll have it tomorrow, and I'll have it tomorrow.'

'I have a reputation, you know what happens to people who screw with me, Eddie.'

The phone went dead and he tossed it onto the seat beside him, cursing under his breath.

His hand found the ignition key and he was about to start the car when a loud tap on his window made him jump almost out of his skin.

'Jesus!' he said to himself, spinning round.

He swallowed hard as he raised his hands into view. The longer his day went on, the worse it seemed to be getting and he wondered how much worse it could possible get.

Actually, he knew the answer to that question. He hit the window button and the glass slowly dropped into the door.

'Afternoon, PC Carey, and what exactly can I do for you on this fine day?'

'Get out of the car please, Eddie, and it's *Sergeant* Carey now.'

'A promotion, well congratulations.'

'You can congratulate me down at the station. I have a few questions I would like to ask you about Nancy Reed? Know her?'

chapter nineteen

Jonny was really busy with work and apart from a couple of flirty texts back and forth and some sneaky phone calls, things had gone a bit quiet. Probably for the best, as things were getting a little out of hand and the space had given me a couple of days to fully consider what I was doing.

I was half asleep as I stood vacantly in front of the ironing board, and had been for longer than I am prepared to admit. Feeling overwhelmed by the leaning tower of laundry that was looming on the chair beside me, my attention was mostly directed at Tom Hanks, who was plunging to his fate in *Castaway* on the TV in front of me. I hated ironing, and quite honestly, I was rubbish at it, but seeing as there were no other volunteers it was left to me.

I had just begun fighting with a crease in one of Michael's work shirts when my phone vibrated in my pocket and immediately stole my focus.

What are you doing next weekend? x

The whole weekend?

Of course, I want you all to myself, the whole weekend, I've missed you. x

Was he crazy, didn't he know I was married, oh, that's right he didn't.

I looked over at the photo of me and Michael on our wedding day that was next to the TV; apart from being a lot younger, and about a stone lighter, I looked so happy, and so did he. The guilt fairy put her hand up and I knew exactly what she wanted to say, and reluctantly, I tapped my reply into the phone.

Sorry, I can't.

I slid the phone back into my jeans and continued working at the shirt. I so longed for a weekend with Jonny, he made me feel so alive, like I could fly; just thinking about him gave me butterflies. But what about Michael, poor boring Michael? He barely acknowledged me from one day to the next, but did he deserve to be cheated on?

The shirt beat me, as they usually did, but I was done arguing and I hung it on a hanger and took it to the wardrobe, so it could be with the rest of its brothers-in-creases. The phone vibrated in my pocket again, but my attention was taken by Michael, who was sitting by the leaf-topped pool in the garden. I watched him from the window, and he looked distracted, lonely even – and cold. It *was* November, after all. And then it occurred to me.

What I liked most about seeing Jonny was how exciting it was. It was naughty. Maybe me and Michael just needed a bit of excitement in our marriage, a little spontaneity, a change of pace. Maybe I didn't need to cheat on my husband at all. So I unplugged the iron. The kids were both out and I had an idea. I quickly checked the text message; it was, unsurprisingly, from Jonny.

Pleeeeeeease ☐ xx

I ignored it and rummaged through my dressing room for my sexiest clothes. It took me half an hour to squeeze myself into the black and red lace Basque that had been squished into the back of a drawer, including the time it took to find the stockings and the dangly bits that connected it all together. I found my sexiest heels and my warmest winter coat, a mocha, ankle length, imitation fur lined faux suede coat that I had fallen in love with, paid a fortune for and never worn.

I checked out the window and he was still there, so I unclipped my hair and ruffled it out with my fingers, applied a touch of bright red lipstick and a dash of perfume and I was ready.

I hurried down the stairs, pressing my lips together to make sure the lipstick was even, the coat draped over one arm and the shoes dangling from my free hand.

At the back door I quickly wrestled the shoes on, pulled the coat on and with a big smile on my face I wobbled out into the garden.

'Hey.' I said, trying my best to look casual. 'Everything all right?'

Michael looked round. He looked heavily preoccupied and I reminded myself not to ask again.

'New coat?'

'No, I've had this for ages.' I know that's the party line, but at least this time it was true. 'You look cold.'

He shrugged.

I mustered my sexiest face, 'Well, maybe, you'd like me to warm you up.'

I allowed my coat to *accidentally* fall open and spell out to him exactly what I meant as I sauntered over, as best I could in the heels, and I perched myself on his knee.

'What are you doing?' he said, his eyes wide.

I ran my hand over his chest and started kissing his neck. 'Well, we have the place to ourselves, and you looked so miserable, so I thought I would come and *perk* you up.'

He jumped up from the chair knocking me onto the freezing ground with a thud.

'I don't know what's come over you this last week, have some class woman, you look like a cheap whore!'

My jaw dropped as he snatched the chair he had been sitting on clear off the ground and plonked his arse back into it a few feet away. My cheeks were on fire and if I could've found a hole to crawl into, I would have.

I'm not sure what hurt the most, my back side or my pride, but I sure knew which was going to heel the quickest.

'Sorry,' I mumbled.

I got to my feet and pulled the coat tightly round me. I didn't know if I wanted to cry, shout or just slip into a deep coma. He didn't even turn his head as he spoke to me again.

'What are we having for dinner?'

I took a deep breath, and bit my lip.

'Haven't decided yet.'

I fought back tears as I turned and wobbled back across the garden as quickly as I could. Once inside, I snatched the heels off and ran through the kitchen and up the stairs, dragging the coat off my back as I went. I threw the shoes and coat to the floor and as quickly as I could, I tore the Basque and stockings off my trembling body and tossed them into the pile. Certainly not how I had hoped they would be removed.

I couldn't hold the tears back as I pulled on my comforting fleecy pyjamas and curled into a ball on the bed. Sobbing into a pillow, I had never felt so humiliated.

When the tears started to subside, I heard my phone vibrate again from the back pocket of my jeans, which were draped over the end of the bed. I reached over and pulled the phone out to check the message. It was a picture message from Jonny entitled *What if I beg?* And sure enough, the picture was of him on his knees, his hands clasped together in a begging pose, I laughed out loud, he was so funny, and that beautiful smile was very hard to say no to, especially after that performance from Michael.

I wiped away my tears and texted back. Michael had made a big mistake tonight. I felt awful, but I knew just the thing to make me feel better.

Yeah ok, but can I see you now, I know you're busy with work, but can I come over, just for a bit.

His reply hit my phone almost instantly.

You ok?

Just need a hug. Can I come to yours?

Meet you there in half an hour? xx

My whole body trembled, this time with joy. A whole weekend alone with Jonny and even better, I was going to see him right now for some much-needed TLC.

Sorry Michael, I did try. The guilt fairy put her hand up again but then thought better of it and quickly retreated back into her box. After Michael's performance, she had no case to make. Michael should be ashamed of himself, he deserved this, and I deserved better, I deserved Jonny. Now, just to come up with a decent enough excuse to go away for a whole weekend, and to go out right now.

He was still sitting by the pool when I stepped out the back door, this time with jeans and my favourite fluffy jumper on, his back to me.

'I'm just heading out.' I shouted across the garden.

'Ok,' he replied without even looking round, or asking where I was going, so I didn't bother to make something up in the end. I just turned and left.

chapter twenty

Eddie was slumped in a black plastic chair positioned on one side of a basic wooden desk, he watched intently as the second hand on the noisy white wall clock did its sixty-fifth sweep.

Apart from one torn poster advertising the Samaritans, another one saying *Do you know your rights?* with a helpline number and some graffiti, the room was plain, boring and downright depressing. He glanced back at the Samaritans poster and looked at the number. *Another hour in here,* he thought, *and he might need it.*

He fidgeted with a crumpled paper cup that had once contained an interesting and unique blend of coffee; java and pond water. He tossed it back and forth between his hands before throwing it angrily across the room. Despite the force, the lighter-than-air cup floated gently through the air and barely made it halfway across the room before it fluttered to the ground. It was very unsatisfying.

He glanced at the clock again as he stood up and stretched out his back and legs. Patience was not his strongest card and waiting was painful. He listened for any sign of life as he did a lap of the room, but there was not a whisper, so he slumped back onto the uncomfortable chair again, clasped his hands behind his head and sank deep, sighing loudly as he lifted his feet one by one, onto the table.

It was not the first time he had been stuck in a police interview room, not by a long shot, but it was one of the few times he wasn't under arrest, at least not yet. He hoped to keep it that way, which was why he had been abandoned with his awful cup of coffee in this awful room.

'No comment,' doesn't make for a compelling conversation apparently, so they eventually gave up asking him questions and called his lawyer as per his initial and repeated requests.

The police officer had spotted him coming out of the club, purely by chance, and had recognised him from the case board for the missing girl - Nancy Reed. He had only been asked to come down to the station to answer a few questions to help with their enquiries, but there was no way he was going to let himself get tangled up in their clever questions and incriminate himself, and he had immediately demanded his lawyer, Ash, who unfortunately had been in court all day and was busy celebrating a victory on the other side of town, so they would all just have to wait.

He had almost given up all hope when the door to the interview room opened just enough to squeeze a frazzled looking, unruly blonde head through the gap; the head of the sergeant who had collared him outside the club.

'No sign of Ashley Banks. Still not feeling chatty?' said Sergeant Carey.

'I'll wait.'

'You sure, it won't take long?'

'I'll wait.'

'Just a few harmless little questions?'

'I'll **wait**!'

'Suit yourself.'

The head disappeared, and he went back to watching the clock.

The second hand was on its seventy-first sweep when the door opened again, this time granting passage to his very welcome and long overdue legal counsel.

'Thank God.'

He sighed loudly and stood up to shake his hand before sitting back down in his own chair.

'Hi Eddie, sorry, I came as quick as I could.'

Ash took out a reporter's note pad and took the seat on the opposite side of the desk.

'No problem, Ash, I'm just glad you're here.'

'So, what's going on?'

'They want to talk about Nancy Reed.'

'Ok, but you're not under arrest; they've not charged you with anything?' Ash confirmed.

'Yet.'

'Right ok, it's like that,' he said scanning through the top sheets of his note pad. 'I wondered, when she went missing last week...' He retrieved a pen from his breast pocket and tapped it on the desk twice. 'Give me ten minutes.'

Ash lifted his notebook, scraped his chair backwards across the concrete floor and marched out through the door, leaving his very impressive looking leather case on the floor by the desk.

Eddie sat alone again, with only the clock for company, tapping his foot and wondering what on earth Ash could possibly be doing out there.

Ash was the guy you wanted to be on your side if you got in a scrape, he was a legal miracle worker and Eddie just hoped he never developed a conscience and started working for the prosecution. The very thought made him laugh out loud, he doubted that prosecution lawyers got paid nearly as much as defence lawyers did; he had seen Ash's house and car, and immediately reassured himself - Ash would never defect.

Nine and a half sweeps of the minute hand later and Ash reappeared in the doorway.

'Sorted, let's go.'

'That's it?'

'Of course, come on, before they do find something to charge you with. My guess is, they wouldn't have to look too hard,' he said with a raised eyebrow. 'Lucky you got one half of Beavis and Butthead out there.'

Eddie grinned widely and laughed as he enthusiastically followed his knight in crocodile skin armour out of the station.

'Good evening Gentleman.' Ash nodded to the desk sergeant and Sergeant Carey as they left.

They both looked pissed, *good*, Eddie thought, but he knew he'd had a lucky escape this time.

He followed Ash out to the car park, where his very impressive black and white Pagani Zonda Roadster was parked. He had seen the car before and it never failed to provoke a reaction, especially now that it was parked next to a couple of police panda cars. Prosecution lawyers never drove cars like this, and they say crime doesn't pay.

'You need a ride?'

His jaw dropped, 'are you kidding?'

Eddie rushed round to the passenger door like a, well, like a normal guy who had been offered a ride in a Zonda. This was gonna be better than Space Mountain at Disneyland.

The car roared as the engine fired up and for the second time that day he felt something inappropriate stirring downstairs. Thank god Ash's eyes were fixed on the windscreen.

'Where's your car?' Ash boomed over the roar of the engine, and the cold wind.

Only Ash would drive a car with the roof off in November in the West Country.

'Hopefully, still outside The Green Room.' He shouted back, the chill ruffling through his hair.

'No problem.'

'So, what's happening with the cops?' Eddie said.

'They got nothing, they'll not be bothering you again, forget about it.'

'You're a fucking genius.'

'It's easy to look good when you are dealing with a bunch of polished monkeys. Just threaten to take away their bananas and they'll do anything you want.'

'Yeah well, thanks anyway.'

'No need to thank me, bill's in the post, what's your address again?'

Eddie's heart stopped until he realised that Ash was just kidding.

Ash grinned and Eddie joined him, but inside he was having serious concerns about TJ. This was a close call, but his reckless behaviour was going to get everyone into serious trouble sooner or later. Something needed to be done about him, and hopefully before Eddie found himself doing a stretch in jail on TJ's behalf.

chapter twenty-one

I was early to Jonny's flat and he wasn't back yet, so, like a homeless bag lady I was sitting on the floor waiting patiently. Sitting on the floor by his front door, by myself, was still better than sitting at home with Michael; it made me shudder that he could be so cold, so cruel.

Jonny's next-door neighbour, a bleach-blonde girl in her twenties with the tightest body I had ever seen, gave me a dirty look as she passed me to get to her door. I felt like smacking her in her smug little face, but instead, I just smiled and wished her a good evening.

She smiled back as she scuttled down the hall, but it was such a fake smile that it just made me want to slap her even more.

I had almost given up hope when Jonny finally bounced breathlessly around the corner. Just seeing him, I felt better already, and I couldn't help but smile.

'Sorry, sorry, it took longer than I thought to get away,' he said, his hand stretched out for mine. 'You ok?'

'I'm ok,' I said, taking his hand.

But apparently, I was not OK, and I was the only one who hadn't noticed.

'You don't look ok, you look really sad, have you been crying?' he said, helping me off the floor, and before he even had his door keys out of his pocket, I had burst into tears again and was weeping shamelessly in his hall.

He wrapped one arm tightly round my shoulder as I sobbed onto his chest.

'What's happened, are you hurt, did someone hurt you?' he said, as a burning look took over his features. I didn't answer, couldn't if I had wanted to, a head shake was all I could muster, and it was enough to soften his face.

'Come on, let's go and sit down, tell me all about it.'

We went inside, and I was already feeling much better by the time we made it over to the sofa. He gave me a box of tissues and sat down beside me, waiting patiently for me to dry my eyes and blow my nose.

'Feeling better?' he said.

I nodded that I was and snuggled into his chest and arms for that hug I had come for.

'Good, now tell me, what happened?'

What happened, well, let's see. My husband, who you don't know about, well, I tried to seduce him in the back garden by the pool, then he called me a cheap whore…

I guess not.

'Just had a bad day, that's all.'

But was it really that that had overwhelmed me? Did I even care what Michael thought anymore or was it the fact that my boyfriend, who has only known me for only a couple of weeks, can tell when I am sad whereas my husband of more than twenty years would need a segment on the news before he noticed something was wrong. Is that what was so overwhelming?

'That's all? You sure? You can tell me,' he said, tracing patterns on my back with his finger.

'Honestly, I feel a hundred times better now, thank you.' And I did. 'Sorry for dragging you away from work for this.'

'Nowhere else I'd rather be.'

With my legs folded up on the sofa and my head resting on his lap, we spent the rest of the night in front of the telly. It was quiet, uncomplicated and comfortable, it was heaven, and I was now even more impatient for the weekend to come.

chapter twenty-two

Wednesdays were always quiet days at the 'New Shoo' shoe shop, and as I often did at quiet times, I was sitting in the office with Jackie drinking tea out of polystyrene cups. Note I didn't say *enjoying* a cup of tea, there was nothing to enjoy about the tea from the café next door, but their donuts were good and that more than made up for it.

The office was little more than a stuffy broom cupboard with a computer in it, although she had managed to squeeze in a filing cabinet and two chairs. Beside the computer was a stack of papers and receipts which were patiently waiting for me to do something about, maybe later this afternoon.

As usual, the hot topic on the agenda was Jonny and Michael; I'd had the day off yesterday, so I hadn't had the chance to tell her about what Michael had done on Monday night, or about Jonny inviting me away for the weekend. Naturally, she was disgusted with Michael too. But just like me, she was far more interested in my weekend plans.

'What are you going to tell Michael?'

'I already said that Gayle was still upset about our dad's anniversary, so I was going to stay with her for a couple of days.'

'So where is he taking you?'

'No idea, but he said to wear warm clothes and flat shoes. I'm gonna go shopping after work on Friday to treat myself.'

She squinted and started rubbing her jaw line with her finger. Detective Jackie was hard at work.

'Did he say to bring a passport?'

'No.'

'Hmmm. Going somewhere cold, but staying in the UK?'

'That could be anywhere Jackie; everywhere is cold in the UK.'

'That's true.'

Jackie 'Sherlock Holmes' Barnes went back to her sleuthing and I took a mouthful of tea and picked up my donut.

There's nothing like a fresh jam donut. That first hazardous bite is the best, not yet knowing where the jam is, but knowing that just one bite could see the jam shoot out at you, so you had to be ready for it otherwise you could end up with it everywhere. Gently does it is my motto, and I tentatively took a small bite, no sign yet.

The shop door joyfully ping-ponged, alerting us that there was a customer. I replaced the donut and hastily started licking the sticky, sugary glitter off my fingers, one by one.

'I'll go.' Jackie said, leaping up from her chair. 'You're not putting those sticky fingers anywhere near my McQueens.'

She grinned and left, and she was right, these were extra sugary today, and delicious. I took another bite, but I forgot the rule and the jam shot out.

'Shit.'

It had gone everywhere, just like I knew it could and it was extra jammy as well as extra sugary. I dropped the donut back in the cardboard box it came in, scrapped the jam off my chin with my finger, sucked the worst off my arm and searched for some tissues to take care of the jam that had dropped onto my pretty white blouse. There were none that I could see, so I crawled under the desk to see if there were any in my handbag. I was in luck; I retrieved the tissues and started backing out, suddenly becoming aware of a pair of man's work boots standing in the door way behind me.

The boots spoke, 'Nice view.'

I grinned. I knew that voice very well, but I was surprised to hear it in Jackie's office and as I stood up, I clocked my head against the bottom of the desk.

'Shit.' That hurt.

The boots bent down beside me and Jonny's upside-down face grinned at me as he rubbed the back of my head and guided me carefully out from under the desk, avoiding further incident or injury.

'You ok? You took quite a knock there.'

'Yeah, I'm alright,' I said, hopelessly spreading out the jam stain with the tissue in my left hand. 'What are you doing here?'

'I was with a client down the road and thought I would pop in and surprise you,' he grinned.

'Well, you sure did that?' I said, rubbing the back of my head.

'You got time for a quick lunch?'

I opened my mouth to say no, but it wasn't me that answered.

'Susanna *has* got time for a very long lunch, actually,' Jackie said, glaring at me. 'But first, I quickly need a very urgent word outside.'

Jackie was standing behind Jonny, grinning and beckoning me to come out,

'One sec.' I said to Jonny, and followed Jackie out the door. 'What is it?'

'You're wearing your wedding ring,' she whispered in my ear.

'Shit, do you think he saw it?'

'Doubt it. Men rarely notice anything; besides it was mostly covered by the jammy tissue.'

'Jesus!' I pulled the ring off and tucked it in my pocket. 'Thanks. You know I'm starting to wonder about you, you seem to be very good at this.'

'It's all those romance novels I read.'

'And in any of those romance novels, does it ever end well?'

'Every time,' she winked. 'Now go get some lunch.' She made inverted commas with her fingers to punctuate the word *lunch*. I hate when people do that, but I was in a good mood and I let it ride, and went back into her office.

'I guess I do have time for lunch after all,' I said, but then I noticed the stain on my shirt. 'But I can't go looking like this; I look like I've been attacked by an angry toddler.'

'Cover it with your jacket.' Jackie said, handing me my jacket.

'How long has she got?' Jonny asked Jackie.

'As long as you like,' and she winked at me again. 'Enjoy your "*lunch*".'

Jonny took my hand and led me across the shop floor as I waved behind me. He guided me across the road to an impressive looking, metallic grey Subaru WRX that was glinting in the autumn sun. He yanked open the passenger door, and I climbed in. Actually, it might have been more accurate to say that I climbed down into the red trim, leather sport seat, this was definitely a boy's toy.

'How did you know I worked here, there are tons of shoe shops in town?' I said, battling with the six-point seatbelt. I'm glad I was wearing trousers, but what was wrong with just a standard seat belt?

'I know there are, this was the fourth shop I tried,'

He leant across and, stifling a grin, he systematically straightened out all the straps and plugged them all into the right holes, firmly pinning me into my seat.

We sprinted out of town and found a cute little pub on the outskirts of Ottery St Mary.

He parked his car right at the back of the car park under some trees. Apparently, that prevented some 'careless bastard' scratching his precious paintwork by accident. Boys and their toys, jeez.

The pub was nice; quite traditional. I'd been here years ago for a wake for someone Michael knew through work, and from my memory it didn't look like it had changed very much.

We found a little, out of the way booth, and a casually dressed waiter brought over two menus and a funny little chalk board with the specials scribbled on it. He took our drinks order; two cokes, and left us to ponder the gastronomical selection that was on offer.

The menu was typical for a country pub; anything you like, with chips, just my kind of place, and when the waiter returned with our cokes I ordered a vegetarian lasagne – with chips, and Jonny ordered a rare 16oz Ribeye with, you guessed it, chips.

The steak was a monster, never mind the poor cow that sacrificed itself for Jonny's lunch. It was making *my* eyes water just looking at it.

'You are never going to eat all that?'

'Yeah, why not?'

I shook my head. Then he cut into the enormous brick of meat, exposing its virtually raw insides. Blood oozed from the middle and I almost expected it to start mooing in protest. Seriously, a vet might have still been able to revive it. I couldn't watch, it made my stomach turn.

'That's gross.'

'What?' he said, forking a chunk into his mouth.

'It's still bleeding,' I said, strategically positioning the wine list to hide his plate from my view.

'How it should be.'

'You can't be serious.'

'Here,' he said, as he cut into the steak again. 'Try it, it's good.'

I screwed up my face and shook my head. There was no way I was going to put that in my mouth, and I started picking at my lasagne, which looked fabulous, but I had suddenly lost my appetite.

'Try it,' he said again.

I started to politely say *er no*, but my mouth had been plugged with a forkful of dead cow. Spit or chew?

The meat hung in my mouth, *spit or chew?* Jonny was staring at me with anticipation, chew, it was the only polite option, and then straight after, explain to Jonny that I was a vegetarian; I can't believe that hadn't come up yet.

'See, it's good huh?'

I had to admit, the steak did taste quite good. Actually, it tasted bloody divine. Where have you been all my life, dead cow meat?

'Jonny, I probably should have mentioned that I am a vegetarian, have been for years.'

His face dropped, 'Shit, I'm so sorry.'

'It's ok, you didn't know.'

'Yeah, but shit, I'm not stupid, you got a vegetable lasagne, a monkey could have worked that out. I'm really sorry.'

I laughed, 'You can make it up to me later.'

Then I leant forward across the table to whisper quietly in his ear. My message delivered, I sat down and quickly changed the subject to our weekend away before his jaw hit the table, or something else did.

Thankfully my appetite returned quickly, and I started eating my lasagne, still not ready to look at the steak. I can't stand the sight of blood at the best of times, least of all on my plate, but I did wonder whether it was possible to eat without seeing what you were eating. I would ponder it more later, that steak was damn good.

'Did you always want to work in a shoe shop?' he asked.

'Me, God no, I wanted to be a vet.'

'A vet?'

'Yeah, what's wrong with that?'

'Nothing, but I thought you didn't like the sight of blood.'

'I hoped I would either get over it,' I laughed, 'or, if not, I would just have to only help animals that were a little bit sick.'

'You must like animals a lot, do you have pets?'

'None, Mic, er, my mum is allergic.'

'You never told me you lived with your mum.'

Jesus woman, change the subject, this is getting a little too dangerous.

'Didn't you wonder why I had not invited you to mine yet? Anyway, what are we doing this weekend?'

Over lunch, I took several opportunities to interrogate Jonny over the finer details of our weekend ahead. I clearly haven't missed my calling at MI5, as my lackadaisical interview skills weren't cutting it and he seemed determined that he wasn't going to tell me what he had planned, only informing me that, if he did tell me, I would probably change my mind and not go, but that I would have a great time and I should just trust him.

If he thought I probably wouldn't want to go, then maybe he was right, and I shouldn't go, but he also said I would have a good time, which appealed, and he hadn't let me down so far.

Two hours into lunch, I thought I had stretched my half hour lunch break far enough and we headed slowly back to the car.

He strapped me back into the passenger seat, minus the bottom two straps. Why didn't we need those two? I didn't know if I would ever get used to the daft contraption, and I braced myself for the car to get going again, but instead he flicked a lever at the side of the chair and the seat, including me, fell sharply backwards.

'Whoops,' Jonny said with a glint in his eye.

Then he grabbed both my hands and, holding them tightly above my head, he crawled on top of me, his hungry lips pressed firmly against mine, his fiery eyes fixed to mine. It was so hot I nearly let go right then.

The world stood still as the heat welded us together in the back of his car. I couldn't hold back a second longer and neither could he.

'I need you now,' he whispered in my ear.

I yanked the button on his jeans and unzipped his fly, he was free and by the feel of him he was not kidding about needing me now. Then he ripped down my trousers; panties round my ankles and still pinned to the seat, he slammed into me so hard he took my breath away. Again and again, my hands gripping his back, one foot on the dashboard the other on the roof, this wasn't love making, this wasn't even sex, this was sub-primal.

Deeper and deeper, I bit my lip and closed my eyes. I couldn't hold back, and I cried out as the pleasure waves rippled up and down me, and a second later Jonny did the same, and we held each other tight as we came together, gasping for breath.

A few minutes later I opened my eyes and suddenly became very aware again of the fact that we were in a car park, half naked. This sudden realisation mobilized every ounce of my blood northwards and immediately filled my face, although the windows were so steamed up that even if someone had wanted to look in they couldn't have seen anything.

'Come on,' I said, tapping him on the back. 'As much as I would love to lie here all day with you, half naked, in this very public car park, I have to get back to work before my arse gets fired.'

'Urgh, Ok,' he said.

It took us a couple of giggly minutes to untangle ourselves and get the seat upright again, and then a couple more minutes to un-steam the windows, and then we were sailing back into town.

My mind reeled from all the new experiences I had just had; rare steak and public, animalistic sex. My mother always assured me that those types of escapades would make you go blind, if that's true then bring it on and then, as a bonus, I could eat the steak too because I wouldn't be able to see it.

'Thank you,' I said, as the car pulled up outside the shop.

'You're welcome,' he said, and blushed.

'No, really. Thank You. You don't know what you do to me, you make me into someone I like again.'

He didn't speak. Instead, he leant over and pushed the release button on the harness and pulled me into his arms, holding me tighter than he ever had before.

'I'll see you Saturday ok, warm clothes, flat shoes.'

'I'm counting the hours.'

I kissed him lightly on the lips and climbed out of the car.

Jackie closed early on a Wednesday, and by the looks of it she was long gone, so I skipped across the road, waved to Jonny and found my car.

I really was counting the hours, sixty-nine and a half of 'em to go.

chapter twenty-three

'I can see her from here,' TJ said into his phone from the inside of his blacked-out Golf. 'She's sitting at the counter reading a magazine.'

'Is she alone?'

'Well, apart from another woman.'

'Well, don't lose her, I need to know exactly what she's doing, where she's going and who she's with.'

'Got it boss, if she's cheating, I will soon know.'

'She *is* cheating, just get the proof, and remember to keep this just between us ok? I'm trusting you TJ, don't mess this one up!'

He hung up the phone and lifted his newspaper, holding it in front of his face in just the right position so that anyone walking past would think he was reading it, but low enough that he could easily see over it. He had already read the headline on the front page; Seedy Club Owner Suspected of Arson. He knew rightly what had happened at The Green Room, shame, he liked that club.

It was approaching lunch time and he was sure she would be leaving soon; the boss said she only worked till one on a Friday.

He was right too, and shortly after one she disappeared briefly before emerging from the shop with her coat on and her handbag over her shoulder.

He was expecting her to go straight to her car, which was parked three cars in front of his, but instead she turned left out of the shop, and headed up the high street.

Adrenaline surged as he jumped out of his car to pursue on foot; this type of work always gave him a buzz. He hadn't had to follow someone in a long time, and he loved it, so much so that, without concentrating, he dashed between two cars, only narrowly avoiding getting run over.

Think, for God sake, think, he scolded himself.

She's not bad to look at, he thought, as he tracked her step by step along the high street, not his usual type. She had a nice figure for her age, but he liked his girls at least fifteen years younger. He liked 'em naïve and giggly, and he suspected she was neither.

'We'll see,' he said to himself.

He followed her at a good distance, ignoring the bustling crowd, past the flower shops, a couple of charity shops, bargain basements and travel agents, weaving in and out of the town's oblivious shoppers as she headed further and further away from her car.

He stopped to check his phone when she paused to look at a shop window. One eye on the phone, the other on his target as he pretended to punch out a text message. He got a whiff of chips from the chippie across the road while he waited, it was making him hungry and for a moment he wondered if he had time.

No time for chips, focus, concentrate.

The whole job had him tingling from head to toe and he had to work hard to keep himself under control and suppress a keen grin from completely taking over his face.

She smiled smugly to herself, he wondered what on earth she had to smile about, and then she stepped through the door into a store. He tutted, from his spot he couldn't see her at all. He didn't want to lose her, so he crossed the road and resumed his fake text message from his new position, still wondering about those chips.

Much better, he thought, he had a great view of her from there, and of the chippie too. She was trying on a coat. A cream, fur lined, half-length coat. He thought it was quite nice, but clearly, she didn't agree, as she took it off and handed it to the shop assistant, who walked her across the store to a different one.

The black leather, full-length, fur lined trench coat was a better choice, he thought, as she swished from side to side in it. She appeared to share a joke with the assistant as she paraded up and down in front of a full-length mirror.

He watched his target showing off in front of the mirror as the assistant disappeared, returning a few minutes later with a pair of gloves, which she also slipped on. She nodded, laughed again and followed the assistant to the till; the old coat was bundled into a large plastic bag as she handed over a plastic card from her purse.

She left the shop looking very pleased with herself and turned into a coffee shop that was right next door to the chip shop. He put the phone back in his pocket and was going to cross the road to follow her from a safe distance. He waited, as car after car suddenly appeared from nowhere, and by the time he found a gap, she had returned with a takeaway coffee and was heading back up the street in the direction of her car.

He had an idea, but he needed to look alive, so he rushed ahead, keeping one eye on her as he arrived back at his own car well ahead of her.

Out the corner of his eye he watched her cross the road and head straight for her car.

Aaand action.

He pressed his phone against his ear and started shouting into it as he walked straight for her, his eyes glued to the floor and seconds later he *accidentally* bashed straight into her, catching her coffee arm with his elbow and throwing the coffee and its cup across the path and down her new coat.

'Eish, I'm so sorry,' he said in his South African accent that the girls dig so much. 'Are you ok?'

If looks could kill, he thought to himself, *I would be in a body bag by now.*

'Ah, my new coat. Look where you are going, for God's sake'

She flicked spots of coffee off the bottom of her new coat, tutting.

'You're right, of course. I'm such an idiot. I'll pay for that to get cleaned, and of course get you a new coffee.'

'No that's ok. It's fine,' she said, nervously walking away.

He darted ahead and stopped in front of her.

'I won't hear it, at least let me buy you a coffee to replace that one.'

'No thanks,' she sighed. 'I really have to go.'

'It won't take a minute.' He took her firmly by the arm and started escorting her involuntarily down the street to a nearby coffee shop.

What's with all the coffee shops he thought? *How much coffee does one town really need?*

'I'm Tatsuo, but no one can pronounce that. So my friends call me TJ.'

'Alice.'

'Alice?'

'Walker.'

'Well, nice to meet you Alice,' he said, opening the door for her and gently pushing her in.

He walked her up the aisle to the counter,

'What'll it be?'

'Just black coffee, to go,' she said.

'You heard the lady,' he said to the barista.

'You running late for something? Work maybe, boyfriend?'

'Neither, just got to get home.'

'I'll bet you are a lawyer or doctor or something like that.'

She laughed awkwardly. *Tough crowd*, he thought, and he was reminded why he liked 'em young and naive.

The barista handed her the coffee.

'Thank you, TJ,' she said, turning and walking quickly back out of the shop.

TJ chased her out to the street, 'Maybe, you and me could get together some time, maybe tonight, I'll bet I could show you a good time.'

She half coughed and half laughed.

'And would that good time include my husband?'

'Ah.'

'Yes, exactly, thanks again for the coffee.'

He watched her go back to her car, her new coat swishing behind her as she went. Then he reminded himself of the job he was supposed to be doing, he wasn't on the pick-up, *damned shame*, he thought, and sprinted to his car before he lost sight of her.

At a safe distance, he followed her all the way home, where she stayed until The Boss showed up in his BMW a few hours later.

He considered that meant he was off the clock. Michael Walker could stalk his own wife for the rest of the day, surely, and with nothing to report, he headed back into town for some well-deserved chips.

Tomorrow was a new day; maybe he'd catch her at it then.

chapter twenty-four

I woke up at five this morning buzzing all over. Only a couple of hours till I start my weekend with Jonny. In the interest of plausibility, I booked return tickets to Jersey, just in case Michael asks. He won't, he never has before, and I forewarned Gayle to cover for me, which she seemed very happy to do.

Although she was never a big fan of Michael either, I chose not to tell her exactly why I needed a cover story, but I'm sure her bullshit-ometer was raging. I could never lie to her.

My "flight" was due to leave at 11:30 am, got to be there two hours before for "check in and security" and a fictional forty-five-minute drive to the airport meant I was counting down to an 8:45 a.m. departure from home. Perfect, as Jonny wanted to get an early start.

I glanced again at the clock, 8:35 a.m., close enough. I might explode if I had to wait a second longer.

Ben and Sara were in their rooms, fast asleep as expected, and I quickly popped my head round their doors to say good-bye. I got the usual grunts and I headed downstairs to the intercom. Michael was, predictably for a Saturday, in his den upstairs, and I let him know I was going and advised him of the location of the pre-plated meals I had left him in the fridge. He seemed unimpressed. Oh well.

I grabbed my flight case that I had left by the front door; a beautiful fuchsia pink bag on wheels that was stuffed with my warmest clothes, and headed out to the car.

No farewell party for me, no tears or white hankies as I pulled out of the garage. I shrugged, was I really expecting any? At the end of the drive I paused, and tingled all over as I pulled off my wedding ring and hid it in the glove box of my car. Won't be needing that for a couple of days, at least.

A blacked-out Golf was parked down the street and I had to strain awkwardly to see past it. *Stupid place to park,* I thought, as I pulled tentatively out of the drive and turned left.

Jonny was standing by his car when I arrived, dressed top to toe in camouflage. Clearly, he was as excited to see me as I was him and he rushed over to my car as soon as he spotted me, barely giving me time to get the handbrake on before he yanked the door open and planted a kiss on my very appreciative lips.

Despite begging, Jonny still refused to tell me where we were going, but he was as excited as a boy on Christmas morning, so I went with it. The two-hour journey passed swiftly as we both howled along with Jonny's collection of 90's hits. I was eighteen all over again, running away from my parents with the boy they disapproved of, only this time I had left that boy at home and found a new, more exciting one. I was alive.

'What are we doing here?' I said, as we pulled into a small car park signposted for the Brecon Beacons.

'You'll see.' Jonny winked as he hauled a giant rucksack out of the boot of his car and dumped it on the ground.

'What do we need all that for?'

'You'll see,' he repeated, chuckling as he handed me my fuchsia flight bag that now looked particularly poorly thought out.

He heaved the enormous bag over his shoulders and started walking along a gravelly path.

'Come on then,' he turned and beckoned.

Quickly, I extended the handle of my bag and rushed after him, the tiny wheels skipping and bouncing over the uneven ground. Definitely a poor choice, and I was starting to get a really bad feeling.

Hand in hand, he dragged me up the path for about half an hour. The views were amazing, no doubt about that, and apart from one very committed dog walker there wasn't a person in sight, just miles and miles of rolling hills, trees, heather, rivers and grass. I guess hiking in the forest was not so popular in November. I wonder why? Then Jonny turned off the main path and dragged me over a fallen tree and deep into the thick of the trees.

Another thirty minutes later, my two throbbing, cold and wet feet arrived at our destination; a tiny clearing in amongst the dense trees, miles from anywhere. Jesus, you could scream all day here and no one would ever know.

Way to look on the bright side, Alice. I thought.

'Well, what do you think?' he said, dropping his bag carefully onto the ground.

What did I think? Good question. Well, the view was breath-taking, the rolling hills making a perfect backdrop for the small lake in front of me. Behind me, thick forest, and all set to a mellow sound track of chattering birds and a babbling river that was running through the trees about twenty feet away.

But what I was really thinking, or should I say, what was worrying me, was what was in Jonny's bag. I suspected I knew the answer but decided to leave Schrodinger's bag alone and continue my fantasy that we were just here for a lovely picnic. Instead I dug my new leather gloves out of my own bag, adjusted my scarf and headed down to a tree truck to rest my tired feet and fully appreciate the view.

'I come here when I need to get away from it all.'

Jonny had sat down beside me on the fallen tree trunk. He didn't seem his normal chipper self as I took his hand.

'Get some perspective, do some thinking, you know.'

'I can see why.'

I gave his hand a squeeze.

As I looked round, I realised how special this place was. We were in the middle of no-where, not a soul in sight. He was right about one thing though. If he had told me I was going to spend my weekend in a forest, I would have said *no thank you very much*, but now that we were here, it might not be so bad.

Jonny never stayed down for long and moments later he had jumped up from the log.

'Come on, Susanna, we've got a tent to build.'

'We?'

This should be interesting.

I estimated, while I was helpfully holding a pole for him, that the tent would have taken about twenty minutes to put up if he had done it by himself, but with my help, we finished in an impressive forty-five.

We spent the rest of the day chatting, walking round the lake, gathering firewood and generally just mucking about. Being November, the night started to draw in early and at about six o'clock we brought a two-man sleeping bag out onto the ground and huddled in it by the fire to keep warm. With a tin cup each full of rum and a large tin full of hot baked beans for supper, we were set for the night.

Apparently, I should have been grateful for the vegetarian dinner, he usually gets the ones with little sausages – so thoughtful.

I had some impressive holidays before the kids came along, comes with being married to a wealthy man I guess; St Lucia for our honeymoon, weekends in the south of France, the odd fortnight in Marrakech or Dubai to name a few, all in five-star resorts I might add. But none of them quite compared to the intimacy of sitting under the stars with a large can of baked beans and just one spoon.

I wrapped Jonny's arms around me tighter as I watched the sun slowly sink from view and thought about how lucky I was to be here with him, a man whom I suspected I had fallen head over heels in love with.

chapter twenty-five

The sun had long since departed and the view was looking quite different than it had when we had first settled in front of the fire.

The moon cast eerie shadows across the gently rippling water, trees stretched out over the lake like they were reaching out for something. It was deathly quiet apart from the soft crackle of the fire and the occasional flock of yammering birds, it was kind of creepy, and I was grateful Jonny was with me. Without him, this whole night time experience would have been upgraded to utterly terrifying.

The sky was perfectly clear, and the stars glinted and twinkled high above us. Jonny had done his best to point out some of the main constellations, but just like I did when I saw my first scan, I just smiled and nodded along, completely ignorant of what he was talking about. It just looked like a random bunch of stars to me.

'You know, you're the first person I have ever brought here,' he said.

'Really, why?'

'I usually come here to be by myself, to get away from people. You're the first person I have ever met that I feel completely safe with.'

I gave him a squeeze. 'How long have you been coming here?'

'Since I was about ten.'

Jesus, ten years old? What does a ten-year-old have to get away from that he needs to feel safe?

'I used to live nearby, and when things got rough at home, I would get on my bike and just ride and ride, then one day I found this spot, I stayed here all night. I got the hiding of my life when I got home the next day.'

He laughed when he said the words *got a hiding*, but I didn't. If my kids ever went missing, no matter how long they were gone for, I could only imagine hugging and squeezing them to death when they came back to me, I couldn't imagine any circumstances where I would ever feel the compulsion to beat them and I tightened my grip around him again as I imagined his frightened little ten-year-old face.

'I love you Susanna.'

I sat up and looked straight at him; he had taken me totally by surprise, 'I ur…'

I was grateful when he put his hand over my mouth, what am I supposed to say to that, of course I loved him, more than anything I think, but was I ready to say those words to another man?

'Don't,' he said, his eyes deadly serious. 'I didn't say it to hear it back, I just want you to know how I feel, that's all. We've only known each other a couple of weeks; you'll say it one day when you're ready, if I haven't made a total mess of things before then. But I'll be glad if or when you do, but for now, let's just leave it there. I don't want you to say it just because I did.'

Our eyes locked as he spoke, and I could feel the atmosphere thicken in the sleeping bag. He loves me. Just the thought made me tingle all the way down, but the awkward silence was starting to eat me up and I needed to lighten the mood and quick. I did what any normal person would do under these circumstances, and I stuck my tongue out and licked the inside of his palm.

He retracted his hand quickly. 'Ewww,' he said, wiping his hand on the sleeping bag. 'That's so gross.'

I laughed out loud and so did he and we wrestled in that sleeping bag as I tried my damnedest to lick his face as he tickled me, but playful wrestling soon turned to kissing and kissing could only lead to one thing and soon enough I had forgotten I was married, how cold it was, or how scary the shadows were, and we were making love under the stars in the middle of nowhere. I didn't even notice when it started pouring with rain.

It's amazing how noisy a forest can be during the night.

As well as the trees rustling in the wind and the rain tapping against the sides of the tent, there was an occasional hoo hoo from an owl and the deathly screech of a fox, and if that wasn't enough, you can add Jonny's snoring to the cacophony. I think I managed about ten minutes of sleep, although I might be exaggerating, it was probably closer to five.

Of course, Jonny slept like a baby, this was his nirvana after all, and I had sat up for much of the night jealously watching him peacefully breathing in and out.

Then, in between clutching at my pounding chest every time an animal called out or something hopped past, casting its enormous shadow over the side of the tent, and the moment I was sure I had seen a man standing outside the tent, I was busy contemplating the best way to tell him that I was not going to spend another night in this tent.

How he ever felt safe here I will never understand.

In the nick of time; just as the fear of being eaten alive by a killer fox/owl tag team was about ready to finish me off, the sun finally started to poke its head up, casting a comforting glow over my imagination, and I finally started to relax, a decidedly good thing, I thought. As prepared as Jonny seemed to be, I doubted there was a defibrillator in that ruck sack of his and if my heart continued to labour the way it had all night I suspected it might have just conked out.

Reassured that the sun would protect me from the murderous forest animals, I grabbed the loo roll, crept out of the tent and attended to some private business that I had been putting off for more hours than I care to admit - another experience that I prefer never to have to repeat.

Jonny was still snoring, so I wrapped myself up in my scarf and gloves and bravely took myself for a short walk by the lake. My feet crunched through the frosty grass as I plodded over to the edge of the water. It's funny how friendly the lake seemed with the sun casting its eye over the place. Barely an hour ago, this place felt like a set from a horror movie.

'SUSANNA!'

Shit. That's my cue, I hurried back to find Jonny, completely panic stricken, standing next to where the fire had burnt out.

'Susanna,' he gathered me up in his arms. 'I was worried, where'd you go?'

'Just over to the lake, I didn't go far.'

'Don't do that to me, I was worried sick.'

He squeezed me again, tight as he could, and I realised that whilst I had survived being eaten alive by a fox, the real threat was standing right beside me, slowly squeezing the life out of me. Thankfully, I was able to wriggle free, but that was when the verbal assault started.

'Jesus, you look like crap,' he said.

'Why, thank you.'

I curtseyed sarcastically.

'I take it you didn't sleep well last night.'

'No actually, and I am glad you brought that up, because after last night I will never be able to read *Watership Down* again without having nightmares.'

He laughed, 'Sorry. You should have woken me.'

'I couldn't do that, you looked so peaceful.'

'Well, why don't we spend the night at mine tonight then, although I still can't guarantee you'll get much sleep.'

'That would be great.'

There are lots of things that can induce a sleepless night, I realise, some good and some not so much, but I thought I might approve of this one. Actually, I knew I would.

'Thank you for coming,' Jonny said, giving me a hug, 'And sorry you hated it.'

'I didn't hate it, not all of it anyway, just the overnight bit.'

After a hand-in-hand walk around the lake, we packed up, hiked back to the car and headed back to his flat, just in time for a late sandwich, made by Jonny I might point out. He put on a movie, don't ask me what it was, I don't even remember seeing the first trailer, I was so tired I was asleep before the opening credits.

chapter twenty-six

'Did you like the movie?' Jonny asked as I yawned along with the credits.

'Oh, yes,' I lied. 'It was great.'

I started uncurling myself and stretched out my legs, leaving my heavy head resting comfortably on Jonny's lap. It was very content there, and I rolled onto my back and dangled my feet over the armrest so I could see his face, especially his beautiful blue eyes and smile. I was blissfully rewarded with a kiss for my efforts.

'Did you like the bit with the robots?' he said, peering down at me, his hand draped lazily across my tummy.

'Oh yeah, that bit was great.'

'Uh huh,' he nodded, 'I particularly liked the bit when you snored like a blocked drain.' he said laughing. 'And especially the bit that had me pinned to the chair and afraid to move in case I woke you up.'

'Oh, sorry.' I felt my cheeks reddening. 'What was the movie anyway?'

'You missed *This is the End* and *White House Down.*'

Two movies, damn it. I loved *This is the End* too. Ah well, I will catch it again sometime. Then I realised something and sat up.

'Hey, there are no robots in either of those movies.'

'I know that, I stayed awake,' he said and shot me a wry smile. 'Hungry?'

'Maybe in a bit, can I use your shower first?'

'Just try not to fall asleep in there,' he grinned.

'Ha ha.' I got up and headed for the bathroom, commenting over my shoulder as I put my hand on the door handle, 'Then again, maybe I will, and you'll have to come rescue me.'

'Well, in that case,' he said, jumping onto his feet. He hurried over and held me round the waist, pushing himself against me. 'Maybe I had better just come and keep an eye on you, or perhaps I could think of something that might just keep you awake!'

I turned around and wrapped both arms around his neck and gave him a deep but brief kiss. 'Well let's see if you can succeed where Seth Rogan and James Franco failed, shall we.'

He moaned quietly as I pulled him backwards into the bathroom with me. I had only one thing on my mind, but Jonny was in no rush today.

I threw my head back and moaned loudly as he stood behind me and slowly washed my body, the heavenly chocolate aroma of his lynx shower gel stirring the last of my senses. My skin quivered as he teased every inch of it with his soapy hands. I closed my eyes, the water spilling over both of us as his wet, curious hands led his mouth from my toes all the way to my lips. I could hardly contain myself as his fingers took their time and massaged shampoo into my head and down the length of my hair; so erotic, it was the most incredible form of torture.

With my hair still soapy I found his hands and held them tight as I dropped to my knees. I looked up into his eyes, lightly nuzzling him with my nose. I never dropped my gaze as I closed my mouth around him and slid my lips all the way down, feeling him grow inside my mouth. Then neither of us could wait any longer and the door to the shower was thrown open.

He pulled me on top of him as he fell backwards onto the bathroom floor. I quickly found my rhythm and rode, gripping his hands tightly until we both came noisily together.

Feeling giddy, gasping for breath and very content indeed, I groaned and collapsed onto his hot, sweaty chest, my wet hair still full of suds. He wrapped his arms around me and we lay there, on the soaked bathroom floor, listening to the shower that was still pumping out water.

'Well done for not falling asleep, by the way.'

I lifted my head just enough to see him grinning like a Cheshire cat.

'No one could sleep through that,' I said between breaths. 'You are unbelievable.'

He blushed, and I dropped my weary head back onto his chest. Who'd have thought getting your hair washed could be such a turn on. I'll never be able keep a straight face at the hairdresser again.

I could have laid there forever, but I was starting to get hungry and his small bathroom floor was not the comfiest of places, so I dragged myself up and we both hopped back in the shower for a rinse off.

Wrapped up in towels, Jonny ordered a pizza while I cleaned up his sodden bathroom. It looked like someone had been drowned, as there was water everywhere. I smirked as I picked up all the clothes from the soaking wet floor and dumped them in his washer/dryer. Another new experience for me, and one that I intended to repeat soon.

While I was getting dressed in Jonny's bedroom, my phone vibrated to tell me I had a text message. I found it in the bottom of my handbag and opened the message. I'll be honest; if I had been given a hundred guesses as to who it was from I would never have guessed Michael.

Missing you, can't wait to see you tomorrow night. Love you.

I sat down on the edge of the bed and my heart sank as I read the message. I had never had one like that before and especially not from him. He was missing me, he loved me. Shit, now I felt really bad. I sat on the end of Jonny's bed, still naked, staring at the message, what should I say, shit, I quickly typed a safe reply:

Me too, xx

I turned off the phone and threw it back into my handbag, now totally and utterly confused. Things were simple when I thought he didn't care about me, didn't love me, but maybe I was wrong.

Damn you Michael! I was having such a good time until now.

'Everything ok?' Jonny said, poking his head round the door. I took a deep breath, smiled and shrugged Michael off, I had to, I was naked in my lover's bedroom, of all places, and I went back to my suitcase to find something to wear for the rest of my evening with Jonny.

'Just trying to decide what to wear.'

'Well, I think what you have on is just perfect.'

I laughed, 'You would,' and continued rummaging through my case.

I was in my fleece pyjamas and his long robe by the time the pizza arrived, so I wasn't allowed to answer the door when the delivery guy arrived. Instead, I was in charge of opening a bottle of wine and we started our last evening of the weekend together eating pizza on the sofa and getting drunker and drunker on red wine, and when we ran out of wine, dark rum.

chapter twenty-seven

On Monday morning I woke up alone and very hung over. *Why did I have to have so much to drink last night?* I rubbed my sore head and pulled on Jonny's black dressing gown and plodded through the bedroom door in search of life, but there was no one about, just me. It felt weird to be in Jonny's flat by myself.

Clutching my aching head, I wandered into the kitchen to make a cuppa and found a folded note propped up against the kettle, with Susanna scribbled on it and a key.

Morning Susanna,
Sorry, I had a work crisis and had to rush off, didn't want to wake you.
Thanks for a great weekend, can't wait to do it again, maybe book a hotel next time!
Jonny xxxxxxxxxxxxxx
PS Please lock the door after you.

I sighed, refolded the letter and put it back next to the kettle, which I flicked on. Oh well. While I waited for the kettle to boil I glanced at the clock on the oven.

Shit. It was half nine. Suddenly the adrenaline started flowing. Forget the tea; I had to get to work.

I rushed round the flat, heart pounding, as I quickly gathered up my stuff, which was strewn all about the place. Handbag in the bedroom, clothes in the dryer, shoes, one by the telly, the other by the sofa, and my pyjamas, which were scattered around Jonny's bedroom. I could feel my cheeks redden as I found my top by the window; *how did it get all the way over there?*

Never mind, I had to get to work, so I quickly dressed, grabbed my coat and bag and legged it down the three flights of stairs and out to my Audi, which was now completely frosted up.

With little time to properly defrost it, I scraped a small hole in the windshield with my credit card and fired up the car. I screeched out of the car park and hurtled along the street in the direction of town, at the same time, fumbling through the glove box for my wedding ring, one eye on the road.

I should've been at work forty-five minutes ago. My indicator on, I swung the car into the oncoming lane to overtake a dawdling Nissan and tore past at the speed of light. I flung the car back onto my side of the road as soon as I was clear of the Nissan. I was still fighting to get my ring back on my finger when I noticed the brake lights on the van just ahead.

'Shit.'

I pumped the brake but there was no grip on the icy road and the lights were getting closer. The back of the car swerved to the side, while I fought frantically with the wheel. Twenty feet and thirty miles an hour. Shit, shit, shit. I pushed harder on the brake, begging the car to stop. Ten feet. Twenty miles an hour. I closed my eyes and braced myself as my screeching car crashed straight into the back of the innocent van.

In a split second a heart pounding bang reverberated through the car, then everything turned white. It sounded like a bomb had gone off, and then I heard the piercing crunch of metal as I was thrown backwards into the seat.

For a moment, I had thought I was dead. But I wasn't dead; the excruciating pain in my arm proved that, as did the acrid smoke that was now filling my choking lungs. I flung the car door open gasping for breath, popped the seat belt and fell out onto the cold ground, clutching at my aching chest as I searched desperately for a breath of fresh air.

Voices echoed all around me.

Are you ok, are you ok?

Was I ok? I turned and saw the front of my car, the beautiful *guilt car* that Michael had bought me after forgetting my fortieth birthday, now reduced to a crumpled lump of metal. The enormity of what had just happened hit me in the face like a juggernaut and I crumpled into a hysterical mess on the freezing ground.

More voices, shouting, sirens, bright lights, the world spun in breathless circles. Someone wrapped a blanket over my shoulders, they were talking softly to me, asking me things. I couldn't make out what they were saying.

Oh my god, oh my god!

Tears shot out of my eyes. Coughing, I still couldn't breathe.

I felt an oxygen mask being pushed onto my face and a few minutes later the world stopped spinning. I could breathe again, and I was feeling much better.

The man rubbing my back was a paramedic called Clive, he had a nice smile and nice eyes too. He helped me stand up and I walked with him to his ambulance, and sat in the back breathing in the lovely oxygen, while he stuck lots of wires to me and plugged them into his machine.

I watched the chaos I had caused while he worked. A policeman directed the heavy traffic around my smashed-up car, another spoke to the van's owner, who looked particularly irate at the state of the back of his van. I suppose I couldn't really blame him, at least he didn't look hurt, that was something. People milled around gawking, chattering with each other, gossiping. I kept taking the lovely deep breaths of oxygen.

Clive asked me my name. I knew that one,

'Alice Walker.'

Where I was? A little trickier, 'High Street' – was it?

Where did it hurt? Easy, 'face, left arm and chest.'

Where had I been? I swallowed hard, where had I been, with my lover? No, I couldn't tell him that. A tearful 'I don't know,' would have to do.

'Just keep taking deep breaths,' he told me, and walked over to a waiting policewoman.

The policewoman spoke to Clive for a while and eventually they both came back to see me. I had a good idea what this was about, as flashbacks to last night and the many glasses of rum reminded me, I was probably still drunk. I wanted to cry again.

The policewoman asked me a bunch of questions first and then recited me a very well-rehearsed statement; this was not her first time, clearly.

'Mrs Walker, I require you to provide two specimens of breath for analysis by means of an approved device. The specimen with the lower proportion of alcohol in your breath may be used as evidence and the other will be disregarded. I warn you that failure to provide either of these specimens will render you liable to prosecution. Do you agree to provide two specimens of breath for analysis?'

I nodded; this was turning into a nightmare.

I barely had enough energy to stand up, but sitting in the back of the ambulance, I somehow managed to give her two sufficient breath samples. Then she started talking; terrifying, stomach churning words.

'Alice Walker, I am placing you under arrest for dangerous driving and driving a vehicle whilst over the legal alcohol limit, you do not have to say anything, but it may harm your defence if you do not mention, when questioned, something which you later rely on in court. Anything you do say may be given in evidence. Do you understand?'

I felt sick, but I nodded and then I sobbed.

I understood alright, if only she had taken the test after reading her little statement. Hearing it was enough to sober anyone up.

Michael was waiting for me at the hospital. How did he even know I was there? Two police officers; the girl that had read me my rights and a taller male who I didn't recognise were also at the hospital, making sure I didn't try and escape now that I was technically their property, for at least the next twenty-four hours anyway.

Michael's wrinkled up face was a picture as he dashed over to the stretcher I was being carried out of the ambulance on. He gripped my hand and gave me a kiss on my forehead; his eyes were intense and full of concern as he walked alongside the stretcher that was wheeling me into the hospital and into a private room that Michael had, apparently, insisted on. I don't even know why I still had to be on the stretcher, I felt fine now, well apart from the pain in my head and my arm, but I didn't need a stretcher for that, surely. The two officers stood vigil on the other side of the door as the paramedics left me and Michael alone in my tiny room.

I lifted my head, 'I'm sorry,' I mustered. My head hurt more than I thought, and I let it fall backwards onto the stretcher again. Michael perched on the side of the bed and squeezed my hand.

'It's ok, I'll get this cleared up, don't worry about it.'

'Michael, they arrested me for drunk driving, I could go to jail, or worse, I could've killed someone.'

He smiled warmly, 'but you didn't, I'll sort it.'

Tears pooled in my eyes, 'and the beautiful car you bought me, it's ruined.'

'Then I'll get you another one.'

He smiled down at me and squeezed my hand again.

'I'm just relieved you are alright. Listen, I need to make a few phone calls, will you be ok for a bit?'

I nodded, and he stood up and walked out the room. I saw him speak to the police officers waiting outside, then they all disappeared.

I was alone, staring up at the bright white ceiling, and I decided then and there that this all had to stop. Seeing Michael so concerned, so supportive, only reminded me why I married him all those years ago. He did love me, and he definitely didn't deserve this.

I knew now, more than ever, that I had to end all of this. I had to get to my solicitor, to sign divorce papers, and preferably before anyone else got hurt.

chapter twenty-eight

Michael closed the door to Alice's private hospital room softly behind him. Officers Fletcher and Whiteman were standing diligent guard outside the room.

His head was almost ready to explode under the pressure that was fast building. He had enough on his plate already with the police sniffing round his business. He didn't need his soon to be ex-wife's reckless behaviour giving them any more excuses to pry into his family's affairs.

'Take a break!' he ordered, trying his best to maintain at least some element of control.

'Mrs Walker is under arrest.'

'Not anymore. I think you'll find that you don't have any evidence.' He glared at them both. 'Or are you calling me a liar?'

'No sir.'

'Well good, then you can both run along.'

Problem one sorted, well superficially at least. He retrieved his mobile phone and called Ash. The cops were gone for now, but he needed a little more reassurance.

'Michael, I'm glad you called.'

Michael headed straight for the nearest exit, the phone pressed firmly to his ear.

'Ash, things just got a lot worse.'

'Jesus, what now? I'm just a barrister you know, not God, there's only so much I can do.'

'Yeah, well you better get real good at performing miracles, and fast. Alice's been charged with drunk and dangerous driving.'

'Shit, really, is she ok?'

Michael forced his way through the hospital's automatic door and made a bee line for a bench, which looked fairly private.

'She's fine.'

'Ok, well that I can sort easy enough. She didn't kill anyone did she?'

'No.'

'Well, that makes a refreshing change. It's the other charges I am most concerned about. They found a dead prostitute in the bottom of the river Exe. A dog discovered the body this morning, they have identified her as Cheryl Kid, goes by the name of Pixie. Apparently, she was last seen when she was dropped off by her pimp at your house.

'They are putting together a case against you, Michael. I'm holding them back for now. They don't have enough evidence to charge you now, but after Nancy mysteriously disappeared they are becoming a bit itchy. They only need one more witness to come forward and it's all over for you.'

Michael sat on the bench and rubbed his temples. His world was crumbling around him. *Just keep fighting* he told himself, he'd been in worse trouble than this in the past, he just had to trust in his guys, just like he always had. Ash continued as he popped two little white tablets from a blister pack of aspirin he found in his pocket.

'They even had Eddie in last week, trying to lay Nancy's disappearance on him. They said a food delivery guy ID'ed him, and there was another guy there, but they don't know who it was. My guess is TJ, as it was at TJ's mum's house.'

Michael bowed his head.

'Ash, just keep doing your job, we've been here before, more than once if I remember rightly. The case will fall apart, and they will have nothing on any of us.'

'I don't share your optimism this time, Michael.'

'You said they don't have any other witness. As long as that doesn't change, they will have to drop it. Leave the rest to me.'

'All right then.'

He dropped the phone back into his pocket and looked out across the emergency entrance of the hospital as an ambulance pulled in, lights and sirens spoiling his moment of peace and quiet. He watched the crew rush someone out the back of the ambulance and through the hospital doors on a stretcher, and sighed heavily.

He only managed about ten minutes of deep thought before he was interrupted again.

'Hey, Boss.'

He looked up and spotted a familiar figure running across the lawn in his direction. He sighed again, it was TJ.

He had once been pleased to have TJ on staff, but recently he had started to go off the rails. He was crazy and impulsive, and he couldn't help thinking that things had been smoother and more efficient before he came along.

An interesting thought entered his troubled mind – maybe TJ would prove useful after all. *Maybe TJ could take the bullet for this*, he thought, after all Nancy was spotted at his mum's house. That would solve two problems rather nicely. He would have to look into that and make sure he couldn't be linked back. In any case, TJ had to be kept in the background from now on, he couldn't afford any more of his petulant cock-ups.

'Boss.'

TJ was standing about six feet away, puffing away with a frenzied look on his face.

'What is it TJ?'

'You were right about Alice, definitely having an affair.'

TJ retrieved his cigarettes from his coat pocket. Still panting, he took one for himself and offered one to Michael.

He nearly shook his head, he hadn't smoked a cigarette for years, but he thought under the circumstances one wouldn't hurt and slid one out of the box.

'Tell me something I don't know.'

'I can do better than that,' he said, leaning forward so he could light both cigarettes simultaneously with his zippo. 'Look at this.'

TJ unlocked his phone and opened the gallery app before handing it over to Michael. A very angry, evil looking grin consumed his face. Michael continued to scan through the pictures, there were ten in total, each one adding fuel to the throbbing rage he was already feeling. His hands tightened into fists as he stood up from the bench, the cigarette hung listlessly from his dry lips. He hurled his phone to the ground and found it with his angry boot as he glared at TJ.

'Boss?'

He snatched the cigarette from his mouth and started moving, his long legs striding out across the grass, his feet pounding his anger into the ground with each heavy step.

'Boss?' TJ chased after him, jogging to keep up. 'You want me to cut him up?'

'Go home TJ.' Michael said without stopping.

'But...'

Michael turned, rage spilling out from every trembling pore in his body. Without thinking he lifted his fist and smashed TJ across the face with the back of his hand, forcing him onto his hands and knees.

'Go. Home.'

He turned and continued on his destructive path, stomping over flower beds and barging people out of his way until he found himself back at his car.

He sat in the driver's seat and banged his head against the steering wheel three times before breaking down in tears. People screwed him over all the time; he was used to it, hardened to it, but his wife, like this, with him? That, he could not take, and it would not go unpunished.

He took a few moments for that thought to sink in. Revenge always had a calming effect on him, it soothed him, comforted him when nothing else would. He wiped his wet face, took a deep breath and gathered himself; he needed to consider his next move, he needed a steady head. There was only one way he knew to deal with people who took advantage of him and he took five slow, deep breaths before pulling out his phone, scanning for the right number and hitting dial.

The phone rang twice before it was answered.

'Yeah?'

'Eddie, I have an important job for you, meet me at the house at Redmarsh Road tonight.' He hung up and dropped his head back onto the steering wheel. Just one more call to make.

chapter twenty-nine

Thanks to the lovely people at the Royal Devon and Exeter Hospital I was quickly checked over and released. My wrist was only badly sprained thank goodness, that and my bruised face had come from smacking into the car's airbag, while the chest pain was from the white powder I had inhaled when the airbag popped open.

'So, if it weren't for the airbag, I would be fine right now,' I joked.

Sounded like a reasonable statement, in my muggy head anyway, since all my injuries had been caused by it.

'Mrs Walker. I don't think you realise that if hadn't been for the airbag I might well be sending you off to the morgue in a body bag, I think a little discomfort and bruising is a small price to pay for your life.'

Cheery chap.

So, after being royally scolded, Michael walked me out to his BMW and helped me into the passenger seat like I was an invalid, and minutes later we were sailing home.

The police standing guard at my hospital room door had long disappeared, which seemed weird considering I was supposed to be under arrest. Maybe they would come to the house to cart me off to jail later.

'I have a surprise waiting for you at home.' Michael said, smiling, as he navigated the car through the tea time traffic.

'Oh, what is it?'

My head was still a little muggy from an injection I had been given by the paramedic to help me calm down, but I did my best to feign interest.

'You'll see.' His grin widened.

I was in no mood though. Whatever it was, I was sure it could wait, I just felt tired and wanted to crawl into my warm and cosy bed. I hadn't had a good night's sleep for two days, probably best not to mention that and blame the accident for my exhaustion.

The car pulled up on the drive and Michael dashed round to help me, but I was already half out by the time he got around to my door.

'I'm fine, Michael,' I said. 'I'm just exhausted, that's all.'

He scowled but gave in and let me get out by myself.

Waiting for me in the hall were Sara and Ben, who couldn't wait to give me a hug when I came through the door, a pleasant change from the usual reception I got from them. Did I have to have to smash up a car just to get some love from my husband and kids?

Standing next to the kids was a woman I didn't recognise, about 5' 4 and petite, maybe in her late thirties, and irritatingly attractive. She looked like a waitress or something in her black, perfectly ironed trousers and white blouse.

'This is Brenda,' Michael said proudly.

Was this my surprise?

'Brenda, this is my wife, Alice, please take good care of her.' He pushed me toward Brenda. 'Alice, Brenda is our new housekeeper, she will take care of your every need, do the house work, the shopping, you won't have to lift a finger.'

'Hi Brenda.'

I took Michael's arm with my good hand and dragged him into the kitchen,

'Michael, I don't need a housekeeper, I am fine.'

'I won't hear a word of it. I have noticed you've been struggling around here, you're not yourself and I think you need help. I thought you would be pleased.'

'Well, I'm…'

'Uh!' He threw his hands up in the air. 'She's already been paid a month in advance; give it a try at least.'

'Fine, *one* month.'

'I've also called Dr Sage in from London, he will be here first thing tomorrow to see you, and Dr Bentley will be here in the afternoon also to make sure you are ok.'

'Michael, I don't need a shrink or a doctor.'

'Dr Sage is the best there is, let's let him decide if you need help or not, ok?'

I sighed heavily, there was no point in arguing with Michael, just bite your tongue and get on with it was my motto. In fact, that was the story of our marriage, as was his ability to outsource his problems. If only he had invited a lawyer to visit.

I followed him out to the hall where Brenda was looking a little nervous. I threw her a half smile. These next four weeks will be agony, well they will be if I am still living here myself.

'Brenda, would you help my wife up to bed, she's had a difficult day and needs her rest, and I have a lot of work to catch up on and need to pop out for a short while.'

'Of course, Mr Walker,' she chirped. 'This way Mrs Walker.'

Of course, Mr Walker! I followed her up the stairs, as if I didn't know where my own flipping bedroom was. *This way Mrs Walker.*

Stupid cow.

I gasped as I followed Brenda into my own bedroom, I hardly recognised it. The duvet and sheets on the bed were changed for clean, properly ironed ones, and all the throw cushions were arranged beautifully behind a large box of chocolates that had been laid out on the bed. Flowers had been beautifully arranged in a vase on the side table and their sweet scent filled the room.

I had cleaned the bedroom before I left for the weekend but somehow it looked and smelled cleaner. I hadn't noticed that it had looked so drab normally. Maybe, I *could* get used to this after all, but one thing had to change, and that was non-negotiable.

'I guess you have noticed I am not all that keen on having a housekeeper.'

'That's ok, Mrs…'

I threw my bandaged hand up. 'Stop right there, if I hear you call me Mrs anything again, I will have your arse fired quicker than a shot. My name is Alice.'

The girl blushed and looked at her feet, 'Sorry, Alice.'

'That's better.'

I sat on the edge of the bed, which felt strangely more bouncy than normal, kicked my shoes off and spun round so my legs were resting on the bed, as I snuggled backwards into the scatter cushions.

'Is there anything I can do for you, Alice?'

'Yes, actually, where's the remote?'

I had hardly got through the opening credits of *This is the End* when I heard the doorbell ring. I paused the telly and started shuffling off the side of the bed, but that was as far as I got when Brenda tapped on my bedroom door.

'Yes?'

The door opened, and she was standing in the opening.

'Alice, you have a visitor.'

'Thank you, I'll come down, do you know where my slippers are?'

'It's alright,' the visitor's voice chimed over Brenda's shoulder. 'I'm already up.'

'Well, you'd better come in then Jackie.' I said. 'You're dismissed Brenda.'

Dismissed Brenda, I could feel the power flooding my head already, I will have to keep an eye on that, I might start liking this.

Jackie hopped across the room and met me on the side of the bed with a one-armed hug. I am sure it would have been two if it weren't for the enormous bunch of flowers she was clutching.

'You look like crap.' She said, the epitome of tact that she is.

'Thanks, I *was* just in a car accident.'

'I know, but you look like you've done ten rounds with Mike Tyson.'

I touched my bruised face, 'Is it really that bad?'

'Yu-huh, you shouldn't look in a mirror for at least another week, you might get suicidal.'

'Great.' I wriggled back onto the bed. 'Those for me?'

'Oh, the flowers yes.'

I took the flowers as Jackie perched herself on the side of the bed. They smelt just as good as the other lot; soon I would be able to start my own branch of Interflora.

'Thank you.'

She leant forward and whispered, 'Oh, don't thank me, they are from Jonny.'

'What?'

'Yes, they arrived at the shop this afternoon, with a card.' The card was hidden in her pocket. 'Didn't want Michael to see it. Here.'

Dear Susanna,
Sorry I had to rush off, I meant what I said.
Jonny xxx

'What does he mean, what did he say?' Inspector Jackie said.

'He told me he loved me.'

'Oh my God, you lucky girl.'

'Lucky? I am married in case you hadn't noticed.'

'A minor detail.'

'It might be minor to you, but I don't think Jonny or Michael would agree, and I certainly don't,' I said. 'This all has to stop Jackie.'

'What? You can't dump Jonny.'

'This isn't some fairy tale in a book, people are going to get hurt, I've got two kids, don't forget that.'

'Do you love Jonny?'

'Yes.'

'Well then, you have to follow your heart.'

'But Michael?'

'Mr Mundane will hardly even notice you're gone. Ditch him, take half his money and run away with Jonny, you know you want to.'

I did want to, that was the problem, although Jackie had it all wrong about the money. I couldn't have cared less about that.

But first I had to tell Jonny who I was. I couldn't lie to him anymore, if he still loved me after that, then I would know what to do.

'Listen Jackie, I really appreciate you coming.'

'Say no more,' she gave me a hug and headed for the door. 'Get better, ok.'

'I am better, I just need to get through the parade of doctors Michael has arranged to confirm it. I'll be back to work on Wednesday, ok?'

'No rush. I'll see you later.'

The door closed and I reached for the remote, but I would be denied my fix of Seth Rogan a little longer as a quiet knock on the door preceded Brenda's arrival.

I soon forgave her rude interruption when I saw she had a tray with her. I didn't even think I was hungry until I got a whiff of the spaghetti and vegetarian meatballs she had prepared. Michael hated *foreign food,* and I giggled as I imagined his face when he saw what he was getting, but I thought I was in heaven.

Dinner and a movie, all I needed was Jonny to curl up with and I would be the happiest girl in the world.

chapter thirty

Eddie's car was already parked outside the house when Michael arrived, at least that was something to be thankful for, he wasn't in the mood to be kept waiting.

He took a long deep breath as he considered his decision one last time. No, this had to be done, no one gets away with humiliating him, and this time would be no different. He had enjoyed his performance at home though, he was pleased by how well he had pulled off the role of caring husband.

He got out the car, pulled his shoulders back, his head up, and strode purposefully towards the house.

Eddie was waiting in the kitchen reading the paper.

'I see that guy at The Green Room has been charged with arson.' Michael said, pointing to the paper.

The story had made front page news again.

Eddie looked up, and folded the paper to acknowledge the story with a knowing smile. 'Yeah, how about that?'

'I knew you wouldn't let me down.' Michael said. 'Come, have a scotch with me.'

Michael led Eddie into the front room, the room he came to when he needed to relax, to regain perspective. He didn't share it very often, occasionally with Ash, but more recently he would invite Eddie in, and today he decided the occasion deserved it.

He poured two very large glasses of his favourite scotch and gestured for Eddie to sit down in the spare leather lounge chair.

Michael remained standing and tested the aroma of his drink before taking a satisfying sip and turning to Eddie.

'I have a special job for you Eddie, one that I can't trust to anyone else, only you. Do you understand?'

Eddie nodded and sipped his drink.

'This is highly sensitive, there can be no mistakes. I need to know I can trust you.'

'Of course, you can trust me. After all these years, I would think you should know that.'

'Yes well, it seems that just recently I have had my trust challenged in some unexpected ways. I am finding it hard to know who I can depend on these days.'

Michael sipped his drink and continued after a momentary pause, 'This is very hard for me, Eddie. I have found a new enemy, one that I never imagined, and they need to be dealt with in a very particular way.'

'Ok, I can handle that.'

'Good, good.' He paused for another mouthful of Scotch; the more alcohol he consumed the easier this was becoming. 'It seems that my, not so, good lady wife has taken leave of herself and is betraying her vows. I can't have that, you understand.'

He paused again, to give one last thought to what he was about to say. He had ordered people dead before, many times, and it was always as easy as ordering a pizza, but this time it was different, very different, and it surprised him how much.

He took a deep breath and continued. 'I need you to deal with her, Eddie, make her suffer a bit for her unacceptable behaviour, traumatise her, then I need you to find out who the bastard is that's screwing her, find him and deal with him, appropriately, if you understand me, then bring her to me. I'll deal with her after that.'

Eddie sat firm.

'There's fifty-grand in it for you and an extra twenty-five if you make him suffer and her watch. She needs to learn her lesson.'

Eddie was quiet throughout, thoughtful almost.

'Eddie, am I right to trust you with this?'

Eddie looked over his glass and paused while he considered the right response.

'Do you remember how we met?' Eddie said.

'Of course, but what has this…'

'Do you remember saying that I only had to work for you as long as it took to settle mine and Mum's debt?'

'Well yes, but…'

'I think I'm there now, and some, wouldn't you agree? I'll do this for you, but after this, I'm out. I'm done. I'm done with threats, with looking over my shoulder, I'm done with TJ, with dead bodies. I'm just done. I'll take my money and you'll never see or hear from me again. You won't have to worry about me, I won't cause trouble for you, it'll be as if I never existed.'

It was Michael's turn to be silent and thoughtful for a moment as he digested Eddie's speech, but of course he was going to agree, how could he not, it just made it more fun?

'You have a deal,' he said, offering his hand. 'There's no rush, she is not well at the moment anyway, and besides, I have a housekeeper now who won't let her out of her sight. I've made sure of that, so they'll be no mucking around for a few days at least.

Eddie nodded.

'I'm going to be staying here from Friday, so you'll have your opportunity then. I don't want to be there when you take her.'

Eddie took his outstretched hand and they shook on it as Eddie stood up to leave.

'I'm doing the right thing, aren't I?' Michael asked.

Eddie smiled.

'Of course, if some bitch cheated on me, I would want them both to suffer.'

He grinned and raised his glass of Scotch.

'To cheating bastards and making them suffer.'

'I'll drink to that.'

Michael smiled and they both drained their glasses.

Then Eddie left. Michael felt uncharacteristically emotional for the second time in in one day. He poured another drink and took a cigar from the wooden box on the side table. These next few days were set to be the hardest ever. He felt impatient, but he would just have to bide his time and continue playing nice, for now.

chapter thirty-one

Things finally seem to be getting back to normal, the good Dr Sage didn't certify me, although he did have some interesting insights that only confirmed to me that my marriage had run its course. Dr Bentley declared me fit to go back to work, which was nothing I didn't already know, and the Docs were able to convince Michael, who would otherwise have had me on house arrest if it weren't for their professional opinions.

My car has been declared a write-off; I could've told them that would be the case just by looking at it – the engine compartment had shrunk by at least a third, but the insurance company insisted on a *professional* opinion. I guess that's their prerogative, but in a couple of days I should expect a shiny new one to arrive on the drive. In the meantime, I have been left at the mercy of the local taxi company to get me about – apparently, I neglected to request a courtesy car come as is standard with my insurance, whoops.

There has been no sign of the police yet either, which is weird as I was expecting a visit from them days ago. Don't get me wrong I'm not complaining. When they do catch up with me I will most likely lose my license and I am in no hurry for that to happen, but I think it's weird to have heard nothing from them.

While all this has been going on I have been dodging Jonny's texts and more specifically, dodging the difficult conversation I need to have with him, in the main because

I wasn't sure how he would react. My imagination was offering me an entire spectrum of possibilities that ranged from stabbing himself, or me, with a dinner knife, to proposing marriage. Of course, neither was likely, but I hoped to stay closer to the marriage proposal end of the spectrum. Jonny or no Jonny, I had at least committed myself to one decision, and had made an appointment next week with Alistair, only this time I wasn't going to wimp out. I would petition for divorce, I promised myself.
So here I was, back at work, my wrist still bandaged up, rummaging in the stock room for a pair of very nice-looking Valentino boots in a size four.

Because this is a posh establishment, I have been banished to back room activities, owing mostly to the fact that my face still looks like Mike Tyson got the better of me, more than once.

The boots retrieved, I gave Jackie a call and she dutifully collected them, leaving me with a huge pile of boxes of re-stack. Never a dull moment, I thought to myself, as a nervous voice came from behind me.

'Hi.'

I closed my eyes and grinned, I didn't need to turn around to know that Jonny was standing behind me. I spun round to give him a much-needed hug and kiss, but as I turned, he didn't look at all pleased to see me, he looked downright angry and was now charging straight for me.

'What the hell happened to you?'

'Me, why?' I had forgotten about the shiner.

'Your face, who did this to you?' He snapped, reaching out to touch the side of my face, wincing on my behalf.

'Oh, that. The airbag did it to me when I crashed the car on Monday.'

His face relaxed a bit, but he still looked cross.

'You crashed the car? You're ok though? Why didn't you tell me?' he said, gently holding up my sore hand.

When the Mask Falls

'I'm fine, and I didn't tell you because I've had a lot to deal with the last couple of days and I didn't want to worry you.'

'You should've said something, don't keep things like that from me.'

Flip, if he didn't like that, he isn't going to like my other news.

'You're right, I'm sorry, my head's just been all over the place, I didn't think.'

'It looks really sore.'

'It looks worse than it is, honestly.'

'Jesus, I thought I had scared you away when you didn't answer my texts. Because of what I said. You should've told me. All kinds of things have been going through my head.'

'Oh Jonny, I really am sorry.'

I held out my arms and we made up with a very welcome hug.

'Do your lips hurt?'

'My lips.' Weird question. 'No why?'

'Just if they did, I might have to kiss them better.'

'Well, now you mention it, maybe they are a little sore.'

His face relaxed into a smile and we shared an extraordinarily gentle kiss.

'Listen Jonny, I'm glad you're here actually, there is something we need to talk about.'

'Oh no.'

There goes that smile I love so much. I took his hands and we sat down on the floor of Jackie's stockroom.

'Is this because I said I love you, I knew I shouldn't have said anything.'

'No, it's not that, I liked it when you said that.'

'Then what?'

'Knock, knock.' Jackie was at the door. 'Do we have those boots in a five, she thinks they are a little tight.'

'I think I saw some, hang on.' I looked back to Jonny. 'Wait there a sec.'

While I rummaged for the boots I caught the look on Jonny's face, poor soul, he looked like he had the world on his shoulders. Maybe this was a bad idea. No, it wasn't fair to keep on lying and it was making me crazy anyway, for better or worse, no pun intended, he needed to know who I was.

I located the boots and handed them to Jackie, who was eagerly waiting on them.

'Sorry about that.' I said to him.

'It's ok.'

I sat back down in front of Jonny and held both his hands again, 'the thing is.' Jesus, this is harder than I thought it would be. I tried again. 'The thing is, I…'

Then his phone started to ring, he looked at the screen and sighed.

'I'm sorry, I have to take this.'

'That's alright.'

'I'll be back in a bit.' He answered the phone as he walked out the room. 'Yes?'

I don't know how long he was gone for, probably only a couple of minutes, but it felt like hours, as I considered exactly what I was going to say. I had hoped I could have planned it a little better, but here he was.

'I'm really sorry,' he said, poking his head through the door. 'I've got to run; can I see you tonight?'

'I can't tonight.' I would be on house arrest for at least the next few days. 'Saturday?'

'That's three days away.'

'I know, I'm sorry.'

'Ok, I'll try to contain myself until then.'

I gave him a quick hug and a kiss and then he was gone.

Jackie replaced him at the door, and I looked up at her stupid grinning face, as I nursed my sore hand.

'Jackie, in those romance novels you read, what happens after the girl tells the love of her life that she is married with two grown kids?'

'Well, his heart breaks and he runs away…'

'Thanks Jackie.'

Who needs enemies right?

'Haaang on,' she continued, 'then he realises what an idiot he has been and comes back to rescue her from her boring husband, and they both live happily ever after.'

Let's hope so.

chapter thirty-two

Michael had been called away by his work at the last minute and would be gone for at least the next few days. He had left a couple of hours ago with a large suitcase and a tuna roll for the journey. He didn't tell me where he was going, I probably should have asked, but as soon as I heard he would be going away I could think only of Jonny.

Brenda had gone home too, thank goodness, she was starting to make me look bad. I caught her cleaning the skirting boards and the lampshades earlier. I don't think I've ever done that.

Sara was in her room with her girlfriend, I wouldn't see or hear from her again, and Ben had gone to a party with his mates, so I had the house and the night pretty much to myself.

Of course, the first thing I did as Michael's BMW rolled off the drive was reach for my phone.

The guilt fairy was a distant murmur in the back of my head by now, occasionally raising her feeble hand to offer her opinion, but my heart was winning this battle. Jonny made me feel so alive, he gave me energy. With just a smile he made me feel like I could do anything, he made me feel like I mattered. It was intoxicating. Sadly, he had to work tonight.

Husband away, boyfriend working, so I did what any self-respecting girl would do and scheduled a Friday night date with a bottle of wine, a mud pack and Tom Hanks.

I had kicked my movie marathon off with *The Terminal*. I followed that with *Apollo 13* and now it was time for the best of all – *Philadelphia*, which I would sob along to, as always, from the sanctuary of my bath tub.

The lavender scented hot water was billowing with foamy bubbles, the movie was loaded into the back of the waterproof telly, the candles were lit, and the wine poured. The smell coming from my ensuite bathroom was just begging for me to get in and I padded across the bedroom floor.

I had just about made it as far as the ensuite when my phone stopped me in my tracks. I considered ignoring its incessant ring, but visions of my sixteen-year-old calling me from jail tortured my conscience, and in the end, I couldn't help myself, the bath would wait for a couple of minutes while I find out what new kind of hell my little angel had brought.

I pulled my dressing gown over my fleece pj's and rummaged through my bag for my phone. It was Mum.

'Hi Mum, you ok?'

'Yes love, just wanted to check in, say hello.'

'Well, I was just about to jump in the bath actually.'

'I won't keep you then.'

Famous last words, she kept me on the phone for at least another ten minutes telling me all about her aches and pains that even the doctor could not work out, quelle-surprise; it's hard to find the cause of a sore ankle when it's all in your head. She needed a shrink, not a GP. Maybe I should give her Doctor Sage's number.

'I don't think you need to worry mum, just keep taking the pills the doctor gave you...' Hopefully antipsychotics. 'And I'll come and see you in a couple of days ok?'

'If I'm still here.'

The doorbell rang; the perfect excuse to get rid of Mum and get in the tub before it got any colder.

'Mum, don't be so dramatic.'

Although asking Mum not to be dramatic is like asking Brian Blessed to keep it down. 'Look the bath is getting cold and there's someone at the door, I have to go now.'
'Alright love, see you for coffee on Wednesday.'
'Yes Mum, love you.'

The phone clicked off and I dropped it into my dressing gown pocket. Now just to get rid of whoever was at the door and I would finally get to relax with the lovely Mr Hanks, preferably before my face mask dripped off my face.

chapter thirty-three

Eddie had parked his fake Sky engineers van about a hundred yards from The Boss's house; a very nice detached townhouse with sweeping lawns and a nice pond in the front, not quite the grandeur he had imagined given the amount of cash this man surely had, but still very nice.

The van was half way between his and his neighbours house, tucked neatly behind a cluster of trees at the end of the drive, which had given it some cover, although in all the years he had been doing this, no one had ever questioned the presence of the Sky van, even at half nine in the evening.

Danny sat on a mattress on the floor, nestled neatly between the side of the van and a cardboard box containing duct tape, a black hood, rope, plastic tie wraps and amongst other things a large bottle of Eddie's finest homemade chloroform. He had his feet crossed and resting on a wooden lock box.

'Any sign?' Danny said, without looking up from his Muscle and Fitness magazine.

Eddie was sitting in a plastic camping chair by the door, his night vision binoculars aimed through the rear window. He massaged his temple and tossed the bins into Danny's lap crumpling his magazine.

'Nothing, you're in.'

Danny lifted the bins out of his lap like they were toxic and sent them clattering back across the floor of the van, only narrowly missing an M4 rifle that was lying by the door.

'Nope. Your deal.' he straightened his magazine. 'Wife stalking, not my thing, call me when you need her dumped in the canal.'

'Thanks.' Eddie frowned.

He lifted the binoculars with his leather gloved hand and peered back through the rear window again.

'If you are just going to sit there, why did you even come?'

'Kicks.'

'You get kicks from sitting in the back of a freezing van?'

'Huh.' he frowned, closed his magazine, pushed himself off the mattress and stooped towards the door. He squeezed past Eddie, pushed the rear door open and hopped out, slamming the door behind him.

Eddie frowned and shook his head as he watched him disappear down the street.

He didn't need Danny anyway, this was straightforward – break in, grab the girl, beat her up a bit until she gives up the name of her new boy toy, grab him, carve him a new smile, drop her off at the boss's house, collect seventy-five g's and home in time for bed and his new life. He could do it in his sleep.

But this was monkey work, not his style at all, not anymore anyway. It had been quite a few years since he stalked someone's cheating wife, but seventy-five large and a promise was hard to say no to. He had already started thinking about the future and his new life in America. Seventy-five grand plus the money from the sale of his place and car would go a long way to getting him on his feet over there, either that or he could test his luck at the roulette wheel.

Three hours into the stake out, the coffee had run out, and despite his thick coat, he was so cold he was convinced his kidneys were shivering out of protest. Even the gun in his shoulder holster was starting to irritate him, and there was still no sign of her leaving or of anyone for that matter. This was a bloody boring street, not even a dog walker had passed since he had set up shop, so he tucked his night bins inside his jacket, hopped out the back of the van and went for a walk about, hoping that a bit of movement might get some warmth into his blood before it froze completely solid.

Using the trees for cover he snuck round the side of the house. Silently and athletically he pushed himself up and over the back gate and dropped down into The Boss's back garden. The back matched the front, except the back was three times the size and the pond had been substituted for a good-sized pool. The garden was lined with trees and hedges, perfect cover for a stalker, he thought, obviously the boss didn't worry too much about security. He didn't even have a sensor light.

He shrugged, crouched low and practically crawled round the perimeter of the garden until he found a gap in the hedge to crawl into which would give him a good enough view of the back of the house, and he made himself comfy.

From the back he could hear music playing, a light was on and he could easily see a young girl through the window, just a teenager. She looked like she was talking to someone, and then another girl of similar age got up and walked across the room, and then they both moved away from the window. He made a note to watch out for them later, but they were not who he had come for.

An hour later neither girl had left the room. He could see the top of the door from his position and it hadn't moved an inch, but there was still no sign of The Boss's wife either, and it was starting to rain so he climbed out of his hiding spot and headed back to the van, where he took up his original position.

It was getting late and he was seriously considering calling it a night when a light came on at the front of the house. He peered through the bins, and saw that his luck had finally changed just in the nick of time. There she was, or at least someone who matched the Boss's vague description of his wife. Standing with her back to him by the window, wearing a dressing gown by the looks of it, she was holding a DVD in one hand and a wine glass in the other. Bingo, she was home. The game was on.

He reached over and dragged his box of kidnapper's tricks across the floor and pondered his options for a second, tie wraps or rope? He went for the tie wraps, quicker to get on and off. He had used the rope before and there were still blood stains on it, and he made a note to chuck it out when he got home.

He dragged an old t-shirt out of the bottom of the box and tore a chunk of fabric off, grabbed the bottle of chloroform and a plastic food bag and unscrewed the lid.

He had learnt the hard way to hold his breath while he soaked the cloth, and chuckled out loud as he recalled one of the first jobs he had done; a kidnap for ransom. He still had no memory between soaking the cloth and being woken in his car at 5am the following morning, with a very sore head, by a concerned passer-by. Suffice it to say, the rich man had to wait an extra day before being offered hospitality at hotel Eddie.

He tucked the hood into his inside top pocket and the tie wraps into the back pocket of his jeans. Hopefully, he wouldn't need either before he got her back to the van, but better to be safe than sorry. The bagged cloth was tucked neatly into his left pocket and his trusty lock pick, a SouthOrds Snap Gun, with tensioner and spare picks, was nestled in his right pocket.

The floor of the van sported an array of weapons that included a bowie knife, the M4 and a couple of hand guns, no place for a lady he thought, as he locked them all up in a metal cabinet that was strapped to the inside of the van.

Wouldn't want her waking up and getting her cheating hands on any of those.

He pulled his Glock 41 out of its shoulder holster and slid the safety lever to the Auto position, pulled back the guns slide to cock it and slid it carefully back under his left arm, slid his spare magazine into the holster under his right, both fully loaded, well almost.

He checked the window again with his binoculars; she was still there, by the looks of it on the phone, perfect. Something about the way she stood was familiar.

Time for the first quarter.

He felt his gut clench and his heart start to race, he was now under the influence of the newly injected adrenaline; there was no feeling like it, even though this was child's play, he still got a buzz when the starter's whistle was blown on a gig.

He pulled his balaclava over his head, for warmth as much as anonymity, and hopped out the back of the van and darted straight for the front door.

The racket still boomed from inside the house; how on earth did she put up with that? Then an idea struck him, and he rang the doorbell. It was a long shot that anyone would even hear it at all above that din, but he felt certain that if anyone would, it would be her. The teenagers wouldn't have a hope. Besides, why go to the hassle of picking locks and creeping about the place when he could just as easily get her to come to him.

His instincts were bang on, and seconds later he could see her distorted shadow coming down the stairs through the patterned glass in the door. He rummaged for the plastic bag and hood, and as her hand turned the handle he ripped the feeble plastic open.

As soon as the door was wide enough he grabbed her, pulled the bag over her head and spun her round quickly so his arm was tight across her neck. It took seconds and before she even had a chance to scream the poisoned rag was pressed firmly over her mouth and nose.

She wriggled weakly for a second then slumped limply into his arms. He quickly pulled the hood over her head, threw her over his shoulder and tucking the cloth back into his pocket, quietly pulled the front door closed and walked her back towards the van.

'Well good evening Mrs Walker, how nice to make your acquaintance.'

chapter thirty-four

The world spun around me as I tried to open my burning, scratchy eyes. I was lying on my side. My banging head was light and fuzzy. I tried to sit up, but my stomach turned over, threatening to evacuate its entire contents, and I dropped my exhausted head back down onto the thin mattress.

My shoulders were sore too and I tried to wriggle them. Only then did I realise that I couldn't move my hands at all, they were tied together with something, a plastic wire maybe. Was this some kind of horrible nightmare? I took a long, deep breath into my aching lungs and coughed violently.

There was a terrible taste in my dry mouth and nose. I swallowed to clear it, but it just got worse. Then I remembered the man at the front door and I felt my whole body suddenly start to tremble. This was no nightmare.

I forced my stinging eyes open, but it was pitch black. Where was I? There was no clue other than a toxic smell of solvents and paint.

A vision of the man, dressed all in black, flashed back into my head, and I was back there at the front door, his arm tight around my neck, his hot breath on my face. My pulse started racing and I could hear my heart thumping in my chest. I tried to wriggle my hands free, but the wire cut into my skin. I closed my eyes and listened to the pounding in my head and the rasp of my chest as a single tear slid across my cheek, then another, and soon my whole face was wet from crying. I couldn't even lift my hand to wipe my own tears away, they just fell, forming a wet patch on the mattress.

Then I heard a noise. I turned my head to follow it, what was it, who was it? I could just make out a shape in the darkness, possibly a person, and I lifted my head slightly to see if I could get a better look. Bad idea. My stomach turned over again, and my body lurched forward as the remains of my dinner were propelled, at speed, out of my stomach and onto the floor. My forehead smacked the cold concrete in front of me.

Then there were hands on me, two large, strong hands, and I was being sat up. A cloth appeared and wiped the vomit away from my face and the front of the dressing gown that I was still wearing.

Holy hell, I was still in my pyjamas and dressing gown and, now I knew I was not alone.

A whiff of the vomit snaked up my nostrils and my stomach contracted again, throwing me off balance, and even more of my stomach's contents onto the floor beside me. The stranger's hands caught me before I smacked my head again.

The hands lifted me off the floor and I was dragged away from the vomit and plonked down again. At least I didn't have to smell it anymore, but I'd lost my mattress, and the little comfort it had offered. The hands left me, and I sat still for a moment taking deep breaths. Panic had struck me dumb, but the tears were still flowing.

'It's the effects of the Chloroform; it'll wear off in a while.'

The voice was familiar, but my mind was racing, and I couldn't concentrate. My heart was sprinting out of control, my head felt light, my stinging eyes glazed over as an intense heat spread through me. My head felt like it was on fire and I couldn't breathe, shit, I couldn't breathe. My lungs contracted, I sucked for air, oh my god, still panting, urgently.

'Shit!' I heard the stranger say.

Then his hands were on me again and I was being stood up, his strong hands gripping my shoulders firmly, parading me around on my wobbly legs as I panted and sucked for tiny gulps of air.

Gradually, I started to calm down and as I snatched ever increasing mouthfuls of air, I was knelt back down on the floor. I tried to concentrate on my breathing as my mind raced to hell and back trying to understand what was happening to me.

I glanced at his face. I wanted to know who he was, but my eyes were still sore, and I couldn't see properly. It was just so dark.

My whole body was trembling, and the tears started falling again as I could hear the stranger pacing back and forth in the room. What was he doing, what was he going to do to me? I focused on his footsteps, three to the right, then four to the left and back again, while I calmed myself and my breathing.

My options were limited, an understatement I know; run – out the question, I could hardly stand up. I could fight – although that was unlikely to have a good outcome, given the wire cutting into my wrists and I was so tired that there was no way I could perform an all-out assault, even if I *could* see what I was doing.

But the more my brain strained, the more obvious the situation became. This had to be about money. You hear about people being kidnapped for ransom money all the time. I relaxed a bit, this would all be over as soon as Michael gave them what they wanted.

So, for now, do nothing seemed the only sensible option, do nothing and start negotiating.

'Who are you? How much do you want, I can get you money?'

The footsteps stopped. There was a deathly silence for what seemed like an eternity, then he inhaled deeply and moved across the room.

'Surely the question should be. Who the FUCK are you?'

The light suddenly flicked on, forcing my straining eyes temporarily closed.

I looked, blinking as my eyes struggled to adjust to the sudden brightness. The man had stepped back away from me and as my eyes adjusted to the light I ran my gaze from his feet all the way to his very angry looking, tear stained face. My stomach turned again, but this time it managed to hold on to whatever might have been left in it.

'Jonny?' I said.

'Hello. Susanna, is it, or maybe you'd like to tell me your real fucking name?'

Fuck, fuck, fucking fuck!

I had wanted to tell him, I had tried to tell him, but not like this.

'Alice Walker.'

I dropped my eyes to the floor; I couldn't bear to look at his crumpled face.

'Nice to meet you Alice Walker,' his voice was pained and tight. 'I'm the hitman your husband hired to sort out you and your fucking bit of rough.'

'Michael hired you?' My voice trembled, this was getting worse.

I knelt with my head hanging and let the information sink in as I watched a puddle growing, one tear at a time, on the floor in front of me. My chest was tightening again, *just breathe, in, then out*, I told myself, as if it was that easy.

I could see his boots starting to pace back and forth again.

'He wants the head of your filthy little toy boy on a stick, an extra twenty-five large my way, if I make you watch as I cut the horny little smile off his face.'

'You're a hitman?'

'Yes, I'm a hitman, and thanks to you, I have taken a contract on my own fucking self.'

'Wait, I thought you worked in security?'

'Yes well, seems none of us are being particularly honest here. Fuck sake!'

'Wait, if you knew it was me, why did you do all this?'

'I didn't know anything until I got you back here and I got the hood off your head. Fuck. Susanna!'

This was all so overwhelming, my head felt light again, emotion streaming through my body like a deadly tidal wave, I tried to stand up, forgetting about my woozy head and instead flopped forward, banging my head sharply against the floor again. Jonny shot forward and put his hands on my shoulders, but the searing pain that was shooting from my head had drastically altered my mood.

'Get your hands off me,' I blurted out.

'But you're bleeding.'

'Then let me bleed.'

I slumped to the floor and as I felt the blood trailing down the side of my head I closed my eyes and audibly wept. This was a disaster of titanic proportions.

'At least let me clean it up.'

'Don't touch me.'

I heard Jonny walk out and slam a door. I sighed and listened as he started talking loudly. There were no other voices, so I presumed he was on the phone. He introduced himself as Eddie.

I didn't know his real name either.

He came back about five minutes later, and I could still feel the blood oozing out of my head. On a good note I was feeling much calmer. Maybe that was due to the blood loss, I don't know.

'You ok?' Jonny, or Eddie, or whatever he called himself said.

'No. I'm having a very bad week and now my head is bleeding.'

'Will you at least let me look at your head?'

'Yes, ok.'

He sat me up and I caught his eyes with mine, and my stomach clenched, but not with desire.

'I was going to tell you, I was going to get a divorce. I made an appointment.'

He ignored my comment.

'Wait here.'

Where was I going to go?

He came back with a rag and started dabbing at my head.

'Your name is Eddie?' I asked.

'No, my name is Jonny, Edmondson is my surname, so they call me Eddie for short. I've always been called Eddie since I was a kid.'

'Whose they?'

I winced as he caught the wound with the cloth.

'Sorry,' he said. 'They, are your husband and two others who work for him like I do.'

'And what do they do?'

'You don't know what your husband does? Where did you think all his money came from?'

'I just thought he was a really good accountant.'

Jonny started to laugh, a little at first, then more uncontrollably. His laugh was infectious and for a moment I completely forgot what was going on and joined in with him. For a moment we laughed together, it was quite a relief, and for a moment at least I got a glimpse of the Jonny I knew.

'So, what now?'

I sat, helpless, on the ground in front of him as his strong hands tenderly bandaged my head.

'Well, first we are going to delete me from your life, and then I'm going to give him what he paid for.'

'You're going to kill yourself?'

'No, dumbass, he doesn't know who you've been dicking around with, I'd be dead already if he did, believe me. We'll just find some unlucky guy, and you are going to convince your husband that he was me. Then I'll collect my money and get the hell out of here and you can go back to playing happy families with your husband.'

'Just like that?'

'Yep, just like that,' he said with a coldness that shocked me. 'How's your head feeling now?'

'Better. Thank you.'

I don't really know why I was thanking him.

'Good, then we need to get moving.'

'Where are we going?'

'Are you going to come calmly?'

'Yes, why? Where are we going?'

chapter thirty-five

Jonny helped me onto my feet. I turned and held my hands out so he could cut them free, but he shook his head and started dragging me by my elbow to a van parked outside.

I had no idea what time it was, but it was very dark. He yanked open the door and bundled me into the passenger seat, pulled round my seat belt and clicked it in for me as I sat uncomfortable and helpless, with my hands locked together behind me. I looked around as he slammed the door and walked round the van, locking the door of his storage unit as he passed, and climbed into the driver's seat.

'Where's your car?'

'At home, I prefer not to carry dead bodies around in the boot of my car, does things to the carpet.'

'Dead bodies?'

'Yeah, what do you think is going to happen here?'

The van revved to life and reversed away from Jonny's unit at breakneck speed. He slammed the gearbox into first and shot forward, forcing me back into the seat.

'Jonny slow down, where are we going to get a dead body?'

'Oh, it's ok, they sell them on eBay!' He stared, unblinking, at the road. 'Where the fuck do you think you get a dead body?'

'I don't know, Jonny, I am a housewife, usually my biggest concern is whether my Yorkshires will rise or not.'

'I beg your pardon, you're right. Let me explain how dead bodies are made. You take a live body, fire something hard and fast into its skull until its brains start spilling out, and then, voila, you have a dead body.'

'You're going to kill someone? Tonight? Now?' He didn't answer, but he didn't have to, the glazed expression said it all. 'You don't have to do this, I can talk to Michael, get this sorted out.'

'Susanna, Alice or whatever, just stay out of this. We're not in your 'meat and two veg' world any more, this is *my* world, and this is how we sort out problems in *my* world.'

'This isn't you Jonny, please, I know you.'

'You don't know nothing.'

This was a nightmare. Less than a week ago I was camping in the woods with this guy, now I was in a speeding van with his homicidal alter-ego. Hours ago, I was ready to give up everything for him. Well aren't I the fool. I twisted my body round in the car so that Jonny couldn't see the waterfall of tears tumbling down my cheeks.

I sat staring out the window as my world fell apart around me, and the worst thing about it was, I knew things would only get worse. Much worse.

The van thundered along the deserted road. Only the faint glimmer of the moon and a few stars that had managed to peak out between the clouds were visible in the sky. The tired looking hedges and trees that lined the road hung their branches gloomily, as if in sympathy for me as we rattled quickly past.

Ahead, walking at the side of the road, was a lone man, probably heading home after a night out, full of hopes and dreams, and beer, unsuspecting of the fate of his evening. The van drew to a stop and my heart stopped. I knew why.

'Jonny, please, I'm begging you.'

He jumped out onto the street and opened the rear doors of the van; I could hear him rummaging in the back and banged my head against the back of the seat out of frustration. I can't let him do this. Twisting in the seat, I just about managed to get my hands to the door latch, my fingers curled round the handle and started pulling and tugging frantically at it, *why won't it open, come on.*

I pulled harder, and harder still, praying for that click that meant the door had released. Jonny jumped back into the driver's seat, with a gun in his hand.

'What are you doing?' he said.

'Nothing.'

'Nothing is right, that door is locked, you can only open it from the outside.'

'Jonny, stop this now, I am begging you.' He wasn't listening as he screwed a silencer to the end of his gun. 'That man is innocent. He might have a family, kids, a wife, you can't do this, his kids will grow up without their daddy. Please.'

He pulled back the slide and let it snap back into place with a heart stopping crack.

'Jonny, don't, please. Jonny!'

He pulled a piece of cloth out of his pocket and before I could do anything it was being stuffed into my mouth, all I could do was shout muffled pleas through the foul-tasting rag and stamp my feet against the floor of the van.

'I had to grow up without a dad, they'll be fine,' he said. 'Now calm down, put your head between your knees and don't sit up until I tell you to, otherwise you'll be joining the corpse in the back, clear enough?'

I nodded and sobbed into the rag as the van pulled slowly forward and then stopped. Jonny hopped out and slammed the door shut behind him. My eyes fixed on the floor, I listened as he asked the poor unsuspecting man if he wanted a ride. I prayed he would say no and just keep walking, and he did at first, but Jonny was so charming and seconds later I heard the rear doors open. There was muffled conversation, then a loud thud briefly stopped my heart. I felt sick as I waited for the rear doors to slam shut. That was it, the line had been crossed. Without a doubt those noises would haunt me for the rest of my life.

I sobbed for that poor man. I might be naïve, but I knew exactly what had just happened only a few feet away from me, and it was all my fault.

Jonny hopped in beside me and slipped a knife through the tie-wraps that bound my hands and silently removed the gag. I shuddered and fixed a stare out the window as the van pulled away from the side of the road and back onto the carriageway.

There were no more words, no more tears, just emptiness. Hope had been lost. Jonny had been lost. I settled back into my seat and prepared myself for the journey ahead.

As the van picked up speed my attention was drawn to a fast diminishing object in the rear-view mirror, and in that moment hope was returned, and so was my Jonny.

'I knew you couldn't do it,' I said, trying to conceal my pride.

He made no comment.

chapter thirty-six

Jonny manoeuvred the van onto a long sweeping drive which already had three cars parked on it; Michael's BMW and two others. The drive led up to a bungalow I had never seen before. How did he own a house without me knowing about it?

'All you have to do now is make your husband believe your fancy man is gone then I can call an end to all this bullshit.'

'What do you mean?'

'This was supposed to be my last job, the one that got me off the hook. I was going to sort my life out and run away to Vegas with the woman I loved, guess that's off the table now.'

I looked back at Jonny. He was deadly serious, and I felt so sorry for him. How did he do that to me, half an hour ago I could've seen him hang for what he had put me though.

'Now do as you're told, or I'll shoot you myself,' he said coldly.

He pulled a gun out from a holster that was concealed under his jacket. Surely he didn't mean it, but I wasn't going to take the chance. There were moments where I barely recognised the man sitting beside me.

He hopped out and made his way round the front of the van, his eyes careful to never meet mine as he yanked my door open.

'Get out.'

No sooner were my feet on the ground, and his hand was pressing firmly into my back pushing me forward, his gun clearly visible under his jacket, as if to remind me to behave. As if I needed reminding of this horrendous situation.

My trembling legs carried me slowly towards the front door of the cottage, where we were greeted by a very smug looking young man Jonny addressed as TJ. It was the same guy who had spilt my coffee in town last week.

'Hey TJ, where's the boss?'

TJ nodded us in through the front door and hopped across the hallway to fling open a closed door. With the gun protruding from his pocket an effective incentive, I chose to behave myself as I was pushed through the door into a very civilised looking gentleman's room. I wondered if this is what his loft looked like at home.

It was dark, but a roaring fire lit up the dark wooden floor and a gold mantle clock indicated it was 1.30 am. The flames cast a warm, flickering light over a man I used to call my husband, but I barely recognised the confident man who sat proudly smoking in the leather chair in front of me.

'Well, good evening Alice. I thought I would never see you here. But then this past few weeks have been an unwelcome source of surprise for me, haven't they dear?' He turned to Jonny. 'I see you ruffed her up a bit, I like that.'

'She put up a bit of a fight, nothing I couldn't handle.'

'Thanks Eddie, and the other guy?'

'It's taken care of.'

He nodded to Eddie and the hand disappeared from the small of my back. I could only listen as his footsteps diminished, leaving me and Michael alone in the room for the first time in what seemed like forever.

'You know, I always thought you were such a good girl,' Michael said calmly from his plush chair.

'Michael, I'm sorry, but I was upset, we never go anywhere or do anything together anymore, it's not your fault, but it wasn't his either, I'm really sorry.'

'Don't try to put the blame on me.'

'I'm not, but you have to admit that things have fizzled between us. I tried to spice things up the other night, but you were so nasty.'

'You looked like a hooker.'

'I was trying to be sexy for you.'

I stifled a tear and urged myself to stay strong. This was not the time to succumb to weakness. I'd been doing that all my life, not now.

'You could have had anything you wanted, and this is how you thank me.'

'You're wrong. I had tons of nice *stuff*, but all I wanted from you was a husband. Someone to love, someone to love me back, to care about me, to make me feel special,'

'I do love you,' Michael said, standing up, looking me straight in the eye. For a moment I almost believed him, but I quickly reminded myself that people that love each other don't behave like this; it was all just a line.

'But I don't feel it. I need someone to take care of me, show interest in me, support me, you never did any of those things Michael. He did, he did all those things and more. He made me happy.'

I could see the rage building in Michael's face with every word I had spoken. His face had turned red and he was starting to shake. I had seen that look before, it had been a long time since I had pushed him like this and even though I sort of knew what was coming, the back of his hand still caught me off balance and I squealed as I fell to my knees, cradling my throbbing face in my hands.

I nursed my sore face; my cheek bone felt like it was on fire. The door opened, and Jonny stepped back in, not even flinching at the sight of me on the floor. Maybe I should take back my last speech.

'Sorry to interrupt.'

'Come in Eddie, I have your money right here, seventy-five wasn't it?'

'Seventy-five *and* out.'

'Hmm, just one last thing before you go Eddie.' Michael said. 'Alice, what was the name of your little hobby boy?'

I panicked for a second, this was my bit, and I had to get it right. I looked over at Jonny and then at Michael and took a deep breath.

'It doesn't matter what he was called, it's finished now and I'm sorry.'

'Hmm, yes, I'm sure you are sorry,' he said. 'Please indulge me a little, just for a second. You know how I like to get value for money. I'd like to know what did Eddie do to him. Did he make him beg?'

'Erm, I…'

'Beat him up a bit, cut bits off?'

He started to grin as he reached into a drawer in the side table beside his chair. He was suddenly as calm as day again.

'Come on Eddie, you're awfully quiet, spill the beans, and don't leave anything out now?'

There was an awkward silence as Michael's hand withdrew from the drawer, but instead of taking out a pile of cash as I was expecting, he took out a small hand gun, pointed it and pulled the trigger.

My heart stopped for a second as the world slowed down around me. I twisted round, the booming shot still ringing in my ears.

'No, no, no!' I called out as Jonny dropped to the floor.

TJ snatched the gun from Jonny's holster as he dropped onto the floor in agony, I crawled over to him and grabbed at his bleeding leg.

'Oh my god, Jonny.'

His blood oozed through my fingers as I tried to stop the bleeding.

'Michael what the hell did you do that for?'

'Do you think I'm stupid? I know what the pair of you have been up to,' Michael said. 'TJ!'

TJ was standing at the door still holding Jonny's gun and standing behind him now was a very large, scary looking black guy.

'Get rid of this piece of shit, will you.'

The big guy wrestled me off the floor, kicking and screaming; he was unbelievably strong, and I had no hope of wriggling free of his vice grip, meaning I could only watch hopelessly as TJ dragged Jonny's silent, bleeding body away from me.

'No,' I called out after him. 'Jonny, it's gonna be ok.'

The black guy released his grip and I was free. I ran straight to the door as TJ pulled it tightly closed behind him. I briefly turned to face Michael who was sitting righteously in his chair, looking about as smug as I'd ever seen him. I wanted to kill him.

'It's gonna be ok, Jonny.' He mimicked me. 'You're so funny.' Michael laughed. 'Nothing about this is going to be ok.'

'You're a monster. Let him go. This is not his fault, he didn't know who I was, he didn't even know my real name.'

'You know, I pushed you away the other night because you reminded me too much of the whores I pay to come here. You're supposed to be my wife – demure, respectful, not some two-dollar harlot.'

My jaw dropped. Who was this man sitting in front of me? I pulled off my wedding ring and tossed it into the fire.

'You'll be hearing from my lawyer, you can be sure of that, now let Jonny and I go.'

'Jonny and me dear. But, no, he stays here. We have got urgent business to settle. I'll have TJ drive you home. TJ!'

Like an obedient puppy; TJ appeared almost immediately at the door, and the black guy disappeared out past him. TJ looked a little ruffled, with blood pouring

When the Mask Falls

from a cut by his right eye. By the looks of it Jonny put up a bit of a fight.

'Is he secured?' Michael asked.

'Ja, boss.'

'Good, now take Mrs Walker home would you.' He turned to me. 'I'll deal with you myself when I get home.'

Deal with me? What the hell did that mean?

'Yes, sir,' TJ said.

'Oh, and be careful with this one, she can be a little feisty too by the looks of it.'

'No problem, sir,' TJ said, taking my arm.

'No, I'll wait. Jonny comes with me,' I protested, shaking his hand away.

I may not have liked him, but I wasn't going to leave him here with Michael and a gun, not if I could help it. But a cold metal sensation on the back of my neck was a surefire way to convince me to shut up and move.

I closed my eyes as my hands were being dragged behind me to be tied again. TJ folded me over his shoulder and I was marched back out, kicking and screaming, into the dark and onto the backseat of Michael's BMW. Michael followed us out the door a few steps and I could see him waving gleefully as the car pulled off the drive.

Deal with me when he gets home, good luck with that, I thought, *I will be long gone by then.*

I lay sideways on the backseat of the car and sighed, at least I was out of there, and the gun was not pointing at me anymore. Jonny would just have to sort out his own problems. This was not a world I felt comfortable in, they are all just as monstrous as each other.

Unfortunately, I loved one of them and I couldn't turn that off that easily, no matter how awfully he had behaved. But there was still something I needed to know.

'TJ? Jonny, I mean Eddie said to me that this last job would get him off the hook, what did that mean?'

'I'm not going to talk to you,' he said from the driver's seat.

'Come on, it's just talk.'

He paused and shook his head for a second before answering me.

'Boss helped him out a few years back. Eddie has been working off his debt, that's all.'

'So, he didn't choose to do this.'

'Trust me, from what I know it's still better than what he did before. And that's all I'm saying.'

'Just one last question – will Michael kill him?'

'Not today, and it won't be Michael, not his style.'

My heart started thumping.

'What the hell does that mean?'

A gun pointed over the shoulder rest.

'Just shut up.'

I bit my lip and those words whirled around my head, *not today, not Michael*. I wanted to scream out, fight back, but the sight of a gun barrel was very persuasive and instead I just dropped my head onto the back seat of the car and kicked at the soft leather until we arrived back home.

TJ pulled open the door and I climbed out. I waited for him to untie my hands and gave him a swift kick with my slippered foot before I headed to the front door, leaving him bent double and cursing on the drive. He could've come after me, shot me, I didn't care anymore, I was done.

He chose to let it go, and I listened as the BMW scuffed the gravel and left.

chapter thirty-seven

I walked slowly through the front door, up the stairs and turned into the bedroom. Standing at the end of my bed, sorry, *the* bed, it wasn't mine anymore, and neither was the room, I took a moment to reflect. Then I glanced the closet, at all my things beautifully laid out by Brenda. But I couldn't stay here tonight, or any night, even if it was nearly three in the morning.

My suitcase was at the top of the closet and I pulled it down. It was heavy, and I remembered I still hadn't unpacked after my weekend away with Jonny. My wonderful, carefree weekend with Jonny, the weekend he told me he loved me. Was it just a line? It hadn't felt like it. The memories overwhelmed me, and I crumpled onto the bed, sobbing loudly.

A quiet knock at the door caught my attention, and when I looked over, Sara was standing in her night dress, yawning.

'Mum, you ok?'

I flopped back onto the bed and wept.

'I've done a terrible thing,' I managed through the sobs.

Sara's hand found my back and rubbed it quietly for a moment.

'Mum, do you love him?'

'Dad?'

'No, not Dad, *him* the man that has made you so happy for the last few weeks.'

'What?'

'I'm not stupid, Mum, or blind, am I right?'

I nodded, and her hand rubbed a little harder.

'Then, you've got to go fight for him.'

She tapped my back twice and stood up, taking hold of my blood-stained hand, and dragged me upright.

'It's not that simple, I've been really stupid.'

'Course it is, love conquers all, isn't that what they say, go get him Mum.'

I've never felt so proud of my daughter. I thought she didn't care. Hell, she barely seemed to acknowledge my existence most days, nor me hers, how wrong was I? And here she is standing in front of me, so grown up, knowing exactly what to say, knowing exactly what to do, if only she knew the whole story, I wonder if she would still be offering me the same advice.

'Get dressed,' she said. 'I'll call you a cab.'

Ten minutes later I was cleaned up, out of my pj's and more suitably attired in jeans, a dark red jumper and my new leather trench coat. A cab was already waiting downstairs.

'Right, where to?' the cabby said, looking through the open window.

'Winchester Street, the apartment block, do you know it?'

'Yep, I know it.'

The car pulled out of the drive and my mind flooded with thoughts. I had Jonny's spare key in my pocket. I knew he left his car behind tonight, so hopefully I could find his spare key and borrow his car. After that the plan sort of faded into nothing.

Of course, if his car wasn't at home, or I couldn't find a spare key, the rest of the plan would be moot anyway. Assuming I *could* find a key, and assuming I *could* find the cottage again, and assuming I *could* find out where he was being held.

I still don't even know how I really felt about the whole situation and whether I could get past what has happened. I know his behaviour has sickened me, but he wasn't doing it willingly and I don't think he deserved any of this, not to die. This was all my fault. Of course, I am assuming that he even wants to see me again after all this, I know I wouldn't.

The taxi pulled up, so I paid the driver and sprinted for the main door to Jonny's building. I could just about see the Subaru parked round the side, so that was one assumption confirmed. Next for the spare key and I started running up the stairs to the third floor. This was crazy. I didn't even know how long I had, could he be dead already. No, TJ had said not today, but could I trust him? What a nightmare.

Where does a thirty-something year old man keep his spare car key anyway? I quickly scanned the apartment for obvious places. The kitchen drawer maybe? He didn't use it for kitchen things. I dashed in and started yanking the drawers open and spilling out the contents, but no key.

Next the coffee table, but its drawers contained only loose batteries and a bottle opener.
Shit, it was only a tiny flat.

I headed for the bedroom and pulled the drawer out of his bedside table and flipped it over onto the bed, revealing a key taped to the bottom of the drawer. But it wasn't a car key. And neither were any of the items in his bedside drawer.

I was starting to panic. Maybe I should've brought Ben with me, he knows how to steal cars apparently, just not very good at the not getting caught part.

I glanced at the clock radio by the bed, it was already 3.30 am, the night was racing away from me and I picked up the pace as I systematically tossed his clothes drawers, but still no key.

I stood rubbing at my aching temples with my left hand as I scanned the room for any other possible places a key could be hidden, but there was nowhere left to look.

Was this it? Had I fallen at the first hurdle? No key meant no car and no cavalry. I started scooping the items I had scattered onto his bed back into the drawer and accidentally dropped his old Nokia phone onto the floor. I stretched my arm under the bed to retrieve it, but instead of the phone my hand found something cold and metallic. I pulled back the covers and found a large, cold safe box under the bed. The box was seriously heavy, but I gave it a good tug, and it eventually gave and peaked out from under the bed, enough at least that I could get to the lock. Emptying the drawer back over the bed, I tore the key off the bottom and tried it in the lock.

Lady luck was back gunning for me, and it pinged right open.

I opened the narrow door and scooped out the contents with my arm. I found exactly what I was looking for, plus a few extras to boot. First a black shiny gun. *That might come in handy*, I thought, and laid it on the bed. There was also a passport, some foreign money in a wallet, his driver's license and a far more exciting looking item. I glanced at it for a moment before reminding myself that I was supposed to be on a time critical mission and I shoved it in my pocket.

I jumped onto my feet, grabbed the car key and poked the gun down the back of my jeans and dashed out, making sure to lock up before I took the stairs two at a time down the three floors and out to the parked Subaru.

Engine revving, windscreen automatically defrosting and Jonny's gun for company on the passenger seat, I braced myself as I very gently put pressure on the accelerator. The car threw itself forward toward the road, as keen as I was to save Jonny.

Stage Two, done. Assumption number three: could I even find the house again? Directions have never been my strongest suit, but as I broke land speed records hurtling down the empty carriageway the road at least seemed familiar, but was that because I had crashed my own car on it less than a week ago.

Just don't get caught, don't get caught, I repeated to myself over and over. I am sure, if the court is not already considering putting my driving license behind bars, they most definitely will, and me with it, if they ever catch me driving at these speeds.

The car flew effortlessly past the spot where we had previously stopped and almost picked up that hitchhiker, and I was at least glad I was heading the right way, although the memory of those awful hours that led to that moment were taunting me all over again. And now I knew that Michael knew it was Jonny the whole time. Will I ever be able to forgive myself or forget about that? For now, I had to. I was in charge of a death machine and had just shot past my turn at over 120mp. Thankfully, the brakes on the WRX were exceptional, and as I jammed on the breaks I saw, and felt, the benefit of the six-point harness.

There was no one around so I slammed the car into reverse. The engine squealed as I forced it at breakneck speed backwards down the road, snapped back into first and off the main carriageway onto the country road I am sure we had taken earlier – only a little slower this time. I really needed to concentrate.

chapter thirty-eight

Apart from the last six or seven hours, the last few weeks of Jonny's life were the best he'd ever had. He'd been at a bar that night to collect the final payment on a loan, and in a move that was completely out of character for him, he had stayed afterwards for a drink.

He put on a good enough act, but he hated his job and he liked the landlord of this pub, a family man in his mid-forties. The man hadn't told his family he was in financial shit. They thought Jonny was just a friend who called round every week for a quick chat, albeit without having a drink. Surely, they knew something was up, or maybe it was easier to pretend they didn't.

Life as he knew it had changed the moment he had looked up and his eyes caught those of an attractive, but nervous looking woman who was sitting at the bar just a few feet away from him. Fireworks had lit up inside of him. It was a feeling he had never felt before, one he didn't know how to deal with, but one he kind of liked.

Paranoia ran through his veins thicker than blood most days, it comes with the job, and he initially put the strange feeling down to that, and instinctively considered marching her outside with his very persuasive Glock stuck in her ribs to *ask* her what her problem was.

But he had thought better of it, as it wasn't paranoia he was feeling. She was just waiting to meet someone, who by the looks of it hadn't turned up.

There was something about her though, and despite his best efforts, he just couldn't stop thinking about her. She wasn't like other woman he met, most of whom he met while *at work*. Young, coked up, skinny girls who wore too much make-up and not enough clothing, who were just looking for a free ride and a good time, and he was usually happy to oblige. But she was different.

Then she took the last mouthful of her drink and bent down to get her bag and at that moment he had started to panic that he might never see her again, so he had hopped out of his chair and just in the nick of time ordered her another drink, and then another, and that's where it all began.

He'd been working for Michael Walker, the Boss, for many years, and until he met her, he had never thought about doing anything else. She did something no one had ever done in his life, she made him feel safe, she made him feel like he mattered. She didn't care about how much stuff he could get her or how fast his car went. It was intoxicating, and he soon realised what those fireworks were all about. He was head over heels in love with a woman who, by the looks of it, would now end up getting him killed.

How ironic. He thought to himself as he sat hunched up against the metal pipe in Michael's basement.

He'd been in this basement many times before.

The basement was reserved for people that had truly pissed off The Boss.

Those that didn't pay on time, or just irritated him, usually just got away with a bullet in the back of the knee or a fire somewhere inconvenient; a quick and painless lesson and a stark warning to others. But he knew what happened to people that made it to the basement, and he knew what it was like to look into those hopeful eyes as they looked up, convinced that someone would come and rescue them, convinced that maybe they would be beaten up a bit and then let go on a promise to be good. If only they knew what the following days would hold, they wouldn't be so optimistic, they would be praying for the bullet. Just as Jonny was now, although he knew he wasn't going to be that lucky. No one left this room alive, or even in one piece.

So far, he had got away with just a bit of a shoeing, a couple of size ten boots to the head, face and ribs. It hurt, no denying it, as did the bullet that was embedded in his thigh, but that was just the appetizer.

No use trying to escape either. He had personally made sure the basement was secure long ago. He had done a great job and remembered celebrating his work with The Boss and laughing at the poor saps that would end up staying for a few days or longer if they were unlucky.

How ironic.

He could hear TJ and Danny laughing through the floor, and a lone tear carved a path through the dried blood that stained his face.

He shivered, and not just because it was freezing cold in that basement. The door at the top of the stairs had suddenly opened.

Time for the salad course?

He sighed into his lap, he was exhausted, hungry, thirsty, cold, but more than that, he was terrified. The guys that once called themselves his friends had, in a split second, become his enemies. He knew their style, how sick they could be, especially TJ, who liked to play games. The boss was seriously pissed, and there would be no holding back, no mercy.

He didn't look up, but he could feel their eyes boring into him, and he tightened his fists. What were they doing up there, just watching him? He had to look, but the light was too bright and his eye too swollen to see anything other than one figure standing perfectly still at the top of the stairs. He closed his eyes and his exhausted head flopped back onto his knees.

Whatever you are going to do, just get it over with. He thought. *Please, God forgive me.*

chapter thirty-nine

Lights off, engine off. I let the car roll the last few feet. The cottage sat in almost complete darkness at the end of the sweeping drive, which was home to two cars and the Sky van, but no BMW. Had Michael gone home already, or perhaps TJ had not yet returned? Only one light glimmered through the window on the right side of the house.

Against all the odds I had made it here and in miraculous time too. If the floor falls out the shoe business I should retrain as an ambulance driver, or a detective.

But now things were getting serious. I needed a plan, and urgently, but my only point of reference was the movies, and we all know how reliable they are. Unfortunately, I couldn't recall a movie about a middle-aged housewife storming a building guarded by at least two crazy men, both armed and more than prepared to kill. If the last few hours had taught me anything, I could be in big trouble here.

I rubbed my head, poked the gun back into the back of my jeans and let out a huge sigh. There was no plan. I was no Bruce Willis, but I was smart, and I got this far by riding the seat of my pants, so why not keep riding.

Death or glory awaits.

I rested the car door on the latch so it wouldn't make a sound, and keeping my back to the hedges that surrounded the cottage, I made my way all the way round to the window with the light on. The room was the kitchen, and inside I could hear voices. I sunk down against the cold brick wall to listen.

There wasn't much to hear, just some typical boyish banter, so I crept round the back, not much to see there either, except a back door that suddenly had started rattling. I stepped backwards into the hedge and knelt down, praying I wouldn't be seen. I held my breath, and my heart thumped so loudly that I was convinced whoever had come through the door could have heard it if they had just listened hard enough. I stayed as still as I could.

It was TJ, just putting something in the dustbin. I watched intently as he looked straight at me, but he didn't seem to take any notice and went back into the house without locking the door. I sighed loudly, relief overflowing.

I dashed back round to the kitchen window and listened again. More muffled boyish banter, and then TJ shouted out and stamped his foot on the ground.

'You ok down there?'

Down there? Was Jonny in a basement?

They both erupted in riotous laughter and then they were moving, I shifted to the side of the house and watched them both walk out into the drive, laughing and joking about Jonny's predicament by the sounds of it.

Absolutely sickening, A couple of hours ago he was their friend. Is there no loyalty? Is that what it means to be friends with criminals?

I saw my opportunity and rushed around and in through the back door. The two men were still laughing and joking on the drive as I entered the kitchen, and I searched frantically, I had no idea how long I had before they would come back, there was no hatch in the floor, so I started pulling open every door I could find – nothing. Then the front door clicked closed.

'Shit!'

For a moment I was frozen to the spot. If I got caught now, I would be in serious trouble. I needed a place to hide, and quick, for the footsteps were heading my way.

A door on the opposite side of the kitchen offered my only possible chance of escape and I darted across the kitchen, my pulse racing, and ducked into the darkness behind it just as the black guy came back into the kitchen. I held my breath as he came in. I could hear the fridge door open and close again, and then his footsteps left the kitchen.

Once I was sure he had gone, I allowed myself to breathe again and eased open the door. The gap allowed some light to fall into the larder room I was in, which was host to amongst other things, another quite narrow door.

I carefully turned an ancient looking key that had been left in the lock and pushed the door open to find a set of concrete stairs. This was the basement all right, it smelt damp and rotten and it was pitch black. On the other side of door was a string pull, which lucky for me turned on the light and illuminated the entire room.

'Holy shit.' I said under my breath.

As well as a steep set of concrete stairs, dusty cobwebs and paint tins, there was also an almost unrecognisable, shrivelled up man chained to a pipe in the far corner of the room.

I could've wept for the battered and broken soul before me. I wasn't sure what I should expect, but this was not it, and in that moment, he was my Jonny again.

He lifted his head. The light must've hurt his eyes. as he was squinting, either that or he was in too much pain. Or both, as his eye was quite swollen and covered in dried blood. It took my breath away, and I stood staring for longer than I should, frozen and stunned.

He looked at me then dropped his head onto his knees. I pulled the door closed behind me and called his name as I walked over to him. This wasn't bad Jonny who was chained and beaten, this was my Jonny and I couldn't help but put my hand round his shoulders for a second.

'I'm so sorry,' I whispered into his ear, before kissing the top of his head. I felt his head rest against my shoulder. 'I'm so, so sorry.'

We sat quietly for about a minute before I broke away. It would have been easy to forget why we were here, but we couldn't stay. Apart from the imminent threat, the stench was starting to get to me.

'I need to know something Jonny, before we get out of here.'

'What?' he mumbled into my shoulder.

'I need to know that this is it, that you'll never get involved in anything like this again.'

He lifted his head and looked me square in the eye.

'NEVER again.'

I believed him.

'Then let's get out of here, and quick before that other guy finds us.'

I worked behind him to untie the rope that bound his hands together; it was putting up quite a fight, but I nearly had it.

'Who's up there?' he asked as I struggled behind him.

'The black guy,' I said, fighting with the last bit of the knot.

'Danny. He's tough, but as thick as horse shit, we'll be fine getting past him.'

'You think so huh?' Danny said, standing at the top of the stairs.

chapter forty

I spun round and crouched in front of Jonny, my legs shaking. Danny was holding a kitchen knife, the whites of his eyes popping against his dark skin, making him look even more menacing as he descended slowly down a few of the steps. I glared back, my heart in my mouth; this wasn't part of my plan.

'Usually people try to escape out of here, not get in,' Danny said, grinning an insane and scary grin.

'Just leave him alone.'

At least, I think that's what I said, my voice was trembling so much.

'Leave it, Sus - er Alice, just go ok, I'll be fine,' Jonny said softly behind me.

'Well, your boyfriend is right about one thing at least, you *should* go,' Danny said. 'Unless you wanna join him maybe. I've never done a couple before, might be kinda fun.'

'I'm not going anywhere without you Jonny.'

I knelt with my hands out to the side as if to somehow shield him from the madman with the knife.

'Danny, come on, you and me, we go way back. Don't do this.'

'Way back, yeah, that's true, but you broke the code.'

The giant man paused thoughtfully, and for a moment I thought Danny might be softening.

'Danny?' Jonny said.

'This is how its gonna work, she can go or stay, I don't care, but you ain't goin' no-where.'

'Go Alice, get out of here.'

'No, not without you.'

'You really are stupid you know,' Jonny snapped. 'Just get the hell out of here.'

'What? No,' I said, not taking my eyes off Danny and his glinting knife. 'How dare you? I came here to save you.'

'Well you shouldn't have bothered, you're gonna get us both fucking killed now.'

'This is priceless,' Danny said, grinning. 'Carry on like this and I'll give *her* the knife, and she'll kill you for me.'

Rage brewed from a place I didn't even know you could get rage and I felt every muscle in my body tense. How dare he?

'Fuck you Danny, this is between me and her,' Jonny said.

'Her? Who the fuck are you calling "her"?' I shouted.

'Please, just one nut job at a time for fucks sake,' Jonny said. 'Danny, let her go, this is between you and me, she's just a stupid loved up bitch who she doesn't know what she's doing. She can't help herself.' I felt my jaw drop. 'Now duck.'

'What?' Danny and I said at the same time.

'I said Duck.'

I felt his hand on my back a split second before he pushed me down off my knees and fired a shot past my ear and into Danny. I hit the ground and threw my hands over my head, tilting my face just enough to watch blood splatter over the wall behind Danny.

His body jerked with the second bullet, the look in his eyes contorted with fear, staring as the knife slipped from his limp hand and bounced down the remaining steps, flipping and cartwheeling off each one, until it came to a rest at the bottom.

A third bullet followed straight past my head, and then a final shot dropped his lifeless body onto the concrete steps with a thud.

I closed my eyes and exhaled loudly. Was it over? A tear rolled down my cheek onto the floor. I didn't dare even look up.

After a couple of minutes, I felt a cold hand on my back,

'Are you ok?' Jonny said, and I almost believed he meant it.

'Am I ok? There's a dead man bleeding out on the steps, and you ask if *I'm* ok.'

'Well, I can see *he's* not ok from here, it's you I'm not so sure about,' he said, then paused and I could feel his hand rubbing up and down my back. 'You know I didn't mean any of those things, I was just stalling so I could finish untying the rope round my hands.'

'Really?'

'Of course, come here.'

I looked up into his eyes, he was smiling, and his dimple was back. My Jonny was back, and I crawled into his arms. For a moment he held me so tightly I almost forgot what was happening, but a glance at the steps soon snapped me back to reality.

'We've got to go,' I said.

He'd already untied his ankles and I helped him to his feet, well his foot, for even though the other leg had stopped bleeding, he couldn't put any weight on it.

'Who keeps a gun down the back of their trousers?' he said, as he hobbled up the narrow steps in front of me.

I was careful to avoid looking at Danny's dead body.

'They do it in all the movies.'

'You knew it was loaded, didn't you?'

'Yeah, course.' I lied.

'And you knew you had the safety *off*?'

'Duh!'

Didn't know it had one, oops.

'You could have shot yourself in the arse.'

'Yeah, well, I didn't, and if it hadn't been there, you wouldn't have been able to get to it, and we'd still be down there.'

'That's true, I'll shut up.'

chapter forty-one

The house was deserted when we emerged from the basement, just as I had presumed it would be, and apart from the kitchen light, the rest of the cottage was still in complete darkness. It had a strange eeriness to it. I don't know if that was because of the silence or because I knew there was a dead body a few feet away from where I stood, or if it was something else, but I was keen to leave anyway.

I expected Jonny to feel the same and head straight for the front door, but instead, he holstered his gun and hopped down the hall, past the front door and towards the front room, where he had not long ago been shot in the leg.

'What are you doing?' I shouted in a whisper.

'Nothing, just wait there.'

He hopped through the door and out of sight, leaving me standing in the hall, one eye on the front door, the other eye on the doorway that led to God knows what he was doing.

'Sus, sorry, Alice, you still out there?'

'Yeah,' I said, curiosity beckoning me in.

A preliminary scan of the room revealed nothing interesting at all. Michael had long gone, and the fire had all but burned itself out. Even Jonny seemed to have completely disappeared.

'Down here.'

The voice came from behind the chair in the corner of the room; he was on the floor and it looked like he had started taking the wall apart.

'What on earth are you doing?'

I crouched down beside him, and my question answered itself.

'Just keep an eye out for me. What's Michael's birthday?'

'Erm, the 21st of June, 1965.'

Jonny punched the numbers into the digital keypad on the safe that was hidden in the wall.

'Twenty-one. Oh-six. Sixty-five.'

The safe door remained defiantly shut.

'Is this a good idea?'

He ignored my question.

'Damn it. Your birthday?'

'October the seventh,' I paused before I added the year. Hopefully he wouldn't notice. '1974.'

He turned his head to the side and hesitated for a second.

'But I thought you said you were thirty-six?'

I cringed.

'Shouldn't we just go? Just being here is making me nervous.'

He sighed and punched in my birthday digits as I kept watch over the drive through the window. Not much was going on out there.

'It could be anything. We could be here all night, just leave it, let's go.'

'He owes me money. Now think, he likes birthdays and anniversaries, it used to be the date he bought this house, but he must have changed it.'

'Oh, you could try our wedding anniversary, oh-three, oh-five, ninety-four, but hurry, this place is giving me the creeps.'

I continued watching out the window as he tried the kids' birthdays, the day we met, the registration number of the car, any six-digit numbers I could think of.

'Where did you get the gun from anyway?' he asked as he worked at the safe.

'It was in the safe under your bed,' I said casually.

'When were you under my bed?'
'Earlier, when I was looking for your car key.'
'My car key?'
'Yes, remember my car got crushed. I needed a car, so I could get here to rescue you.'
'So you stole mine.'
'Yes, no, borrowed. Look can we talk about this later. I am trying to rescue you here, and quite frankly, I wasn't expecting so much of your attitude.'
'Sorry ma'am.'

We ran out of numbers and I had given up.

'It's hopeless, let's go.'
'Damn it, ok.'

He started to push himself off the floor and then I had a thought.

'What about yesterday's date?' I said. 'The day my marriage ended.'
'Worth a try,'
'If not, we go right, I can't wait around here any longer?'
'Yeah, ok.'

He punched the numbers in, twenty-eight, eleven,
'Jonny, there's a car.'

Adrenaline surged through me in powerful waves as a black car pulled quietly onto the drive, with the lights off.

'Shit.' Jonny looked up. 'What kinda car?'
'It's dark, I can't tell, but its black, small.'

The car door opened, and TJ stepped out.

'It's TJ, we gotta go.' I grabbed his arm. 'Come on, he's come back.'

'Just one second.' He tapped all he numbers into the safe and this time it clicked open. 'Yes.'

'He's coming to the door, hurry.'

Jonny started unloaded the contents of the safe. I watched through the window, horrified, as the front door opened. My pulse was raring to go, run, run, run, it screamed at me, and then it stopped dead.

'Danny?' TJ called through the door.

Jonny dragged me down onto the floor behind him with his finger over his lips. He had the gun out of his holster and it was pointing straight at the door, *oh my god, oh my god, this was bad, please not another death.*

'Danny, you here?'

The footsteps got louder in the hall, and I watched, frozen as the door moved slightly. I held my breath as I saw his head come around the door and peer into the room, *shit, shit, shit*. My stomach vaulted, and I covered my mouth with my hand.

'Danny?' his head disappeared but his feet didn't move. Why didn't his feet move? My heart pounded against my ribs, as my lungs selfishly clung on to the air I had sucked in minutes ago. I could feel Jonny's hand tighten around mine. I closed my eyes, the tension unbearable.

After an eternity TJ's footsteps started back along the hall. The relief was incredible, and I grabbed a greedy breath, but we were not out of trouble yet.

Jonny gathered up the money, forcing it into bulging pockets, and crawled slowly, dragging his bad leg behind him towards the door, I followed tightly behind him.

His gun raised, he listened hard at the door and after what seemed like a lifetime had passed, he peered round the door, his finger firmly on the trigger.

He looked back at me and gripped my hand, and then we were running. I dashed after him, out the front door and across the drive. Even on one leg, he was seriously fast.

I took one last glance behind me before we dashed behind the hedges at the end of the drive. Still, no sign of TJ, thank goodness. I allowed myself a breath of fresh air as I found the car key and walked, panting a little, the last few feet to the car.

Jonny bumped into me by the driver's door.

'What do you think you are doing?' I said.

'It's my car.'

'And you're going to drive it in that state? You can hardly walk.' He looked straight at me, almost with an air of disbelief. 'Go on, mush, passenger seat, now, I've got this.'

Like a cute scolded puppy, he hopped round to the other side of the car while I got in the driver's seat and waited for him to strap himself in. I watched him fold his fingers tightly round the door handle and press his good leg into the floor as the car lurched forward.

'Relax, I might be a good driver.'

'You wrote your own car off on Monday, forgive me for being sceptical.'

'Psht, we'll be fine.'

chapter forty-two

There were only ever two possible reasons why Carrie's phone might be ringing at five on a Saturday morning. Neither of them were good, and she seriously considered ignoring the phone and pulling the warm duvet back over her head.

Duty got the better of her though, as it always did, and she clicked the side light on. The sudden brightness temporarily blinded her as she picked up the phone.

'What?' She rubbed at her itchy eyes, trying to get them to focus.

'Carrie. A double murder at the Walker house on Redmarsh Road just got called in.' said the voice on the phone.

That got her attention and she sprang forward on the bed, clutching the edge of her duvet.

'Do you know who?'

'Not yet. I'm in the car now, I'll pick you up in five.'

She hung up the phone and tossed it onto the duvet before she punched the air with her fist.

'Yes!'

Five minutes wasn't much time though, so she would have to prioritise.

She dashed into the kitchen, clicked the kettle on and rushed back to the bathroom. She was good at this and had perfected the art of brushing her teeth with one hand, smoothing down her unruly shoulder bob hair with the other, all the while balancing over the toilet seat to have a pee.

She found new underwear in the drawer and threw last night's jeans and grey t-shirt over the top, a puffa jacket over the top of that and she was nearly ready. She bounced through to the kitchen just in time to hear the kettle click off, ready to make up a travel mug of tea, to go.

She cringed as her partner, Detective Sergeant David Rowlands, honked his horn. There would be complaints from the neighbours, again.

Impatient to get going, she snatched her phone, tea and handbag and belted out the front door, into the harsh cold and out to the waiting car.

It had taken a year of begging to get transferred onto the Walker case team, and the thought of a development had her buzzing from head to toe. Her lucky break had come only a week ago when the previous Detective Inspector was unexpectedly removed from the case. She had studied every detail, read every report and watched every interview. David had been working on the Walker case for years, too many years actually, and she hoped to breathe some life into the case, and a long overdue resolution.

He had come close to nailing Walker a couple of times, but each time he had managed to wriggle free. It would be hard to wriggle out of two dead bodies in your house, or so she hoped.

She hopped in beside David, who was looking surprisingly chipper, considering the hour, and before she had even plugged in her seat belt, he had pulled away in his unmarked, police car. At the end of the street he flicked on the blues and twos and catapulted the car through what little there was of the very early morning traffic.

'So, what do we know?' she said, gripping the arm rest to stop herself from swinging across the car as he took a fast corner.

'Not much, it was called in at approximately 4:15 this morning. Two dead, one in the basement, one in the back of a van.'

'Who called it in?'

'Uniform has his name, a South African, said he saw two people running away from the scene.'

'Is he still at the house?'

'Yep, uniform were interviewing him when I got the call.'

She grinned smugly to herself, as the car threw her against the door going around another sharp bend in the road. She had a good feeling. After four years of hard work, they were finally going to get him.

'This is it David, I can feel it.'

The car skidded to a halt between two panda cars outside 15 Redmarsh Road. David barely had the handbrake on before they were both leaping from the car and heading for the police tape. A uniformed officer met them just in front of the tape, but waved them quickly through when they flashed their IDs. Carrie searched the many faces; uniformed police, medical examiners, ambulance crews, forensics, the place was packed, but her eyes found the face she was looking for, and she led David through the crowd, heading straight for him.

'Jack!' she called over the crowd, waving.

He looked up and smiled as she pushed past all the uniforms.

'Hey Carrie, I wondered how long it would take you to get here.'

'What have you got for me?'

'Ok, straight to the point. We'll start with the body in the van.'

'David, have a sniff around, would you?' she said.

David disappeared whilst Jack led her over to a Sky engineers work van. The back doors were wide open and despite the tiny amount of room, two people were busy working round the covered body inside.

'Prepare yourself, this one's pretty brutal,' he said, indicating the zip on the bag.

She pulled the zipper down far enough to get a clear view of the face in the bag. She winced at the pungent aroma that escaped. She never really could get used to seeing dead bodies, or smelling them for that matter. The poor girl had clearly been badly abused, her face was covered with cuts and bruises, and even worse, she recognised the face.

'Oh my God!'

'I know, poor girl.' he said.

'No, it's not that.' She said, although that was part of it. 'This is that witness that went missing, Nancy Reed, I'm sure of it.'

'Ok, we'll get that confirmed ASAP.'

'Any other forensics yet?'

'The van is covered in fingerprints, but her body was dumped here quite a while after her death, post mortem will confirm how long. We also got some hair fibres from her robe, might be something, might be nothing.'

She nodded.

'It looks like the killer could have been Jonathon Edmondson, a well-known associate of Walker's. Better still, it looks like he had help, as we got fresh prints from the handle of the passenger door.'

'Michael Walker's?' she hoped.

'Maybe, I'll get back to you on that.'

'Ok, so what about the other body?'

'Follow me.'

She followed him into the house; something wasn't right about this at all.

The second body belonged to Daniel Perez, who was very well known to her. He had taken three shots to the torso and one in his arm and was laying on the concrete steps that led down into the basement.

She tip-toed past the body and looked at the blood splatter and the position of the body and did a rough estimate as to where the shots had come from. There was blood on the floor there too and she quickly stuck a proverbial boot up a forensic examiners arse for the results of the DNA.

She followed another trail of blood that led from the kitchen out to the front room. There was blood in three different places, one large pool by the door, a smaller smear further into the room and another smear on the door frame, but what intrigued her most was the open but empty safe.

'Where's David? We need to speak to the guy that called this in,' she said out loud to no one.

chapter forty-three

It was half past five in the morning and I was completely knackered. I glanced over at Jonny who, after the initial horror of letting me drive his car, had relaxed after about two minutes and then immediately fallen asleep. I guess he was tired too.

It was awful to look at him in that sorry state, so battered and bruised, but that at least could be fixed, and I leant across to the passenger seat and gently nudged his arm.

'Jonny.' I whispered. 'Wakey wakey.'

'Hmmm?' he murmured as his eyes slowly blinked open.

'It's only me. We're at the hospital.'

His eyes shot open, and he glared at me.

'What?'

'We're at the hospital. It's ok.'

'Are you insane?' he said, pulling himself upright in the seat.

'I'm sorry, isn't that what normal people do right after they get shot, they go to the hospital to get fixed.'

'Yeah, normal people. Don't you think they might have a few questions though as to how I got shot in the first place?'

He had made a good point, I will never get used to the crazy world he was living in.

'So, what then?'

'Back to my flat.'

'What about your leg?' I said, backing out of the parking space and heading for the exit.

'Don't worry, we'll get it fixed soon enough.'

Thankfully, Jonny managed to stay awake this time and we drove straight to his flat. Twenty minutes later we parked and headed upstairs. After warning me to 'stay here' he unlocked the flat door and went inside, his gun unholstered and ready for action.

I rested my head on the wall, just praying the next sound I heard wasn't gunshots. Thank goodness it wasn't, and five minutes later he appeared in the doorway.

'It's clear, come on,' he said, waving me in. 'By the way, thanks for leaving my flat in such a mess.'

I laughed, but as I followed him in I realised that the mess he was talking about had not been made by me. I closed the door behind me and leant back against it, gobsmacked.

'Jonny, this wasn't me, I went through a few drawers, that's all.'

I felt sick looking around; the place was completely ransacked. The TV had been smashed, the sofa was upside down and the cushions torn and strewn across the floor. The coffee table was on its side and the drawers had been pulled out and emptied on the floor. A side table that had once had a couple of bottles of spirits and some glasses was on the other side of the room and the bottles and glasses were smashed on the floor.

'Jonny, who did this?'

'I'll give you three guesses, come on, we can't stay here.'

I followed him into the bedroom, which looked much the same except that the floor was covered with all his clothes, the stuff from the drawers was on the bed, as was his safe, which was now empty.

Jonny wasn't being sentimental about the mess, and he quickly gathered stuff up into bags, which I then hauled out to the car and squeezed into the tiny boot and back seat. Bags loaded, I ran back up the stairs to find Jonny on his hands and knees next to the bed, searching frantically for something.

'You ok?' I asked.

'Yep, just wait in the car, I'll be there in a sec.'

'What are you looking for?'

'Nothing, just go wait in the car.'

I knew what he was looking for, or at least I thought I did.

'I can help, what is it?'

He was visibly sweating now. 'NOTHING! I'll be down in a sec.'

I reached into my pocket and pulled out the tiny ring box I had found in the safe earlier. 'You looking for this?'

His face was a picture, a twisted mixture of relief and anger.

'What are you doing with that?'

'I found it earlier and just took it with me, I don't know why.' I tossed it to him and he opened it to check it.

He got up off the floor, closed the box and dropped it in his pocket.

'Was it for me?'

'*Was.*'

Ouch, I guess I deserved that.

'Come on, we're not safe here.' He said.

In silence, I followed him as he hopped down the stairs and out into the brisk early morning air, and in no time we were back on the road again, this time heading south for Torquay.

chapter forty-four

As Carrie entered the bedroom of the Walker cottage, she saw a young man sitting on the edge of the bed. He was clutching a mug and on first impressions he looked quite shaken, a natural reaction to the discovery of two murders, she thought.

'Can I go now,' he pleaded to her. 'I've told them everything I know already.'

'I know this must have been a shock for you, but I just have a few more questions if you don't mind.'

She pulled over a stool from the dresser and sat in front of the trembling man. He nodded wearily. David remained in the doorway scribbling notes, ready to jump in should a bad cop be needed. She was always so good at playing good cop, he rarely was.

'What's your name?' she asked.

'Eish, just call me TJ, no one can pronounce my real name.'

'Ok, TJ, I'm Detective Sergeant Carrie Longwood. Why don't you start by telling me in your own words what happened here tonight.'

He hung his head, and wiped away a large tear before it had a chance to drop.

'I arrived at about four, I had been at the house earlier, but I thought I had left my phone and came back to look for it.'

'That's quite late to be looking for a phone, don't you think?'

'Maybe, I couldn't sleep thinking about it, so I just thought it was better to look for it and get it out of my head.'

'Did you find it?'

'What?'

'Your phone.'

'Oh Ja.'

'What kind of phone is it?'

'It's an iPhone, why?'

'I wanted the new one, but ended up with a crummy Samsung instead. can I see it?'

His eyes darted as he searched through two pockets looking for it. He found it in his inside coat pocket. She unlocked it, clicked a few buttons and looked admiringly at it for a second before handing it back.

'Very nice,' she smiled. 'Ok, so you came back here and then what happened.'

'Oh, I don't live here.'

'My mistake, sorry, go on,' She said, drinking her now cold tea from her travel mug.

'Well first I went into the front room, saw blood on the carpet and the empty safe, then I went into the kitchen and saw more blood by the door to the cellar. I opened the door and saw Danny just lying there and I must have panicked or something. I ran back to the living room and then I heard a bang from outside. I looked out the window and saw two people running away from the Sky van.'

'Can you describe them to me?'

'I can do better than that, one was Eddie, and the other was Alice Walker. They left in Eddie's car.'

She crossed her legs and leant forward on the stool. 'Eddie?'

'Yes, Jonathon Edmondson, and Alice Walker, my boss's wife.'

'Who is your boss?'

'Michael Walker,' TJ said.

'And what kind of work do you do for him?'

'He's an accountant; I do admin and visit clients sometimes for him.'

'Visit clients?'

'Yes, sometimes.'

'And he lives here?' she said.

'It's his house, but he doesn't live here.'

'Ok. Does Danny work for him too?'

'No, he just knows him.'

'And Eddie?'

'Same.'

She looked round to David who, despite having learned nothing new, was busy scribbling away on his pad.

'Ok, so could you tell me how Alice and Eddie know each other?'

'Ag, I don't know, you would have to ask the boss.'

'I will. I was just interested in your opinion.'

'Well, the money has gone from the safe, maybe they were trying to rob him.'

'That's right, you mentioned the safe before. Did Mr Walker keep a lot of money in there?'

'A few thousand maybe, I never really looked.'

'Sure, sure, so you think this was a robbery gone wrong?'

'I didn't say that.'

'David, anything you would like to ask TJ?'

David looked up from his pad and paused for a second while he read through some of his notes.

'Just want to clarify; you were here to look for your phone?'

'Ja.'

'At five a.m?'

'Yes.'

'Just seconds after two murders and a robbery took place.'

His eye twitched, it was only subtle, but she noticed it.

'Yes, that's what I said.'

'That's right, you did,' David said. 'That's all from me.'

'Thanks TJ, you've been really helpful. I really appreciate it,' Carrie said, standing up and offering a reassuring shoulder pat.

'Can I go now?'

'I'm sure they won't keep you too much longer,' She said.

She took his contact details and left with David and a nagging doubt in her head. Something was not right. There were no missed calls on his phone, but surely the first thing you do when you lose your phone is call it. Plus, he didn't correct David when he challenged him on the timing, why not?

She wandered out of the house and stood at the end of the drive looking back at the house. The familiar buzz of police radios and chatter echoed around the cars and police tape, and the welcome smell of coffee wafted around. No coincidence, where there were cops, there was usually coffee, especially at seven am.

She watched as they brought the girl's body out the back of the Sky van in the fastened body bag and she thought about her poor family and shook her head. The body was loaded into the back of an ambulance ready to be whisked back to the Coroner for a forensic autopsy.

She picked up her phone and made two phone calls.

The first wasn't answered; the second was to the control room back at the station.

'Any sign of our two fugitives?'

chapter forty-five

Thirty-five minutes later we were parked at the back of a very modest looking hotel just outside Torquay. The sun was just stirring after a restful night's sleep, if only I could say the same, as I dragged a huge bag off the back seat and threw it over my shoulder. With a smaller bag in each hand, I nudged the car door shut with my knee.

Even with his bad leg, ribs, well everything, Jonny still insisted on carrying the biggest bags. *What a foolish gentleman*, I thought.

Mr and Mrs Craft checked in, paying cash for a double room, and we were directed to a lift which would take us to room twelve on the second floor. I leant against the wall and sighed, my eyes barely having the strength to stay open, as we waited for the lift.

Room twelve was, let's just say adequate. There was a bed, a kettle, a toilet and a shower, but then I am sure I wasn't expecting the Hilton on £32 a night. At least it seemed cleanish, and even in its barely adequate state the bed looked so very tempting.

We had hardly spoken since we'd left the flat, apart from polite directions, and I decided to break the tension and address the elephant in the room.

'I should hate you for what you did to me,' I said.

'Ditto,' he said, without looking up.

I shrugged. I guess that seemed fair.

'Do you?' he said.

'No.'

'Ditto.'

He smiled.

And that was the full extent of our deep and meaningful.

Jonny's phone vibrated as he gazed out the window. He looked at it then closed it up and sat back on the edge of the bed.

'Who was that?' I asked.

'No-one.'

He looked exhausted as he emptied the wraps of money onto the bed.

'How much is there?' I said.

'Each one is five grand.'

I counted them as he pulled them out of his pockets. Seventeen packets. Wow. Then he started unpacking one of the other bags, wincing periodically as he caught either his sore ribs or sore leg.

'Let me do that, what are you looking for?' I said, pulling the bag away.

'The first aid kit is at the bottom.'

He gave in and fell backwards onto the bed with a cough, followed by a laboured 'ow'.

I hoped when he said first aid kit, he meant mini A&E with surgeon included. He didn't. At the bottom of the bag was a slightly larger than standard first aid kit.

'You think a sticky plaster is going to fix this?' I said.

I started wondering whether I should physically force him to go to a hospital, if I even could.

'It's fine,' he coughed again. 'There is a needle in there, just stitch the hole closed.'

I was horrified, this was a joke surely, please let this be a joke. I looked across at him. He had his eyes closed, and he didn't look like he was joking. Shit.

'Listen, you need to see a proper doctor, it could get infected. I'm not doing this.'

'I've told you, I can't go to the hospital.'

'I don't care how many questions they ask, this is so wrong, I would rather see you in jail than a coffin.'

'It's fine, I've done it before. It's just sewing. Anyway, didn't you say you wanted to be a vet?'

'And the bullet?'

'Just leave it, they only take them out if they are near arteries and stuff.'

'No!'

'Alice…'

'I said no, I won't do it. What if it gets… just what if…?'

I could feel myself starting to shake; this whole thing was like a terrible nightmare, except it wasn't a dream. People were getting shot around me; dying, bleeding, DIY surgery. I couldn't cope anymore. I was too tired, and I stormed into the bathroom and locked the door behind me, so I could sit on the toilet and weep in private, without having to look at him.

Half an hour later I was woken from a toilet nap by Jonny as he knocked softly on the door.

'Alice?'

'Go away.'

'I just want to talk to you, please just come out.'

'Just talk?'

'Yes. Just talk. Please.'

I wiped my face on a strip of wafer thin toilet paper that reminded me of school, stood up slowly from the toilet and walked quietly over to the door and unclicked the lock. The door opened, and Jonny was standing on the other side with his leg all bandaged up. The medical kit was gone from the bed, so I stepped out into the room.

He took my hand and I followed him over to the bed. He was starting to put some weight on his leg again, not so much hop-a-long, more limp-a-long, that's progress at least. Maybe it wasn't as bad as it looked. Had I over reacted? Then of course reality hit me.

'You did it yourself, didn't you?'

'Do you really want me to answer that?'

'No.' And I didn't.

I decided I liked living in ignorance and I desperately wanted to get out of this insanity and back to the "meat and two veg world" I had previously sheltered myself in.

'And what about your ribs?'

'They're just bruised.'

'Oh, you're sure about that, you have a portable x-ray in that first aid kit too?'

'They're fine.'

He stretched his arm around my shoulders, but I shrugged it off and just rolled over on the bed for a much-needed nap by myself.

When I woke up it was already half past twelve, Jonny had gone, but a note on the bed saying *back in a mo* reassured me he hadn't gone far.

I needed those few hours of sleep. My head had cleared, and I finally felt like I could think straight. The last twenty-four hours had been the most insane of my life and I wouldn't soon get over the things I had witnessed, but at least it was no longer *all* I could think about.

In the early morning haze, the hotel room had looked quite clean, but now that the sun was in full glow it showed up every stain and smudge. It was quite disgusting, so I pulled the curtains across the window to numb the sun and the horror of a bed I had slept on this morning. Thank goodness I hadn't made it under the sheets, God only knows what filth lurked under there.

The room had a slightly damp feel and smell to it. I hadn't noticed that this morning either. God, I wished Brenda was with me, she would have this place sparkling in no time.

My train of thought was quickly interrupted by a knock at the door.

'Room service, Mrs Craft.'

He had faked a silly accent, but I knew it was Jonny and I pulled open the door. He stood on the other side of the door with a brown paper bag in one hand, two paper coffee cups in the other, and a daft grin on his face. His clothes were wrinkled and dirty, but then mine were probably just as bad, and I wondered what the girl on reception must have thought of us when we arrived at the crack of dawn.

'Where have you been, and how's your leg?' I said, as he limped gently past me.

'Burger van for breakfast and fine, thanks for asking.'

'Burgers for breakfast?'

'It might be breakfast in here, but the rest of the world thinks it's lunch time for some reason, can't think why.' He winked.

Fair enough, I thought, 'You are in a surprisingly good mood.'

'Am I?'

Yes, he was very surprisingly upbeat. Breakfast or lunch or whatever he wanted to call it, those cheeseburgers smelt damn good and I was starving.

There was no table in the room, so we sat with our feet up on the bed and Jonny handed me a paper wrapped cheeseburger, hold the burger, from the brown bag. Surprisingly, it tasted even better than it smelt although I don't think I will start a new breakfast habit. In any case, I polished mine off in minutes and my stomach thanked me profusely.

Despite Jonny's good mood, something ugly hung between us, and I'm not talking about the lampshade, although the cigarette stained atrocity would have qualified. No, I'm talking about *Me and Jonny,* and more specifically, was there a *Me and Jonny* anymore? Did I even want there to be a *Me and Jonny*? Interrogation time.

'Jonny, I need to ask you a question and you need to be brutally honest with me ok?'

'Yes, ok.'

'Promise me.'

'I promise, what is it?'

'You said last night that your last job would get you off the hook? What hook? What did you mean?'

I watched as he covered his face with his hands and waited for him to answer. When none came I took one of his hands and clasped it between mine. 'Jonny?'

'No. Ask me something else.'

'Jonny please, you promised.' His face contorted in all different directions and he turned his head away and he pulled his hand away from mine. 'We need to start being honest with each other.'

'No.'

I sighed, I had my answer and the look on his face did not invite me to push harder, I knew what I had to do.

'Then I have to go.'

I stood up, found my coat and my handbag and without looking back I opened the door.

'Please, don't go,' I heard him say.

His voice was high pitched. I knew he was holding back tears. *Just don't look back*, I told myself, *if you do you'll end up staying, you know you will.*

My problem is that I always give in and then hours, weeks or years later, I curse myself for not following through. Not today, not now. Not anymore.

'Goodbye Jonny,' I said, as I walked through the door and closed it firmly behind me. 'God, I hope I know what I'm doing.' I said under my breath.

Then I ran for the stairs, ran down two flights and out the front door of the hotel.

It had been a long time since I had been in Torquay, but I sort of knew my way around. I was heading for the town centre, but after that, God knows.

My phone buzzed in my pocket. No prizes for guessing who that was, so I ignored it.

'Just keep walking, Alice. Just keep walking,' I said to myself.

I found Sea Road, dug my hands into my pockets and followed it along the coast. If I had been in a better mood, I would have stopped at a lookout point and taken in the beautiful view.

I marched past hotel after hotel, including one that was boasting of having won Hotel of the Year in 2012, deservedly so by the looks of it. Every one of them looked better than the one we were staying in. I continued past an elderly couple who were sitting on a bench holding hands; they looked so happy and in love and wished me a good afternoon as I passed. There was nothing good about it, but I nodded and forced a smile anyway.

My phone had rung another four times since I had been gone, but I managed to resist the urge to look. I just kept walking and about half an hour after I left Jonny and the stinking hotel, I reached the Mallock Memorial, a pretty clock tower that stands in the middle of a roundabout at The Strand.

I crossed over the road and sat quietly on a bench to gaze out over the water. I had plenty to think about, but I couldn't help be distracted by the amazing view. Even in November, it was something to behold. The houses on the hill in the distance, the boats bobbing on the water and of course the controversial big wheel in the distance; it was magical.

But of course, I still didn't know where to go, or what I was supposed to do. Should I just go home? It was an option. I still had to sort out my divorce, and there were the kids. Even though they were fast growing up, they still needed me. But Michael would be there, and I didn't want to face him, not yet anyway. Maybe I could stay at Jackie's or go to Gayle's? What a mess. In the space of twenty-four hours I had lost my husband, my boyfriend, my home, my ignorance of the world, and now I was even afraid to go home to my own kids.

I watched a girl, probably in her early twenties, walk past with three greyhounds trotting along beside her, and it made me smile. I had always wanted a dog of my own. Mum didn't like dogs, and Michael was allergic, so maybe now I could get a dog. The thought made me smile, maybe I would get two. On second thought, maybe I should just get a house to live in, and worry about filling it with dogs later.

Half an hour later, I was still sitting on that very same bench staring out to sea, listening to the insistent squawk of the seagulls, and still undecided about where I was going to go, and getting colder by the minute.

My attention was momentarily taken by the screeching of car tires and the sound of car horns. I looked round to see what the fuss was about. By the looks of it, someone had cut someone else off on the roundabout and they were not best pleased. I sniggered and turned back to the boats.

Then I heard my name being called. My head snapped round to find the source of the panicked voice, just in time to see Jonny vault over a bench, running straight for me.

'Alice!'

I sighed loudly and turned back to the water. Don't get me wrong, my heart was tap dancing I was so happy to see him, but it didn't change anything. I loved him, no doubt about that, but was that enough? He still couldn't answer my question; it was total honesty or nothing from now on.

Stay strong, I reminded myself as he stopped in front of me.

chapter forty-six

'Hi.' She said, not looking up.

It was only by pure chance that Jonny had seen Alice sitting by the marina. He had started to lose hope he would find her at all, and the longer he had looked, the more hope he had lost.

When she had pulled the hotel door closed behind her, he felt instantly paralysed. She was the best thing that had ever happened to him, he knew that, even given his current predicament.

He had thought it was all over the moment he opened the rear doors to his van last night and pulled the hood off her head. He was hysterical when he realised what he had done, inconsolable. But at that moment he knew he still had a job to do, and he couldn't get emotional about it. That's what would get you killed in this business, and it still might.

But even after he was so awful to her, she still came back for him. He couldn't believe it. She had given him a second chance, and he knew he didn't deserve it, but there she was. The question was, was he going to let her go again and could he even stop her?

'Hi,' he replied humbly.

He sat down on the bench beside her and glanced out at the boats.

The silence was awkward. She looked so despondent, just staring out across the harbour. He had no idea what to say that would make this all better, if there even was such a thing.

She spoke first. 'I've been married for twenty years, you know that? Me and Michael had our twentieth wedding anniversary this year,' she said, her eyes fixed out to sea. 'I have two teenage kids, and yesterday I found out that my husband is not a successful accountant like he had led me to believe, for all that time. He is actually some kind of mafia boss or whatever you want to call it.' She took a breath before continuing. 'My boyfriend, who I thought sold burglar alarms for a living, is actually a hitman, and I found out that he actually works for my husband. I don't know who he is, who you are, and I'm not even sure I know who I am anymore.'

He hung his head and stared at the floor. 'You do know me, bet…'

'Please, don't,' she said, cutting him off. 'Yesterday, you found out that the woman you said you loved…'

'I do love…,' he protested.

'Fine, yesterday, you found out that the woman you love hadn't even told you her real name and was married to your boss.

'All those lies have *cost* lives and *destroyed* even more – my life. I don't want to wake up tomorrow and find out anything new. I can't take anymore. I can't. I just need you to be honest with me, whatever it is, but I can't take any more surprises.'

She looked up for the first time since he had sat down, and he caught a glimpse of her sad, confused eyes and it broke his heart.

'I'm sorry, but that's how it is,' she said.

She leant forward and stared back out to sea. He knew what she wanted but he just couldn't give it to her.

'I can't,' he said.

'Do you think it was easy for me to come back for you, after everything you did to me?'

He shook his head.

'But I did it because, well, I just did. You said you loved me, and if you really do, you should be able to tell me anything.'

'Not this, you'll leave me for sure.'

'I have already left you, Jonny.'

She used his knee to push herself off the bench, and he watched her walk slowly along the harbour, walking away, again. He couldn't he let her go again; this was his only shot. She had already left him; he knew that, so it couldn't get any worse.

'Ok,' he shouted after her.

She stopped. He watched anxiously as she turned around to face him. She was smiling. Thank God, she was smiling.

Now just keep buying time, just like you did at the pub when you first met her, just keep buying that extra time, he told himself.

'But not here, please. Come back to the hotel with me.'

She nodded, and she smiled a little more. He had never felt a rush of relief like it.

'Thank God,' he said, rushing her for a hug.

It felt good to have his arms wrapped around her again, really good, and it was all he could do to stop himself crying with relief. He had bought some time.

He had bought cokes and sandwiches, and even more time, from the twenty-four-hour Subway before they headed back to the hotel. That had bought him another hour. All that was left now were the wrappers and empty paper cups. They had sat quietly, awkwardly, on the bed, since they had finished eating

Alice was impatiently looking straight at him. He took a deep breath. Time was up.

'I'm gonna tell you about me, but I don't want to look at you when I do.' There was no way he could take seeing the look of horror, disappointment or just pure loathing on her face when he told her what a screw-up he had been.

'Ok.'

'Listen, when I'm done, don't say anything. If you still hate me, which you will, the door is there, just go. Take my car, I won't come after you.'

He wouldn't be needing a car again anyway when she left, so she may as well have it. At least he would know she could get home safely, before he ended this whole sorry mess and texted Michael the address of the hotel.

'Ok.'

He sighed heavily and turned on the bed so that he was sitting on the edge facing out the window and away from Alice. He started talking quietly.

'My mum was an addict ok, since long before I was born. She ran up a serious debt with her dealer that she couldn't pay, and your husband paid it off for her. I've been paying him back ever since.'

He paused for a moment to gauge her reaction, if there was one.

'I was expecting much worse than that.'

So far, so good. He continued, 'he paid off my dealer too.'

'Oh.'

'Listen, I know I'm not Mr Perfect ok. I told you, the doors over there, I don't need you judging me.'

He felt the bed move and his whole body tensed. He closed his eyes and held his breath, while he waited for the hotel room door to click closed behind her. Instead, he felt her warm hand on his shoulder.

It was the most wonderful feeling, he thought, as he nuzzled her hand with the side of his face.

'He helped me. He got me back on track, kept me out of trouble, I owe him a lot. I would be dead by now if it wasn't for Michael. I was just a kid then. You know, when your mum's a junkie and turns tricks for money instead of a proper job, there's really no hope for you, is there?'

She didn't say a word as her hand gently squeezed his shoulder. He had never talked like this before; it felt so good to finally let it all out.

'You don't know what it's like growing up with a junkie for a mum, she did her best, it wasn't her fault. I had no friends or family, just her. There was no money, I hardly ever went to school.

'The drugs numbed all that. It's easy to be an addict when your life's a pile of shit and you've got no future.'

'What happened to her, your mum?'

'She died when I was seventeen, overdose.'

'What about your dad?'

'Never had one, I had plenty of *uncles* though, that's what Mum made me call 'em when I was a kid. One of them might have been my dad, don't know. When I got older, I knew who they were and what they were doing there. Some were ok, some weren't.'

'That's why you went to the forest? They hit you.'

'Some did. Some worse. I told her once, about *Uncle* Theo when I was twelve. She just said that sometimes we had to do things we didn't like to get by. I thought it was normal, but it wasn't normal, was it? I think I knew it wasn't'

He bit his lip and fought back the tears as the memories flooded back.

She moved on the bed again and he felt her sitting right behind him now. He felt her warm breath on his neck as her arms and legs stretched around him. He didn't deserve her. She was being so nice, and he was completely overwhelmed.

'Why didn't she stop him?' He said, turning around and pressing his face into her shoulder. He wrapped his arms round her waist and hung on tightly as he let go of decades of hurt in one big flood. 'Why?'

'I don't know, its ok, I'm here now, I'm here,' she said, rocking him gently from side to side.

His face still buried, he composed himself for a moment.

'I never wanted to get away from all this till I met you. You made me feel like there was something else, something better. This was supposed to be my last job, and then I was going to be free. It was going to be just me and you. I was going to... It doesn't matter now does it?' he said, and started sobbing quietly again.

He felt her take a deep breath.

'Do you still want that? Just me and you?'

Of course I want that, more than anything, Jonny thought, his face still buried in her shoulder. But he was far too emotional to give her an answer, so he settled for a simple nod. He felt her relax and smiled to himself. That was the answer she was hoping for.

He surprised himself at how emotional he had been, especially as he had left the worst bits out. He hadn't told her that he had tried to overdose when he was fourteen and again after his mum died; he also hadn't told her how angry he was when he woke up in hospital, angry because they had saved his life when he only wanted to die. He hadn't told her what it was like to be so angry and desperate that they had to strap you down on a hospital bed and fill you with even more drugs while your body detoxed in the most agonizing way.

He had never told anyone about his past before, not like that anyway, not even the shrinks they made him see when he was a kid, or in rehab. He would make the occasional blunt aside maybe, a flippant comment, but nothing so raw. It felt was like he was back there all over again. It brought back memories, memories he had suppressed. And he was reliving it all.

His hands started trembling and he was overcome with a sudden chill. He tightened his grip around Alice as a piercing headache forced his eyes tightly closed.

He was ten years old again; heavy footsteps clunking on the dusty wooden stairs. Alone in his room, he caught his breath as he silently scrabbled to his feet and tucked his tiny self in his closet, and pulled the door closed behind him. Uncle Theo was knocking on his bedroom door again. He held his breath as the door handle turned, his heart pounding so loudly he could hear it over the sound of the door creaking. He hugged himself tightly, praying he would just go away. Watching through the crack in the door. Theo was calling for his special boy.

He took deep breaths and concentrated hard. More than ten years clean, it had been a long while since the last time he had a craving, but he recognised the symptoms instantly. He would never forget them, no matter how much time passed.

When the fog cleared he sighed. It had passed easily this time. After all he was in his happy place, right here with Alice.

He should enjoy it while he could. If TJ's text earlier was anything to go by, his days were well and truly numbered. TJ was right about one thing though. If his luck was in Michael would catch up with him first. He shuddered at the thought.

It was a good hour before he lifted his head. Her fingers had been running continuously through his hair. It felt amazing, but he couldn't stay there forever, nature was calling.

He wasn't sure quite what to expect when he lifted his head and sat up beside her. Frankly, he was just glad she was still there; he certainly hadn't expected her to be.

She wrapped her arms around his neck and gave him another hug and at the same time she whispered the sweetest words he had ever heard.

'You're not alone anymore, Jonny, never again. I love you too.'

He held onto her like he had never held onto anything in his life. No-one had ever said those words to him before.

chapter forty-seven

I let Jonny go to the bathroom and settled back against the rigid head board. I bit my lip and fought back a sympathetic tear. I couldn't even begin to imagine what it was like for him growing up. I had two loving parents, went to gymnastics after school and horse riding on the weekends. Never once did I think I was lucky, in fact, I often complained that my trainers weren't good enough, or my curfew was unfair.

How guilty do I feel now? My kids are just the same, probably worse. Maybe they could do with a bit of grounding, maybe they will appreciate the things they have. Jesus, Sara didn't even have to buy her own car.

Despite all that, I still felt about as content and happy as I ever had, no mean feat considering the circumstances. My mind digressed as he came back from the bathroom. Jonny's limp had almost vanished and the swelling on his face had gone down an awful lot just since last night, and apart from walking with his left arm hugging his ribs he was almost looking human again.

'So, what do we do now?'

'I got a text from TJ earlier, saying they are looking for me. Michael won't rest now until I'm dead, Alice. I have to find them before they find me. It's the only way this will ever be over.'

'Are you sure he's not just saying that to scare you?'

'Alice, he blew the head off a prostitute for touching his phone, so how do you think he's gonna feel about the man that screwed his wife?'

I sighed. This wasn't going to get any better, but I think I already knew that.

'This is a nightmare, I need to think.' And I was sure I was stinking the place out. 'Time for a shower.'

'Oh, goodie.'

'No, *I'm* going for a shower. I just need some space for a bit.'

'Ok.'

'I'll not be long.'

The shower was divine and it had given me the space I needed to come to two conclusions. The first was that I wasn't going to be able to have a life with Jonny until this whole mess was properly sorted out, whatever that meant. The second was that I needed to speak to my kids and make sure they were safe. Thankfully, the second was easy to deal with.

'Feel better?' Jonny said, stretched out on the bed.

I nodded, 'Much, I just need to call my kids.'

I picked up my phone, but I had no signal. Seems the hell hole that was this hotel was good for absolutely nothing.

'Damn it, this stupid phone has no signal; I'm just going to head out for a bit. See if I can get one outside.'

I grabbed my coat and turned the door handle and the door popped open, but Jonny pounced off the bed and slammed it shut again before I could step out.

'Wait,' he said, hopping back. He started frantically pulling things out of his bag again. 'Take this with you.'

He had found a strange looking piece of moulded plastic.

'What's that?'

'A belt holster,' he said, with his hands round my waist. When he finished attaching it to me he took a gun out from under his side of the bed, clicked some buttons and slipped it into the holster. 'Just in case.'

'I don't need this.'

'Good, then you'll bring it, and you, straight back, safe and sound. But if you do?'

There was no point arguing. I closed my coat tightly around it and walked out the door shaking my head. It was Torquay out there, not the Wild West. Likely the most dangerous thing I would encounter would be a hungry seagull.

I walked out of the hotel with my phone in my hand, holding it out in front of me and waving it about to find a decent signal. On the outside I looked like your everyday crazy woman, but under my coat was Jonny's very heavy gun, hanging awkwardly on my hip. How do people walk with these things attached to them? It just felt ridiculous and another reminder of how much of an action hero I am not.

I sighed and took a left out of the hotel. It was already starting to get dark. After about ten minutes I still hadn't found a decent signal, but I had found the coastal path. *That'll do nicely*, I thought. Soft sand underfoot, the smell of seaweed, the hushed sounds of the waves. I felt quite nostalgic. I hadn't taken a walk on the beach since the kids were little.

The kids. I was really missing their grumpy teenage selves and I re-checked my phone. I nearly cheered out loud when I saw a good enough signal. I found Sara's number and hit dial.

'Hi Mum,' said the cheery voice on the other end. 'Well, did it work out?'

'Erm, sort of.'

'I knew it, that's why you didn't come home last night, isn't it?'

'Yeah, listen, I was just ringing to check you and Ben were ok.'

'We're fine, Ben's in his room.'

'And Dad?'

'Hardly seen him. He was home late last night and left early this morning. Are you getting a divorce?'

'Erm, yes, maybe, probably.'

She started telling me about one of her friends whose mum was getting a divorce, but I wasn't really listening, just enjoying listening to the chatter. As I walked further along the path I noticed a large rock and sat down to gaze out across the sea. The salty air was cold but affirming. The place was deserted; no surprise considering it was late November, and I sat quietly, mesmerized by the sea gently lapping at the shore.

I adjusted the gun that was now pressing into the top of my leg and listened to Sara chatter on as I considered my own crazy life. Maybe I could just convince Michael to leave him alone, or was I just being naïve?

I watched a pair of seagulls fighting on the beach, the larger of the two had clearly injured the smaller bird. I was dismayed. How could it behave that way, towards one of its own? The weaker bird was fighting back and trying to get away, but the more powerful bird was determined, squawking and flapping its giant wings in between bouts of violent pecking. But this was the way of things, wasn't it? My dad always used to say to us when we were kids, 'If you don't get them, they'll soon get you.' Now I know what he meant.

'What Mum?'

'Oh, nothing.' I hadn't even realised I'd spoken out loud. 'Listen, I need you and Ben to do something for me, it's very important.'

'Ok, what?'

'In my bedroom, go to my jewellery box. The bottom is loose, and if you lift it out, you will find a credit card. It's there for emergencies. The pin number is five-oh-six-nine. I need you to use it to buy tickets for you and Ben to get to Gayle's in Jersey. You need to go straight away. Promise me you'll go now.'

'Why, what's happened?' She sounded worried, and I didn't want to scare her.

'Nothing. I would just feel better knowing you were both there. I'll come for you when this is all sorted out. Promise me.'

'But what about Maddy, I can't leave her now?'

'Then buy a ticket for her too. Promise me, just don't tell your dad what you're doing or where you are going.'

I felt a tear sliding down my face. My poor kids, I had to know they were safe. I didn't have a clue what was going to happen over the next few days, at least at Gayle's they would be spared the heartache of getting dragged into this mess.

'Ok, I promise, you sure you're ok?' she said.

'Text me the time of your flight as soon as you book it. I love you both.'

I hung up and dropped my face into my hands. What the hell was I doing? I sat shivering for a minute as the enormity of the situation sunk in. Was I doing the right thing? Time would be the judge of that.

I looked back out to sea and sighed. No use in hanging around. The smaller bird had fallen and was now seagull food. I took a deep breath and stood straight up from the rock, took one last look at the beautiful coast line, then checked behind me, and marched straight back to the hotel. There was no way I was going to end up like that little bird.

I hadn't taken a key with me, but it turned out I didn't need it. Jonny must have been watching out for me from the window, as he was waiting in the open doorway as I made my way down the hall.

'Quick, get in here.' He looked really worried.

Jeez, I was only gone twenty minutes. But I couldn't wait to get that door closed and get rid of the hunk of death metal that was hanging on my hip, so I rushed the last few steps. That gun was starting to make me paranoid.

'We've got to go,' Jonny said, dragging me into the middle of the room.

'Why. What's happened?'

'Look.'

He spun me round to see the TV; the news was on.

'What am I looking at?' I said. 'Oh no.' My stomach shifted violently.

'Exactly, we have to go, right now.'

'Shit!'

We started bundling everything into bags as quickly as we could; my heart was doing some serious overtime. Just seeing my own face on TV was scary enough, but they had superimposed my picture over one that had been taken at Michael's cottage.

It was a picture of the front of the house. The Sky van was still parked on the drive with the rear doors wide open, police tape everywhere. But it was the words underneath the picture that just finished it off for me; they were just gut-wrenching.

Wanted for Double Murder – Armed and Dangerous.

Double murder? Bags packed, we raced down the stairs. Thankfully, the girl manning the desk seemed more interested in her phone than us, and we quickly snuck out through the front doors.

'What now?' I said, as we threw everything in the back seat of the car.

'Back to the forest, no one'll ever find us there.'

My stomach sank as Jonny skidded the Subaru out of the car park and onto the main road.

What was scarier, a night in the woods or a night on the run. Oh wait, what about both?

chapter forty-eight

Carrie watched the interview through the one-way glass that looked into the interview room next door.

Michael looked cool as ever as he sat beside his very smart, and very sexy looking lawyer. He leant back casually in his chair, his legs stretched out under the table, his hands resting loosely on the table as he answered question after question about the events of last night.

Her partner David and Detective Constable Frankie Daye were conducting the interview that so far had not come to much at all. *That's ok,* she thought to herself, she knew how these two worked, they were good, and he would trip himself up soon enough, he had to.

After an hour of gentle questioning from Frankie she watched David start to stir and begin to turn up the heat on Michael. That was his trade mark and it usually worked. He asked him about the bruise on the back of his hand, for a second time.

Michael surprised everyone when he exploded out of his chair, hurling insults into the air. His uncharacteristic rant continued for a good few minutes, ending only when emotion got the better of him and he broke down in front of the shocked detectives, and his even more shocked looking barrister. Carrie watched the floorshow through the glass, her mouth hanging open, as his lawyer gave him a comforting shoulder rub and requested a drink of water for his, apparently, distraught client. Carrie wasn't buying one word of it.

When Frankie returned with the water, the barrister reminded them, in no uncertain terms, that his client was suffering because of his wife turning out to be a double murderer, as well as the fact that his wife of twenty years was cheating on him and had left him only hours previously. This was the woman he apparently loved beyond words, and they should remember that as they proceeded.

Bullshit! Carrie coughed.

They continued, more gently this time, for a further twenty minutes.

'So, let's recap some of the facts. Alice and Jonathon were having an affair,' Frankie confirmed.

'Behind your back?' David added.

'Of course!' He snapped. 'I knew nothing about it before that night. I just thought things had got on top of us. I hired a maid so she wouldn't be so stressed at home, and I was going to take her away to St Lucia. She loved it there. I had no idea.' He paused to take a drink of water.

'They had come to the house together and she told me she wanted a divorce, she said they were in lo...' He paused to recollect himself again. 'I was devastated and begged her to stay, to work things out, but she refused and that's when she got violent. She had a gun. Danny had tried to intervene, and that's when she shot him. After that was a blur. I ran out the house, got in my car and just kept driving.'

'Where did she get the gun?' Frankie said.

'I don't know.'

'Did you know she had a gun?'

'Not until then.'

'May I remind you that Mr Walker is here of his own free will; he's trying to help you,' Ashley injected.

'Of course,' David said. 'You said Danny was still alive when you left the house?'

'Yes, I think so.'

'And you didn't stop to help him, or even take him with you in your car?'

'No, I was afraid for my life, and my kids. She just went mad.'

'Right. Now remind me why you didn't report this to us this morning.'

'He was afraid she might go after him, so he didn't come forward at the time.' Ashley said. 'Michael has already admitted to knowing about Danny's shooting, but he didn't know he had died, and he also knew nothing about the body in the back of the van. Now if there's nothing else, I think we are done here, don't you?'

She had watched every inch of the interview with interest, watched his face for any sign he was lying, anything at all, but he was giving nothing away. He was either a really good liar or completely innocent, and she cringed as she considered the possibility.

She scrunched her fists as she watched the detectives shake hands with a still slightly teary Michael Walker and his stone-cold lawyer, and they walked free from the interview room.

'Damn it!' she said, kicking the wall.

A few moments later David joined her in the adjoining room with a cup of tea.

'Thought you could use this,' he said, handing her the polystyrene cup. 'Milk and three?'

'After that performance, I might be up to four by tea time.'

'What did you think?' he said, perching on the corner of the table.

'He's lying.'

'Oh, absolutely, but which bit Carrie?'

'He said she was having an affair, that part might be true. I just don't get how the rest of it falls together. What happened David?' she asked, almost rhetorically.

'I know I want to get that TJ guy back in here. Michael said he was just a friend, so why would TJ say he worked for him?'

'I'll have uniform track him down.'

'You know,' David's leg swung under the table like a pendulum as he spoke, 'I've interviewed Michael Walker so many times, and he was always a cool guy, very collected. That performance with the tears surprised me. He has never tried that on before. He's a liar, no doubt, but I just don't know how much of *this* we can pin on him. I don't know how we can get it all to stick.'

'That had crossed my mind too.'

She thought to herself, maybe *Jonathon and Alice had shot those two people, but that wasn't going to bring her any closer to Michael, dammit!*

David's phone started ringing.

'Yes?' He hopped down. 'You're sure?'

She watched him pace the room.

'Great, thanks,' he said, before sliding the phone back into his pocket.

'Well, what is it?'

'The blood on the floor in the basement has been identified as belonging to Jonathon Edmondson and Daniel Perez. The large pool of blood in the front room and the smear on the door frame and floor is Jonathon Edmondson and the smaller patch is Alice Walkers.'

'So, they are both hurt, is anyone checking the hospitals?'

'Already done, nothing.'

'Do you think they did it David?'

'Dunno. I think she wanted her divorce, Michael said no, I think she got angry, but shooting people and emptying the safe? I just dunno, evidence sure points to her though.'

'You think she could have shot Jonathon too?' Carrie paced across the room, her hand rubbing her right temple as she considered the possibilities.

'Someone did, we know that much, and he lost a lot of blood. We need to find him, I'll bet good money he has a gunshot wound. If so, and we can retrieve the bullet, we can see if it matches the bullets found in Daniel Perez. If they match, we will have our answer.'

'I am just not so sure. It doesn't feel right. I feel like they are being set up.'

'Listen, I want it to be Michael as much as you, but we've got the pissed off wife, an affair, a gun, and a robbery, what if that's all it is, it just happens to be in Michael Walker's house'

'And Jonathon?'

'Just an unfortunate accessory. He's probably bled to death by now judging by the amount of blood found in the house. If it continued like that he would be in big trouble. She's probably looking for somewhere to dump his body right now.'

'And the body in the van?'

'Hmmm.'

His phone rang again, interrupting his train of thought.

'Yes? Really? Text me the address, we're on our way,' he said.

'What is it?' Carrie said.

'You can ask her yourself in about twenty minutes.' He grinned. 'Alice Walker has just been spotted entering a flea-bitten bed and breakfast in Torquay.'

'Then what are we waiting for, let's go.'

chapter forty-nine

Back at the forest, *again*, and feeling surprisingly safe this time. I guess I was starting to get a feel for what Jonny had been talking about before. I suppose it helps when two crazy madmen are after you, and the police want you for two murders. Whether I would still agree in an hour when the sun disappears, we shall see.

The car journey was stilted to say the least, no karaoke like last time, just two hours of obsessive staring every time a car went past that looked even remotely like a police car. And then almost hysterical panic when one drove by with its lights and sirens on. Thankfully, it was after someone else; heart attack over.

Jonny was sitting on the ground by the fire staring pensively into the flames, absently picking bark off a bit of stick, seemingly miles away. I stood and watched him quietly for a few minutes before interrupting his deep thoughts and snuggling up beside him for a hug. We both needed one by the looks of it

'What are you thinking about?'

'Just stuff. You, me, Michael.'

'Did he really kill a girl because she touched his phone?'

'Yep, just shot her, just like that and that wasn't the first time. He's a bad man, Alice.' He paused. 'Sad thing is, I know I'm no better.'

'But you said you didn't want to do those things.'

'Yeah, so?'

'Then you are a hundred times better than he could *ever* hope to be.'

'I s'pose.'

I squeezed him again, 'So what's next?'

'Well, I am going to spend the day tomorrow doing the only thing I know how, and for the last time I might add, and then when I'm done we can run away into the sunset together and live happily ever after.'

'That easy, huh?'

He laughed. 'Yep, that easy.'

'Only got one problem with that.'

'What's that?'

'You said I. You meant we, right?'

He turned and looked at me square in the face, 'God no, it's I, you stay here where I know you are safe.'

'Both of us, or neither of us.'

'But, you understand that I have to kill your husband.'

'How many people have lost their lives because of him? He needs to be stopped, as does the rest of his lot. Clearly the police aren't going to do anything about him. It would be like killing Hitler, I can live with that.'

'You're sure.'

'We are a team now, right. I told you, you're not on your own anymore, and I meant it.'

'Yeah, but...'

'But nothing. I'm coming, end of. Then we will sort out the police, don't know how yet, but we will.'

'You're amazing.'

'True, but first, there is some more urgent business I would like to attend to.' I said, pushing him backwards onto the ground. 'You owe me some serious make-up sex.'

'Shit!' He cried out as I rested on his *not broken* ribs. I winced for him and bit my bottom lip as I quickly sat back. He rolled over the ground with his arms wrapped around himself.

'Ooh, sorry,' I said.

He nodded as he hugged himself, his face all scrunched up. Probably for the best he didn't answer me; he might have said something we both regretted.

After a few minutes his face started to relax, and I risked asking him if he was ok. He didn't say much other than to direct me to a packet of morphine tablets in the bottom of his bag. So that was how his limp has mysteriously cleared up. I fetched him the pills and a bottle of water as I made a promise to myself that when this was all over he was going to see a proper doctor, no arguments.

The to-do list of the damned was getting longer by the minute.

My phone buzzed to let me know I had a text message. Good timing. I certainly did not want to know how many of those little tablets you needed to make the pain of broken bones go away, but I suspected it was more than the recommended dosage, so I left Jonny with the pills and his water and stepped away from the fire, happy in my ignorance, for now, and I opened the message.

Hi Mum, got flights, take off at 6.30am, land at 7.55, packing now will text you when we get to Aunt Gayle's. Sara and Ben xo

That's all I needed to know, they were on her way, sort of, and would be safe in the morning. The relief was overwhelming, and I chuckled nervously.

I turned back to Jonny, who was still lying on his back on the ground.

'You ok?'

'Yep, just give me twenty minutes,' he said through gritted teeth. 'Who was the text from?'

'Sara, she's going to Jersey with Ben in the morning, I needed to know they would be safe, and out the way.'

'Good idea.' He grimaced and lay back, staring at the stars.

Thirty minutes later Jonny's smile had grown into a proper, if not slightly spaced-out looking one and his dimple was back, that's morphine for you, and he was ready for some, slightly gentler this time, but still good al-fresco make-up sex.

chapter fifty

After another sleepless night in the forest, we spent the morning killing time. I did my best to distract myself from the enormity of what was happening, but my message box was jammed with texts and my voice mailbox was full. Clearly, I had been spotted on the news by everyone I knew over the last few hours, including, apparently, my mum, who had tried to call me a record eighteen times since 8:15 this morning. Mum was afraid of technology so there were no texts or voicemails

The fire was out when we got back from a walk around the lake, so I sent Jonny off to get some more wood. There was no way I was going to eat another tin of cold beans.

I found the last tin and headed over to a sit on a log by the fire pit to wait for Jonny.

I froze when I saw what was in the fire pit.

'Jonny.' I shouted. 'JONNY!'

My chest was pounding. The fire had not gone out by itself, it had been put out, and in the middle of the wet ashes there was a postcard.

Jonny bounced back into camp.

'What, what is it?'

'Look,' I said, pointing.

He picked up the card and looked at the back.

'Shit,' he said, spinning round in a circle.

'What does it say?'

'You don't wanna know,' he said sharply. 'Let's go, we'll get lunch out.'

So, once again we threw everything into bags at the speed of light and hiked quickly back to the car. I didn't know what was written on that card, only that it was from TJ, but Jonny kept his gun drawn all the way back to the car. He was rattled.

The plan was to get something to eat and then we were going back to Jonny's lock up to get 'tooled up', as Jonny put it. I don't know how I felt about that, especially after the last time I had been there – against my will.

'I can see why my dad didn't like Michael much now,' I said, once we were in the car.

Jonny laughed. 'He was obviously a good judge of character.'

'Maybe. I guess you had to be in his job. I always thought he was just being an over protective dad.'

'What was his job?'

'He was Detective Chief Inspector of the Devon and Cornwall Police.'

Jonny went quiet for a moment.

'What happened to him?'

'He killed himself.'

He took one hand off the wheel and reached across to hold mine in my lap.

'Sorry.'

Me too, I thought to myself, *if only I knew why*.

I went back to watching out the window, this time for a blacked-out VW Golf and police cars. Jonny was being extra careful and was keeping his speed to a conservative sixty-five on the motorway, to not draw attention to the car, and it must have been killing him. So far there had been neither, not that I had spotted anyway.

We stopped at a Welcome Break on the M5, just after we passed Bristol. It was so good to get out the car and walk about for a bit. The car park was busy, as it always was, but we found a free spot near the back and started walking, hand in hand, towards the main building.

As well as some decent food, I was also very keen to get to a proper toilet. I was really starting to appreciate some of the simpler things in life; running water, toilets that flush, toilet paper, it was heaven in there, and as a bonus there was no draft, and no homicidal owls.

Jonny was waiting for me outside with a rolled-up paper in his hand, and he didn't look happy.

'What is it, what's happened?' I said.

He ushered me around the corner into a door way and unrolled the paper.

I felt sick again. My face was plastered all over the front page of that too. The story made me out to be a cold-blooded murderer and warned the public not to approach me in case I was armed, *just call the police* it advised. I shrunk down into my coat as I read the rest of the article. It said Michael, Sara, Ben and Jonny were also missing, and they were treating that as suspicious too.

'But I didn't kill anyone, I didn't do anything?' I protested to Jonny.

'I know that, and when this day is over we'll find a way to prove it.'

He gave me a big hug in the door way, but as I looked over his shoulder, I watched the world shrink and spin wildly around me, and suddenly I didn't feel so good.

Everywhere I looked, people had a newspaper in their hand. It felt like people were staring, talking loudly, laughing at me. The place was packed with people. A man scooted past on a disability scooter, my face draped over his handle bars. *Jesus, if he looked up now,* I thought, tucking as much of my face as I could into Jonny's shoulder.

Don't approach her, just call the police, that's what it said, what if someone already had. I searched the faces. No one looked at me, maybe that was all part of the plan. A security guard walked by and I felt my legs weaken when he caught my eye. I hung on tighter to Jonny, anything to stop my hands shaking.

'What's wrong?' he said, bending down to see my face.

I shook my head frantically and glared at the security guard who had stopped by a payphone and was looking in our direction. I could hardly breathe let alone speak.

'He's just a security guard,' he said, holding my head firmly in his hands. He looked straight at me. 'You have to calm down, no one cares who we are in here. Everyone is more concerned with their own stupid lives. Just take deep breaths ok.'

I nodded again, but it wasn't helping.

'I'm sure he's looking at me. What if he's called the police already.'

'Just look at me and smile for God's sake,'

I tried a smile as he slipped his hands into mine.

'He doesn't care who we are,' he said. 'He's probably looking at you because it looks like I am trying to harass you, right. Just relax. We are just two people, going on a trip like everyone else.'

I nodded again and took a deep breath, *just two people on a trip*, but he was still looking straight at me. I felt sick.

'I'm sorry, I need to get out of here, get some air,' I said, pulling away from Jonny and heading briskly toward the doors.

'Alice, wait up,' he said, catching up beside me. 'You just need to calm down. It's ok.'

I looked back, and the security guard was following us.

'He's following us Jonny, are you sure everything's ok.'

My phone started ringing, it was Mum, and I panicked and answered it as I scurried towards the main doors.

'Mum, I can't talk now, I'll call you later ok.'

'But your picture is all over the news.'

'I know, Mum, I'm sorting it. I'll call you later.'

Only a few meters to the exit now.

'Well, what's happened, where are you, are you ok?'

'Mum, I'm ok; don't believe what you see on the telly.'

Why did I answer the damned phone? Nearly there, just keep going.

I hung up the phone. Jonny was right behind me.

We both looked over our shoulders as we passed through the automatic glass doors. The security guard was still following us, and at a pace too, and it looked like he was talking into a radio on his shoulder.

'What now?' I said.

'Just run.'

I gripped his hand for dear life as I followed him at full speed along the side of the building towards the main car park.

Two more guards appeared from a Starbucks just as we approached the edge of the car park. One behind, two in front.

'Just keep running,' Jonny said, as his hand slipped out of mine and we both ran in different directions.

'Hey, stop,' One of the guards called as I heard a car skid and swerve behind me. God, I hoped that wasn't what I thought it was as I just kept running.

One guard, at least, was not far behind me as I ran across the car park. I couldn't even think straight anymore, and my heart was screaming at me to stop. I could hardly breathe, the cold air biting in my throat and chest.

Just keep running.

The footsteps behind me were getting louder, I was desperate to turn around. Where was Jonny, I couldn't see him, shit, shit, shit. I needed to get back to the car, that's where he would go.

I veered round and accidentally sprinted out in front of a Ford Escort. The car swerved and only just stopped as I folded over his bonnet, slamming my hands down on the metal. Another second and I would have been under his car. He yelled something impolite out of his window and I smiled apologetically, as I caught a quick breath and started running again, this time, in the direction of the Subaru.

I was panting, but the security guard wasn't, and I knew he was right behind me. There was no sign of Jonny. I searched the car park as I ran, darting haphazardly between parked cars, barging my way through a coachload of families with their tiny kids, desperately trying to shake off my pursuer. I continued to scan the car park. Where the hell was he?

The chatter of the guard's radio was getting louder. I could almost make out the words. Still no sign of Jonny, but I was nearly at the back of the car park, *just keep going, you can make it,* I told myself. I caught a glimpse of flashing blue lights heading straight down the motorway.

'Give me a break.'

I still couldn't see the car; it wasn't where I thought we'd left it. I stopped for a split second to scan the car park just as a pair of hands wrapped round my waist and I was yanked down onto the gravelly car park. I yelped as my hands and knees scuffled against the rough ground. He had a firm grip and I kicked out with my feet as I tried desperately to crawl away from him on my bleeding and sore hands. He momentarily lost his grip and I scrambled to my feet, but he caught me and dragged me down onto the floor with him again.

'Get. Off. Me,' I yelled, kicking at him and wriggling to get free.

He crawled over my back, fighting with me the whole time, and eventually he had pinned me to the floor with his heavy body. He grabbed my arm and pulled it backwards behind me.

My face was being forced into the ground as he fought to twist my arm behind my back. I winced. It felt like it was going to break.

I heard the screeching of tires and a car door open and close. Had the police finally arrived? I couldn't see; my face was being crushed into the freezing ground.

I sighed and stopped fighting. I let him bend my arm, it was over, the rabbit was caught.

Then the guard mysteriously disappeared from behind me.

'Come on, quick!'

My head snapped round as Jonny dragged me off the floor and back towards his waiting car. I looked back at the guard who was lying on the ground beside me, his nose and eye bleeding heavily. Jonny must have hit him hard.

In a state of shock, I fell into the car. Jonny already has his foot pressed firmly on the accelerator before I even had the door closed.

He raced the car towards the exit, slowing down considerably just as we exited the car park and turned towards the motorway slip road. My heart temporarily seized as we passed two police cars driving into the service station with their blue lights flashing urgently.

'Are you ok?' Jonny asked as he thumped the pedal again, forcing the car to accelerate like a rocket down the slip road and onto the motorway.

'I'm still hungry.'

In hindsight, I think he was more concerned about the blood that was oozing out of my hands and torn jeans. But it was all I could think of to say. I was still in shock. But we both laughed, gently at first, then more hysterically as the relief of escaping such a close call sunk in.

When would this end? I thought to myself as the car cruised towards Exeter, and Jonny's infamous lock-up.

chapter fifty-one

The first order of business, once we had arrived at the lock up, was a little first aid. I had bad memories of getting first aid in that horrible place, memories I would much rather forget, so I insisted that Jonny dig the gravel out of my hands while I sat in the passenger seat of the car, even if it was getting dark.

If I hadn't been in love with this man before, I was now. Especially after he patched me up, again. He had such a gentle way about him. Once my hands were cleaned up and kissed better, we were free to get on with the business at hand.

Jonny couldn't wait to get inside his lock-up and get the door closed. My jaw dropped as he unlocked a large metal cabinet and I got a glimpse of the kind of *tooling* he had been talking about. The back of the cabinet was covered with guns in all shapes and sizes and the doors were the same. I had never seen anything like it. There were some scary looking weapons in there; it looked like something from a movie.

Snapping on some surgical gloves, he unclipped one from the back, a very mean looking item indeed.

'What is that?' I asked, naively.

'This, is a HK MT27 Infantry Assault Rifle, the US Marine Corps uses 'em.'

He held it up to his shoulder, grinning like a five-year-old as he peered along the full length of it like he was going to fire it, then brought it down and placed it on a work bench. He threw me a pair of gloves and went back to his cabinet to retrieve a much smaller hand gun, which he gave to me.

'You can have this.'

'What is it?' I said, holding the thing in my hands.

'My old Glock 17.'

'Is it loaded?'

'No.'

Knowing it wasn't loaded helped and I tossed it gently in my palms. It was heavier than I imagined it would be. I turned and flipped it round to have a proper look at it from all angles. I'd never really taken time to look at a gun up close before.

'What the hell?' Jonny shouted, snatching it away again.

'What?' Then I realised that I had been staring straight down the barrel, whoops.

'Never, never, ever point a gun at anything unless you don't mind it dying, ever.'

'You said it wasn't loaded.'

'Doesn't matter, jeez you'll give me a friggin' heart attack. I'll just hold onto this for now, I think. Just wait and don't touch anything.'

'Fine. What are you doing anyway?'

'Loading rounds into the mags.'

'Oh, right.' Whatever that meant, just keep nodding and smiling. 'Am I allowed to pick that up?' I said, pointing to a small rectangle of metal.

'The mag, yeah you can't hurt anyone with that, unless you throw it at them.'

I picked it up and looked at the neat little bullets that were lined up inside.

'Is there supposed to be a gap here at the bottom?'

Jonny looked at me, his cheeks flushing as red as beetroot, 'The Glock 41 only takes thirteen rounds, but that's unlucky so I only ever load twelve.'

'I didn't think you were the superstitious type.'

'Yeah, well I am. Listen I don't tell you how to mash potato do I?'

'Guess not.'

I stifled a grin and put the magazine down on the bench. Although I wish someone would, since my mash is terrible.

The smell of solvent and stale vomit was overwhelming, so I left Jonny to play with his toys and waited in the car. Clearly, I was superfluous anyway.

In the car I tried not to think too much about how insane my life had become and instead tried to catch a few zzz's. I couldn't remember the last time I had gone to bed or woke at a normal hour. I put it on my to do list, right after don't die, don't get arrested, get Jonny to a hospital, and just ahead of learn to make proper mash.

I must have just dropped off and I woke with a start. Jonny was making a racket as he loaded his artillery into the boot. He wanted to show me how to use the gun he had handed me earlier, which was probably wise given the circumstances, so I followed him back into the lock up where he had set up some old plastic bottles for me to shoot at.

After a quick rundown of which bits slide and why, what to press and what not to press, he finally let me point the gun at something and with a very shaky hand I held the gun out in front of me. My finger curled round the trigger and I winced in anticipation of the imminent bang. I closed my eyes and pulled hard on the trigger, but after a loud click nothing much else happened.

Contrary to the look on Jonny's pained face, he insisted I had done a good job, although he was relieved he had left the safety on, and I earned myself a pat on the back and a kiss. I had done so good a job, in fact, that I was asked *never* to fire the gun again unless it was a *real* emergency.

So, he showed me how to take the safety off, in case of an emergency, and I slid it into the holster that was still dangling from my waist, and we headed off in the car again, this time we were headed to TJ's house.

chapter fifty-two

It was actually TJ's mum's house, but his mum was spending so much time back home in South Africa that he pretty much had the place to himself.

Jonny parked the car about a hundred yards away, just outside the neighbour's house; we would have to walk the last bit.

'I would prefer you didn't come, you know,' he said for the hundredth time, before we got out the car.

'No, one for all and all for one.'

'We're not the three musketeers you know. There are only two of us.'

'And there were *four* of them, what's your point.'

'Then why were they called the *three* musketeers?'

'I don't know,' I said. 'Point is, I'm coming.'

'No. You wait in the car where you will be safe.'

'What if he comes out and finds me here?' I said. 'Alone. Vulnerable.'

He handed me a balaclava and took back the gun he had given me earlier, so he could insert the magazine in it.

'Fine. But you don't blink without my say, ok. This is dangerous,' he said, handing it back to me with a spare magazine for my pocket. It wasn't even loaded before, probably for the best.

'Only use this in an emergency, and for God's sake, don't close your eyes.'

I nodded and gave him a kiss and a hug,

'Whatever happens, I love you,' I whispered into his ear.

'I love you too.'

He threw the rifle over his back and I followed him, in the dark, up the street to an alley behind the houses that led to TJ's house.

Clearly the alley was rarely used, or at least it hadn't been recently, as it was completely overgrown with weeds, some of which were nearly as tall as me. We made our way to a spot that Jonny liked the look of crouched down and waited.

There was a light on in one of the rooms upstairs and TJ's car was in the drive, so we assumed that he was home, and decided to just to sit and wait for him to come close enough to a window so that Jonny could take a sniper shot through the glass.

'Easy,' he insisted.

So, we waited, and we waited, and just as I thought my fingers and toes were about to snap off in the bitter cold air, we waited a little bit more. My legs had started to go numb and if it wasn't for the fact that my nose was dribbling inside the balaclava, I might have believed it had frozen solid and already dropped off.

I rubbed my double gloved hands together just as the light switched off in the upstairs room, but I needn't have bothered getting my hopes up. A few seconds later, a light flicked on downstairs, but there was still no action at the window.

'Wait here, I'm gonna see if we can get a better shot from over there.'

I nodded and watched as he crunched further along the path and deeper into the darkness, and then turned back to the window. I knew perfectly well that he was only humouring me by bringing me along, just because I had insisted on coming. He clearly didn't need me. This was his life I was intruding in, and he was used to working on his own.

As I gazed at the inactive window, I wondered what the range on my gun was and if I could have made the shot

When the Mask Falls

without him. Of course, I would have to keep my eyes open if I was ever to hit anything. It didn't matter though, as I never saw anything behind the window.

After what seemed like a frozen eternity, but was probably ten minutes at the most, there was no sign of Jonny and I was now completely bored and so cold I could feel my insides shivering. I looked through the empty branches up at the sky, which was looking lighter, a sure sign that snow was on the way.

I squinted to find where Jonny was, but it was too dark, and the weeds were too thick to see anything at all, so I decided to go after him. In a squat, I worked my way along the alley way, my hands getting scratched to bits by a hibernating wild rose bush.

'Jonny?' I called out in a whispered shout. *Where the hell was he*, I thought, as I pushed passed another large weed. 'Jonny?'

Forcing my way through the undergrowth, the weeds were getting thicker and thicker with every step. I barely managed to contain my cursing as I caught my foot on something and fell face first onto the ground in front of me. I brushed my hands together and reached back to unhook my foot, which as it turned out wasn't caught on a plant or root as I had imagined, but was actually tangled in the shoulder strap of Jonny's rifle.

'Shit!' I cried, louder this time, my eyes searching the dark. 'Jonny, where are you?'

The abandoned gun was heavy to lift and I stared blankly at it as my gut turned on itself. It dawned on me that I was now alone. I sat perfectly still, my backside nailed to the floor as my eyes darted up and down the dark alley frantically searching. I held my breath, never before feeling as lonely and afraid as I was at that moment.

Something had happened and I allowed myself a couple of moments to think before I took a deep breath and acknowledged the fact that he wasn't coming back for his gun or me. This wasn't good, and it was all up to me now.

I hooked the monster of a gun over my shoulder and looked back at the house. Two lights were on now, but still no sign of TJ or Jonny, that's if he was even in there. Think fast. I had two guns I hadn't a hope of operating effectively. This needed something a little cleverer than firepower and I scampered back down the alley and back to the car.

From the safety of the car, I spotted a young lad walking down the street towards me and stopped him. Thankfully, in the dark he didn't recognise me, although he didn't look like he spent much time watching the news or reading newspapers, so he might not have even in the fresh light of day and with an arrow pointing at my head.

For a fiver he agreed to go to the front door and ask for the charity envelope he had supposedly left there the week before. I stood and watched from behind a wheelie bin and nearly cheered when I recognised TJ as he finally answered the door. He looked stressed. Bingo. And I got a good look at his hall which was a bonus.

The lad looked pleased with his fiver, and even more pleased with the twenty I waved at him in exchange for another job. He took the money and waited patiently for me to get into position on the far side of the house, and when I waved at him, he headed back down the drive. This time I told him to be persistent, and boy was he. Just as the kid was about to give up, and with another fiver that TJ was trying to buy him off with, he pretended to hear a noise and ran around the side of the house, distracting TJ and leading him away from the door.

It did the trick and gave me just long enough to sneak in behind him. I jumped behind a door I had spotted from the road, which turned out to be a toilet and not a very clean one by the smell of it. It suited me to hold my breath in there, and not just out of pure terror.

After a couple of minutes, TJ came back, and I followed the sound of his footsteps to my right for about twenty feet. Then a door slammed and the place went quiet again.

No shouting or screaming, no telly, no radio, it was very eerie. I slid the holster on my belt behind me, pulled the rifle forward, found the trigger and with the barrel leading, I slowly inched the toilet door open. It was dark on the other side, but there was no one there, so I confidently stepped out. My heart thumped as my finger trembled over the trigger. *God help us all if I actually have to fire this thing*, I thought, as I inched slowly down the corridor.

I could hear muffled voices behind a door at the end of the hall, most prominently TJ's South African inflected voice. I continued to the door and pressed my ear up against it to listen to the raised voices on the other side.

'I should've just killed you when I had the chance,' Jonny said.

'Yeah, well you didn't, and now here we are. The police are looking for you, by the way, especially your girlfriend, someone must have tipped them off.'

'You grassed?'

'Of course.. You'll be taking the rap for Nancy too. They'll find you soon enough, too, just you won't be in a very chatty mood when they do, not if I have anything to do with it anyway.'

'Listen TJ, you're just a kid, you've got your life ahead of you, just like I did when I was your age. Don't do this. Don't make the same mistakes as I did.'

'Giving me advice granddad?' TJ shouted on the other side of the door. 'I don't fucking think so.'

Then I heard something crash to the floor. That was my cue. I charged at the door, the heavy gun just about poised and ready.

'Everyone get down,' I shouted as I burst through the door.

chapter fifty-three

To my enormous surprise everyone did. In fairness, Jonny had been handcuffed to a radiator and had little choice, but TJ had hit the ground almost immediately and was on his knees with his hands over the back of his head. I forced the gun into the side of his head.

'On the ground. Now.'

The room was a very cosily furnished living room. The walls were decorated with family photos and art from Africa. I doubted TJ had much to do with it; he didn't seem the type, to be honest. I noticed a long cream sofa and two single chairs that were crowded round a TV at the opposite end of the room in front of a large window.

In front of me there was a plastic Christmas tree decorated garishly in brightly mismatched lights, baubles and tinsel, and just behind me to my right an upended cabinet. Glass had been smashed everywhere and I wondered if the family's Crystal had once been kept in there.

I kept the gun firmly against his ear as TJ lowered himself onto the cream carpet, pushing his outstretched hands in front on him. I glanced over at Jonny who was kneeling to my right, his hands pulled tightly behind him. Blood trickled slowly from his eye and the corner of his mouth and I briefly wondered how much more of this his poor body could take.

'What now?' I mouthed to Jonny.

'Shoot him,' he mouthed back.

Of course.

I looked down at TJ and my finger tightened slightly on the trigger of the heavy rifle. I could feel sweat on my neck and my hand felt cold and clammy, despite the gloves. My mouth was suddenly dry. I licked my lips and focused back on the target.

A bead of sweat had dripped into my eye and for a moment I was as good as blind. There no way I was removing either hand from the gun at this point, so I tried to mop it away with my shoulder. That didn't work. I could feel my heart rate shifting up a gear as I focused all my energy on the one finger that was gripping the trigger. *Just do it, come on, it's like shooting Hitler,* I reminded myself, but no matter how hard I tried, I just could not bring myself to squeeze that trigger.

I turned back to Jonny, 'I can't,' I mouthed, 'I'm really sorry.'

'Then get the keys, I'll fucking do it,' he mouthed back.

'Where are the keys to the handcuffs?' I poked the gun into the back of TJ's neck. I could do that alright, but a killer I was not.

'In my back pocket,' TJ mumbled into the carpet.

I looked down and sure enough I could see them bulging in his jeans, and hesitantly, I held the heavy gun in my right hand and slipped the fingers of my left hand into his pocket to retrieve them. Just as I got a finger to them he twisted, and I squealed as his elbow caught the side of my head, sending me and the gun flying sideways.

Everything went fuzzy for a second. I'd lost the gun and the keys. I blinked to clear my eyes just as TJ took a flying leap over me for the gun.

'Shit!'

I snatched at his trouser leg and he came crashing down on top of me, knocking the wind clean out of me and catching his shoulder against the corner of the cabinet he had pulled down. I heard Jonny shouting as I fought to reinflate my lungs and TJ scrambled to get over the top of me.

I could not let him get to that gun.

I caught a quick breath and reached up and found the top of his jeans and dragged him back on top of me again. A swift knee, right between the legs, left him in agony for long enough that I could roll him off and climb out from under him.

The gun was only a few feet away, nestled under the tree. Merry Christmas kids. My trainers bit into the carpet as I clambered to get to it, but TJ was already recovered and had taken hold of my hair and yanked my head sharply backwards.

His evil eyes met mine as my body arched backwards, pulled by his fierce grip on my hair. He leant forward, and then his disgusting mouth was on mine. I shouted into his mouth as his cigarette lips violated mine and pushed his face away with my free hand, but he grabbed my wrist and held my hand away. He was determined and much stronger than me. I was stuck fast as he forced his tongue into my mouth, and without even thinking, I bit down hard.

'Fok!' he screamed, releasing his grip on my wrist. 'Boss was right, you are feisty, maybe you come with me.'

I briefly saw the fist as it came straight for me. I winced, then the lights blinked out.

The pain shooting out of my face was unbelievable. I could feel blood dripping off the side of my face, again, and I could hear Jonny shouting something, but I couldn't make it out. Even my vision had blurred as I felt myself being dragged out of the room by my arms and hair.

'You don't mind if I borrow her for a bit, do you bro?' TJ shouted behind him. 'Didn't think so.'

The lights blinked in and out again. Jonny was still shouting, but I couldn't concentrate at all through the pain in my face. He dragged me as far as the bottom of the stairs, right outside the toilet where I had hidden, and then he was on top of me.

'Time for you and me to have a little fun of our own,' he said.

He had one foot on each of mine, his heavy arms holding mine down against the floor. I was well and truly pinned. Staring down at me, his eyes looked evil. I could feel his hips against mine as he rocked them against me. Now I was wide awake. My heart paused as I worked out exactly what he was going to do next. That was no gun in his pocket, I almost wished it was.

I panicked, screamed at him and tried to push him off, but he must have weighed twice what I did. He just smiled down at me, laughing almost, as if he was getting off on me struggling,

I spat in his face, but that didn't stop him.

He pushed my hands together. He was so strong he gripped both in just one of his, and then his spare hand was working at the fastener on my jeans. I felt my stomach clench as it turned over. He let my hands go and with his full weight pinning me down, pressing the last drop of air out of my lungs, his hands were pushing at the waist band of my trousers. I snatched at tiny morsels of breath and thumped and pushed at him with my own hands, screaming and shouting. He barely seemed to notice.

'Come on Alice,' he laughed. 'Don't be such a prude.'

He had his own fly open and I could feel his rock-hard penis on my leg. Tears flooded my face as he pushed my feet apart, his hands forcing my shoulders into the floor. He rocked his hips and angled himself as I frantically searched the carpet with my hands for something, anything to stop him.

My belt holster was empty, and my hand searched the floor for the missing gun. I found metal and in a panicked heartbeat the gun was in my hand and on a collision course with his head. I caught him right on the temple, spraying my own face with his blood, and he dropped like a stone right on top of me.

chapter fifty-four

It took all my strength to push his heavy body off me, but after a couple of moments I was free. I curled up on the hall floor beside him for a moment and allowed myself a few minutes to sob as I caught my breath. Panting, exhausted, I pulled up my jeans. It was over. Well nearly.

I spat on the floor, anything to get rid of the bitter taste TJ had left in my mouth, before turning around, rolling TJ over onto his front and finally retrieving the keys from his back pocket. I crawled, keys in one hand, gun in the other, down the hallway towards the living room where I had left Jonny.

He looked broken when I crawled back through the door. His head was pressed tightly between his knees and his wrists were bleeding badly from the metal cuffs.

'Jonny?' I said, with all the strength I had, which was not much.

He didn't hear me. His knees must have muffled the sound. I crawled across the floor and touched his face. His eyes popped open when he felt my touch and that smile was back.

'Oh my God, I thought...it doesn't, just thank God.'

I had almost caught my breath by then, and my trembling hands fumbled with the key in the lock of the handcuffs, while we both asked each other the same question, 'Are you ok?' and replied with the same lie, 'I'm fine.'

He held me tight when the cuffs finally clicked open, and I allowed another couple of tears to fall onto his shoulder.

'I'm so sorry,' I sobbed. 'I should've shot him when I had the chance.'

He didn't say anything, just squeezed even harder, which made me want to cry even more. I took a deep breath.

'Come on let's get out of here,' I said.

We both knew what had just nearly happened, but it would remain unsaid. Jonny wiped my blood and tear stained face with his sleeve, collected the rifle from under the Christmas tree, and I followed him out of the room, gripping his hand for dear life.

'Where'd he go?' Jonny asked.

I followed him into the hall and sure enough TJ was gone. There was just a puddle of blood on the carpet as evidence he had ever been there at all. Then the sound of an engine roared from the front of the house. We both looked at each other and had the same thought as we bolted for Jonny's car.

'You drive,' he said, as we skidded round the end of the driveway towards the car.

We both leapt in. I grabbed the keys from Jonny and seconds later I had done a super-fast U-turn and we were in pursuit.

He was already out of sight, but I had the accelerator floored and we were soon closing in on him.

I swung the car into every oncoming gap to overtake the painfully slow drivers that were standing between us and TJ, the sound of horns fast becoming the soundtrack to our impromptu car chase.

There were only two cars between us. Jonny spotted him turning right onto a country lane and we quickly followed behind. It was a mistake for TJ. Nobody else turned, and moments later there was just him and us and I was able to really floor it and close the gap.

When the Mask Falls

Only then did it become clear why Jonny wanted me to drive as he reached out of the window with the Glock and fired off a couple of rounds at the swerving Golf.

The sound it made was deafening and it seemed to echo round the car, but the first few bullets missed. Moments later he let off another couple; one shattered the rear windscreen, another embedded itself in the back of the VW.

TJ's car was veering all over the place as he tried to stay ahead and dodge the bullets. I tried to keep up, but we were already doing over seventy on a tight country road, and I was really struggling. I chased him round a tight corner. Jonny was still shooting, and I was sure he caught one of the rear tyres.

TJ's car skidded badly on the bend and I quickly slammed on the brakes just in time to watch the Golf suddenly skip up into the air in front of me. We fishtailed as I pushed harder on the brake, willing it, begging it to stop in time as we screeched to a sideways halt.

Then we could only watch as TJ's car landed crudely on its roof, just feet away from ours. It skidded across the road, the metal screeching against the tarmac, and then it rolled backwards down the embankment and into a ditch.

The cars wheels were still spinning, and smoke was billowing out from the engine, when Jonny jumped out of his Subaru. He darted over to the upside-down car, his pistol leading. I was helpless, still reeling from the adrenaline of the chase as he disappeared down the embankment. I banged my head on the wheel out of frustration, and braced myself for the *bang* of the gun.

There was no bang, just Jonny dragging TJ by his collar, alive and kicking, out of the car and into the middle of the road. I jumped out of the car as Jonny struck the side of his head with his fist. TJ dropped to his knees, begging Jonny for his life, but he wasn't going to show any mercy, not now. I knew by the fierce look in his eyes and he waited until TJ was back on his feet before he battered him again. He fell onto his side crying out.

My heart thumped, it was all I could do, with my hand over my mouth, as the life was slowly being kicked out of TJ in front of me, thud after ear splitting thud.

When he stopped trying to get up, Jonny dragged him off the floor and back over to the ditch. His opponents face bloody and swollen, it he was virtually unrecognisable. Jonny gripped him by his blood-stained coat. TJ's face only inches from his own.

Jonny was much calmer now and he whispered something to TJ before he punched him to the ground again. I watched his crumpled, broken body as it lay still, but I felt no sympathy for him. He was a monster. I climbed out of the car and headed over. He had no energy, no strength; he didn't even try to crawl away when I walked over and knelt beside him.

'TJ?'

His right eye blinked, his left might have too, but it was far too swollen. His right eye stared up at me as his lungs strained for a gargled breath of air, and then he closed his eye and sighed loudly. He hung in his clothes for a moment, then I lifted his limp wrist and closed my eyes; he was gone.

Jonny looked at me. He was expecting me to say something, or do something and so was I, but there was nothing. I felt nothing. I just got up, sighed heavily, turned and walked solemnly back to the car.

I heard Jonny's gun fire twice behind me. A few moments later, I felt his arms reaching round me.

'You ok?'

I nodded. 'Why did you shoot him?'

'Making sure.'

It scared me that I was glad TJ had died, but then I guess that was normal after someone gets an inch away from raping you. I shuddered and quickly put the thought out of my mind.

'Where to now?' I asked.
'Well, I'm starving, don't know about you.'
Jeez, how could anyone eat after seeing that, I was mystified.

chapter fifty-five

We opted for McDonalds drive thru as we thought the sight of two battered and bleeding people might draw unnecessary attention, plus I didn't want to get recognised again, so we just grabbed the food from the oblivious employee and disappeared to the back of the car park.

Being on the run from the police, and now with a third murder that would surely be placed on my head, meant my stomach was already full of epileptic butterflies. Food was the last thing I wanted, even though I hadn't eaten since that morning, but Jonny was starving, as usual, so we had taken the risk.

It did smell good though, I had to admit. *Well maybe I could squeeze in just one little chip,* I thought, as I dipped my hand.

'Hey, get your own.'

'I only want one, and besides, I did just rescue you, *again,* that's twice now, if anything I should get two.'

'Hard to argue with that kinda logic,' he said, offering me another, then moving the bag out of my reach with a cheeky grin.

'Although,' he continued, 'didn't I rescue you from the security guard at the welcome break?'

'Nah,' I said with a cheeky smile. 'I had him just where I wanted him, if anything, you just got in the way.'

I giggled nervously, it was either that or cry, and left the man alone with his precious chips.

I slumped in the chair, put my feet up on the dashboard and checked my phone again. It was nearly nine and I hadn't heard from Sara since yesterday. She should have been at Gayle's house hours ago. I was sure she was having so much fun that she had just forgotten to text, but still, I couldn't help worrying and I finally gave in and sent a text myself.

Hi, it's mum, just checking you arrived ok. x

The phone bleeped almost instantly. It was Sara and I let out a big sigh of relief as I unlocked my phone to read her message. But it was not the message I was expecting.

Checkmate.

That's all it said. What the hell did that mean? Then the phone bleeped again, and it was a photo message.

I felt sick and held my breath. It was a photo of Sara and Ben. They were kneeling by the fireplace in my living room with tape over their mouths and their hands behind their backs, both looked terrified. The line under the photo read:

Want to trade?

I looked up at Jonny who was still stuffing chips into his gob; he glanced over and caught my gaze.

'What?'

The phone beeped again. This message was from Michael's phone:

Your answer, ten minutes.

I could feel the blood draining into my feet. Suddenly I felt hot and sweat was starting to bead on my forehead. My hand trembled as I handed the phone to Jonny.

Checkmate was right.

I needed air and yanked sharply at the door handle, pushed open the car door and ran to a patch of long grass behind the car. I dropped to my knees and started dry heaving over the grass.

Jonny joined me and held me tightly across my shoulders. Out the corner of my eye I noticed two people staring. I had no energy to run and just continued to heave.

'Come on,' he said, his voice emotionless. 'It's over. Let's go get your kids back.'

'No, no, no,' I said, beating my hand against the frozen ground.

'I texted him back, said we would be there in forty-five minutes. Come on, we have to go now.'

He guided my numb body back to the passenger seat and closed the door behind me. I leant against the door, hugging my knees to my stomach, staring blankly through the windscreen as the car pulled out of the car park. It took one devastating photo to suck every last ounce of energy from my body. After everything we had been through, we were just going to give up, just like that? But what else could we do, I was tired, and I had no fight left.

Checkmate was right.

God knows what was going through Jonny's mind as he drove himself to what was essentially his own execution. I hoped he had something up his sleeve. He hadn't spoken a word since starting the car. Is that how he did those horrible things? Just shut himself down, close his mind, get the job done. I wondered if he learnt how to do that when he was a little boy and Uncle Theo had knocked on his door. The thought made me shudder.

We had made it home well ahead of time, and Jonny pulled over in a side street about two hundred yards from the house.

We both sat quietly in the car. I couldn't even bear to look at him. What could I possibly say? Only one thing came to mind and I reached out, took him in my arms, and as I choked back tears, I simply muttered into his chest, 'I love you' and 'I'm sorry.'

He held me tightly and I think he said, 'I love you too.'

chapter fifty-six

It had been a long day and Carrie had decided it was time to take a break. She and her partner received a severe talking to from their DCI after missing Alice and Jonny at the hotel by only fifteen minutes yesterday, and then again today at the service station by mere seconds. Extra patrol cars had been sent out, and had been on patrol the rest of the afternoon, but the trail had gone cold, again. They had been so close.

They had spent as little time at the station today as possible, trying to keep a low profile. It seemed they were not the only ones trying to keep a low profile though; there had been no activity on Alice's or Jonny's debit or credit cards since yesterday, no activity on either of their phones and no further sightings. To say she was feeling frustrated would be an understatement.

'So, what do we know today that we didn't know yesterday?' David asked, as he unwrapped his Big Mac.

'McDonalds couldn't put together a burger if their golden arches depended on it.' She laughed as she reassembled her McChicken Sandwich.

'I already knew that yesterday.'

'Ok, what do we know?' she said, jabbing her finger against the greasy table. 'We know that our suspects have not left the country, but it looks like they intended to. We searched both their homes yesterday morning and both their passports were found at Alice Walker's, as well as a wallet full of Euros.

'We also know that three tickets were bought for a flight to Jersey for her two kids and one other girl on her credit card yesterday afternoon, just after she phoned her daughter,' Carrie added.

'Yes, and that none of them boarded the flight.'

'So, what now?' she said. 'I feel so close, yet so far away. What are we missing?'

He swiped a blob of ketchup with a couple of chips and shoved them inelegantly into his mouth. Carrie sighed, *what are we missing*, she thought as she stared out the window, watching the cars queuing for the drive thru.

'You know, I am starting to wonder about the Walker cases,' David said. 'Hear me out here ok. What if Michael Walker isn't behind any of the crimes we have been investigating for the past God knows how many years.'

She was intrigued.

'What if it was her, the wife, all along?'

'That would make some sense, but we have had witnesses in the past who have placed him at crime scenes.'

'Yes, but no one has ever actually seen him do anything. What if we got so bogged down thinking it was him, what if we were wrong all this time?'

She drank her coffee and held the cup in her hand as she pondered the idea, occasionally picking at her chips. *What if he was right, and it was her all along? No, couldn't be.*

'We need to get back to the station and start going through all the evidence again, find a new lead, something. Shit David, Michael's no innocent, but we had her down as a harmless victim who worked in a shoe shop.'

She was already out of her chair when her phone rang, and she listened with intrigue as the DCI relayed the details of a serious RTA, one fatality.

Carrie didn't usually attend road traffic accidents. That delightful job was usually left for uniform, but this one was different.

'Come on David,' she said, gathering up the last of his fries and dashing out the restaurant. Change of plans.'

He followed her to the car and five minutes later they were standing beside an upside-down VW Golf. The driver was their South African witness – TJ.

She scanned her torch over TJ's dead body and winced at the sight of what was left of his face. Another murder, and a nasty one at that. Two point-blank shots to the head. This wasn't a murder, this was an execution. And now there was one less witness to the murders at the house in Redmarsh Road.

She thought about the other witnesses and called in for police protection to be assigned urgently. They couldn't afford for any more witnesses to go missing, if they hadn't already. She hadn't been able to contact Michael, Sara or Ben since yesterday, and after this, she was worried about their safety. She shuddered as she imagined them laying in a ditch somewhere.

This was turning into a nightmare, she thought, as her phone rang again. She turned away from the car and started walking slowly back towards David's car as she answered.

'Yes?'

'Carrie?' The DCI. 'The alarm has just been raised at the Walker house at Princess Gardens, get yourself and David there now. Tactical are on their way.' She hung up.

'Shit! David, we gotta go.'

David was talking to a forensics officer by the car.

'Why? What's up?' he shouted.

'It's all kicking off at the Walker house. Tactical have been called in. Come on let's go, this is it.'

chapter fifty-seven

We held each other for as long as we could before it was time to go, and with moments to spare we approached the house slowly by car. But something was wrong, very, very wrong. I couldn't see the drive, and I didn't need to. The flashing blue lights were a big giveaway that something wasn't right.

We sailed casually past and to my horror the front door had police tape across it, the drive was covered in police cars and half the neighbourhood had gathered. There were two ambulances, and a crowd of police were swarming on the drive, talking to each other and into their shoulder radios.

'Oh no, no, no, please no.'

I felt like I was coming apart. Jonny grabbed my arm and pulled me across the car as I struggled to get to the door handle. He just about managed to pull over the car without crashing. I had to get to my kids; I had to know they were ok.

'Alice, stop it, Alice!' He shouted, wrestling to keep me in the car.

'What happened? He said forty-five minutes, what's going on? He killed them didn't he, oh my God?' I could feel myself getting hysterical as my imagination ran wild. He held me tight in his arms while I shouted into his chest, my world unravelling around me.

'I'm gonna check it out,' he said, as I calmed down a bit. 'Wait here.'

I didn't have much choice. He locked me in the car and I buried my head in my hands and prepared for the words no mother ever wants to hear.

After the worst two minutes of my life, the car door opened, and Jonny got back in. His hand quickly found my shoulder.

'It's ok, they are both ok. I saw them standing by the back of the ambulance.'

I sighed and laughed. I was so overcome with relief.

'What happened?'

'I don't know, text Sara and get her to come to the car, and you can ask her yourself.'

I did and a few anxious minutes later she scared the crap out of both of us by tapping on the window. She climbed into the back seat. Apart from looking a little traumatised, she seemed to be unharmed. I still asked though, and she insisted several times that she and Ben were both completely fine.

'I guess you're Jonny,' she said.

'Yeah, Sara is it? Nice to meet you.'

'Same, but listen, you have to go,' she said. I looked at Jonny, but he didn't react. 'Mum they are saying you killed three people. Is that true?'

'It's complicated honey, just tell me quickly what happened?'

'There were two men and Dad,' Sara said. 'They must've got Ben first and then they grabbed me in my bedroom while I was packing to go to Jersey. The men tied us both up and sat us by the fire, and then Dad took a photo and sat watching us for, like, hours. The two men had gone by then. He didn't speak or anything, just sat there smoking a massive cigar and staring at us until you texted to find out where we were.

'Then he smiled, but not his normal smile. He looked evil. He started sending more messages on his phone.

'He was distracted, and I had been working my hands free, so I pressed the panic alarm that Brenda had given me when she had first come.

'About ten minutes later there must have been a noise or something. I didn't hear anything, but Dad suddenly shot over to the window, started swearing and then disappeared. A couple of minutes later Brenda burst in with a gun.'

'Brenda?'

'Yeah, the cleaner dad got, 'cept she isn't really a cleaner, she's a cop and she was working undercover, spying on him all this time. That's why she gave us the panic alarms.'

Me and Jonny just looked at each other; he looked as shocked as I felt.

'She's been trying to catch dad for years, she's really pissed that she missed him. She's pretty keen to find you too, you have to go.'

'Did your dad say where he was going?' Jonny added.

'Nothing, just got up and left.'

'Thanks Sweetie. You'd better go back, do what they tell you ok.'

I got out the car and hugged her tightly, 'I love you and Ben so much, tell him that from me.' She nodded into my shoulder before running back into the hedges, and back to the safety of the police.

I leant on the side of the car and smiled to myself as I watched her sneak back into the garden through a gap in the fir trees. I still had all my babies. I said a thank you prayer under my breath as Jonny made me jump by starting the car. I peered through the window to see him waving frantically at me.

'I think I know where he has gone, get in.'

We were back on the chase, and I was suddenly buzzing with energy again.

We ducked as an unmarked police car flew round us, lights flashing, heading straight for my house. Then, coast clear, we raced away like a bullet from a gun and headed straight for Michael's lawyer's house, the house of Mr Ashley Banks, otherwise known as Ash.

The wiper blades worked hard to keep the screen clear of the snow that had started falling. The house was surrounded by a high wall and an elaborate electric gate; clearly the lawyer was doing well for himself. We had pulled up a few feet away and had paused to take a deep breath and check we were ready. Guns, check. Spare mags, check. Balaclavas, check. We were ready, nearly.

'Jonny, I need to ask you something. I never understood why my dad suddenly killed himself. There was no note, he seemed happy, and even his partner at work couldn't understand it. Do you think Michael could have had anything to do with it?'

'I, er, you should ask him.'

'I will, but I want to know if you think he was capable of it.'

'Listen Alice, don't…'

'Jonny, I need to know.'

'I suppose, he could have, he's done worse.'

'Thanks.' I kissed him on the cheek. 'That's all I needed to know.'

Jonny knew the code for the gate, but it sends a signal inside whenever it opens, so we decided to take the side gate, an un-monitored access point that Jonny had noticed one day whilst checking on the security.

The gate was so overgrown that you wouldn't even have known it was there from the outside, so he hadn't mentioned it as a security concern at the time, thank goodness.

I squeezed myself through a gap Jonny had made when he pushed open the gate. I waited while he followed me through. It was getting colder by the minute and the snow was getting heavier. I checked the gun in my holster, took one last look at Jonny, smiled and took his hand.

The hedges gave us some cover, but there was no view of the house. I turned to follow Jonny. We only made it a few feet when the hedges that had offered us cover suddenly came to life with a series of clicks and I was staring down the barrel of a gun.

I shuddered. We were in big trouble.

Checkmate indeed.

chapter fifty-eight

'Hands in the air,' a voice demanded.

My hands went up and my stomach sank. I looked around at darkened faces. Like me, they were wearing balaclavas; they didn't want to be identified either.

With my hands still in the air, I closed my eyes and bit my lip as a pair of strong hands roughly ran all over my body searching for weapons. I only had the gun Jonny had given me, but the guy continued searching for long after he found it, lingering for longer than I would have cared for in some of my more intimate areas, but I was in no position to complain.

I looked past the end of the gun barrel, past the flakes of snow that had started settling around us, to Jonny, who was getting a similar treatment. He stood confidently, almost defiantly, as they stripped him of two guns and a knife that he had tucked inside his boot. He mouthed *love you* then immediately looked away. He was so brave. I was like jelly.

The gun barrel disappeared, and I felt something on my back. I assumed it was the gun that belonged to the frisky frisker.

Another man with a gun walked Jonny over to the front of the house. A light in the house illuminated the flecks of snow that flickered playfully down to the ground, a magical sight under normal circumstances.

The gun jolted in my back and persuaded me to walk behind Jonny and across the lawn. We stopped and waited for the front door to swing open and Michael, and a man who I presume was his lawyer Ash, stepped out into the light.

Michael smiled and rubbed his hands together before striding out towards me. He was handed the gun that the masked man had taken from me.

He looked quizzically at it for a moment, released the mag, checked and returned it to the gun and yanked back the slide. He pointed the gun at the ground and didn't hesitate before firing it, sending a patch of damp lawn, snow and mud spraying over everyone.

He seemed satisfied and he turned and walked over to me. Standing inches away now, he held my face in his left hand. I locked eyes with his. Those once loving eyes were long gone, or very well hidden behind cold, heartless ones.

Michael turned towards Jonny and ordered him to 'turn round.' He did, and I could see his eyes were fixed on the floor. I looked back at Michael and a moment later my face exploded with the impact of his ringed hand against my cheek.

'Alice!' Jonny shouted.

I squealed as he knocked me off my feet, and I steadied myself with one hand as the other clutched at my throbbing face.

A fight had broken out behind me as I tried to get to my feet. Michael grabbed the front of my coat and dragged me back up so that we were nose to nose. My blurry eyes tried desperately to focus, on him, on anything. God, I hope this is in your plan Jonny.

'Did you think you could bring shame on me like this and get away with it, did you?'

I hung my head silently.

'Alice, answer me!'

I shook my head from side to side, trying to ignore the excruciating pain in my face.

'No Michael, I'm sorry.'

'I'll bet you are,' he said, dropping me back onto my knees.

'Look, there's your boyfriend,' he said, kneeling beside me and pointing at Jonny. He was now being held round the neck. My vision was still blurred, and I could only just make out the shape of him. I'll bet he wished he could say the same about me.

'I *was* going to have him killed, but then I thought maybe we could have a little game first. I like games. You like games too, don't you Alice.'

I nodded gravely.

'Good. A quiz then. Get it right, your boyfriend can go home. Get it wrong, tut, tut, and he will get one of these little bullets somewhere unpleasant.' He grinned inanely. 'This is fun, don't you think Alice?'

I nodded again as a storm of terror filtered through my body. I had pushed through that gate full of confidence and rage, now I was just a bumbling mess again. *Remember your dad, remember what he did to your dad.*

He leant in close and whispered in my ear, 'your boyfriend will be keen to listen, so do speak up. Make sure he hears you ok, Alice.' He turned to look at Jonny. 'Oh, just look at him, he looks so sad, why don't you cheer him up a bit, why don't you tell him how much you love him, huh?'

I looked up. The fuzz had cleared enough that I could see Jonny standing in front of a masked man, a gun pointing straight at the back of his head.

'No,' I said in shaky voice.

'Alice, I am disappointed.'

I looked at Jonny, *please tell me what to do*, I silently begged him and in his own way I guess he did as he stood there, straight as a dye, a blank, cold expression fixed on his face. He had shut down, as I would have to.

I paused to ready myself and looked him straight in the eye, 'I love my husband, always did, you're nothing to me Jonny, just a toy, nothing more.'

Inside falling apart, outside solid as a rock(ish).

'Ooh, you almost gave me chills. That was good. You know, when this is all, over you should consider a career on the stage. Shame, as I was really looking forward to shooting him. On second thought, you know what, it's my game, my rules, I can do what I like.'

I was horrified as he lifted the gun to take aim. I was desperate and in a panic- what could I do?

Remember your dad, Alice, do this for him.

I thought quickly. The odds were stacked heavily against me, but I did have one thing left in my favour, and I lunged forward, grabbing Michael by the shoulders and pushing him backwards. I must have taken him by surprise as he lost his balance immediately and fell back, landing heavily on his arse and dropping the gun behind him.

I grabbed for the gun and straddled him, pressing it straight between his eyes, and I looked him square in the eye.

'It's ok, just leave her, she's not got it in her to pull the trigger,' Michael said, holding his hand up to the man behind me.

Was he right?

'Bet your life?' I said, as he smirked back at me. 'You killed my dad, didn't you?'

'Alice, of course I did. I am surprised it took you this long to work it out.'

'You're a Bastard!' I said, my finger trembling on the trigger.

'Oh, don't be like that,' he said calmly. 'I didn't do it by myself. Your boyfriend was very instrumental.'

I looked around. Jonny was shaking his head and staring at the ground.

'You're lying.'

My fingers tightened around the grip of the gun, my index finger gently squeezing the trigger. My heart pounded as I closed my eyes for a moment.

'If you don't get them, they'll get you,' my dad screamed into my head, again and again. I opened my eyes.

What would Susanna do?

And in a sudden moment of clarity, Susanna looked him straight in the eye and pulled hard on the trigger.

I waited for a bang, or a click or something. Nothing happened.

Shit! What the hell? I stared blankly at the inanimate gun.

'Cock it,' I heard Jonny scream out from behind me. 'The slidey bit.'

My hand shook as I pulled back the slide. A brass coloured bullet sprung out the top and landed on Michael's chest. I pulled the trigger again, harder this time and Michael started laughing out loud.

'Its empty sweetie,' he chuckled. 'See, the slide didn't snap back, you're out, bad luck.'

I tossed the useless gun and wrapped my hands round his neck. I pushed him backwards onto the ground and squeezed as hard as I could. I was out of control and all I could think about was squeezing the life out of him, somehow. Apart from trying to part my hands, he didn't even try to fight me.

He didn't need to, did he? I couldn't hurt a fly, even if I wanted to. If only Jonny had shown me how to do that thing with my thumbs. The guy that had been standing silently behind me decided to intervene and started dragging me backwards by my waist. But I was determined I wasn't going to let go and I just squeezed harder and harder, sobbing noisily, screaming in his face, as it started to turn blue.

The world around me had shrunk. It was just me and Michael and the guy behind me, who now had a knife.

I felt the icy steel press against my skin. He knelt beside me and whispered in my ear, and I realised I had no choice but to let go.

Michael coughed a few times, stood up in front of me and straightened his shirt and collar as if he had just put a tie on; not the behaviour of a man who had just been half strangled by his estranged wife. He pulled his own gun from inside his jacket and pointed it at Jonny.

I was furious, but beaten. Only shameless begging could save us now. Jonny if you have a plan, please God, now's the time.

'That was unpleasant, Alice.' He coughed again.

'Please Michael, I'm sorry. I'm begging you, whatever it is you want, I'll give it to you. I made a mistake with Jonny, I realise that now. I've missed you so much.' I could feel my voice getting higher and higher as desperation started to take over.

'Please, he's not even a quarter the man you are, I can see that now. He's not even worth a bullet. Just let him go, anything you want,' I continued in vain. 'We can start again, just you and me, please.'

Michael lowered the gun slightly; his eyes were hard, staring past the heavy clumps of falling snow. I desperately hoped I had done enough, but then he started to laugh.

'Bullshit. You seriously expect me to believe any of that. You deserve each other.'

He flicked his hand and I was spun round to face Jonny.

'Make sure she watches. I'm bored with this crap now,' Michael said to the guy with the knife. He bent forward so I could see his face. 'Don't struggle Sweetie, you could get a nasty nick off that knife.'

I could feel the cold edge of the knife against my skin, pushing firmly. Still on my knees, eyes closed, my heart thumping so hard it hurt. The snow was starting to settle. I could feel maybe an inch or more under my knees.

My heart stopped as I heard a gunshot. My eyes snapped open to watch Jonny fall to the ground in front of me, the splatter of blood stark against the fresh white snow.

He wasn't dead, but his labouring lungs sounded like they were sucking for air under water. A moment passed and then the gurgling noise stopped, and he lay still.

Silently, I begged him to move, a foot, a hand, anything, but he just lay there, perfectly still, face down in the snow.

Then another deafening bang and the sky turned brilliant white, and then another, and there was thick, acrid smoke. I was deaf and blind. The arm and the knife had gone, and I struggled forward on my hands and knees to where Jonny had been. I called out his name, he couldn't have heard me, I couldn't hear me, or anything else. I kept crawling, kept calling, choking on the caustic smoke.

My eyesight started to clear, and I could just about make out a shape on the ground in front of me. I blinked to clear my eyes further.

'Jonny, oh my God, Jonny.' He was right there in front of me, the snow settling on his lifeless body. I felt a thud in my leg, and my hand shot back, I was bleeding, but I had to get to Jonny. I dragged myself over the snow, warm tears rolling down my frozen cheeks as I found his cold hand.

'I love you, Jonny. I'm so, so, sorry.'

Then another thud in my back. I collapsed over Jonny's unresponsive body, took a final gulp of air, and a second later the lights went out.

chapter fifty-nine

Michael frowned at his reflection in the washroom mirror. He had aged about twenty years in the last week. His eyes were baggy; his skin looked wrinkly and grey, not beautifully aged in an oak barrel like Richard Gere's, more like one foot from the grave.

He had gone well beyond the fashionable two-day stubble too and was starting to look a bit feral. His hair was unruly, and he fingered it with wet hands in an attempt to regain some order to its lanky strands. It was futile. He had run out of time to argue with it anyway, as the queue behind him was growing impatient.

He was escorted, in silence, eyes down, away from the washroom and back to his cell by his guard who, once back at his cell door, locked the door and left him alone again. He winced at his sore ribs as he sat down on his bed, a painful reminder that he wasn't the boss in here, he wasn't likely to forget it.

He cheered himself up by remembering that any time between now and four thirty this afternoon he was expecting a visitor, his first since he had entered his plea in court.

He didn't mind admitting he was getting excited. Everyone in here wanted to kill him, or rape him. It would be nice to talk to someone who liked him. He sat staring at the door, full of eager anticipation.

He whiled away the next three and a quarter hours e-reading Richard Branson's autobiography to a vivid soundtrack of rattling keys, vibrant cursing and slamming doors, until finally his door was opened, and he was summoned. His visitor had arrived.

Butterflies partied in his stomach as he felt a rare moment of excitement; it's amazing what the simple promise of a visitor can do to a man held in virtual solitary confinement.

His hands were cuffed and he eagerly followed his guard down several corridors, waiting at each heavily locked door for the loud buzz and a green light, before he passed through and headed to the next one. Further and further away from the tiny cell he had recently come to call home.

His eyes lit up at the sight of Ash sitting on the far side of a desk in the small interview room. The door was locked behind him and he sat down, wincing, but still beaming from ear to ear. Even the pain in his ribs couldn't bring him down at this moment.

Ash wasn't grinning.

'Thanks for coming. it's so good to see you. I'm going crazy in here.'

'How are you Michael?'

'I'm ok, I'm ok.'

'They told me what happened,' Ash nodded to his ribs.

'It's nothing, don't worry about it.'

'Michael, I am fine. Thanks for asking. So are your kids Sara and Ben if you want to know.'

'I should've asked, sorry.'

'Yes, you should've. They are living in a safe house with two armed cops playing mummy and daddy, at least I assume they are ok. Nobody knows where they are. Funny, the cops get a bit over-protective when the kids' dad puts bullet holes in their mum.'

Michael hung his head. He hadn't even given them a thought.

'You're right.'

'Listen Michael, I am not here to make small talk with you. I'm only here to inform you that I won't be defending you this time.'

'What?'

'I can't help you Michael. I am a witness for the prosecution. I saw you shoot Jonny, your *own* wife *and* two cops. You're on your own now.'

Michael dropped his head onto his cuffed hands. This couldn't be happening.

'Then who should I get?'

'Michael, they've confiscated your assets and you're penniless. The court will appoint someone for you via legal aid.'

Legal Aid! The room started spinning. He closed his eyes to shut it out as his stomach threatened an immediate evacuation of the cornflakes he'd had at breakfast.

He lifted his head as far as he dare, and looked up at Ash, who was standing up, presumably to go.

'Help me, please.'

'Michael, there isn't a lawyer in the land that can get you out of this mess. Take my advice. Change your plea to guilty, play nice, cooperate and you *might* see sunlight before you croak.'

'There must be something?'

Ash pushed the chair neatly under the table and lifted his leather case. 'Michael, listen to me. The list of charges is as long as my leg. You've got more than a dozen counts of murder including three cops, plus attempted murder, soliciting to murder, false imprisonment, arson, you've got possession of illegal firearms, corruption, money laundering, and that's just off the top of my head. Even the inland revenue wants a piece of you. They've got witnesses now and good ones.'

'But I own a judge.'

'The only way Henderson is ever going to be allowed back in a court room is if he gets caught doing over a post office. Michael, it's over.'

Ash knocked on the inside of the security door. 'You are out of options. Do yourself a favour, plead guilty.'

Michael hung his head. 'I can't do that.'

'Then I'll see you and your legal aid team in court.'

The heavy door clunked and pushed inwards to let Ashley out.

'Good luck Michael.'

He was alone again, completely alone, but there was no way he was going to plead guilty. Not a chance in hell.

Witnesses can still be influenced, even from jail. He wanted his day in court. He wanted to watch as all those insufferable witnesses stood in front of him and dare to disparage him. He wanted to memorise their names and faces.

He might be destined to a permanent change of address, but that didn't mean he couldn't have a little fun while he sought revenge on each and every one of the filthy traitors.

chapter sixty

I don't know how long it had been since the lights went out, could have been hours, maybe months, I really had no concept of time any more.

What I did know wasn't much. At the start, I wasn't even aware of my own body, but it floats in and out now. When it's here I test my fingers and toes, wriggle my nose, it's become a bit of a ritual, but nothing ever happens. I don't even know which way is up, sometimes it just feels like my empty head is floating about in this dark place.

I thought I could smell something earlier, it smelt good, whatever it was, but I never smelt it again. I often wonder if I just imagined it, just like the voices that sometimes come and go, all familiar, but I have no idea who they belong to or what they are saying.

In the beginning, I couldn't even remember who I was, but I concentrated for ages and ages and eventually it came to me. I am Alice. But that didn't really help much, as I have no idea who Alice is, or why she is here in this dark place.

Ah well. Back to my thoughts. But how is anyone supposed to think with that God-awful racket going on. Wait. Now I could hear? I recognised the noise, it was familiar, but I didn't like it. Then voices, then the noise went away, thank God. I sighed.

My hand felt warm again. *Move fingers.*
They moved.

Holy shit, this was news. I was getting quite excited. I flexed them again, more this time. Someone had their hand in mine, and they squeezed back. What was that smell? Oh no, TCP, I hate that smell.

Ben and Sara were arguing, no surprise there, they always argued, worse than Tom and Jerry. But it made me smile. I hadn't smiled for a while, and it felt good. Light shined around my eyes, it was bright and painful, *stop it*. I tried to move my head, to ask them to stop, but nothing came out. I tried my eyes again – nothing.

When I woke up again, I felt exhausted, like I'd run a marathon. The bed was not comfortable at all, but when I tried to move nothing much happened. I was just so tired.

It was quiet, aside from the irritating bleeping of the heart monitor – wait, now, I'm not a doctor, but I am almost sure the bleeping means you are not dead.

A good sign, I think.

I took a few deep breaths and found some energy from somewhere. I forced my dry scratchy eyes to open. I could hardly see anything at all at first. Blinking helped a little, but then I realised it was just dark.

I lifted my head slightly and dropped it down onto the pillow again; just that small act was simply exhausting. The monitor continued to beep, irritating and reassuring at the same time. I couldn't move, even if I wanted to. I had wires and tubes coming out from virtually everywhere, even my mouth.

A stream of light was making my eye twitch. I squinted as I opened it. It was blinding, and I tipped my head to avoid it. Then there was a flurry of activity and suddenly two strangers were staring down at me.

One of the people, a man, spoke gently to me while the other, an ageing woman, started scribbling on a clipboard.

'Good morning Alice, my name is Brian. I'm a nurse here at the hospital,' he said softly. 'How are you feeling this morning?'

The woman took my hand and lifted my arm off the bed. I couldn't see what she was doing but I think she was taking my blood pressure.

I looked up at Brian and opened my mouth to speak. The tube was gone, but my throat was so dry I must have sounded like a chain smoking frog as I made a series of random noises.

'That's ok, you've been sleeping a while, just nod for now, ok?'

'Are you in any pain, Alice?' the woman asked.

I shook my head. I wasn't.

'That's great,' Brian replied.

The female nurse shined a light in my eyes. I could feel myself getting irritable and imagined what it would be like to punch her. I laughed, then coughed.

'Do you know where you are?'

I nodded. He already told me that, didn't he?

'Do you know why you are here?'

I shook my head.

'Why?' I just about croaked.

My voice was loosening up.

The female nurse asked me to squeeze her fingers with my right hand, and after a moment of resolute concentration I lifted what I thought was my right hand and grasped her fingers.

'Your kids will be so happy to see you're properly awake,' Brian said. 'Can you tell me their names?'

'Sara and Ben. Where's Michael?'

'Who's Michael?'

'My husband.' I coughed again, this was hard work.

'What ages are your kids?'

'Fifteen and Seventeen.'

There was some sort of commotion outside, and then moments later Sara and Ben burst through the door and into my little room. I beamed at the sight of them, both safe.

'Mum!' they both shouted at once.

Brian smiled. He had nice eyes and a friendly smile, and I smiled back, 'Looks like you have visitors. I'll come and talk to you again later. You're doing great.'

I watched him whisper to the kids and then leave.

I got a kiss from each of them as they sat on either side of me, both looking really worried. They had one of my hands each in theirs. It felt nice and for a moment I forgot about everything else and just closed my eyes and listened to them rattling off their dramas.

When I woke up the kids had gone. I felt stronger this time and pushed myself into a half- seated position. It was a little more comfortable than lying down, but only just. My throat was still really dry, so I filled a plastic cup from a jug beside the bed and started sipping it. It was so cool and refreshing; it felt amazing on my sore throat.

It wasn't long before Brian, the friendly nurse, came back to visit.

'Hey, you're up, how are you feeling?'

'Much better, thanks.'

'You sound better too,' he said. 'Any more clues as to why you are here?'

'No, not yet, please just tell me?'

He perched sideways on the bed and looked straight at me, 'Well, you were in an accident and you were shot.'

'Oh God. Why? What happened?'

'The important thing is that you are ok, but you have been in a coma.'

'How long?'

'Just over three weeks in total.'

Three weeks. How could this happen? Memory, damn you, let me in.

Then later, during a nap, it did, and the whole bloody scene flashed in front of my eyes; snow, gun shots, smoke, Jonny.

'Oh no, Jonny?'

I woke up shouting and screaming and seconds later Sara came bursting in.

'What is it, are you ok?'

'Where's Jonny, is he alright?'

'Jonny is fine.' She looked very relieved. I can't imagine what she thought I was screaming about.

'Where is he, why isn't he here?' I said, trying to get out of bed.

'Mum, I think you need to get some rest for now, just try to stay calm,' she said, pushing me back into bed.

'No, tell me about Jonny, where is he? I want to see him.'

'Get some rest.'

'Sara!'

Moments later a nurse came in. She had obviously heard the commotion I had made.

'Is everything all right in here?'

'I just want to know what's happened to Jonny, why won't anyone tell me?'

'Jonny is just fine, but you are not, you need to rest,' she said. 'Just rest.'

'Why won't anyone tell me?'

'She's right mum, you do look tired. I'll call back tomorrow ok.'

And just like that they disappeared, and I was all on my own again with only my over active imagination for company. I curled up in the bed with a spare pillow to hug and tried to imagine what on earth had happened that they couldn't tell me about.

I knew he was ok, Brian had said so, but if that was true, why wasn't he here and why was everyone being so coy? I desperately wanted to see him though, to make sure he was ok.

They were right about one thing – I was tired. Clearly, three weeks uninterrupted sleep just wasn't quite enough.

'Jonny!' I sat bolt upright in the bed, drowning in my own cold sweat, but it was just another dream. I held my chest and sighed. That was the third one. They were so real. I banged my head against the head board and decided to get out of bed and go for a walk.

My wobbly legs barely kept me upright as I took the two steps needed to get to the door. I was met by two men camped outside the door, both sitting, gazing into nowhere on very uncomfortable looking chairs.

The one with the moustache quickly nudged the other one, who looked half asleep.

'Good evening Mrs Walker, do you need something. I'll have someone bring it to you?' He got out of his chair.

'Who are you?'

'I'm Detective Pull, and this is Detective Whiteman,' said the moustached officer.

'What are you doing here?'

'Mrs Walker, you should go back to bed, I'll get a nurse for you.'

He held my arm as I glanced along the bright white hospital corridor. Not a soul in sight and barely a sound either, just the feint bleeping of a monitor in the distance and a quietly ringing phone. I turned back to Detective Pull, who was the only thing keeping me upright.

'You didn't answer my question.'

'We are just here to keep you safe. You need your rest, please go back to bed,' he said, walking me back towards the bed.

'Fine,' I said, gripping on to him for dear life.

He helped me across the room and back into bed before returning to the corridor.

That was exhausting, even with his help.

I curled up on the bed and remembered the picture on the telly from the hotel room, the newspaper, getting tackled in the service station car park, and I sighed.

Jonny wasn't there for me because he was in jail. It was obvious now and as soon as I was better, that's where I'd be too. The coppers weren't there to keep me safe; they were there to make sure I didn't escape.

chapter sixty-one

The man pulled the balaclava over his short blonde hair and rolled it down his neck, leaving only his blue-grey eyes visible to anyone that looked, but they wouldn't look. It was just after three a.m., no one would look, at least they wouldn't until he was long gone, and then all they would have to look at was the grainy CCTV images he would inevitably leave behind.

He climbed out of his battered Ford Escort and slammed the door shut behind him. He inhaled sharply and shivered violently as he took in a bracing, minus ten-degree breath. He quickly glanced over the frozen car park. Apart from a couple of people taking a brave smoke just outside the main entrance, the place was deserted, just as he expected.

His leather gloved hand drew his fifteen-inch Delta Force survival knife smoothly from the sheath that was fixed to his hip and, pulling his leather jacket tightly closed, he angled the knife vertically along the length of his arm and marched straight for the hospital's maintenance entrance.

He punched in the key code and the door popped open. He poked his head through the door, cautiously checking for any sign of life. There was none, just as he expected, so he committed his whole self and pulled the door closed behind him.

So far, so good. Of course, he had had three weeks to plan, re-plan and plan again his unwelcome hospital visit.

Nobody expected her to stay in a coma for three weeks, and there had been doubt for a while she would even come out of it at all. The Boss would probably have preferred that, he thought. But now that she was awake, he had a job to do, a job for which he had already been paid handsomely.

He walked along the maintenance corridor and turned into the kitchen; empty just as it had been the four times he had practised this journey. The service elevator waited patiently for him as he swiped his staff pass across the sensor. The lift co-operatively drew its doors back and he stepped into the vast space.

His heart started racing as the lift rose through the building, cheerfully dinging as he passed each floor; eleven, twelve and the final ding. Floor thirteen. His heart skipped, and he could feel sweat dripping down his back as he waited for the doors to slide open again.

This was the bit he had never practised, never at night anyway. He was running short of breath as he turned out of the lift and headed straight for the bathroom.

'Get a grip of yourself,' he snapped, as he glared at his black woolly face in the mirror. He had taken everything into account, left no detail unchecked, but never had he considered the effects of the adrenaline. How could he? He had nothing to compare it to. He rested the knife on the top of a waste bin and placed both hands on the edge of the sink while he took deep breaths and reminded himself of the script he had practised a million times in his own bathroom. He had it word perfect, just as he had the last few times. He just needed to calm down, and after a few minutes of deep breathing he felt his thumping pulse starting to ease off.

He checked his watch. He had to hurry. The two coppers that he was told would be on duty would be knocking off soon, and then he would be too late and would have to start over tomorrow. He didn't think his heart could take another battering like the one it was getting tonight.

It was now or never.

He checked his pockets. Two syringes, just to make it look like they weren't in on it. He picked up the knife, had a good shake and growled at himself in the mirror.

He was ready, and he stepped out into the corridor and marched towards the ward. His stolen staff pass granted him access and he turned right and headed for room one, which was fortunately the first room he would come to. The place was empty. *Thank goodness,* he thought, as he headed straight for the two guards who sat dutifully outside her room.

They looked straight at him as he approached, head held high, trembling inside.

'Pull, Whiteman?' He said, disguising the tremor in his voice.

'Yes,' they both said together, looking him up and down.

'Time for a nap,' he said, pulling two preloaded syringes from his pocket and jabbing one each into their legs. The officers obligingly slumped and peacefully drifted off to sleep in their chairs.

Without hesitation he quickly pushed into the room. The nurses weren't due to check on her for at least another thirty minutes, so he had time; the plan was working perfectly.

The room was pitch black, but he could clearly make out the outline of Mrs Walker under the sheets, and he watched for a minute as she snored peacefully, completely unaware of the danger she was in.

He was getting turned on just thinking about the power he held in his hand and he could feel himself getting hard. He cursed himself for getting distracted and took a deep breath and re-focused.

He padded quietly around the bed, gazing at her. *She really was a very attractive woman,* he thought, as he sat down beside her. Placing the sharp edge of the knife against her throat, he ran his fingers through her hair, teasing and stroking as he gently brought her out of her peaceful sleep.

'Wakey, wakey, sleepy head,' he whispered.

chapter sixty-two

Jonny looked at the alarm clock beside the bed. It was one a.m. and so far he had managed exactly zero hours of sleep. At first, he put it down to the strange bed. Lots of people have trouble sleeping in a strange bed or a strange room, but as the days ticked past he realised it had nothing to do with the room.

'Well, at least I tried,' he said to himself as he rolled out from under the duvet and pulled on a pair of tracksuit bottoms. He padded slowly down the hall to the living room.

The TV, decorated with a solitary strand of silver tinsel, the only evidence of Christmas in the flat, was already on. Brenda was sitting with her legs folded under her on the dark brown sofa, laughing at an Irish comedian on the screen. She looked up and followed him with her eyes as he walked barefoot across the room, crouched on the floor and clinked through a cabinet filled with bottles.

'What happened to the bottle of scotch?' he said, looking over his shoulder at Brenda.

'You finished it yesterday,' she answered, and then burst into fits of laughter at another of the Irishman's jokes. 'You should watch this, he's hilarious.'

'Did I? Shit,' he muttered under his breath.

'There's beer in the fridge.'

He stood up and headed to the kitchen for a beer instead. He snapped the lid off the bottle and Brenda watched him pad back across the living room in the front of the TV. She watched him pace back across the room for a second time before interrupting.

'Still can't sleep huh?'

'Uh uh.'

'I don't know what to suggest.'

'Yes, you do.'

'You know it's not up to me.' She unfolded her legs and sat forward on the sofa to pick up a glass of coke.

'Brenda?'

'You can either join me on the sofa or go back to staring at the ceiling in bed, best I can do, choice is yours.'

'Brenda, I am never going to get a wink of sleep until I know she's ok.'

'I told you, she's ok, and I shouldn't have even done that.'

'Yeah, you *told* me,' he protested, glugging the last drop of beer. 'I need to see for myself. I need to know how ok.'

Brenda huffed. 'She sat up, ate some food and she's been talking. She's weak, but she's ok, please just drop it.'

'Did she ask for me?'

'Jonny, please.'

'Did she?'

'We've been over this.' Brenda relaxed back into the comfy chair and turned her eyes back on the screen.

'Come on, it's the middle of the night. No one even has to know. Just let me poke my head round the door, see she's ok and then I'll come back quietly, I promise.'

'I don't even believe *one* word of that. No.'

'Come on, where's your Christmas spirit?' He strode across the room and stood firmly in front of the screen.

'No.'

'Brenda!'

'You will have my arse fired,' she said, trying to peer round the side of Jonny.

'They would never fire your arse, it's far too pretty.'

'Begging and flattery now. How could a girl resist? Unfortunately having a pretty arse doesn't get you as far as you'd think in the police.'

Jonny dropped onto his knees and put his hands together, and with his best begging eyes, said 'Please.'

Brenda flicked the TV off, lifted her gun off the seat beside her and stood up out of the chair exhaling loudly.

'Five minutes?'

'Not even.' His smile started growing.

'You are supposed to be under house arrest, you know, for your own protection.'

'Yes, yes, I won't tell, so we can go?'

'If we do, it'll be the last I hear about it from you?'

'Yes, yes, promise.'

'Fine,' she huffed, poking the gun into her belt holster.

Jonny threw his arms around her, giving her a squeeze so hard she could barely breathe, then bolted out of sight as Brenda shouted down the hall after him.

'I always wondered what it would be like to work as a security guard. Hey maybe I'll get one of those scary Alsatian dogs. I'll call it Lollypop.'

'You're very funny.' Jonny grinned as he skipped back into the living room minutes later, fully dressed except for the trainers he was awkwardly hopping into. 'Ready?'

His feet barely touched the floor as he bounded out to the front door. He waited anxiously for Brenda to unlock the door and brief one of the officers standing guard at the front door. The second one would tag along for the long drive.

Jonny tapped his foot nervously in the back seat of Brenda's car for the entire two-hour drive. He had originally figured three hours but had failed to take into consideration the fact that at that hour of the day the roads were virtually empty. He had also failed to consider the enthusiasm of Brenda's right foot to get there and back before she got found out. He wasn't complaining.

At exactly ten past three in the morning, the black Mercedes roared into the car park of the St Helens Private Hospital. If it wasn't for the security doors of the unmarked Mercedes, he would have been across the car park already and banging on the front door, but he was forced to wait for Brenda to open the door for him.

She turned in her seat and winked at him before checking her lipstick in the rear-view mirror. Jonny was about fit to explode as she casually licked her finger and slicked back her eye brows before slowly pushing open her own car door.

She exchanged words with her partner, who laughed while Jonny knocked petulantly on the window. Brenda bent down and waved playfully back at him, teasing him. *Cruel bitch*, he thought, and he waved back, but with only one finger.

When the car door finally popped open he jumped out and continued his solo fingered wave as he sprang across the car park towards the front door.

The door slammed shut after two nurses who had just snuck out for a sneaky fag.

So, he waited, not so patiently, until his guards caught up.

He was reminded in no uncertain terms to stay calm and quiet. He nodded as she reminded him how serious this was and that her job was on the line if he were caught anywhere near the hospital. He didn't want that. Brenda was, without a doubt, an angel, so he took a deep breath and reluctantly fell in behind the two detectives as they led him over to the lift.

The lift took its time, and he watched impatiently as the numbers lit up in descending order, indicating it was on its way. Four, three, two. Then the doors slid open and they all piled in.

He had no idea where she was in this hospital and was completely at the mercy of Brenda, who seemed to know her way around well enough.

The elevator stopped at floor thirteen. Unlucky for some. He shuddered at the thought of it and followed Brenda to a security door, where she turned and pressed her finger over her lips, to remind him again to be calm and quiet.

chapter sixty-three

My heart pounded like a stampeding army of horses as the cold steel of the knife cut into my shivering skin. I looked across the snow and there was Jonny's still body, lying face down in the blood-stained snow. Then my eyes shot open and I lurched forward, swimming in my own sweat again, my hands on the bed propping me up. I gasped for breath as I had already done so many times that night.

But, this time I could still feel the cold steel against my neck. Maybe I wasn't fully awake after all.

'Careful Mrs Walker, we don't want any accidents, do we?' a voice whispered into my ear.

I gasped again and my eyes pinged open as his leathery hand pressed down over my mouth.

This wasn't a dream, and I could feel blood trickling down my neck. I closed my eyes, and tried to scream through his gloved hand, but nothing more than a feeble mumble came out. Where were my guards, for God's sake?

'Now, now, things will go a lot smoother if you just relax Mrs Walker. Just take some deep breaths and then we will talk ok.'

Just do as he says. Someone will be along soon to help you. Just do as he says, and this will all be over soon. I couldn't shout or run, and even if my legs could carry me away fast enough, my arse felt like it was nailed to the bed. I was trapped.

I nodded slightly and started breathing as best I could through my nose. I used to like the smell of leather – not anymore.

'Now, I'm going to take my hand away from your mouth. Can you stay calm for me?'

I nodded again. The sharp knife cutting into my skin certainly persuaded me that I could give it a bloody good try.

The hand slowly slipped away from my mouth and his shadowy body came into my eye line. He changed hands on the knife and sat round on the bed facing me.

In the darkened room I could only see his eyes. They looked afraid. Not as afraid as mine though, I'm sure.

'You look tired,' he said, as he put a hand behind my back and laid me down on the bed, the knife still reminding me to be quiet. 'There, that's better, isn't it?'

'What do you want?' I think my trembling voice said.

'Mrs Walker, I am not here to hurt you, I have a message to deliver, that's all.'

A message? Most people send a text or an email these days, this was no ordinary message.

'You are very pretty, Mrs Walker.'

I closed my eyes and cringed as he leant forward, allowing his whole weight to pin me to the bed. He stroked the side of my face with his free hand, and whispered in my ear.

'Mr Walker wants you to know how happy he is that you are getting better. But he thinks it would be a mistake for you to talk to anyone about him. He thinks it would be much better if you somehow forgot what had happened.' He spoke slowly and carefully. 'No witness has ever lived long enough to testify in court against him. They all just seem to keep disappearing. He wanted me to warn you that he would hate for that to happen to you, your kids or your precious boyfriend. I'm in no doubt you'll make sure the message gets around.'

I coughed a little as he pulled his heavy body away from mine. I flinched, and my hand grasped at my throat as the sharp knife caught my skin.

'Woops, see how easily accidents can happen,' he said.

He held a finger over his masked lips reminding me that this was not over yet, and I forced myself to hold in a scream. The pain in my neck was getting worse, and I could feel the blood oozing through my fingers. He wiped the knife on his trousers and leant forward with one final message.

'This didn't happen? Oh, and wait for at least fifteen minutes before calling for help or I'll be back and next time I won't be quite so friendly.'

I nodded, gripping the wound on my neck with both hands now, panting quietly, as his shadow walked slowly round the end of the bed towards the door.

chapter sixty-four

'Five minutes, you promised,' she said, adjusting the holster under her coat.

'Yes, come on, come on.'

She shook her head, resigned. 'I am so fired.' She said as she waved her pass over the sensor and the door clicked open.

He followed them calmly down the hall, trying not to get seen, but by who? No one was there, but he did it anyway. Then, for no obvious reason, Brenda started sprinting, drawing her gun as she ran, followed closely by the other detective, who was shouting random numbers into his ear piece.

As they pulled away, the problem became obvious. Two police officers were slumped in chairs by the door of what he presumed was Alice's room.

Horrified would have been an understatement. He was frozen solid, watching, as his own body guards left him in the hall and crashed through the door to Alice's private room.

He came to his senses when he heard shouting coming from the room and charged after them, pushing through the door, only to see Alice curled up on the bed, trembling, her hands tightly covering her face.

'...find him, he might still be here.' Brenda barked into her radio, one arm round Alice. The other officer pushed out past him. Then he noticed the blood, lots of it, all over Alice's clothes and sheets.

'Get a nurse,' he screamed, as he pushed past Brenda to get to Alice.

'Alice, it's Jonny,' he said gently, pulling her arm away from her face. 'It's ok, I'm here, you're safe now.'

She looked up at him, and he could see the blood trickling down her neck, 'Get a fucking nurse, Brenda!'

He wrapped her up in his arms and rocked her as she sobbed and bled onto his shoulder, until the nurse arrived, and he was dragged out by Brenda.

The door closed loudly behind him. He stepped out of her private room and into the chaos that had kicked off outside. A team of nurses were working on the two vaguely familiar officers that were taking a bewildering nap in the hall.

He was seething, anger boiling inside him. He stepped over one of them and looked down the hall to a group of police officers standing by the lift. One looked up and saw him coming and quickly started backing away. Brenda saw him too and broke away from the herd to meet Jonny just ahead of the group. She raised a hand to the rest of the officers as Jonny picked up the pace, blood boiling, eyes fixed on her.

'God help you if she's not ok.' His voice crackled. 'This is your idea of protection?'

She put her hand on his chest, which he batted straight off, so she walked towards him, backing him away from the group of now gawking officers, with her hand raised as a sign to the other officers to stand down.

'Come on Jonny, just calm down.'

At 5' 4, she just about made it up to his chin, but she was not intimidated by his size, not for a second.

'Calm down? What the fuck? She could've been killed in there, on *your* fucking watch, who are these...'

'Jonny, I am asking you to calm down,' she said gently, backing him further down the hall.

'You know, I only agreed to all this because you said it was the only way you could keep her safe, well. What. The fuck. Is this, Brenda? Those two arseholes let a man with a fucking knife into her room.'

'She's fine and we'll find him. I can see you're upset, but this is not helping.'

He raised his fist at her, and she didn't flinch, so he thought better of it and smashed it down against the wall with a thud.

'Jonny, I don't want to arrest you, but I will if I have to. Please, just take a deep breath and calm down.'

'I should've been here, Brenda. You should have been keeping her safe, you promised me.'

chapter sixty-five

Turned out it was only a surface cut, my first bit of luck since I got here, if you don't take into consideration that I was just threatened by a knife wielding psycho.

I listened to the shouting outside as the nurse tenderly cleaned up the blood that had managed to get just about everywhere, and dressed the cut. It felt like my whole throat had been opened and I must admit I felt a little embarrassed when she told me it was less than an inch.

After she left, I listened to Jonny shouting outside the door. I couldn't hear what he was saying, but I knew a thud when I heard it and wondered if someone had punched him to get him to shut up.

I couldn't just sit there listening anymore, so I dragged myself off the bed and wobbled over to the door and pulled it open. The two guards were being piled onto stretchers, which explains why they didn't stop the man with the knife. But I was more interested in all the commotion and my eyes followed my ears down the hall.

Jonny was rubbing one hand with the other, obviously he had lost it and taken it out on the wall. I sighed as I gripped onto the door frame. He was shouting at Brenda, my housekeeper, and I smiled apologetically as she glimpsed me in the door.

'Jonny,' she said, trying to get his attention.

'Police fucking protection, do you even check the people you put on to guard people …'

'Jonny,' she tried again.

'Jesus, he could have killed her, Brenda...'

'Jonny!' she snapped.

My right leg wobbled, and I instantly realised I had less than half a second to find something solid to lean on. My eyes darted for something suitable. I caught Brenda's glance, but it was too late.

'Whhoooops,' I said, as I hit the floor.

Now on my hands and knees with my arse poking out the back of the hospital gown they make you wear, there were at least a dozen or more cops and nurses looking on. Just peachy! But hey, at least it got their attention and a millisecond later Brenda was crouching beside me, followed quickly by Jonny, both barraging me with 'are you ok?' and 'are you hurt?'

'See what I have to do to get you to visit.' I joked with burning cheeks.

I grinned as Jonny lifted me clean off the floor and took me back into my room, followed closely by Brenda and then a nurse I didn't know. Jonny put me back on my bed and sat down beside me, and the nurse told me once again that I needed to get some rest. *Broken record love*, I thought as she and Brenda left.

'Hi.'

Jonny opened his mouth to speak, then changed his mind and started crying, and so did I. It was such an overwhelming relief to see him again, so much better than the residual image I had of him lying face down in the snow. I held him till it hurt, but that didn't take long, for every inch of me seemed to ache.

'Seriously,' Jonny said, wiping his eyes. 'Are you alright?'

'I'll be fine, honestly, just stop picking fights with people ok, you promised me, remember.'

We both laughed, and it felt good to laugh.

'I've missed you. I've been going out of my mind this past few weeks.'

'What happened?'

'Oh, well, that is a very long story.'

'Well, I'm not going anywhere,' I said.

'But you look knackered. I'll tell you tomorrow, I promise.'

'Only if you promise.'

Brenda appeared in the door, 'Ready to go?'

'You are kidding me!' Jonny said, looking over his shoulder.

'I promised you five minutes, we've been here for over an hour. I'm in enough trouble as it is.'

'I'm not leaving now, not after...'

She took his arm and dragged him into the corner of the room, and I watched them argue in a whisper for a few minutes.

In the meantime, a nurse checked on me and reminded me that I should get some rest. This time I agreed with her and curled up on the bed with a pillow and drifted off, leaving Jonny and Brenda to argue quietly by the window.

chapter sixty-six

Jonny must have won the argument with Brenda, as he was snoring in the chair beside me when I woke up the next morning. Brenda was sitting by the door doing a Sudoku puzzle.

'Don't you ever get any sleep?' I said quietly, so as not to wake Jonny.

She looked up, 'I'll sleep in an hour when I get off. How're you feeling?'

'You know.'

'Hmm.'

'I should apologise for being so mean to you, you know before, when I thought you were a housekeeper.'

'Don't worry about it, Mrs Walker!'

'I guess I deserved that. Did you really clean the skirting boards?'

'Cleaned and bugged!'

I wriggled into the pillows to get comfortable.

'Brenda, tell me what happened. Last thing I remember was Jonny lying in the snow. I thought he was dead.'

'So did everyone. He was in a very bad way when the paramedics got to him, you both were.' She tucked her pen into the book and closed it as she spoke. 'You have your daughter to thank for the fact that neither of you are dead. She is such a bad liar.'

I chuckled, that was true.

'She had disappeared for a few minutes at your house and I just knew something was wrong. When I asked her where she had been, she had a bit of trouble coming up with a cogent answer, so I took her phone off her and saw she had met you out the front.

'We had everyone out looking for your car and eventually we found you, just in the nick of time.'

'They told me I got shot.'

'Twice.'

'Who shot me?'

'Michael did. We found your car and stormed the house. It was chaos. He tried to run, but we got him. Unfortunately, not before he killed two police officers and shot you. Lucky for you; you caught one in your backside and one in your shoulder. He wasn't a very good shot, turns out.'

I laughed, 'You should tell him that, it would really piss him off. He likes to think he is good at everything.'

'I'll make a note do that.' She grinned and re-opened her book.

'Brenda, am I going to jail?'

'Why, what have you done?'

'On the news, they said I was wanted for murder.'

'You were, but Jonny explained everything, it's fine.'

'He told you *everything*?'

I looked over to him, all hunched up on the chair, muttering incoherently in his sleep. I couldn't imagine he had told her quite everything.

'Yep, everything.' She paused and smirked as she glanced over at Jonny. 'I can be very persuasive.'

'What did you do, shine a light in his eyes, drop water on his head?' I giggled.

'After they finished saving his life, and fixed some very dodgy DIY first aid, we had a little chat, and I offered him a deal he couldn't refuse.' Then she winked. 'He loves you a lot you know. He has been driving me mad for the past two weeks at the safe house.'

I smiled at that. I wanted to ask her more about the deal but two nurses and two, not so subtly armed guards arrived to wheel me off for an MRI scan. I guess that question would have to wait, and I left Brenda watching over Jonny.

When I woke up again I was curled up on my side. Jonny was wide awake and loosely holding my hand while he read a newspaper that was spread out over my body.
'Hiya.'
He looked up from his paper and smiled.
'Well, good afternoon.' He grinned, and that cute dimple was back. Oh, how I missed that; it had been a while.
Apparently, I had massively underestimated how scary the MRI machine might be, and they had sedated me – again. More sleep, just what I needed.
I smiled back and wriggled to sit up. But as I looked around the room, something was different, very different. I was stunned as I took it all in. First, a new person was sitting and reading a book in Brenda's chair; a grey-haired man in his late fifties. I didn't recognise him at all. But that wasn't why I was feeling speechless. I was speechless because Christmas had arrived and had exploded all over my room.
At the end of the bed, on one of those hospital bed tables with wheels on, was a miniature Christmas tree. It was a pre-decorated one with cute little flashing lights at the ends of all the branches. Surrounding the tree were four gifts, all wrapped in brightly coloured paper. There was an assortment of red, gold and silver tinsel draped all about the place; it was wrapped round the end of the bed, the window, even the drip stand and door handle had been decorated.
'You like?'
I was grinning like mad. I liked a lot.
'How? When?'
'Sara helped, and Brenda. Thanks to you having a little wobbly at the MRI, we had more time than we thought we would.'

When the Mask Falls

'You're welcome.' I grinned a little more.

Jonny wheeled the table closer and helped me sit up straight, and I got a better look at all the presents. They were all for me. I picked up the biggest one, of course; always start with the biggest. The tag said it was from Mum and I gave it a squeeze. It felt like a book wrapped up in a jumper. That's what she always got me. There was one from Brenda and one from the kids.

'But now I feel bad. I didn't get anything for anyone.'

'You woke up, it's the best present I ever had.'

'What day is it?'

'December twenty-fourth.'

I picked up the fourth one, a box about four inches square and gave it a shake. It didn't rattle.

'This one is from you.'

'Yep.' He grinned.

'You know, it could be considered very cruel to make a sick woman wait to open her pressies.'

'Really?'

'Definitely. I think I should be allowed to open at least one, under the circumstances.'

'Oh, under the circumstances.' He made a playful frown. 'Go on, you can open mine.'

I peeled back the sticky tape while my mind worked overtime trying to guess what could possibly be inside.

I pulled back the paper to reveal – another layer of paper, red this time. I frowned at his grinning face, and worked on the next layer of paper, which revealed, another layer of gold paper.

'You know, I might need another nap after all this effort.'

He watched intently, his grin growing with each layer of paper until I finally got to a cardboard box. I wrestled the tape off the box and opened it to find handfuls of pink shredded paper, which in turn concealed a very small box.

I pulled the box free of the packaging, shaking off the last strands of paper. I recognised this box straight away.

He took the little box out of my shaky hands before I could open it. I knew what that box was, and my heart did a back flip as he pushed his chair backwards and eased carefully onto bended knee beside me. I held my breath as he snapped the tiny box open. The antique ruby and diamond ring was even more stunning than I had remembered it.

'Alice,' he said, and gazed up into my eyes. 'I can't even begin to tell you how special you are to me, how you make me feel, and how much I love and adore you.

'I came so close to losing you, but just to be here with you now, holding your hand, gazing into your beautiful eyes, I feel like the luckiest man alive. There is nothing I wouldn't do for you and I hope that you will do just one thing for me.

'Alice, will you make me the happiest man in the world and say that you'll marry me?'

I was lost for words, a rare thing for me, and overcome with joy and excitement. I managed a nod at the same time as a strangulated choking sound, just before the happy tears started flowing.

'I'll take that as a yes,' he beamed.

chapter sixty-seven

Jonny had an insane grin on his face as he slid the beautiful ring onto my finger. I'd never seen that dimple so sexy, and suddenly I yearned for more than just a hug, and I wondered if the pokerfaced man in the corner would even notice if we disappeared into the ensuite bathroom. He hadn't batted an eye lid while Jonny proposed so I concluded, probably not.

My improper thoughts were quickly dismissed by the arrival of Sara and Ben. I couldn't wait to get a hug from them both, but a sobering glare from Ben across the bed proved to me that he might not be as pleased for me as I was.

'Hey Ben, Sara,' Jonny tried.

'Hiya,' said Sara.

Bens eye twitched as he turned his shoulder on Jonny. Sara had already told me that Ben was upset about me and Jonny; he had met him briefly at the hospital that morning, and had heard lots of about him, but despite Sara's best efforts, he was not happy at all. This needed handled sensitively.

'OMG! Is that what I think it is?' Sara, said snatching my hand away from Jonny.

I nodded and giggled, as I clearly would be denied a tactful approach as she threw her arms around me. 'Congratulations. Oh, it's so beautiful, I'm so jealous,' she spurted, and rushed round the bed to give Jonny a warm hug too.

Ben stood coldly.

'Ben?'

His eye twitched as I waited anxiously for his response. 'Not my business if you want to marry that piece of shit,' he said, glaring at Jonny.

'Ben, how dare you. I'm so sorry Jonny.' I said.

'Don't apologise for me,' Ben said.

'It's ok, I get it, it's no big deal,' Jonny said.

'You get it do you,' Ben said, walking round the bed, his eyes wild.

I felt so helpless lying there in bed, and the stupid, lazy guard didn't even flinch.

I knew where this was going. I knew what an angry Ben could be like. He was so like his father, poor kid.

'You get it, huh? Poor little boy, getting a new daddy. Having a tantrum. Buy him a PlayStation and we'll all be best friends, is that it?'

'No, I…' Jonny stuttered.

'Ben, you are behaving like a spoilt child, don't you ever talk to Jonny like that?'

He wasn't listening. Sara jumped in front of Ben as he swaggered over to Jonny, her hands pressed firmly against his shoulders, her eyes staring him down. He was at least four inches taller than his sister, but she had never been intimidated by her *little* brother.

'Oh, I'm so sorry, what about, hey new daddy, wanna go for a beer, get some hookers, shoot a little crack, that better Mum?'

'Time to go, Ben.' Sara spun him round and pushed him back towards the door.

'I know all about you,' he said over his shoulder, as Sara forced him to the door. 'Dad told me all about you, says he should've left you to die in the gutter. It's where you belong; you're just a worthless junkie…'

I held my head in my hands as the fight broke out. Sara did her best to stop Jonny and Ben hurting each other, but she couldn't stop the yelling.

In the end, the bookworm in the corner finally got out of his chair and dragged Ben, still fighting and shouting, out of my room. Jonny slammed the bathroom door behind him and Sara followed her cursing brother out of the room.

'Love you,' Sara said and blew me a kiss as she pulled the door behind her.

Then I was all alone again.

'Jonny? You ok in there?'

There was no answer, not that I could hear anyway, so I shuffled round and dropped off the side of the bed. I made three steps over to the bathroom door, but that was all my wrecked body was going to allow me, and before I knew it I was back on my hands and knees, again. Just great.

'Jonny?'

Still no reply.

I looked back at the bed. Could I make it back? It was worth a go, I thought, and I spun myself round on the slippery floor.

That just made it worse. Don't ask me how, but I ended up with one foot trapped under the bed, so I let myself slide down onto the floor and curled up, as best I could, for a bit of comfort while I waited for rescue.

I looked at the ring on my finger, and I wondered if I was doing the right thing. Ben was clearly very angry. I hadn't even considered the kids. In all this mess, I guess I just assumed they would be as happy as me, and to be fair, Sara really was. But Ben, was this fair on him? Was all this happening just a bit too fast?

Ten minutes later, I was still on the floor and there was still no sign of the guard or Jonny, or a nurse or anyone at all. I was starting to get cold and I had lost most of the feeling in my right foot. I needed to get up now, but I was still exhausted from my epic journey of three steps, so I called through the bathroom door again.

'Jonny, I know you want to be left alone in there, but I wonder if I can interrupt for just a minute. It's just, I might have got myself in a bit of a mess out here and I could use some help. Jonny?'

The door opened slowly, and I looked up at his red, strained face. He was still really upset. He looked across the room, presumably for me.

'Down here,' I said, shooting him my best *oopsie* grin.

The sadness instantly drained out of his face and was quickly replaced with a stifled smile, which he tried to cover with his hand.

'What the hell happened?' he said, trying not to laugh. 'Are you ok?'

'Are you going to help me or not?'

He couldn't hide his smile any longer and he started laughing as he bent down to untangle my foot from under the bed.

'How long have you been down here for?'

'Longer than I am prepared to admit.'

He was still laughing as he lifted me onto the bed.

'Are you alright?' I said, giving him a hug. 'I'm sorry about Ben. He shouldn't have said what he did. He's just an angry teenager.'

'I know.'

'He doesn't mean what he says. He just wanted to hurt you, that's all. It'll be ok.'

'I hope you're right.'

chapter sixty-eight

We laughed at the awful roast turkey dinner with Christmas pudding that the hospital had offered me by way of being festive. It was the only effort the hospital had made for Christmas, and they probably shouldn't have bothered.

Poor Jonny had to settle for a turkey sandwich out of the vending machine, with extra turkey and a mini sausage from my plate.

I opened my remaining presents, feeling very guilty, as I hadn't got anything for anyone else. A pretty necklace and earrings from the kids, or more likely from Sara, but with Ben's name scribbled on the card at the last minute. A jumper and the autobiography of Guy Martin, who Jonny assured me was an intrepid motorbike racer, thanks to Mum. Brenda's gift was the funniest, a book called Mash Potato – 85 Mouth-watering Recipes. Finally, I could find out how to make proper mash.

The next few days ticked slowly by. I didn't see much of Ben, but Sara popped her head in from time to time. I was spending less and less of the day asleep, a good sign apparently, but I was getting fed up and was desperate to get me, and Jonny, out of the hospital. He was starting to look awful from all the nights spent sleeping in a chair, and was still refusing to leave. So, after an insisted upon visit from a psychiatrist confirmed that I was just as crazy as everyone else, my consultant finally agreed, under some protest, and after signing a disclaimer as long as a monkey's tail, to let me go home.

I didn't go home. I didn't have one anymore. The house, cars and everything else had been bought with Michael's ill-gotten money, so it had all been confiscated by the court, as well as the four million he had stashed in a secret account. I *was* a millionaire, and I didn't even know it. Shame I couldn't actually spend any of it.

Homeless or not, it didn't matter, especially as me, Jonny, Ben, Sara and her girlfriend Maddy were immediately whisked off to a safe house in the middle of nowhere, complete with a psychiatric nurse to help me regain some hidden memories and deal with everything that had happened, and a physio. That was where we would play happy, if ever so slightly dysfunctional, families for the next few months at least, surrounded by armed guards, while we waited for the trial of the West Country's most prolific criminal, Mr Michael Walker.

chapter sixty-nine

186 days later...

Jonny and I were queuing for Splash Mountain in Disneyland when we heard the news. We had left England as soon as Michael's agonising, five week-long trial had ended. We hadn't even waited for the jury's verdict.

Brenda had been good enough to organise us all new passports, and new names, and as soon as the Judge had sent the jury away, Susanna and Jonny Roper jumped in a cab, with their two kids, and a spare, aimed straight for Heathrow and jumped on the first plane to San Francisco.

A text from Brenda confirmed:

Guilty, and whole of life, with no parole.

The relief was incredible. Michael Walker would never taste freedom again. I had felt sorry for him, for less than a second, but still.

It was strange to walk free of bodyguards, but slightly unnerving too. I had spent my first week in America constantly looking over my shoulder. I soon got used to it though and after a few days I had managed to relax and accept the fact that no one knew who we were. No one was going to hurt us anymore.

The nightmare was finally over.

I smiled as I removed the battery and sim, and binned the phone, just as Brenda had told me to do. A symbolic act for me that meant I was finally completely free of the past. The last piece of the puzzle had fallen into place and I, at last, felt I could properly move on. Jonny felt it too and I smiled at his Goofy smile and Mickey ears.

A week later Jonny had swapped his Mickey ears for a pair of sideburns. and was waiting for me at the front of Graceland Chapel, twinkling with nerves. It was all his idea to get married in Vegas, and I loved it. I had inherited my love of Elvis from my dad, his biggest fan, and grinned broadly as I imagined him looking down with a huge grin on his face.

The chapel was small but beautiful, dressed in swags of pink and white flowers that hung elegantly at the ends of the pews, and I snapped a few quick pictures with my phone before I took my position beside Elvis to take the obligatory selfie.

I had bought a new baby doll dress; pale pink, not white, and a handbag with matching shoes for the occasion. Sara had helped me with my hair and I was wearing a pretty pink flower behind my right ear. Jonny had picked out a white suit. I suppose someone had to wear white and I was glad it was him. It really suited him, and I thought he looked very sexy in it, and only a little bit like a Texan oil tycoon when he added his white panama hat and leather Bolo tie.

Sara and Maddy had agreed to be witnesses to our special day and had new dresses too. Ben wanted nothing to do with it. He still wasn't getting on with Jonny, but he had promised to sit quietly at the back and keep his comments and opinions to himself. That, believe it or not, was progress. But despite all the drama, right then I was the happiest woman alive, and even a tantrum from Ben would not be able to wipe away my beaming smile.

I caught Jonny's wink as I took Elvis by the arm, and after a nod to confirm that I was ready, he led me forward, down the aisle, singing *I Can't Help Falling in Love with You*.

When the Mask Falls

Compared to the ridiculous society affair that was my first wedding, this couldn't have been more different. Hopefully my cheesy wedding would end better than the elegant, but expensive affair that was my first. I was only sad that my mum and sister weren't here to share it with me, although I felt that Dad, in his own way, was with me. Mum would have bellyached all day. She'd have hated everything about it, bless her.

It was corny, but fun, and if it was good enough for Jon Bon Jovi it was sure as hell good enough for me and Jonny. We held hands as we exchanged rings and vows, and after we promised to always love each other tender we were serenaded out of the chapel to *Viva Las Vegas*. It was pure cheesy magic, and just brilliant. I was now officially Mrs Roper and I couldn't be happier.

Afterwards, as I picked rice from my hair, the girls gave us both congratulatory hugs and kisses and disappeared with Ben and the hire car, leaving Me and Jonny to start our honeymoon alone, just how we wanted it. We had promised to treat them all to a proper dinner later, but until then, we had the day to ourselves and I don't know about Jonny, but I only had one thing on my to-do list.

With grins firmly fixed on our faces we took a slow, hand in hand walk in the direction of our hotel, the Golden Nugget Hotel and Casino, as newlyweds Mr and Mrs Roper.

I managed about five minutes before my legs threatened to give up and I needed to sit down. I was much better than I had been, but I still struggled to stand for long periods and the wedding had really taken it out of me, so we found a wall to lean on for a bit.

Jonny was impatient to get back to the hotel though, as was I, if I was honest, but when the legs say no, they say no. However, he had an idea and after a few minutes of squabbling I finally gave in to it.

I couldn't remember the last time I had a piggy back ride, but I think it was when I was about eight years old and it was from my dad. Never-the-less, I was in a funny mood and I hitched up my skirt, commandeered Jonny's hat and climbed onto his back.

We paid little attention to the palm trees or the searing heat as we plodded back towards the hotel. We barely noticed the crowds of people walking the streets and anyone that saw me riding on his back must have thought we were escaped from somewhere. But I didn't care. After all, we had been through so much together. To just get here, to this moment, it was a miracle we were alive. So, I figured we both deserved a bit of silliness.

It took only fifteen minutes to get back to the hotel, giggling all the way, as I clung on round his neck for dear life, nibbling and whispering sweet nothings in his ear. I don't know about him, but I was feeling rejuvenated by the time we arrived, and I slid down his back onto the rug in the hotel foyer.

Jonny had insisted it was the same as carrying me over the threshold, although I thought that had to be the threshold to our own house, and last I checked we didn't actually live at the Golden Nugget. I was also sure you didn't usually take a full mile run up, but still, who am I to mess with tradition.

Anyway, we were both getting a little impatient to make our marriage official, so with the relief of the air-conditioning behind us and my newly energetic legs, we dashed, giggling like five-year-olds, across the polished marble floor in the lobby and headed straight for the lift.

As the doors started to close I caught that look in Jonny's eye, and just as the doors snapped shut I was slammed against the wall with his mouth pressed onto mine.

'God, I love you so much it hurts,' he said, in a pause for air. Still wearing his hat, I grabbed two handfuls of his perfect hair as his hands slid under my dress and lifted me clear off the floor.

Seconds later the lift door slid open, revealing another couple who were waiting patiently.

Jonny gently put me down and with red faces we both stepped out of the lift, excusing ourselves profusely. We walked purposefully away from the lift, and as the door clicked closed behind us, he grabbed my hand and dragged me giggling down the corridor towards our room.

The key card worked first time, and we staggered, joined at the mouth, leaving a trail of discarded clothes across the room. Eventually I fell backwards onto the bed. He leapt straight on top of me, pinning my hands firmly behind my head, and we made love until we were too exhausted and too hungry to do anything other than call room service for provision.

I lay back on the bed, wrapped in the hotel's fluffy white towelling robe and snuggled safely into Jonny, his robed arms wrapped lovingly around me as we waited for room service to bring our steaks and baked potatoes.

I played blissfully with my wedding ring, twisting and turning it on my finger.

'If you had told me this time last year that I would be lying in a hotel room in Vegas next to my wife, I would never have believed you,' he said, kissing me on the cheek.

'Would you have believed you would have got away with murder and were living in the U, S of A?'

'Oh, yeah, I could have believed that,' he grinned, cheekily.

I looked up at his face and that dimple, and he smiled and leant down to kiss me on the lips.

'I love you, Mrs Roper.'

'I love you too, Mr Roper.'

I felt giddy with joy and hunger as I stared at the door, hoping that room service might come faster if I stared hard enough. It didn't seem to make a difference, and instead I caught sight of something on the dresser.

'Were they there when we left this morning?' I said, pointing out the huge bunch of flowers.

'Didn't notice.'

I unpeeled his arms from around me.

'No, come back.'

'I just want to see who they are from.'

'Look later, there are probably just from Brenda. She's the only one who knows which country we are in let alone our exact location. Come back to bed,' he pleaded, patting the bed with his hand.

I ignored him and walked round to the bottom of the bed. The flowers were beautiful; roses, carnations and my favourite flowers, Gerberas, all in various shades of red and pink. I buried my nose in the middle of them; they smelt divine.

'There's a card.'

'Come back to bed Mrs Roper.' I continued to ignore him. 'You know you're not a very obedient wife.'

'Did you expect me to be?' I winked.

I was walking back round to my side of the bed with the card as he lunged over, grabbed me round the waist, snatched the card out of my hand and wrestled me squealing onto the bed.

He laughed as I reached out for the card, snatching at the air as he held it just out of my reach. I cursed him as I crawled up him to fetch it, but just as I got my hand to it, he grinned and tossed it across the room.

We laughed and squealed hysterically as he playfully fought to keep me on the bed and I fought to get off.

I finally managed to break free from Jonny's grip, and still laughing and panting for breath, I slithered over the side of the bed and landed on my backside. Jonny came after me, but I rolled out the way and crawled quickly across the room to get the card.

Before he could catch me, I was on my feet and the envelope had been torn open.

'Too slow,' I teased, still trying to catch my breath. 'I win.'

He slumped onto the side of the bed, catching his breath. 'Fine, you win, well who's it from then?'

I slid the tiny card out of the envelope that was addressed to 'Mr and Mrs Roper'.

On the front of the card was a picture of two horseshoes tangled together with white ribbon, and underneath it said *Congratulations* in fancy gold writing.

'Mr and Mrs Roper,' I said in a silly voice. 'Ooh, I could get used to being Mrs Roper.'

I turned over the card and glared with disbelief at the words that were written on it, the joy immediately sucked out of my stunned body.

The blood drained out of my head, taking my breath with it. The room spun wildly around me, and I couldn't breathe. I felt hot *and* cold. I was tumbling.

'Oh no.'

Through flooding eyes, I tried to steady the twirling room. I felt Jonny's arms catch me as my legs turned to jelly beneath me. The card slipped from my trembling fingers.

I closed my eyes and sobbed into Jonny's bare chest.

Caroline O'Breackin

chapter seventy

To the happy couple

Best wishes on your special day

'Always on My Mind'

Michael Walker